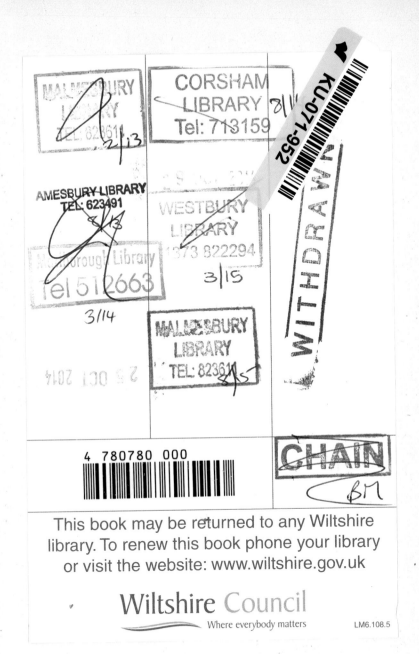

This book may be returned to any Wiltshire
library. To renew this book phone your library
or visit the website: www.wiltshire.gov.uk

Wiltshire Council

Where everybody matters

THE LIMPOPO ACADEMY OF PRIVATE DETECTION

The No. 1 Ladies' Detective Agency

Alexander McCall Smith

WINDSOR
PARAGON

First published 2012
by Little, Brown
This Large Print edition published 2012
by AudioGO Ltd
by arrangement with
Little, Brown Book Group

Hardcover   ISBN: 978 1 445 82821 3
Softcover   ISBN: 978 1 445 82822 0

British Library Cataloguing in Publication Data available

Printed and bound in Great Britain by
MPG Books Group Limited

This book is for Hilary Neville-Towle,
with gratitude.

CHAPTER ONE:
ON A HOT DAY
WE DREAM OF TEA

In Botswana, home to the No. 1 Ladies' Detective Agency for the problems of ladies, and others, it is customary — one might say *very customary* — to enquire of the people whom you meet whether they have slept well. The answer to that question is almost inevitably that they have indeed slept well, even if they have not, and have spent the night tossing and turning as a result of the nocturnal barking of dogs, the activity of mosquitoes or the prickings of a bad conscience. Of course, mosquitoes may be defeated by nets or sprays, just as dogs may be roundly scolded; a bad conscience, though, is not so easily stifled. If somebody were to invent a spray capable of dealing with an uncomfortable conscience, that person would undoubtedly do rather well — but perhaps might not sleep as soundly as before, were he to reflect on the consequences of his invention. Bad consciences, it would appear, are there for a purpose: to make us feel regret over our failings. Should they be silenced, then our entirely human weaknesses, our manifold omissions, would become all the greater — and that, as Mma Ramotswe would certainly say, is not a good thing.

Mma Ramotswe was fortunate in having an untroubled conscience, and therefore generally enjoyed undisturbed sleep. It was her habit to take to her bed after a final cup of red bush tea at around ten o'clock at night. Mr. J.L.B. Matekoni, her husband and by common consent the finest mechanic in all Botswana, would often retire before her, particularly if he had had a tiring day at work. Mechanics in general sleep well, as do many others whose day is taken up with physically demanding labour. So by the time that Mma Ramotswe went to bed, he might already be lost to this world, his breathing deep and regular, his eyes firmly closed to the bedside light that he would leave for his wife to extinguish.

She would not take long to go to sleep, drifting off to thoughts of what had happened that day; to images of herself drinking tea in the office or driving her van on an errand; to the picture of Mma Makutsi sitting upright at her desk, her large glasses catching the light as she held forth on some issue or other. Or to some memory of a long time ago, of her father walking down a dusty road, holding her hand and explaining to her about the ways of cattle — a subject that he knew so well. When a wise man dies, there is so much history that is lost: that is what they said, and Mma Ramotswe knew it to be true. Her own father, the late Obed Ramotswe, had taken so much with him, but had also left much behind, so many memories and sayings and observations, that she, his daughter, could now call up and cherish as she waited for the soft arms of sleep to embrace her.

Mma Ramotswe did not remember her dreams for very long once she had woken up. Occasionally, though, an egregiously vivid dream might make such an impression that it lodged in her memory, and that is what happened that morning. It was not in any way a bad dream; nor was it a particularly good dream, the sort of dream that makes one feel as if one has been vouchsafed some great mystical insight; it was, rather, one of those dreams that seems to be a clear warning that something special is about to happen. If a dream involves lottery tickets and numbers, then its meaning is clear enough. This dream was not like that, and yet it left Mma Ramotswe feeling that she had somehow been given advance notice of something out of the ordinary, something important.

In this dream she was walking along a path in the stretch of bush immediately behind Tlokweng Road Speedy Motors, the building that the No. 1 Ladies' Detective Agency shared with Mr. J.L.B. Matekoni's garage. She was not sure where she was going, but this did not seem to matter, as Mma Ramotswe felt happy just to be walking along it with no great sense of having to reach a destination. And why should one not walk along a path, particularly a comfortable path, without any idea of getting anywhere?

She turned a corner and found herself faced with a large acacia tree, its foliage extending out like the canopy of a commodious umbrella. To dream of trees is to . . . to long for trees, and finding herself under the shade of this tree would have been enough to make the dream a satisfactory one. But there was more to it. Underneath the tree, standing in such a position that the mottled shade of the leaves all but obscured his face, was a tall, well-built man. He now stepped forward, held out a hand

and said, "I have come at last, Mma Ramotswe."

And that was the point at which Mma Ramotswe awoke. The encounter with this stranger had not been threatening in any way; there had been nothing in his demeanour that was suggestive of hostility, and she had not felt in the slightest bit anxious. As for what he said, she had simply thought, even if she had not had the time to say it, *Yes, it has been a long time.*

For a few minutes after waking, she had lain still in bed, mulling over the dream. Had the man been her father, then the dream would have been easy to understand. She knew that she dreamed of her father from time to time, which was only to be expected, given that not a day went past, not one day, when she did not think of that great and good man, the late Obed Ramotswe. If you think of somebody every day, then you can be sure you will dream of him at night; but it was not him whom she encountered under that acacia tree — that was very clear. It was somebody quite different, somebody she sensed was from a long way away. But who could that be? Mma Ramotswe did not really know anybody from a long way away, unless one counted Francistown or Maun, where she knew a number of people. But those towns, although several hundred miles from Gaborone, are both in Botswana, and nowhere in Botswana was the abode of strangers. That was because Botswana, to those who lived there, was home, and familiar, and comfortable, and no place in such a country will seem far away. No, this man under the tree was from somewhere outside the country, and that was unusual and puzzling and would have to be thought about at some length.

"I had a very unusual dream," she said to Mma Makutsi as they attended to the morning's mail in the office.

Mma Makutsi looked up from the envelope that she was in the process of slitting open. "Dreams are always unusual," she said. "In fact, it is unusual to have a usual dream."

Mma Ramotswe frowned. She thought that she understood what Mma Makutsi meant but was not quite sure. Her assistant had a habit of making enigmatic remarks, and this, she suspected, was one such remark.

"Phuti," Mma Makutsi continued, referring to her new husband, Phuti Radiphuti, "Phuti has many dreams, every night. He tells me about them and I explain what they mean." She paused. "He often dreams about furniture."

"That is because he has a furniture shop," Mma Ramotswe said. "So perhaps it is not surprising."

"That is so, Mma," agreed Mma Makutsi. "But he can dream about different pieces of furniture." She paused, fixing Mma Ramotswe on the other side of the room with the cautious look of one about to reveal sensitive information. She lowered her voice. "Some nights he dreams about beds; other nights he dreams about dining-room tables. It is very strange."

Mma Ramotswe looked down at her desk. She did not like to discuss the intimate side of anybody's marriage — particularly when the marriage was as recent as Mma Makutsi's. She thought of new marriages as being rather like those shy, delicate flowers one sees on the edge of the Kalahari; so small that one might miss them altogether, so vulnerable that a careless step might crush their beauty. Of course, people talked about their dreams without too much embarrassment — most dreams, after all, sound inconsequential and silly in the cold light of day — but it was different when a wife talked about a husband's dreams, or a husband about a wife's. Dreams occurred

13

in beds, and what occurred in marital beds was not a subject for debate in the office — especially if the dream *related to* beds, as it appeared that some of Phuti Radiphuti's dreams did.

But if Mma Ramotswe was reluctant to probe Phuti's dreams too closely, the same was not true of her assistant. The topic had now been broached, and Mma Makutsi pursued it enthusiastically.

"There is no doubt about a dream about beds," she continued. "The meaning of that dream is very clear, Mma. It should be very obvious, even to a person who does not know much about dreams, or other things, for that matter."

Mma Ramotswe said nothing.

"Yes," said Mma Makutsi, "if a person says *I have been dreaming about beds,* then you know straightaway what the dream means. You can say to them, *I know what that dream means. It is very clear.*"

Mma Ramotswe looked out of the window, which was high, and gave a view from that angle only of a slice of blue; empty blue; blue with no white of cloud; nothingness. "Is the meaning of dreams clear, Mma? Do any dreams make sense, or are they just like . . . like clouds in the sky, composed of nothing very much? Maybe they are clouds in our mind, Mma; maybe that is what they are."

Mma Makutsi was having none of this. "The meaning is often clear," she retorted. "I have no difficulty, Mma, in understanding a dream about beds."

Mma Ramotswe sighed. "Well, they do say, don't they, Mma, that men have such things on their minds most of the time. They say that men think only of that, all day. Listen to the way Charlie speaks when he thinks you can't hear him. That shows you what men think about — or at least, young men. I do not think that Mr. J.L.B. Matekoni has thoughts like that in his head all day. I do not think that, Mma."

It was as if Mma Makutsi had not heard her. "Yes, Mma. The meaning of a dream about beds is very simple. It means that you are tired. It means that you need more sleep."

Mma Ramotswe stared at her assistant for a few moments. Then, with some degree of relief, she smiled. "Well, there you have it, Mma. That must be what such a dream means."

"On the other hand," went on Mma Makutsi, "a dream about a dining-room table is different. That does not mean that you are tired."

"No."

"No, it does not mean that, Mma. A dream about a dining-room table means that you are hungry. I think that is very obvious."

Mma Ramotswe looked first at the teapot, and then at the clock. She would wait, she decided; if one kept bringing forward the time at which one had tea, then the period after tea time would become far too long. Tea had to be taken at the right time; if anything was clear, it was that.

She decided to steer the conversation back to her own dream. But just as she was about to do so, Mma Makutsi came up with a further observation on Phuti's dreams. "When he said to me one morning that he had dreamed of dining-room tables, I was worried. Was I giving him enough to eat, I wondered?"

"And what did you decide, Mma?"

"I think I'm giving him enough food. I believe in demand feeding. I think that is what it's called. I always leave some food out in the kitchen so that Phuti can pick up a snack if he feels hungry. There are other women who believe that you should only feed your husband at set times, so that he gets used to it. But I am not one of those women, Mma. I leave food out."

Mma Ramotswe suppressed a grin at the thought of demand feeding for husbands. The conversation, although potentially sensitive, had proved to be more amusing than anything else, and she knew that it could drift on indefinitely. It was her own dream that had started it, and it was to her dream that she now returned.

"I had a very strange dream last night, Mma," she said. "As I was saying."

"Please tell me what it was, Mma," said Mma Makutsi. "I cannot guarantee that I will be able to tell you what it means, but we shall see."

"I dreamed that I was walking along a path," Mma Ramotswe began. "And —"

Mma Makutsi interrupted her. "That means you are going on a journey, Mma. There can be no doubt about that."

Mma Ramotswe acknowledged this. "Possibly. But then the path came to a place —"

"That is your destination," announced Mma Makutsi. "That place that you saw in your dream was your destination in life. That is very clear indeed. What was it like, Mma? Was it a very good place?"

"There was an acacia tree —"

Again there was an interjection. "Then that means you are going to end up under a tree, Mma. That is where you will find yourself, under a tree." She looked at Mma Ramotswe sympathetically. "That is not too bad, Mma. There are many worse places to end up."

"But the tree was not all that important," said Mma Ramotswe, raising her voice slightly to prevent further interruption. "There was a man standing under the tree. It was as if he was waiting for me."

"That will be Mr. J.L.B. Matekoni."

Mma Ramotswe shook her head. "It was not him. It was a man I had never seen before. And he did not come from here. He was a stranger."

Mma Makutsi's glasses flashed in a slanting band of sunlight. "Not from Gaborone?" she asked. "Not from Botswana?"

"No. He was from somewhere else. He was not an African at all."

Mma Makutsi was silent. Then she delivered her judgement. "You are going to meet a stranger," she said, with an air of gravity. "You are going to meet a stranger under an acacia tree."

"I thought it might mean something like that," said Mma Ramotswe. "But then I thought that it probably didn't mean anything at all. That it was just a dream, and I would forget about it by this afternoon."

Mma Makutsi looked doubtful. "I don't

think you should forget it, Mma Ramotswe. I think that you should remember it, so that when it happens, when you meet that stranger under the acacia tree, you will be prepared."

She said nothing more, but gave Mma Ramotswe an oblique look; a look that Mma Ramotswe interpreted as a warning. But she had not understood — for all her claims to understanding dreams, Mma Makutsi had missed the point. This stranger was not threatening; this stranger, for whom Mma Makutsi said she should be prepared, was not somebody to be dreaded or guarded against. On the contrary, this stranger was a good man, a kind man, and his arrival — if he were ever to come, which was highly unlikely — was something to be welcomed, something to be celebrated. And there was something else — something that was hard to put into words. The man in the dream might have been a stranger in that she had never seen him before, but somehow she felt that she knew him. *She knew him but did not know him.*

She glanced at her watch again. Resolve can be weakened by time, and by talk about dreams and by heat.

"I know it's a bit early, but I think that we should have tea now," she said to Mma

19

Makutsi. And Mma Makutsi, who had removed her glasses to clean them, looked up, finished her task of polishing the lenses, and said that she completely agreed.

"On a hot day," she said, "we dream of tea."

CHAPTER TWO:
FOOD COOKED WITH LOVE TASTES BETTER

It was shortly after this conversation about dreams, or after the tea that followed this conversation, that an unknown car drew up outside the offices of the No. 1 Ladies' Detective Agency and parked beneath the acacia tree. Had this been followed by the emergence of a tall man similar in appearance to the one who had appeared in Mma Ramotswe's dream, then Mma Makutsi's belief in the prescience of dreams would have been dramatically confirmed. But this did not happen, as the person who opened the car door and stepped out — watched with bated breath by Mma Makutsi — was none other than Mma Silvia Potokwane, matron not only of the orphan farm but also, in a sense, of all she surveyed.

Mma Makutsi let her disappointment be known. "It's nobody," she said. "Just her."

Mma Ramotswe, who had not been looking out of the window, now did so. "But it's

Mma Potokwane, Mma. She is not nobody."
The reproach in her voice was evident and
was picked up by Mma Makutsi.

"I'm sorry, Mma," she said. "I didn't
mean to be rude about Mma Potokwane.
It's just that I thought that it might be the
man you saw in your dream. One never
knows."

Mma Ramotswe let it pass. Mma Makutsi
had never enjoyed a particularly good
relationship with Mma Potokwane — the
natural rivalry, Mma Ramotswe thought,
that results from the juxtaposition of two
strong personalities. That had changed more
recently, though, and in particular there had
been what amounted to a cordial truce
when Mma Potokwane had offered to apply
her undoubted organisational skills to the
planning of Mma Makutsi's wedding. This
offer of help had been gratefully accepted,
and had relieved Mma Makutsi of much of
the anxiety that accompanies a wedding.
Mma Ramotswe hoped that this cordiality
would persist: she did not like conflict in
any form, and it pleased her to think that
these two women, who had so much to offer, might now cooperate rather than seek
to undermine each other. Perhaps Mma
Makutsi might help the orphan farm in its
fund-raising activities, now that she was

Mrs. Phuti Radiphuti and the occupant, therefore, of a reasonably elevated position in the town. Phuti was a man of substance, with the resources of the Double Comfort Furniture Store behind him and a large herd of cattle at the Radiphuti cattle post off to the west of Mahalapye. The size of that herd could only be guessed at — "A very large number of cattle, all of them quite fat," was all that Mma Makutsi had said on the subject — but whatever its dimensions, it meant that Mma Makutsi would now surely have the resources to help the orphan farm in some way.

Mma Potokwane herself was not unaware of the change in Mma Makutsi's fortunes, and it was possible, Mma Ramotswe thought, that this visit was connected with precisely that awareness. The matron of the orphan farm was famous for the vigour of her support for her charges, with every meeting, every encounter being seen as an opportunity to solicit support for the orphan cause. But as Mma Potokwane settled herself into the client's chair in the office that morning, it became clear that it was business of a very different sort that was on the matron's mind. Immediately after the normal greetings, Mma Potokwane cleared her throat and fixed first Mma Ramotswe

23

and then Mma Makutsi with a baleful stare.

"I have come to see you about a very difficult matter," she said. "In all my years as a matron, I have never come across something as difficult as this."

"You must have seen many things," said Mma Ramotswe.

"Many very heartbreaking things," added Mma Makutsi from the other side of the room.

Mma Potokwane turned her head to glance briefly at Mma Makutsi. "You're right about that, Mma Makutsi," she said. "Or should I be calling you Mma Radiphuti now?"

Mma Makutsi beamed with pleasure at the recognition. "That is very kind of you, Mma Potokwane. I shall be Mma Radiphuti when I am in my house — and when I go to the shops." That last qualification was important, as Mma Potokwane and Mma Ramotswe were quick to acknowledge. The Radiphuti name would certainly bring respect — and all necessary credit — when bandied about in shops.

"However," went on Mma Makutsi, "my professional name remains Makutsi. That is quite common these days, you know. Professional people — doctors and lawyers and detectives — often keep their maiden name when they marry. That is because their clients and patients, and so on, all know them by that name."

Mma Ramotswe thought it a bit presumptuous for Mma Makutsi to include herself in the company of doctors and lawyers, but did not say anything.

"It is also the name on my diploma from the Botswana Secretarial College," Mma Makutsi said. "That is it, framed, up there. See it? It reads *Grace Makutsi,* just above the place where it says *ninety-seven per cent.* Right there."

"I have seen it before," said Mma Potokwane, slightly shortly. "You have drawn my attention to it, Mma. More than once, I think." She paused, waiting for her pointed remark to be absorbed, but Mma Makutsi merely smiled encouragingly.

"So, Mma Ramotswe," Mma Potokwane continued. "I have a rather complicated story to tell you."

"I am used to such things," Mma Ramotswe assured her. "Do I need to take notes? Is it that complicated?"

"I can write it all down in shorthand," Mma Makutsi volunteered. "That way, not a word will be lost."

"That will not be necessary," snapped Mma Potokwane. "It is complicated and simple, all at the same time. You do not need to take notes. Have you heard of a man called Mr. Ditso Ditso? He is a well-known businessman."

Mma Ramotswe nodded. She had not met Ditso Ditso, but had seen his name in the papers on numerous occasions. And she knew people who knew him; that was always the case in Botswana — you inevitably knew somebody who knew somebody.

"Rra Ditso is quite a good man, I think," said Mma Potokwane. "Sometimes people like that — rich people — are very selfish and forget where they have come from and who their people are. He is not like that."

Mma Ramotswe felt able to agree with these remarks on the newly rich. The growing prosperity of Botswana meant that there were many who had come a long way, and it was not uncommon to find people who seemed to forget the claims of friends and family once their fortunes were established. Recently there had been a case reported in the newspapers of a wealthy bottle-store owner whose elderly parents were discovered to be living in extreme poverty in a remote village. They had not even heard of their son's success, but were still proud of it when it was revealed to them and declined to express any bitterness over the difference in their circumstances. Mma Ramotswe had been astonished by their response, but then had thought: no, these are the real Botswana values. The son might not have them, but the parents did. And parents — whether they were in Botswana or anywhere else — almost always forgave, whatever happened; or at least, mothers did. Whatever a son or daughter did, a mother forgave.

"It is good that he remembers other people," said Mma Ramotswe. "Sometimes I think that rich people live in a country in which they are the only people. It is called the Rich People's Place, I think."

Mma Potokwane smiled. "I think that's right, Mma. But this Ditso — he's not like that at all. He has been very generous to everybody." She paused. "Including ourselves. He has been very, very generous with his time."

"That's good," said Mma Ramotswe. "You must be pleased with that, Mma Potokwane. You're always asking people . . ." She stopped herself. It was Mma Potokwane's job to ask people to help the orphan farm, and she should not mention it as if it might be a fault.

Mma Potokwane raised a hand. "I should be pleased, Mma, but . . ."

For a few moments there was silence.

Then Mma Makutsi said: "You are not pleased, Mma Potokwane?"

Again Mma Potokwane shifted in her chair and glanced at Mma Makutsi. "No, I'm not pleased, Mma Makutsi. Do I look pleased?"

Mma Makutsi shook her head. "I do not think you are pleased."

"You are right, Mma. You are a very good detective. I am not pleased."

There was a further brief silence. This time it was broken by Mma Ramotswe, who said: "So . . ." It was not much to say, but it moved the conversation on.

"The problem," Mma Potokwane explained, "is that this Ditso is on the orphan-farm board. I have a board, you see, and they are the people who make the big decisions for the orphan farm. They are good people, and they like the orphans. They work very hard."

"Of course they do," said Mma Ramotswe. "I know some of those people on your board. They are on many boards — working very hard for their causes."

Mma Potokwane agreed that this was so. She very rarely had any disagreement with her board, she said, but unfortunately a major disagreement had emerged over a decision that Mr. Ditso Ditso had talked the board into making. "We were given a very big grant by a diamond company recently," said Mma Potokwane. "The board had to decide what to do with all the money. Rra Ditso came up with a project, although he did not consult me — not once. He said the money should be used for building purposes. I had no objection to that: we could do with a few more houses for the children to live in. But then he decided that it would be something quite different, and that was when everything began to be not quite so good."

"He has chosen something unsuitable?" asked Mma Ramotswe.

Mma Potokwane raised her eyebrows. "Unsuitable is not a strong enough word, Mma. His choice is a disaster — a very big disaster."

Mr. Ditso Ditso, Mma Potokwane went on to reveal, had decided that the orphan farm needed a dining hall and a modern kitchen to serve it. This would mean that all the food could be cooked in one place, and that would mean a considerable saving could be made. "It is always cheaper to do everything in one place," he said to the board. "I have always done that in my business, and it has made me a rich man. Do everything at the same time, in the same

29

place, and your costs go down. If your costs go down, then your profits go up."

These words, reported verbatim by Mma Potokwane, hung in the air. There was something wrong with them, thought Mma Ramotswe; they might apply to a business, but . . . but was an orphan farm a *business?*

Mma Potokwane sensed the reservation. "If you're wondering whether that's the right way to run an orphan farm, Mma, then you are right to think that. We are not a business."

"You are a home," said Mma Makutsi.

"That is exactly right," said Mma Potokwane. "We are a home, and although we like to keep our costs down, there are other things to consider."

"The house-mothers . . . ," began Mma Ramotswe.

"Yes, Mma," said Mma Potokwane. "As you know, we have little houses where the children live. They are not big — just eight to ten children in each, and one house-mother for each."

"They are very good ladies," said Mma Ramotswe.

"Yes, they are. I choose them very carefully. Not everybody can be a house-mother. A lady must be kind if she is to be a house-mother. She must also be able to control the children. She must know what it is like to have no parents, and she must make allowances. There are many things for a good house-mother to keep in mind. It is not easy."

"But it works," said Mma Ramotswe. "I have seen those ladies, and they are very fine people. The children love them." She frowned. "Surely the board doesn't want to do away with your house-mothers. Who would there be to love the children?"

Mma Potokwane assured her that the board had no intention of getting rid of house-mothers; there would still be plenty of work for them to do. "They keep the houses clean. They mend the children's clothes. There are many things. But the big thing, Mma, the big thing they do is they cook the children's food and they eat it together, round a table, like a real family."

"And if there is a new hall and a kitchen —"

Mma Potokwane became animated. "That will all go, Mma Ramotswe! That will go! And if that happens, then the heart of our place will be . . ." She searched for the right words. "It will stop beating. There will be no heart any more."

Mma Ramotswe looked down at her hands. Of course Mma Potokwane was right: your family was made up of the people you ate with as a child. Everybody knew that. And how could the people who sat on the board not understand it as well? Had they themselves no people to eat with?

She put that to Mma Potokwane, who thought for a moment before she replied. "I think that maybe they know that, but they are dazzled by all the money that they are being offered. That is what money does, Mma Ramotswe — you must have seen that. Sometimes we need to look the other way when people put money in front of our noses. We have to look at the other things we can see so that the money doesn't hide them." She sighed. "And they are very pleased at the thought of savings. They are always saying to me that we must look for ways to save money. And here is one. They tell me that it will cost only half as much to make the same amount of food in one kitchen. They say that we cannot ignore that."

Mma Ramotswe listened to this gravely. She understood the point that Mma Potokwane was making; she had seen the children eating in their houses with their housemother; she had smelled the rich stews bubbling away in the tiny kitchens of the individual houses; she knew what all of that meant. And now they were planning to have the children sit all together in one great dining hall, served by a kitchen into which they would never be allowed to wander. What chance would a child have of sticking a finger into some dish to taste what was being made? Or of standing beside a house-mother while she made a meal and sang, as some of those women did? Who would teach the children the cooking songs? Not some anonymous chef, she thought, hired to produce large quantities of food with efficiency rather than love. And food made with love, she thought, tasted better — everybody knew that. It just did.

"I'm very sorry to hear all this, Mma Potokwane," she said. "But I'm not sure if we can do anything to help. If you haven't been able to persuade your board to change its mind, then I can't see what any of us can do. They will just say, 'You mind your own business, Mma Ramotswe.' That is what I fear they will say, Mma."

"I know that, Mma," said Mma Potokwane. "I have tried, and I have failed. I cannot expect you to do any better. But . . ."

I should have known she would not be so easily defeated, thought Mma Ramotswe. *Not Mma Potokwane . . .* "But?"

Mma Potokwane leaned forward in her

chair. Mma Makutsi did so too. "I have had an idea, Mma Ramotswe. It's just an idea. I have no proof of anything."

Mma Ramotswe waited. "An idea?"

"More of a suspicion." She paused. "What if we found out that Mr. Ditso was in favour of this project for the wrong reason?"

"I do not think the board would accept it."

Mma Potokwane was triumphant. "Exactly!"

Mma Ramotswe brought her down to earth. "But is there any reason to think that he is behaving dishonestly?"

Mma Potokwane shrugged. "How do you get as much money as he has? By working? I really don't see, Mma, how one man could do so much work that he would end up with so much money. No, there's something else there — something that we don't know about but that must be there, Mma — it must."

That evening, Mma Ramotswe fed the children early so that they could both tackle homework that had taken second place to more attractive afternoon activities — to football, in Puso's case, and to talking to friends in Motholeli's. Both of the foster children were bright, although Puso showed a tendency to be easily distracted.

"It says here," said Mma Ramotswe patiently as she sat with Puso at the table that Mr. J.L.B. Matekoni had made for the boy's bedroom, "that it takes one man one hour to dig a ditch."

Puso looked up at her. "That is very quick, Mma. One hour? Could anybody dig a ditch in one hour?"

"It's just for this sum," said Mma Ramotswe. "And we shouldn't worry about that just now. What else does it say?" She looked at the crumpled sheet of paper on which the homework exercises had been printed out. "It says that if it takes one man one hour to dig the ditch, then how long would it take for three men to dig the same ditch? What do you think is the answer to that, Puso?"

Puso frowned. "It would be very hard for three men to dig one ditch, Mma. They would always be getting in each other's way. So it would probably take longer than it would take one man to do it. Maybe two hours?"

Mma Ramotswe smiled. "We don't have to worry about practical things when we're doing sums," she said. "You can forget about things like that. What you must do is divide one by three. That will tell you." She paused. She was not sure whether he had learned about fractions yet, and the trouble, anyway, was that everything was different these days. Children did not learn to count in the same way as they used to. And she was not even sure whether fractions had been abolished altogether.

"Let's think of it in minutes," she said at last. "One hour is sixty minutes. So if you divide sixty by three, what do you get? That is how long it would take three men to do the work done by one."

Puso closed his eyes. Opening them, he pursed his lips with effort before he replied, "Ten minutes? No, maybe five."

Mma Ramotswe shook her head. "No, that's not right. The answer is twenty minutes, Puso. And do you know how I got that answer?"

The boy shrugged. "They could do it much more quickly if they had somebody like Mma Potokwane ordering them about. She'd make them dig faster, wouldn't she, Mma?"

She did not reply to this, even if what Puso said was quite true. There was nobody like Mma Potokwane to get things done, and that applied, she suspected, as much to ditches as it did to anything else.

"I think you should try to do this by

yourself," she said. "If you can't do these sums, then ask the teacher to help you. I am not sure how you do these things these days — it is all rather different."

And it *was* different, as she discussed with Mr. J.L.B. Matekoni when, an hour or so later, they had their own rather delayed dinner. He said that he was not at all sure if schools taught mental arithmetic any more. "Take Charlie," he said, referring to the older of his two apprentices. "If you ask him to do some simple calculation — such as what the capacity of a fuel tank might be if you take a bit of it off — he looks blank and reaches for his pocket calculator. We can do those things in our head, can't we, Mma?"

Mma Ramotswe thought about this. It was true that she could work out how much change was due at the supermarket till, but when it came to fuel tanks and their capacity, she was not so confident. But the general point that Mr. J.L.B. Matekoni was making certainly stood: there were some things that just had to be learned through effort, and she was not sure how popular effort currently was. "It is all different, Rra," she said. "The world is all different. But people like Charlie can do other things, you know. These people who cannot add up can do other things very well."

Mr. J.L.B. Matekoni looked doubtful. "I'm keen to hear what those things are," he said.

"They are good at . . . ," began Mma Ramotswe, quickly searching her mind. "They are good at computers and things like that."

"Maybe," he said. "But there are things other than computers, Mma. There are proper machines with cogs and grease. Are they good at those? Are they good at fixing ploughs?"

The mention of ploughs reminded Mma Ramotswe of Mma Potokwane, who had recently asked Mr. J.L.B. Matekoni to fix the small plough that they used to till the fields at the orphan farm. He had done it, of course, as he always did, and charged no fee, again as he always did. Now she told him about the visit the matron had paid to the No. 1 Ladies' Detective Agency that morning.

"She came in an unknown car," she said. "She told us that it had been given to the orphan farm by a big donor. Mr. Ditso Ditso."

"Ow!" said Mr. J.L.B. Matekoni. "That man is very big."

"Yes. But the car is only the beginning. He has said that he will give a whole lot more in future."

"He is very kind as well."

"Yes," agreed Mma Ramotswe. "But the trouble is, Mma Potokwane doesn't like a new scheme he has cooked up."

Mr. J.L.B. Matekoni listened gravely as Mma Ramotswe told him about the reservations that Mma Potokwane had expressed as to the effect that the proposed changes at the orphan farm would have. "And then," she went on, "Mma Potokwane wondered about whether his money was honestly acquired. Do you think it is, Rra?"

He did not hesitate. "I don't think so."

She greeted this with interest. "Really, Rra? Have you heard something?"

Mr. J.L.B. Matekoni shook his head. "No, I have not heard anything. I have heard nothing, in fact."

"Then how can you say that his money was not honestly earned?"

Mr. J.L.B. Matekoni looked slightly uneasy. "You will laugh at me, I think."

"I will never laugh at you, Rra."

"In that case, I can tell you. I know this because of his car. He drives a dishonest car."

Mma Ramotswe tried to control herself. She made a supreme effort, but it did not work, and she burst into a peal of laughter.

"There," said Mr. J.L.B. Matekoni. "You laughed at me! You said that you wouldn't, but you did."

"I'm sorry, Rra. I did not mean it. It's just that . . . it's just that I can't see how a car can be dishonest."

"But it can," he protested. "There are certain cars that are always chosen by dishonest people, just as there are cars that only the honest will drive. When you're a mechanic for many years, you become able to notice these things."

"And he drives a dishonest one?"

"Very," said Mr. J.L.B. Matekoni. "Have you seen? It's covered with chrome and flashy bits and pieces. Any mechanic — any mechanic at all, Mma — will say when he sees such a car: 'There goes a bad man.' A mechanic knows these things, Mma. He just does."

Later that night, as she lay awake in the darkness, Mma Ramotswe considered these words. *A mechanic knows these things . . .* It sounded very general, very *unscientific,* but it was, she thought, probably true. Mr. J.L.B. Matekoni had always been a very good judge of character, and if he said that there was something about Mr. Ditso Ditso that was suspect, then he was probably right. But the difficulty for her was that it was one thing for somebody to say that another person was bad; it was quite another thing to prove it. And that was what Mma Potokwane had asked her to do: to provide proof that could be shown to the board of the orphan farm that one of their most influential members was bad, and so was his money. It would not be easy; it is never easy to provide proof even when we feel, in our very bones, that we know something to be the case. She was sorry that Mma Potokwane had asked her to do this, but, as always, when Mma Potokwane asked you to do something, whether it was to dig a ditch or to find out information about a rich man, it was impossible to say no. Completely impossible.

CHAPTER THREE:
YOUR HOUSE HAS GOT
MY NAME ON IT

Mma Makutsi had informed Mma Ramotswe that she would not be coming into the office until mid-morning the next day. It was an announcement rather than a request, and reflected a subtle change in the internal arrangements of the No. 1 Ladies' Detective Agency. This change was not threatening in any way: Mma Ramotswe and Mma Makutsi had always got along together very well, even if it occasionally had to be made clear — in the gentlest way — that Mma Ramotswe was the head of the agency and Mma Makutsi was not. There had also been a disparity in status. Not that this was anything upon which Mma Ramotswe would ever be inclined to founder, but in the past there had been no escaping the fact that while Mma Ramotswe was the wife of a prominent mechanic and garage owner, the daughter of a highly regarded man who knew a great deal about cattle, and a pioneering — indeed the only — private detective in Botswana, Mma Makutsi was none of these things. She had not exactly come from nowhere — Bobonong was not nowhere, even if it could hardly be described as somewhere — but her place, her family, her village all seemed a very long way from Gaborone. And her material circumstances had been very different too. When she emerged from the Botswana Secretarial College she had very little: a couple of dresses and one and a half pairs of shoes, one shoe having been lost in a move from one rented room to another. And to have one and a half pairs of shoes is effectively to have only one pair, unless, of course, the single shoe could in some way be considered a potential substitute for one shoe of the complete pair. This, however, would require that they match, which is rarely the case.

Mma Makutsi had borne her straitened circumstances with dignity. Mma Ramotswe had never heard her complain — not once, not even when, towards the end of the month in those last, trying days before payday, she knew that Mma Makutsi's purse was empty, or close to empty. Mma Makutsi would never ask for an advance on next month's pay, and had declined such offers when Mma Ramotswe had made them.

"If there's one thing they taught us at the Botswana Secretarial College," she explained, "it is this: never take from next month what belongs to next month. That is a good rule, Mma, and if more people paid attention to it, then we would not be in the trouble we are in today."

Mma Ramotswe was not sure that they were in trouble. Some people were undoubtedly in trouble, but not everyone; yet she knew what Mma Makutsi meant in a general sense, and was ready to agree.

Now, of course, it was all quite different. Mma Makutsi's marriage to Phuti Radiphuti meant that she had become a member of a family that was not only financially comfortable, but actually rather well off. Phuti's father, the elder Mr. Radiphuti, had by dint of hard work built up a very successful business, the Double Comfort Furniture Store. This store was now probably the largest furniture business in Botswana, and employed well over sixty people. Phuti, his anointed successor, had shown a real aptitude for the selling of furniture, and had steered the business to even greater prosperity. The profits had been ploughed back into the concern, and also into the acquisition of a large herd of cattle. Phuti did not even know the number of head of cattle he possessed, having only a rough idea; this was unusual in a country where people not only knew how many cattle they had, but also who each beast's parents and grandparents were. On this, the late Obed Ramotswe had once observed that in Botswana there were families of cattle, just as there were families of people; and that within these families there were members who spelled trouble and those who did not, just as there were such differences within human families. A recalcitrant, troublesome bullock was easier to understand if one knew, as Obed Ramotswe always would, that this bullock came from a cattle family in which the young males had a tendency to such behaviour.

There were some who whispered that Mma Makutsi had chosen Phuti Radiphuti because of what he had, rather than what he was. Such remarks were not only uncharitable but quite unfounded. Those who were aware of the truth of the matter — and Mma Ramotswe was one such — knew that Mma Makutsi had had no inkling of Phuti's situation when she first set eyes on him on that fateful night at the ballroom-dancing lesson. She had danced with him in spite of his clumsiness and inability to get the steps right; she had listened patiently to him notwithstanding his speech impediment, the stammer which at that stage had made him virtually unintelligible. That had gone, of course, as his confidence had grown, and she had gently coached him in the ways of less troubled speech. All of that was done out of love and affection, with not a thought to what their engagement and subsequent marriage would bring. And observing all this on the sidelines was that shameless gold-digger Violet Sephotho, who seethed with envy at the unfolding of Mma Makutsi's good fortune.

Mma Ramotswe had been immensely relieved when Mma Makutsi had indicated that she wanted to continue working after her marriage.

"It is much better to do something rather than do nothing, Mma," Mma Makutsi announced. "And when you have professional training, as I do, it is a shame not to use it."

"You are very wise, Mma," said Mma Ramotswe. "You are wise, and I am grateful."

"No, Mma, I am the grateful one," said Mma Makutsi. "You are the person who has given me everything. You gave me a job when I was finding it difficult to get one — in spite of getting —"

"Ninety-seven per cent," supplied Mma

Ramotswe helpfully.

"Exactly, Mma. Ninety-seven per cent, and it was still impossible to find anything. When some of those girls who got barely fifty per cent at the Botswana Secretarial College, girls such as —"

"Violet Sephotho," Mma Ramotswe contributed.

"Precisely, Mma. She is the big example. Anyway, you are the one who took me on and made me into a detective. You are the one, Mma, and I shall be grateful to you until the day I die. Right up to that day and beyond, Mma."

For a moment Mma Ramotswe imagined Mma Makutsi in heaven, dressed in white, as people were thought to be clad there, her large glasses somehow more luminous, more reflecting, than in the mere light of this earth . . . Mma Makutsi sitting, perhaps ready to take dictation from the Lord himself . . . It was a ridiculous thought, but she could not help herself from thinking it, and it made her smile.

The advent of Phuti had certainly changed Mma Makutsi's fortunes, but those had improved slightly anyway by the time of their first meeting. This improvement had come from two sources: the giving by Mma Makutsi of typing lessons to men, and the gradual growth in the revenues of the No. 1 Ladies' Detective Agency, which had resulted in a number of pay rises. This had led to her moving to rather better accommodation, and to the eventual overhaul of her wardrobe, particularly in that department dearest to her, the department of shoes.

There were a number of possible reasons for Mma Makutsi's attachment to shoes. One of these was profound: as a young girl, she had had none, and she remembered looking with envy at those so placed as to afford them. At the age of eight she was still unshod — which was not unusual in a remote village in that rather hard part of the country. But over the next year or so, shoes started to appear on the feet of other members of her class at school, and her heart ached, *ached,* for a pair. The other children's shoes tended to be hand-me-downs — nobody had new shoes then — and Grace Makutsi would have been content even with handed-down hand-me-downs. But she had to wait, though a sympathetic friend lent her a pair of shoes for the duration of her birthday — blissful, remembered hours, even if the shoes in question were slightly too small and pinched her feet in places.

With such memories, what could one do but love shoes, long for them, dream of the day when one might have several pairs safely stacked away; comfortable shoes, shoes that fitted one's feet, shoes with no history of other owners, of other feet? That day dawned for her, of course, and it brought its expected pleasure. But then something rather extraordinary happened — Mma Makutsi began to imagine that her shoes talked to her. It happened quite unexpectedly, and at first she assumed that the voice had come from some passer-by; some person who had perhaps passed by and not been seen, but who had for some reason chosen to mutter *Hallo there, Boss.* But then it had happened once more, again unexpectedly, when the shoes had said to her: *Watch out, Boss, rough ground ahead.*

She had felt none of the alarm that one might normally be expected to feel on hearing voices: a worrying development for some. Rather, she had dismissed it as a mere figment of her imagination, similar to those snatches of melody that we sometimes hear — the memory of music; those half-formed sentences — the memory of conversation; in short, nothing to worry about. Our heads are full of such things, Mma Ramotswe had once pointed out to Mma Makutsi, and she had agreed. If, then, one heard one's shoes talking, it was really coming from oneself, and was nothing more alarming than that.

So she came to accept that the shoes would occasionally express an opinion. And she also accepted that this view might sometimes contradict what she was thinking, or even be slightly rude, or hectoring, perhaps. One cannot expect complete compliance from one's shoes, or unqualified admiration — although that would certainly be nice. One must be prepared, she thought, for at least *some* criticism from one's footwear, the occasional sharp comment, the odd note of jealousy sounded by working shoes of party shoes — that sort of thing.

Now that she was married to Phuti Radiphuti there would be plenty of opportunities to purchase new shoes, but only in good time. Mma Makutsi was very aware that there were people watching her behaviour to see whether her newly acquired position would go to her head. She was determined to deny such people the chance to crow and to make remarks such as: *Give money to a person from Bobonong and that's what you get — every time!* She would not have that; she would be discreet and would not surround herself with the trappings of prosperity.

Except for a house . . . And that was the reason she would be late in to work that morning: she and Phuti Radiphuti were due to meet the man whom Phuti had selected to build the house that they were planning to live in and where, both he and Mma Makutsi fervently hoped, they would raise their children. For this task he had chosen a man to whom he had recently sold two large sofas: Mr. Clarkson Putumelo, the holder of a diploma in building from the Botswana School of Construction and Allied Trades, and proprietor and managing director of the This Way Up Building Company. The sale of the sofas had been an easy and satisfying transaction. Phuti had come across Mr. Putumelo browsing through the soft-furnishings section of the store and had asked if he could help him. Mr. Putumelo had enquired about sofas and had been shown several. He had selected a very large one, in bright green leather, and had gone off to fetch his wife, a woman whose dimensions were almost as generous as those of the sofa. Mr. Putumelo had suggested that his wife try the sofa, which she did, expressing immediate satisfaction with its comfort in a voluble and high-pitched voice. But then, when she had attempted to get up, she had been so embraced by the padding that she had been unable to do so, and both Phuti and Mr. Putumelo had been obliged to pull hard at her outstretched arms to bring her back to her feet. Mr. Putumelo had not been in the slightest bit embarrassed, and had simply said, "This is always happening with this woman." Phuti might have suggested a less commodious option — there were several sofas that had clearly been designed with this issue in mind — but this proved not to be necessary. Mr. Putumelo asked about a possible discount for two, was offered ten per cent off, and immediately committed himself. This painless transaction had put the idea into Phuti's mind that this might be the man to undertake the building of his house. He had heard that building a house could be a traumatic and distressing task: if the builder you chose was as affable as Mr. Putumelo, then presumably that difficult process would be all the easier. He asked, and Mr. Putumelo readily agreed. "I am the man to build you a house," he said with a smile. "I can tell that a mile off. Your house has got my name on it."

The plot that Phuti Radiphuti had chosen for their marital home was well placed from more than one point of view. Gaborone had grown, with the result that many people now had a long journey into work each day, making their way into the city in swaying, crowded minibuses. It would have been easy for Phuti to find a plot of land in one of these new suburbs, but neither he nor Mma Makutsi wanted to spend hours on the roads. So when Mma Makutsi noticed that there was a small parcel of building land not far from Tlokweng Road Speedy Motors and the contiguous office of the No. 1 Ladies' Detective Agency, Phuti was quick to inspect it — and equally quick to snap it up.

"It's perfect," he said, when he reported back to her. "It will take you five or ten minutes to get to work — no more. And I will need fifteen minutes to drive to the store. It could not be better."

The plot was at the end of an untarred road, a cul-de-sac that led nowhere and down which few cars would venture. There were one or two houses not far away, but nothing close by, and on at least two sides of what would become their garden, there was acacia scrub — thorn trees, low-lying bushes with twisted brown leaves, tussocks of hardy grass that would miraculously become green within hours of the arrival of the first rains. It looked like poor earth —

dusty and unwelcoming — but it was enough to keep cattle happy, and they could be seen wandering across this landscape, picking at what nourishment they could find, the soft sound of their bells filling the air.

Negotiations for the purchase of the plot were swift and uncomplicated, and within days of Phuti's seeing the plot it was theirs. Now came the task of designing the house that would be erected on the newly acquired land. Phuti Radiphuti, it transpired, had a friend who was a draughtsman. "You do not need to pay an architect for this," he announced to Mma Makutsi. "My friend can do all the drawings for nothing."

Mma Makutsi was slightly concerned over this. She was not sure that it was a good idea to get a friend to design one's house, even if that friend happened to be a draughtsman. There were many technical issues, were there not? Did you not need to take into account the weight of the roof and the size of the doors? And had there not been a house up in Francistown that had collapsed because these things had been ignored and the walls built far too thin? There had been a picture of it in the paper, she recalled. A woman had been captured standing outside what looked like a pile of rubble, and above it the paper had printed, *Poor lady sees her house fall down.* Mma Makutsi had been struck by the poignancy of this photograph; it must be devastating, she felt, to see one's house collapse. Presumably everything inside was covered by tumbled bricks and pieces of shattered timber: all the poor lady's pots and pans, all her clothing, all her shoes . . .

She did not feel that she could argue with Phuti. It was his money, after all, even if their wedding vows had made reference to sharing everything, and she had to accept that he knew all about how to deal with builders and suppliers and the like. If he decided that his draughtsman friend should design the house, then she would not question his judgement, no matter what private reservations she might harbour. And this view, she thought, would be approved of by Mma Ramotswe herself, who had once remarked to her, "Men are very sensitive, Mma Makutsi. You would not always think it to look at them, but they are. They do not like you to point out that they are wrong, even when they are. That is the way things are, Mma — it just is."

Now Mma Makutsi was gazing at the plot with Phuti Radiphuti beside her, waiting for the arrival of their builder who was coming to discuss the project.

"It is ours now," said Phuti. "Look at it. That is where our house will be, and over there will be your vegetable garden — if you want one, that is. You do not have to have a vegetable garden if you do not want to have it." He looked at her anxiously, almost as if he were concerned that he might be taken to be the sort to impose vegetable gardens on people.

"I will be very happy to have a vegetable garden," she said. "We will start it as soon as the house is built."

"Oh, I am so excited," said Phuti. "I have never built a house before."

Mma Makutsi tried not to look concerned. "I don't think you will find it hard," she said.

"I think there is nothing to it," said Phuti. "As long as everything is straight. You have to get things level, and not like this." He made an up-and-down movement with his hands. "If you do that, then the house will be a good one."

Mma Makutsi nodded. That sounded perfectly reasonable to her. She could hardly believe her good fortune: to be standing here with her husband, her real, legal husband, surveying a small square of Botswana soil that actually *belonged* to them.

56

To own earth was a great and awe-inspiring thing; to be able to run through one's hands the very soil that was yours and nobody else's; that you could stand upon not under sufferance, but as of right; land that you could turn to your own purpose and plant with your own crops, or allow your own cattle to graze — not that they were planning to run cattle in the garden, but if by some whim they chose to do so, then they could. Such things, such freedoms, such privileges were grave things, and might turn the head, unless you were careful to remind yourself of who you were — Grace Makutsi, from Bobonong, daughter of a very humble man and woman who never had much more than a few goats and scrawny cattle, but who had nursed hopes for their children and had encouraged them to make the best of their lives. She had done that, of course, and through hard work and the inspiration provided by a particular teacher, a slight man with spectacles who rode to school each day on an ancient black bicycle and who believed with all his heart in the power of education, she had somehow got herself to Gaborone and become a trained secretary. That powerful word, *secretary* — she was so proud of it; she rolled it about her mouth and uttered it as one might pro-

nounce a shibboleth: *secretary, secretary.*
That would have been enough, she now
thought; to have achieved that would have
been sufficient, but she had gone further
and become an *assistant detective,* and then
an *associate detective,* which was where she
now was. What heights lay beyond? She had
not really thought about it, but now, as she
surveyed the plot with Phuti Radiphuti, it
suddenly occurred to her that she should
become a *principal detective,* if not a *chief
detective.* No, that last description was
perhaps going too far; Mma Ramotswe was
a chief detective, she assumed, and no matter what improvements there might be in
her own status, it was definitely not appropriate for her to claim equality in that
field with Mma Ramotswe. That would
be . . . it would be *pushy:* yes, there was
only one word for it — *pushy.*

They stood for a few moments in complete
silence, and around them, too, there were
no sounds, beyond the faint screech of the
insects that provided that wallpaper of whirring that was always there, but one did not
notice unless one stopped and listened.
There was nothing to say, really; there were
no words Mma Makutsi could use to describe the sense of fulfilment that she felt.
So nothing was said until they heard the

sound of a vehicle making its way up the road and Phuti turned and announced, "That will be Mr. Putumelo now, Grace."

The vehicle was one of those ubiquitous pick-up trucks favoured by people who had things to do: carpenters, gardening contractors, electricians. It was dark brown and on its side bore the legend *This Way Up Building Co. (Pty) Ltd.* In the back were a workman's toolbox, a stepladder, and several rough-hewn planks.

Clarkson Putumelo got out of the van and walked briskly towards Phuti Radiphuti. "Very good land," he said, even before greetings were exchanged. "Good building land."

He did not address Mma Makutsi. He did not greet her in the proper, approved way. He did not even appear to see her.

Phuti smiled at the builder. "I chose it carefully," he said. "Or rather, my wife and I chose it." He turned to Mma Makutsi and smiled as he spoke. *My wife.*

Clarkson Putumelo half turned his head towards Mma Makutsi, but did not look at her. For a moment it seemed as if he was going to greet her, but that moment passed and he turned away again. "Good building land," he repeated. "No problems here. You'll want to put the house over there, in the middle, right? Then you can make a drive which goes from there to there." He pointed out the proposed route of the drive. "There will be no problem with that. Simple as one, two, three."

Mma Makutsi seethed. Nothing was as simple as one, two, three — even one, two, three itself was rarely that straightforward — you could miss something when counting things, even a child understood that. And who was this ill-behaved Putumelo, anyway? Who was he to arrive like this and pay no attention to the wife — the *wife* — of his client? It was a breathtaking display of arrogance, she thought, and she could just imagine what Mma Ramotswe would say when she told her about it. Or Mma Potokwane . . . Mma Potokwane might have her faults, but she would know how to deal with a man like this with a few well-chosen words, such that he would be decisively and deftly put in his place.

"I'll walk around with you, Rra," said Mr. Putumelo. "We can see how it looks close up."

"And me," said Mma Makutsi. "And me too."

Clarkson Putumelo frowned, as if he had suddenly heard something quite unexpected. He looked at Phuti Radiphuti for confirmation. "Everybody can come," he said briskly.

They began their inspection. Mma Makutsi said nothing, but glowered with resentment. She had rarely come across so ill-mannered a man as this Clarkson Putumelo, and she wondered how Phuti Radiphuti could possibly have selected him. But then men do not see things the same way we do, she thought. They have different eyes. *Men have different eyes.* It was a very appropriate observation, she decided, and she would write it down and pass it on to Mma Ramotswe for future use, perhaps, when sayings of this nature would be required, which she knew from experience could be at any time.

CHAPTER FOUR:
I SHALL SIMPLY
LOOK UP IN THE SKY

Mma Makutsi gave Mma Ramotswe a full account of her meeting with Mr. Clarkson Putumelo, sparing no detail of the insulting way in which he had treated her.

"He was very attentive to Phuti," she said. "All the time, he looked at Phuti and not at me. He never noticed nor spoke to me. I am not exaggerating this, Mma Ramotswe — it is as if I wasn't there." She paused, her anger mounting at the recollection of the humiliating encounter. "It was as if I was . . . some nothing, just some nothing."

Mma Ramotswe looked sympathetic. "There have always been men like that, Mma. Fortunately, there are fewer of them than there used to be. But there are still some, and this Putumelo must be one of them."

Mma Makutsi now asked what made these men behave in such a way. Were they like that because they had been badly treated by a woman at some point? Or were they like that because . . . She tried to think of another explanation, but could not. How could anybody ignore the other half of humanity? And did they behave like that to their wives? she asked Mma Ramotswe. Phuti had met Mma Putumelo when she had come into the furniture store to test the sofa, so she knew that Mr. Putumelo was married. Did the poor woman have to put up with being ignored in that astonishingly rude manner? What would it be like to sit down for breakfast with a man who never spoke to you but instead looked over your shoulder as if you were not even there?

"He will be a small man inside," said Mma Ramotswe. "He will feel small and unimportant. That is why he needs to put ladies down, Mma. Men who are big inside never feel the need to do that."

She was right, thought Mma Makutsi. Mr. J.L.B. Matekoni was one of those men who were large inside — kind and generous, and strong too — and he was never anything but courteous in his dealings with women, and with men too, for that matter.

"So what I suggest, Mma," Mma Ramotswe continued, "is that you don't let this man annoy you. Just ignore his bad manners."

Mma Makutsi nodded enthusiastically. "I shall ignore him altogether," she said. "It will be as if he is not there. When he talks I shall simply look up in the sky — like this — as if I can hear something but am not sure what it is."

Mma Ramotswe gently explained that this was not what she had in mind. "Don't repay rudeness with rudeness, Mma. It is much better to show a rude person how to behave. Have you not seen how well that works?"

"I have not seen that, Mma."

Mma Ramotswe knew she would not persuade Mma Makutsi, but she continued nonetheless. "Well, it does work. A rude person wants you to be rude back to him. He really likes that. But if you just smile and are very polite, then he will realise that his rudeness has not hurt you. He has achieved nothing."

This was greeted with silence, and Mma Ramotswe decided that it would be best to move on to another subject. There was work to do: a report to be typed up and sent off to a client, which would keep them busy for the hour or so before lunch time. Both she and Mma Makutsi went home for lunch now — Mma Ramotswe in her van and Mma Makutsi in the car sent for her by Phuti. This car, which had *The Double*

Comfort Furniture Store emblazoned on its side, had been the subject of some remark by the two junior mechanics. "She is very grand now," Charlie had said. "Too grand to go on public transport, like the rest of us. You may have to sit next to some poor person in a minibus. She is now too big for that."

Fanwell, who had at last qualified — though Charlie had not done so, and was still an apprentice — was more charitable. "It must be very nice to have a car with a driver," he said. "Maybe if I marry a girl who has a furniture store that will happen to me."

"That will never happen," said Charlie. "Girls with furniture stores are looking for someone more exciting than you, Fanwell. Sorry about that."

The inference was clear: these furniture-store girls, whoever they were, would be more satisfied with Charlie than they would be with Fanwell. That was probably true, thought Mma Ramotswe, who had overheard this conversation, but the fact that something was true was not always justification for saying it.

Now there was the report to compile, and she and Mma Makutsi began to busy themselves with the task of writing it. The matter to be reported was a routine one — the bread-and-butter, or bread-and-gravy as Mma Makutsi put it, of a detective agency: marital infidelity. This case, however, was rather more sensitive than the usual run-of-the-mill investigation, as the client was a prominent politician, Mma Helen Olesitsi, a former government minister in charge of the police. She had developed suspicions about the conduct of her husband, Kholisani, who was a businessman. She was sure that he was having an affair, but had been unable to find out the identity of her rival; could Mma Ramotswe help?

Mma Ramotswe, assisted by Mma Makutsi, had done her best. Long hours had been spent parked outside houses and in the lobbies of hotels; and more than one evening wasted in bars known to be popular with married men on the lookout for a mistress. Mma Ramotswe disapproved of these bars, which, she said, knew exactly what they were doing. One, in particular, was the object of her derision, a bar that called itself The Second Home — a name that she felt was deliberately and cynically inflammatory to women. This bar advertised itself as a place where "those in need of entertainment they cannot find at home will be given a warm welcome."

"Those words make it very clear, don't you think, Mma Makutsi?" said Mma Ramotswe, pointing an angry finger at the offending newspaper advertisement. "Why don't they just come out in the open and say, 'Married men: you come here to meet other ladies'? That's what it should say, Mma, if they were being honest."

Mma Makutsi was in complete agreement. "As a married woman, I can only say that I agree one hundred per cent. Even if I know that Phuti would never go to a place like that, I know that there are many men who are far weaker and will do that. Shame on them, Mma Ramotswe! Shame on them!"

It was not clear to Mma Ramotswe whether the shame should be heaped on the weak married men or on the bar, or on both, but she nodded her head. Their one trip to The Second Home had been an eye-opener, but had not resulted in any information on Mr. Kholisani Olesitsi. They had shown photographs to the barman, who had been perfectly obliging but who had shaken his head. "Never here, Mma Ramotswe. I have never seen this man. Not once. Are you sure that he has been here?"

Mma Makutsi had been doubtful about the truthfulness of this barman. "I think he probably says that about anybody," she said. "That is why he is the barman in a place like that. He is discreet. If you showed him a photograph of . . . of the Mayor of Gaborone himself, he would deny knowing who it was."

"But the Mayor does not go into bars like that," said Mma Ramotswe.

"You know what I mean, Mma. I did not say that the Mayor goes to bars. I do not think that he does. All I am saying is —"

Mma Ramotswe raised a hand. "It's all right, Mma Makutsi. I know what you're saying. But we have drawn a blank; that is the important thing. Perhaps this man is not having an affair at all. Perhaps it is just another case of a wife who is too suspicious for her own good."

"Perhaps, Mma. But what now?"

Mma Ramotswe had been unable to come up with any ideas for further investigation — at least not at that point — and had explained to Mma Makutsi that it was time for a report. "A report lets the client know what we are doing," she said. "It shows that we are not just sitting around talking about a case; it shows that we are busy looking into possibilities."

"Leaving no stone unturned," offered Mma Makutsi.

"Yes, Mma. That is a good way of putting it."

Sitting at her desk that morning, as Mma Makutsi kept her shorthand pencil poised above her dictation pad, Mma Ramotswe cleared her throat. "Mr. Kholisani Olesitsi," she began, "hereafter referred to as 'the husband' —"

" 'The said husband,' " interjected Mma Makutsi.

"If you wish, Mma Makutsi, although I think that 'the husband' is clear enough."

Mma Makutsi stared across the room at Mma Ramotswe, her glasses catching the sunlight from the window and reflecting it in little dancing specks on to the wall. If she sat in direct sunlight, thought Mma Ramotswe, there might be a danger that she could involuntarily start a fire, in the same way as one risked starting a bush fire if one left a bottle in the grass; the glass could act as a lens and focus the sun's rays down to a point of white incendiary heat. "It is more official to say 'the said husband,' " Mma Makutsi intoned. "It means that you are talking about a husband you have already mentioned, rather than any other husband."

"As 'the said husband,' then," continued Mma Ramotswe.

Mma Makutsi's pencil darted across the

paper. She looked up. "I am ready, Mma."

"We have carried out exhaustive enquiries —"

Again Mma Makutsi looked up from her pad. "Exhausting," she said.

Mma Ramotswe sighed. Mma Makutsi did tend to interrupt dictation with the occasional suggestion, but not usually as frequently as she was now doing. Could it be, she wondered, that her new status as Mrs. Phuti Radiphuti was going to her head? "No, Mma Makutsi, exhaustive means many. It means doing everything you can. Exhausting means tiring."

Mma Makutsi bit her lip. "I know that, Mma," she muttered. "I am not some ignorant lady who has never been to a college . . ."

Mma Ramotswe said nothing. By one interpretation, this was a dig at her; she had never been to a college of any sort, even the Botswana Secretarial College, which was not all that academically distinguished, she thought; not that she would ever say so.

"Let's continue," said Mma Ramotswe. "We have carried out exhaustive . . . no, say, extensive enquiries throughout Gaborone. We have interviewed relevant persons in the list of locations set out below —"

She was interrupted again, this time not

by Mma Makutsi with some suggested improvement to the text of the report, but by Charlie's appearance at the door.

"It is not tea time," said Mma Makutsi.

Charlie smiled unconcernedly. "I am not looking for tea. I have come to tell you that there is a man sitting in a car outside. He's staring at this building."

Mma Makutsi put down her dictation pad and crossed the room to look out of the window, standing to one side so as not to be seen from outside. "You're right," she said. "How long has he been there, Charlie?"

Charlie joined her in staring out of the window. "Maybe about half an hour," he said. "I wasn't really paying attention until Fanwell said something about it. Then I looked and I thought, *That man is staring.* That's when I came in to tell you."

Mma Makutsi screwed up her eyes. "I cannot see him very well," she said. "He is wearing a hat."

"He is a white man," said Charlie. "I've noticed that they like to wear hats."

"The sun can be unkind to them," said Mma Ramotswe.

"He's getting out," said Mma Makutsi. "I think he's coming in."

"He will be a client then," said Mma

Ramotswe. "Thank you, Charlie. You go back to work, and we will get ready to welcome our visitor."

Mma Makutsi knew what this meant. Mma Ramotswe had never liked it when clients arrived to find them unoccupied, staring out of the window, perhaps, or drinking tea. It was far better, she said, if the client came upon a scene of reassuring activity.

"I am ready," said Mma Makutsi, regaining her seat. " '. . . in the list of locations set out below' . . ."

"Yes," said Mma Ramotswe. "Location number one, the office of the said husband . . ."

The knock, which came at the half-open door, was timid — barely audible. Mma Makutsi flipped her dictation pad shut and rose to her feet. "I shall deal with this, Mma," she said in a voice loud enough to be heard by the visitor. "The important report can wait."

She pushed the door fully open. Standing outside was a tall, solidly built man in middle age, rather square-faced, his blond hair in a crew cut. He was dressed entirely in khaki and wore sand-coloured desert boots — the standard outfit of the safari visitor. In his hands was a freshly purchased bush hat with wide brim.

"Please come in, Rra," said Mma Makutsi, gesturing for the visitor to enter. "Do you have an appointment?"

Stepping into the room, the visitor shook his head. "No, I don't have an appointment, but I was passing by and . . ."

Mma Ramotswe rose to greet him. "An appointment is not always necessary," she said warmly. "My door is always open."

"Until five o'clock," chipped in Mma Makutsi. "The office closes at five o'clock."

Mma Ramotswe smiled. "I meant that I am always happy to see people." She gestured to the client chair. "Please sit down, Rra. And Mma Makutsi, perhaps you could take this gentleman's hat."

The visitor handed the hat over somewhat awkwardly. Noticing this, Mma Ramotswe said, "It is a very beautiful hat, Rra. Very beautiful."

He looked up and bashfully returned her smile. "You think so? I had it with me up north, in the Delta, and I must say there were days when I was very happy I bought it."

"It can get very hot up there," said Mma Makutsi.

Mma Ramotswe thought it time for introductions. "This is my assistant, Mma Makutsi."

"Associate detective," said Mma Makutsi.

"Yes. Associate detective. And my own name is Precious Ramotswe. I am the owner of this agency." She paused. "And what is your name, Rra?"

The visitor, who had been about to sit down, straightened up and offered his hand. "My name is Andersen."

"You are very welcome, Rra Andersen."

The visitor seemed to relax. Reaching into one of the copious pockets in his khaki safari shirt, he extracted a card and passed it over to Mma Ramotswe. "This is my card, Mma. You will see it states my profession."

Mma Ramotswe took the card and began to examine it. She stopped, her eyes wide in astonishment. "You are . . . ," she stuttered. "You are Clovis Andersen?"

"Yes, that is my name. I am Clovis Andersen."

There was complete silence. Mma Ramotswe looked across the room at Mma Makutsi, who was sitting bolt upright, the lenses of her glasses flashing signals of amazement.

Mma Ramotswe could barely speak. Her voice, when it came, was faltering. "Clovis Andersen? Who wrote the . . . the . . ."

Now it was the visitor's turn to be surprised. "My book? You know my book? *The Principles of Private Detection?*"

Mma Makutsi could not contain herself. "We know that book very well, Rra!" she exclaimed. "It is here on my desk. Right here. Look."

She picked up the now battered copy of the book and waved it in the air exultantly. A slip of paper marking a place fell out of the pages and fluttered down to the ground. Clovis Andersen watched it fall. "This is an extraordinary coincidence," he said. "I had no idea that the book was read in Africa."

"But we are always reading it," shouted Mma Makutsi. "Mma Ramotswe was the first, and then I read it, and then she read it again. It is always in use. Every day."

Clovis Andersen looked down at the floor. "Well, I must say I'm very pleased by that. And I hope you find it useful. You never know when you write a book — often you don't hear from the folks who have read it, and then . . ." He shrugged. "Then you think: 'Well, I guess nobody's read it after all.'"

Mma Ramotswe shook her head vigorously. "But of course people have read your book, Rra," she said. "All over the world. That book is read all over the world. There are many detectives who have read it — I'm sure of that."

"You're very kind," muttered Clovis Andersen.

Mma Makutsi now made another intervention. "God brought you here," she said.

He turned round in his chair to look at her. "I beg your pardon, Mma?"

"God brought you here," she repeated. "You have been brought to see us by God himself. That is very clear."

Clovis Andersen looked nonplussed. "Well, actually, I was driving past and I saw your sign. I have a rental car, you see, and when I saw the sign I thought that as a matter of professional courtesy I might call in and introduce myself — since we are all in the same profession."

"That is a very good thought," said Mma Ramotswe. "And we are very glad that you did." She looked over the room towards Mma Makutsi. "I think you should put on the kettle, Mma. Mr. Andersen is thirsty and would like some tea, I think."

Mma Makutsi rose to her feet and picked up the kettle. She would not raise the subject now, since they had a visitor, and such an important visitor too, but it occurred to her that she was always the one to make the tea. That had been her lot, in a sense — to make the tea for other people; but why should it always be the case? She was now Mrs. Phuti Radiphuti, and it was about time that people started making tea for her. *Time for tea, Mma Ramotswe. Would you mind putting the kettle on?* It was a delicious, delicious thought, but not one to be expressed just yet.

They talked for almost an hour, well into the lunch break. Most of the talking was done by Mma Ramotswe and Mma Makutsi, with Clovis Andersen making only the occasional intervention, nodding in agreement at some points, expressing surprise at others. From time to time Mma Makutsi picked up the copy of *The Principles of Private Detection* and read out a sentence to illustrate a point; Clovis Andersen, although he seemed flattered at these references to his work, was also reticent, making self-effacing gestures as if it embarrassed him to be considered an authority. Mma Ramotswe told him of the times they had relied on his advice and how his pithy comments had proved to be exactly the guidance needed, and Mma Makutsi added to this with examples of her own.

"You ladies are very kind," Clovis Andersen muttered. "I had no idea that my rather ordinary thoughts on investigation should be taken so seriously. I never imagined . . ."

"We are not kind," Mma Makutsi protested. "You are the kind one, Rra, to have given us all this . . . all this . . ."

"Inspiration," prompted Mma Ramotswe.

"Exactly," said Mma Makutsi.

Clovis Andersen looked down at the floor. He did not say anything. From the garage on the other side of the wall there drifted the sound of metal on metal; something being knocked into place, or loosened; the clanging of a spanner allowed to fall to the floor; the nagging whine of a reluctant starter motor.

"They are busy through there," commented Mma Ramotswe.

Clovis Andersen said nothing.

Mma Ramotswe glanced at Mma Makutsi, and then back at Clovis Andersen. "Is there something wrong, Rra?"

He looked up. His hands were folded in his lap; large, chapped hands, the skin made angry and reddened by exposure to the sun. He moved his head almost imperceptibly. A nod.

CHAPTER FIVE:
I AM YOUR FRIEND,
AND I AM ASKING

That evening, Fanwell left the garage at his usual time, which was five minutes past five. Work ended officially at five o'clock, and Fanwell, being conscientious, insisted on working until the very last moment; Charlie, by contrast, took the view that an eight-to-five day entitled him to leave the building at five o'clock exactly. This meant that work itself should stop a good fifteen minutes earlier, to give him time to put tools away, wash his hands, and spend a vital few moments in front of the mirror in the washroom. Charlie had installed that mirror himself, after the denial of his request that one be provided. "That is a washroom for the use of men," said Mr. J.L.B. Matekoni. "It is a place to wash your hands and attend to other necessary matters. It is not a grooming parlour or a beauty salon. Men do not need mirrors, Charlie."

Charlie had shaken his head. "Oh, Boss,

that is a very old-fashioned thing to say. I do not expect to hear that sort of thing in this modern Botswana."

The effect of this remark was to cause entirely understandable irritation. "What is this nonsense?" asked Mr. J.L.B. Matekoni, his voice rising slightly. He was the most temperate of men, but there were occasions when Charlie tested even him. "Men do not need mirrors. Most men know what they look like. I do not need to look into a piece of shiny glass and say, 'Oh, look, there's Mr. J.L.B. Matekoni.' What other use is there for a mirror?"

Charlie grinned. "These days there are new men, Boss. They are more like their sisters." As he spoke, he watched Mr. J.L.B. Matekoni, assessing his reaction. "Boys and girls, Rra — they are all the same today."

Mr. J.L.B. Matekoni was unmoved. "If you think that, Charlie, you're in for a big surprise."

"Hah!" said Fanwell, who had been following this exchange with interest. "A very big surprise! Maybe you need to tell him about some things, Boss. Maybe Charlie doesn't know yet!"

Charlie had been bettered, and he left the subject at that. But the following day, armed with a screwdriver and drill, he had installed a cheap wall mirror directly above the wash-basin. *For the use of modern men,* he had written underneath. Some time later that day, Mr. J.L.B. Matekoni had taken a pen to the notice and altered the wording to read, *NOT For the use of modernest men.* Fanwell particularly appreciated this: "That will show him, Rra," he said. "That will teach him to think he's so big and handsome!"

The mirror remained, though, and was regularly used by Charlie, even if neither Fanwell nor Mr. J.L.B. Matekoni made any use of it — or admitted to doing so. Vanity was one of Charlie's shortcomings, but it had always been tolerated by Mr. J.L.B. Matekoni, who also put up with Charlie's early stopping of work and unseemly dash for the door, while Fanwell continued at his post until five and then took five minutes to put away his tools and tidy up. Then it was time for him to board one of the swaying, overloaded minibuses that plied the Old Naledi route. If he was lucky, he would not have to wait long before one of these minibuses arrived, and then the journey never took more than fifteen minutes, depending on traffic. Jumping off at his stop, he would cross the road, leap across the storm drain, and walk down the unpaved road that disappeared into the heart of the informal sub-urb.

Old Naledi was the one scar on the neat landscape of Gaborone. While there were other places that had cheap housing, none was as cheap as this, with its rickety houses made half of breeze-block, half of mud daub, their roofs consisting of tarpaulins, odd sheets of corrugated tin, and such other bits of building material as could be scavenged from here and there. It was not quite a shanty town, but at times it seemed to be not far off that, so great was the contrast between its evident poverty and the well-found prosperity of the other parts of the town.

The people who lived there did so because they had no choice. As often as not it was the only place that new arrivals could find — people who came into Gaborone from remote villages, lured by the promise of work and payment they could never find at home. Then there were people from over the border, from countries less fortunate — people for whom the small comforts that Old Naledi afforded, and its comparative safety, were paradise found. These people took what jobs they could, and were often exploited. They painted houses, fixed pipes, patched up roofs. They worked without complaint, and at the end of each month sent home what money they could spare, aware of the fact that every pula, every thebe they wired back to Bulawayo or beyond might be the crucial one that separated a full stomach from an empty one; that meant that a child could stay in school rather than be excluded for non-payment of the tiny fee the schools required.

Fanwell lived in this place, but his lot was infinitely better than that of the migrants. He was a Motswana, a citizen, and thus entitled to the benefits that came with citizenship. He had been well schooled and had — eventually — completed his apprenticeship. He had a trade; he could get a job anywhere now, as there was always a call for qualified mechanics, even for those who did not have a great deal of experience. If he chose to continue working with cars, the fact that he had trained with Mr. J.L.B. Matekoni would stand him in good stead; already he had had an indirect, somewhat veiled offer from one of the big garages. "Ever wondered what it would be like to work in a *proper* garage?" they had asked. "Think about it, Fanwell. Good conditions. Big pay cheque. Latest tools. The lot."

He had turned this approach down, resenting the implication that working at

Tlokweng Road Speedy Motors was somehow inferior. "I'm working with the finest mechanic in Botswana," he said. "That is enough." And it was — at least in the professional sense. From the monetary point of view, though, it was true that he could be earning more elsewhere, although Mr. J.L.B. Matekoni had raised his salary as much as he could. And it would certainly be useful for Fanwell to have more money at his disposal, given his family obligations.

Fanwell lived with his grandmother, an aunt, and four siblings. His father, from whom the family had not heard in a long time, was now believed to be dead, and his mother was working in South Africa. She sent money home, but it was sporadic and could not be relied on. For the day-to-day needs of the family, it was effectively Fanwell's pay that kept the household afloat, eked out by the grandmother with such tiny amounts as she could earn through her skills with crochet or as a potter. Fanwell never complained about this — not once — accepting that this was the way things were. "When they grow up," he said, referring to the younger siblings, "then they will earn money too. Things will get better."

Now, approaching the street corner on which their house stood, Fanwell noticed that there was somebody occupying the stool that his grandmother normally used when she sat out in the yard, working on her crochet. As he crossed the road to the house, the figure stood up and approached him, his hand extended in greeting.

"So, Fanwell, how goes it?"

It took Fanwell a moment or two to place the visitor. Then came the prompt: "Chobie, man. You remember me. Chobie, your friend."

He did remember him. "Of course. Yes, Chobie."

Fanwell took his friend's hand and shook it.

"So," said Chobie. "I've been waiting, man. I've been sitting here for two hours thinking, when's my old friend Fanwell going to come home? That's what I've been thinking. True as God."

Fanwell smiled, but he felt nervous. He and Chobie had been at school together, and he remembered him as frequently being in trouble. There had been some row about something or other — he could not recollect what it was — and this had led to Chobie's being sent away. It was a long time ago, of course, and one could not be expected to remember everything that happened.

Fanwell gestured for Chobie to follow him to the room that served as the kitchen — and as sleeping quarters for three of the children.

"You've got lots of children already," Chobie said, gesturing to the sleeping mats stacked together in a corner.

Fanwell laughed. "Brothers and sisters, Chobie."

Chobie winked. "Myself, I've got some sons. Don't know how many, but more than two. Big boys."

Fanwell acknowledged this confidence with a polite nod of his head. He looked at the shelf; there was very little food, but he could give Chobie a plain slice of bread and jam and some tea. He offered this, and Chobie accepted readily.

"That old lady . . ."

"My grandmother," said Fanwell.

"Yes, her. She said to tell you she's gone somewhere until seven o'clock. Then she'll come back." Chobie paused. "You look after her, Fanwell?"

"Yes."

"That costs money, man."

Fanwell admitted that it did. "But there's nobody else, you see."

"Tough," said Chobie. "These grandmothers eat a lot of food. But I've got the answer for you, my friend."

Fanwell was busy lighting the paraffin stove on which the family cooked and boiled water for tea. His grandmother ate very little, saving as much as she could for the children; he had seen her holding back, had seen how thin she was. He said nothing.

Undeterred, Chobie continued: "This is a business proposition, Fanwell."

"I have a job. I'm a mechanic at Tlokweng Road Speedy Motors."

Chobie made a dismissive gesture. "That's day work. You never make money doing day work. I can give you night work — big money."

Fanwell glanced at Chobie and then looked away again quickly. "I am very busy," he said. "I can't do more work."

"Everybody's busy," said Chobie. "But not too busy if the money's good enough — and it is, Fanwell. It's very good."

"No," said Fanwell.

Chobie got up and came to stand beside him. "I'm not asking you very much, Fanwell. All I want is for you to help me fix some cars. Three or four to begin with — then you can decide whether you want to carry on."

"What is wrong with these cars?" asked Fanwell. "And why can't you take them to a" garage?"

Chobie became animated. "And be charged hundreds and hundreds of pula? Thousands, maybe? No, not me. These are cars I'm selling — that is how I make my living these days. All I want is a little help to get them ready to be sold. Little things. New exhaust pipes, maybe. Fixing lights. That sort of thing. Hard for me, but easy for you. You're a mechanic."

Fanwell remembered now: Chobie had the reputation of being persuasive. It had always been difficult to say no to him.

"I don't have much spare time," he said weakly.

Chobie put a hand on his shoulder. "Thank you," he said. "I am your friend, and I am asking you a favour. I knew that you would say yes." He paused. "Don't bother with the tea, Fanwell. Let's go. I have this car over at my place that needs a new fan belt, and maybe there's something wrong with the brakes — I can't tell. You'll know straightaway. Then, *smack-smack,* it's fixed!"

Chobie had a car parked round the corner. He had paid a small boy to watch it for him while he was waiting for Fanwell, and now he gave the child the rest of the fee — a few coins pressed into an outstretched palm.

"See this car?" Chobie said proudly, patting the side of the vehicle. "You got a car like this, Fanwell? No chance. You could have one, though. Easy, easy. You come in with me and you could have one of these. Turbo-charged. V-8. You name it. It's there for the taking, Fanwell." He paused, looking bemusedly at the young mechanic. "Of course, I forgot: you work at Tlokweng Road Something-or-other Motors."

"Speedy Motors," muttered Fanwell.

"Speedy not," said Chobie. "Ha-ha. Speedy not. Tlokweng Road Old-Fashioned Manual Transmission Motors. That's what that place should be called."

Fanwell laughed weakly. Even a half-hearted laugh, though, felt like a betrayal. "It is a good garage."

"Oh, I'm sure it's a good garage. Good for old ladies and their rubbish, one-horse-power cars. You fix donkey carts in that place, Fanwell?"

Fanwell looked away. "They do not bring them. They do not bring any donkey carts."

Chobie patted him playfully on the shoulder. "Only joking, Fanwell. Anyway, let's get in and go over to my place. I've got this yard, see, and the car I want you to fix up is there. Get in, my friend, get in."

It was getting dark now. To the west, over the Kalahari, the sky was copper red, fading into pink and then into a colour that was somewhere between blue and white, the colour of emptiness; the lights of the town, bright pinpoints, were beginning to punctuate the dusk. Fanwell felt empty. He did not like Chobie; he had never really liked him. But he found it hard to resist the other young man's enthusiastic banter, and there could be no harm, surely, in helping out with this business of his. The second-hand car trade was a notoriously tricky one, and Fanwell had no doubt that Chobie was at the questionable end of it. But if Chobie chose to mislead — and possibly even cheat — his customers, it was not really any of Fanwell's business. Indeed, one might argue — and this line of argument was just occurring to Fanwell — that it would be positively better for him to work on Chobie's cars; that way, the customers would have fewer problems and would get cars in better condition than would otherwise be the case. This work for Chobie, then, was virtually charitable, even if there was payment attached; that is how Fanwell looked at it, and that was how he was looking at things when Chobie turned the car into the gateway of a fenced-off storage yard. On the wall of this yard there was the wording, painted in high letters: *Reliable Autos. We get you there.*

"Get you where?" asked Fanwell.

Chobie smiled. "Where you want to get. That's where everybody's heading, after all. To where they want to get."

Fanwell did not say anything. Chobie switched off the engine and gestured to the single car that the yard contained. "Isn't that a beauty?" he asked.

Fanwell was non-committal. "They can give a lot of trouble, those cars," he muttered. "Mr. J.L.B. Matekoni says —"

He did not finish. Mr. J.L.B. Matekoni took a poor view of cars in which styling played a more important role than mechanical reliability, but Fanwell did not have the chance to relate these views before Chobie interrupted him. "Mr. J.L.B. Rubbish. Of course he doesn't like cars like these. These cars are for successful people, not for people called J.L.B. Rubbish. Come on, let's get going."

Chobie had rigged up a lamp on the end of a long extension cord. This was plugged into the lean-to building at one side of the yard. Fanwell could not help but notice than from this structure there ran another wire, which snaked back to disappear over the wall. Such electricity as the site had, he realised, was drawn from elsewhere — stolen power. Chobie saw him looking at this. "You've got a problem with that, Fanwell? Him over the wall — he's got much more power than he needs. I'm just taking a little bit — just this much." He made a gesture with two barely separated fingers — a gesture that signified inconsequential smallness.

"Where did you get this car?" asked Fanwell, as they approached it across the yard.

Chobie was ready with an answer. "I bought it from a man. Paid good money."

"Where did he get it?"

Chobie shrugged. "How do I know? Do you think you have to know every car's mother? Do you think you have to know its father? Cars are cars, man. They come, they go. You can't ask them all the details."

Fanwell faltered, but only for a moment. He had his suspicions about Chobie, but he did not see what further enquiry he should be expected to make. It might be that Chobie had obtained the car in an underhand way, but it might equally be that he had come by it quite legitimately. Was it his business to find out? No, he thought; not on balance, and he would ask Mr. J.L.B. Matekoni the next day, to see what he said. If he told him that it was wrong to fix cars when there was a doubt about their past, then he would refuse to help Chobie. If, however, he considered it to be all right, then he would help him. After all, the extra money would be useful.

The new fan belt was soon installed, and he then turned his attention to the brakes. This was a comparatively minor problem, and he was able to fix it in spite of the complexity of the braking system installed in that particular make of car. After an hour or so, everything was done, and Fanwell was wiping his hands on the small hand towel that Chobie had thoughtfully provided. As he did so, he glanced at the lettering on the towel: SUN HOTEL.

Noticing this, Chobie laughed. "They gave that to me," he said. "I know somebody who works there. Big time. He gave me that towel as a souvenir."

Fanwell finished wiping his hands. "I should get home now," he said.

Chobie held up a hand. "Not so fast, Fanwell. I owe you." He reached into his pocket and took out a number of folded banknotes. Counting out three hundred pula, he pressed these into Fanwell's hand. "Fee for service," he said. "See? Good money for good work. And there'll be plenty more — plenty more. Tax-free too, ha!"

They began to walk back towards the car in which they had come. As they did so, a nondescript black van drew up at the gate and a man emerged. Chobie looked at the man and frowned. "Yes, Rra? You want something?"

The man nodded. "I need to buy a car, Rra. I need to buy a car for my wife. I saw your sign."

Chobie, who had been tense at the beginning of this encounter, now visibly relaxed. "Well, you're in the right place, my friend. But unfortunately I'm a bit low on stock now — we only have that big car over there. But have you got a mobile? You give me the number and I'll fix you up with something good. No rubbish — something good. And my mechanic here . . . ," he gestured to Fanwell, "my mechanic is top-class. He'll make sure that it's in A1 order when you get it. You won't see your wife for dust. *Bang, bang.* She'll overtake all the other women. *Bang, bang.*"

The man laughed. "My wife would like that," he said. "So, here's my number. You'll call me?"

"Of course I will," said Chobie. "Give me four, maybe five days and I'll call. And I'll get my mechanic . . ."

The man turned to Fanwell and greeted

him formally. "And your name, Rra?"

Fanwell gave the man his name.

"He trained at Tlokweng Road Speedy Motors," boasted Chobie. "They have top-rate mechanics out there. Do all the big cars."

The man nodded. "I know the place," he said.

CHAPTER SIX:
THE THINGS OF WHICH A MECHANIC MIGHT SPEAK

Mr. J.L.B. Matekoni had been in Lobatse and was late home. By the time he arrived, Mma Ramotswe had fed the children and was chatting with Motholeli in her room. The young girl had been in an argument with another girl in school and had been on the verge of tears over dinner. Now it was all coming out and the story, punctuated by copious weeping, was being pieced together by Mma Ramotswe. *This is what I do,* she thought. *During the day I sort out the problems of adults; at night I sort out the problems of children.*

Mma Ramotswe dabbed at Motholeli's tears. "Oh, my darling," she said, "you mustn't cry. Who is this girl, anyway? How can I help you if I don't know her name?"

"She's a girl in my class," said Motholeli. "She's called Kagiso."

"There are many Kagisos," said Mma Ramotswe. "What is her other name?"

"It is Nnunu. Kagiso Nnunu. She's horrid and I hate her. I hate her more than snakes."

Mma Ramotswe put an arm around Motholeli's shoulder. It is so small, she thought, and fragile, as if too great a hug might break it: *the shoulder of a small person.* And there was the illness, too; the illness that confined her to the wheelchair took its toll elsewhere — made it difficult for the body to grow at the rate that it should.

"It doesn't help to hate somebody," she said quietly. "I understand why you want to, but it doesn't help. Not really."

Motholeli looked at her incredulously. "But it does, Mma. If you hate somebody hard enough, then they can die."

Mma Ramotswe caught her breath. Where had the child learned that? Was that the sort of thing that was being peddled around the playground?

"Who said that?" she asked. "Did somebody tell you that?"

Motholeli's answer came quickly. "The teacher told us. She said that if you hate somebody hard enough then they can die. She said that it can happen."

Mma Ramotswe shook her head. "But, Motholeli, that is just not true. That is not true. And . . ." She was about to say that no

97

teacher would express such a thought, but then she stopped herself. Teachers seemed a different breed these days, more like everybody else; when she had been a pupil at the government school in Mochudi, the teacher had been a figure of authority in the village. People respected teachers and listened to what they had to say. She remembered walking with her late father on the road to Pilane when a cart had gone past, a donkey cart, and there had been a man sitting on the back holding a case of some sort and her father had raised his hat as the man passed. She had asked why he had done this, and he had replied that the man was a teacher and he would always raise his hat to a teacher. She did not think that happened today.

"Are you sure?"

"Yes, I am sure, Mma. She said that if you hate somebody then they can die. She told us that. I'm sure about that, Mma."

Mma Ramotswe hesitated. She did not want to further undermine the authority of a teacher — there were enough people doing that anyway — and so she decided to say no more, at least about that side of it.

"But why do you hate this girl, this Kagiso?"

"Because she said I should stay outside in

the parking place — in the place for cars. She said I should have my lessons out there."

Mma Ramotswe was accustomed to receiving shocking confidences, and to receiving them with equanimity; now, however, she gasped. "But why . . . why would she say something like that, Motholeli? What did she mean?"

"She said that my wheelchair is like a car and that it should not be brought inside the school. She said there is no place for cars inside the school. She said I am just like a car."

Mma Ramotswe closed her eyes. It was only too easy to imagine a child saying such a thing; children showed endless inventiveness when it came to devising torment for other children. She opened her eyes and made an effort to smile. "That is the silliest thing I have ever heard, Motholeli. It is so silly that . . . well, I think you should just laugh at that girl. Laugh, and say how silly she is."

Motholeli remained silent.

"Well?" prompted Mma Ramotswe. "Don't you think that's the best thing to do? Don't you think that would be better than hating her?"

"No. I think it would be better to hate her.

Then she might die, and she wouldn't be able to say these things about me."

Mma Ramotswe tried another tack. "Would you like me to have a word with the teacher?"

This brought an immediate reaction. "No, Mma. It is not the teacher's business."

Mma Ramotswe sighed. There was a limit to the extent to which you could fight the battles of children. Down among the children, in the jungle they inhabited, the word of adults could count for very little. An adult's reprimand, or punishment, might get a wrongdoer's attention, but would not necessarily change attitudes, which would revert to their natural state the moment the adult disappeared. No, Motholeli was right: it might not help to take it up with the authorities.

"Well, you think about what I have told you," Mma Ramotswe said. "And here's something you can remember. It's a thing you can say to a person like Kagiso. 'Sticks and stones may break my bones, but words will never hurt me.' You remember that."

Motholeli muttered something.

"What was that?" asked Mma Ramotswe.

"I was practising it, Mma. 'Sticks and stones may . . .' "

"May break my bones," prompted Mma

Ramotswe. "But words will never hurt me."

Watching the child's reaction, her solemn contemplation of what had been said, Mma Ramotswe felt some satisfaction that she seemed to be getting through to her. That was the beauty, she thought, of those little sayings, those proverbs that children could learn and use to help them through life. That one came from somewhere else — she had read about it when she was a child herself — but there were plenty of old Botswana sayings that did the same thing, that gave you little rules for getting through life, for coping with its disappointments and sorrows. And did it matter, she wondered, whether they were true or not? Words *could* hurt you, and hurt you every bit as badly as sticks and stones. So that saying was wrong; but that was not the point. The point was that if it made you better, made you braver, then it was doing its work. The same thing was true, Mma Ramotswe thought, of believing in God. There were plenty of people who did not really believe in God, but who wanted to believe in him, and said that they did. Some people said that these people were foolish, that they were hypocritical, but Mma Ramotswe was not so sure about that. If something, or somebody, could help you to get through life, to lead a life that

101

was good and purposeful, did it matter all that much if that thing or that person did not exist? She thought it did not — not in the slightest bit.

By the time Mr. J.L.B. Matekoni's truck drew into the driveway of the house on Zebra Drive, its headlights describing a wide arc across Mma Ramotswe's garden, illuminating the mopipi tree and the flourish of bougainvillea, the children were asleep and Mma Ramotswe was herself sprawled dozing on the sofa, her feet up on a cushion, a newspaper spread across her stomach. The sound of the truck dispelled tiredness, and she rapidly sat up, folded the newspaper neatly, and slipped back into her comfortable, flat-heeled house shoes. Mr. J.L.B. Matekoni's dinner, a mutton stew rich in grease and lentils, sat warm and secure in the lower drawer of the oven. It was her dinner too, as she had held back from eating with the children so that she could sit down with Mr. J.L.B. Matekoni and recount to him the momentous events of that day. She had planned exactly what she would say, starting with an invitation to guess who had walked in the door that morning. He would never guess, of course, and so she would tantalise him with snippets of information until, almost casually, she would let drop the name of Clovis Andersen. And then she would tell him everything: Mr. Andersen's plans; what he had said to her and Mma Makutsi; what Mma Makutsi had said to him; what she had said to Mma Makutsi after Mr. Andersen had gone and what Mma Makutsi had said to her. No detail would be spared.

Mr. J.L.B. Matekoni came into the house and tossed the keys of his truck on to a table. "There are some people," he began, "who should not be allowed on the road. Maybe they shouldn't even be allowed to walk anywhere, either. Maybe we should hang a large sign around their neck saying *Very Dangerous,* or *No Sense,* or something like that."

Mma Ramotswe spoke soothingly. "You have been on the Lobatse Road, Rra. It always makes you cross."

"The road itself is not the problem," said Mr. J.L.B. Matekoni, stretching out his arms to dispel an incipient cramp. "It is the people who use the road. There was one man, you know, who came up behind me, and although he couldn't possibly see what was coming — we were right on the brow of a hill and there were lines on the road warning you not to overtake — in spite of that, he just pulled past me. And then there was this big Botswana Defence Force lorry coming the other way and it was full of soldiers, I think, and the driver of that had to go right over on to the verge and kicked up a big cloud of dust and little stones flying all over the place, and one of those stones comes — *zing* — and makes a little crack in my windscreen. And this stupid man just drives on like a . . . like a . . . like an ostrich."

"Like an ostrich?"

"You know what I mean, Mma. You know how ostriches run, and how they go this way and that, swerving around. Anyway, he was lucky that he didn't make that Defence Force driver go right off the road because that would have put him in big trouble. It would be like declaring war, Mma. You don't declare war on the Botswana Defence Force."

Mma Ramotswe agreed that such a thing would be unwise. "I'm very sorry to hear about these stupid people on the road," she said. "I'm sorry that we still have such people in these modern days."

"Yes," said Mr. J.L.B. Matekoni. "And so am I." He sniffed at the air. "Is that mutton stew, Mma? Is that what I can smell?"

"It is, Rra. There is a big pot waiting for

you — for us — in the oven. It will be ready after you have washed your hands. And while we are eating, I can tell you of a very strange thing that happened to me today. Or happened to both of us, should I say. To Mma Makutsi and me."

He went through to the bathroom to wash his hands, but they continued their conversation down the corridor. The children were never disturbed by the sound of voices and would sleep through even the most animated conversation elsewhere in the house.

"So something happened," he called out. "You found out some big important bit of information? You won a big prize — ten thousand pula? You saw a lion under your desk?"

She laughed. "These are all quite possible developments, Rra." For a moment she imagined Mma Makutsi suddenly whispering across the office, "Don't make any sudden movements, Mma, but I think there is a lion under your desk. I think I can see its tail." And she would reply, "I shall take what action is necessary, Mma Makutsi, but we really should finish dictation first . . ."

There came the sound of splashing water, and then the gurgle of the basin draining. "So what was it?" Mr. J.L.B. Matekoni asked. "You had a visitor?"

"Yes," she replied.

"What did you say, Mma?"

She raised her voice. "I said yes, Rra. We had a visitor, but you will never, never guess who it was. Not in a year of guessing. Not even then, with twenty, fifty guesses a day; even then you would never get it."

There was a momentary silence at the other end of the corridor. A tap was run again, and then there came the sound of the towel roller turning. "Well, Rra," Mma Ramotswe went on. "Try to guess. I'll give you one clue: he is very important."

"That man who wrote that book of yours. What is his name? That Chlorine Andersen, or whatever he's called."

"Clovis, not Chlorine."

"Him?"

She sounded crestfallen. "Yes, Rra. How did you know?"

He came back into the room, wiping his hands on the sides of his khaki trousers. "I guessed. You said that I would never guess, and so I chose the most unlikely name I could think of. And that was that man, Clovis Andersen. That's how I did it, Mma. Simple."

Over a large helping of mutton stew, Mma Ramotswe narrated the story of her extraordinary meeting with Clovis Andersen. It was the same story that Mma Makutsi had, just an hour or so earlier, told Phuti Radiphuti; but more accurate, perhaps, in Mma Ramotswe's telling of it than in that of her assistant. Mma Makutsi had a tendency to embellish stories for dramatic effect, or at least to tell the tale from her own perspective. In her version, then, Clovis Andersen had introduced himself first to her, rather than to Mma Ramotswe, had been facing her desk when he sat down, and had addressed almost all of his remarks to her. But in this, surely, she could be forgiven; for who among us does not see the world as turning towards him or her rather than towards others? The weather is weather in so far as it affects *us;* great events are great events in that they have an impact on *our* lives; life, in short, was to be judged by what it had in store for Mma Makutsi, or for those within her immediate circle. This was neither solipsism nor selfishness — Mma Makutsi was actually quite generous; rather, it was a matter of *perspective.* It was a universe made up of several key institutions, principal among which was the Botswana Secretarial College and all that it represented (the motto of the college being *Be Accurate*). Then there was the Double

Comfort Furniture Store, to which she was now firmly attached as the wife of its managing director (and the motto of that concern was *Be Comfortable*); the Government of Botswana, its ministers and permanent secretaries; and finally the No. 1 Ladies' Detective Agency and its owner and founder, Mma Ramotswe. This was her world, and these were the bodies to which she was unswervingly loyal.

Mr. J.L.B. Matekoni listened with interest to the story that Mma Ramotswe told, only interrupting her occasionally for clarification of some salient point.

"Out of the blue?" he asked. "He came out of the blue? Just like that?"

"Yes," said Mma Ramotswe. She had not told him about her dream; there would be an opportunity to discuss that later. "He came into the office and, believe it or not, Rra, to begin with Mma Makutsi and I had no idea of who he was. He was a stranger, obviously, but that was all we could tell. And there are so many strangers about these days, there was no reason why we should know; he could have been anyone."

"But do they not have a photograph of him on the cover of his book?" asked Mr. J.L.B. Matekoni. "I thought that they put photos of authors on books. So that you know what you're going to get."

Mma Ramotswe shook her head. "There is no photograph of Mr. Andersen. He is a very modest man. As you would be too, Rra, if you wrote a book. *The Principles of Car Maintenance,* for example. You would have a photograph of a car on it, not of you."

"I have not yet written a book," mused Mr. J.L.B. Matekoni. "I have thought of it, but I have not started one yet."

Mma Ramotswe was eager to continue with her story, but could not let this remark go uncommented upon. "This book of yours, Rra: Would it be about car maintenance, or is it something different?"

Mr. J.L.B. Matekoni looked bashful. "It will be something different, I think."

She looked at him expectantly. "Well, Rra?"

He hesitated, as if deciding whether to trust her with a secret. "I thought of writing something for ladies."

Mma Ramotswe's eyebrows shot up. "For ladies? That is very interesting, Mr. J.L.B. Matekoni! What exactly will this book for ladies be?"

"It will be on how to fix things in the house," he said. "There are many things that a lady can fix herself. Washing-machine repairs, for example, are not all that difficult. Then there are things that can go wrong with cars. There is no reason why ladies should not change tyres, or do simple things like that. You do not need a man to do those things." He paused. "That will be my book, Mma, if I ever write it, which I do not think I shall. I thought I might call it *Mr. J.L.B. Matekoni's Book of Hints for Ladies.*"

Mma Ramotswe clapped her hands together. "It will be a first-class book, Rra! They will sell it at that bookshop at Riverwalk. It will be in the window and take up all the space. Everybody will be buying it."

"I must write it first," said Mr. J.L.B. Matekoni. "And the problem is that I do not know how to do that. I am just a mechanic, Mma Ramotswe — as you well know. I am not a person who can write a book. You need a BA for that, and I do not have a BA."

They returned to the subject of Clovis Andersen.

"What did he want?" asked Mr. J.L.B. Matekoni.

"He did not want anything," said Mma Ramotswe. "He was passing by and he thought he would call in and say hello. It was just because he is a detective too. It is called a professional courtesy call, I think."

Mr. J.L.B. Matekoni took a forkful of his mutton stew. "Passing by? How is it that a famous person like that is just *passing by* the Tlokweng Road? How many famous people do you see on the Tlokweng Road, Mma Ramotswe? I have never seen one — not one. It is not a place where famous people like to go."

"Those were my thoughts too," said Mma Ramotswe. "So I asked him, and he told me."

She waited while Mr. J.L.B. Matekoni dealt with his mutton stew. Then she resumed. "He said that he was in Botswana because he was invited here to visit some lady."

"Some Motswana lady?"

She shook her head. "No, an American lady who has lived here for a few years. This lady is working here on a scheme that the American government has to build libraries in schools. They are building a library in Serowe, I think, and another one at Selebi-Phikwe. There will be many libraries all over the place, and it will be very nice for the children. That is what she is doing."

Mr. J.L.B. Matekoni nodded. "It sounds like good work. And so Mr. Andersen knows this lady, and she asked him to come to see her. Has he not got a wife back wherever he comes from? Is there no wife to say, 'You must not go off and visit library ladies'?"

Mma Ramotswe raised a finger in the air. "No, Rra, that is the point. There was a wife — there was a Mrs. Andersen, but she is late now."

Mr. J.L.B. Matekoni lowered his head, as was polite to do, even if one did not know the late person. "I am very sorry to hear that."

"Yes, it is very sad. So he has no wife now . . ."

"And he is hoping that the library lady . . ."

"No, he is not hoping that. But I think the library lady is hoping that she will be the new Mrs. Andersen."

"You mean she's keener than he is?"

"That is exactly what I mean. He did not use those precise words, of course, but that is the impression I formed. I think that she is keen to marry him, but he has different ideas. I think he wants her just as a friend."

"But what is the problem?" asked Mr. J.L.B. Matekoni. "Do they not like one another? Is that not the most important thing?"

"I think they do like one another. In fact, he said to me, 'I am very fond of this lady, but I do not love her.' That is what he said, Rra."

He shrugged. "There are many people who marry one another without being in love. There are many good marriages like that. I could make you a long list, Mma."

She looked away. Was their own marriage based on love, or was it something else that brought them together? Affection? Friendship? The comfort of sharing their lives? She knew what she felt about Mr. J.L.B. Matekoni: she loved him. It was as simple as that. He was her husband, and she loved him. And she had every reason to believe, she felt, that he had loved her when he asked her to marry him and she had agreed. She was sure that he had loved her when they stood together, before Bishop Mwamba, under that tree at the orphan farm, with the sound of the children's singing rising up into that great, empty sky and the words of the marriage service — those profound words — hanging in the air, proclaimed by the Bishop and repeated by the two of them so that all might hear; she was sure that he had loved her then, and she believed that he loved her still. She would not ask him, though, because you should never ask that question of another; you should wait for him or her to say it, so that you know, then, that it comes from the heart, from that part of us that can never lie, can never conceal the truth.

She acknowledged the veracity of what he said. "Yes, there are many such marriages, but I think that people still like to believe they are in love when they get married. I think that is important."

Mr. J.L.B. Matekoni looked thoughtful. "So he does not love this lady? Then why did he come out to see her here? Surely that is unkind, if she thinks that he's coming out to Botswana so that he can ask her to marry him, and all the time he has no intention of doing that. Surely that is not very kind."

She admitted that it could seem a bit like raising somebody's hopes, but would it not have been more unkind to refuse to come at all? He saw that. "It is a very difficult situation," he said. "It must have been very hard for Mr. Andersen." He stopped for a moment before continuing: "Why does he not love her, Mma? Is there a reason?"

Mma Ramotswe settled back in her seat. "That is the point, Rra. There is a very big reason why poor Mr. Andersen cannot love this lady who builds libraries. It is because he is still in love with his late wife. That is the reason."

Mr. J.L.B. Matekoni finished the last of

the mutton stew on his plate and looked enquiringly at Mma Ramotswe. Sometimes he was allowed a second helping, but these days, following the discovery that a belt he had been wearing for years no longer fitted him, he was on a less calorific regime.

"No more," she said. "We can eat the rest tomorrow."

He sighed, but did not argue.

"So, Mma Ramotswe, what is Mr. Andersen to do?"

"I do not know, Rra. All that I know is that he is sad in his heart." She touched her chest. "That is the place where his sadness is. Right there. And I do not think that it is ever very easy to deal with sadness in that part of the body."

He nodded his assent to that comment. "You are right, Mma. It is very difficult."

"But I shall do my best to cheer him up," said Mma Ramotswe. "I have invited him to come to the office tomorrow to discuss some of our cases. He was very happy to be invited — I think that he has nothing to do all day while the library lady is building libraries. And he is here for three weeks, Rra, which is a long time when you have nothing to do." She paused. "Except to be sad. Three weeks of sadness is a long time, I think."

It was, reflected Mr. J.L.B. Matekoni. Three weeks of sadness was a long time, by any standards, but it would be particularly long when one was far from home in a strange country, when everybody else would have their friends and family about them and would seem so occupied with their own lives. In such circumstances you might easily forget who you were, and how you once were happy. He almost expressed these thoughts to Mma Ramotswe, but did not do so, inhibited, perhaps, by the feeling that he was just a mechanic, not a poet or a philosopher, and that on the lips of mechanics such words might sound false or contrived, and certainly not as authentic as anything they might say on the subject of gearboxes, or fuel systems, or any of those other matters in respect of which he knew he stood on far firmer ground.

CHAPTER SEVEN:
THE THIS WAY UP BUILDING COMPANY

Grace Makutsi, Dip. Sec. (97%), did not accompany her husband, Mr. Phuti Radiphuti (of the Double Comfort Furniture Store), to his next meeting with Mr. Clarkson Putumelo, the proprietor of the This Way Up Building Company. This was not because she was indifferent to the design of the house that Mr. Putumelo was to build for them — she was extremely interested in that — but because she felt that she had not forgiven the builder his rudeness towards her and would avoid being in his presence until such time as he changed his attitude. That, she knew, was unlikely; in Mma Makutsi's opinion, attitudes were qualities with which one was born, and the likelihood of their being changed was, sadly, remote.

That is not to say it was impossible, as in her time she had witnessed a number of marked changes in attitude so profound, in fact, as to be quite astonishing. There was a man in northern Botswana, for instance, who was a known cattle thief; and yet while he was visiting a relative up near Kasane, he had come under the influence of a charismatic preacher and had been baptised in the waters of the Zambezi River. The change in that man had been so remarkable that there was talk of its being attributable to the special qualities of the Zambezi River. People said that as far as washing away sin was concerned, there was nothing to beat Zambezi water and that the religious zeal of those immersed in lesser waters — the No-twane River, to name just one river readily on hand for baptism ceremonies — was far less impressive than those of Zambezi converts. Of course it would be difficult to measure something as elusive as inner virtue, but in the case of this man there had certainly been a dramatic change. Far from stealing the cattle of others, he now actively sought out those that had been stolen, identified the thieves, and then reported the matter to the owners and the authorities. In all of this he was conspicuously successful, owing to his intimate knowledge of the ways of cattle thieves, his having been one in the first place. *Set a thief to catch a thief:* Mma Makutsi had read that somewhere, and it had struck her as containing a valuable insight — almost worthy of elevation into one of Clovis Andersen's famous rules in *The Principles of Private Detection.*

Mma Makutsi did not imagine that Mr. Clarkson Putumelo would change, and she therefore reconciled herself to having to watch the building of the house from a distance, making only irregular visits to the site. She had full confidence in Phuti, though, as she took the view that if you could manage a large furniture store, as Phuti did so successfully, then you could manage just about anything. She had nonetheless been careful to explain to Phuti exactly what she wanted in the kitchen. That would be her domain, and she wanted everything to be perfect. "The fridge," she said, "must not be too close to the door, or you will find that you cannot have the kitchen door open at the same time as you have the fridge door open."

"Very wise," said Phuti. "I would never have thought of that."

"That is because you're . . ." Mma Makutsi stopped herself in time. She had been about to say, "That's because you're a man," but then she thought that this was perhaps a bit unkind, even if it was true. You should not make people feel guilty about things that are beyond their control, and the fact that Phuti was a man was not something he could do anything about. So she completed the observation by saying instead, ". . . because you're too busy thinking about so many other important things. How can you be expected to think about fridge doors when your mind is full of big decisions on things like ordering furniture, and so on and so forth?"

Phuti nodded. It was true that he had many such decisions to make, but he also felt that he should concern himself with minutiae. He called this *micromanagement,* and he had learned about it from a correspondence course he had taken called "Managing the Details in Retail and Related Industries."

"Is there anything else?" he had asked. "Do you need one cooker or two?"

Mma Makutsi was unprepared for this question. Never in her wildest dreams had she imagined that she would be in a position to have two cookers; indeed, it was achievement enough, she felt, to have had the single-plate cooker-cum-oven that she had successfully used for the last few years. Two cookers!

"Oh, I think now that you mention it, we should perhaps have two," she said, trying to sound as casual as possible, as if the choice between one or two cookers was a decision of little weight — the sort of decision one might easily make without giving it much thought at all.

"So you will have two cookers then," said Phuti, proud that he was able to offer his new bride two cookers. "It is best to be prepared."

Mma Makutsi nodded gravely. She was not sure what eventuality they were planning for; indeed, she could not think of any reason why one would need two cookers, but they were now committed to a two-cooker kitchen, and she was happy enough with that.

There were several other minor matters to be settled.

"The floor must be easy to clean," said Phuti. "So I'll tell Mr. Putumelo to lay special tiles that can be easily washed."

Mma Makutsi thought this very wise. "But they must not be too slippery," she said. "Some of these modern tiles . . ." She shook her head, as might one who had only too frequently been wrong-footed on unsuitable tiles. In reality, for Mma Makutsi the thought of any tiles at all was almost intoxicating in its implications; her floors, until now, had been — at best — red-painted concrete, and not all that long ago, in Bobo-nong, the traditional option of packed mud.

They had spent a further half hour discussing cupboards — these were to be plentiful and deep enough to accommodate a vacuum cleaner as well as a full set of brooms and brushes. They also discussed the bedroom windows; these had to be of a sufficient size to let in enough light but not so large as to invite passers-by on the road to stare in at the occupants. "I cannot stand people staring in through your windows," said Mma Makutsi. "What happens in a house is none of the business of people outside that house. Inside is inside; outside is outside. That is what I always say." It was true that she did not like to be looked in on from outside, but what she did not mention was the fact that she herself frequently yielded to the temptation to glance through another's window if the opportunity presented itself. But she was a private detective, and such glances were not prompted by mere idle curiosity, or even nosiness; they were . . . a *professional* matter, an assessment — akin perhaps to the surreptitious clinical glance a doctor cannot help himself but give at a manifestly unhealthy person he passes on the street.

Armed with these requirements, Phuti

met the builder at the headquarters of the This Way Up Building Company. He had stipulated that the meeting should be there, turning down Mr. Putumelo's offer to come to the furniture shop, so that he could cast an eye over the builder's office before he signed the contract. In doing this he was following advice imparted to him by his father, who had always recommended doing business on the home ground of the other side. "If they are no good," he had said, "you will be able to tell that immediately. Look at their furniture. A man who has a rickety chair is a rickety businessman. A man whose table is not straight is himself not straight. These signs will never let you down, Phuti." It was an experienced furniture-seller's view of the world, but it had proved an accurate guide and had on more than one occasion prevented the signing of contracts that would have led to trouble and loss.

Mr. Clarkson Putumelo's office passed the Radiphuti test with no difficulty at all. The company had an impressive office on its own lot, not far from a cluster of prosperous shops off the old Francistown Road. There was an office building on which the company name was painted in large lettering, a garage in which several vehicles, working and otherwise, were parked, and a large yard in which piles of brick and timber were neatly stored under tarpaulins or standing corrugated-iron covers. There was nothing sloppy about the scene, and Phuti was immediately reassured.

"So, here you are, my friend," said Mr. Putumelo, welcoming Phuti into his office. "This is the headquarters of my little enterprise, as you see. It is from here that we go out every morning and build the new Botswana."

Phuti smiled. "And you build it the right way up," he said.

Mr. Putumelo did not appear to see the joke. "We are always building," he said solemnly. "That's the building trade for you. One building goes up, and you start the next."

"It's the same in the furniture trade," said Phuti. "You sell one bed and then you sell the next one."

Mr. Putumelo considered this for a moment before nodding in agreement. "That's business, isn't it? And who would have it otherwise?"

This exchange completed, they sat down to the business of agreeing the terms of the contract. "I have an offer for you," said Mr. Putumelo. "As you know, Rra, there are many people in this business who are bad men. They give the building trade a bad name because they are unscrupulous."

Phuti said that he had heard this.

"You see it in the newspapers," went on Mr. Putumelo. "You read about Mr. So-and-so or Mrs. What's-her-name having a big argument with a builder over some contract that went wrong. He says one thing and the builder says another. Blah, blah. And you know what, Mr. Radiphuti? In ninety-nine per cent of these cases it's because of the sort of contract they've signed. The builder has given a price for the job in order to get it, then he spends the rest of the time trying to do the thing on the cheap so that he ends up with a bit of profit. It's always the same. Agree a low price, then try to cut corners."

"I can see how that happens," said Phuti. "Sometimes with our suppliers we agree on a specification for, let's say, a set of chairs, and then —"

Mr. Putumelo cut him short. "Exactly, Rra. You hit the nail on the head."

"That's for a builder to do," said Phuti.

Again Mr. Putumelo did not appear to grasp the reference. "But," he said, raising a hand to emphasise his point, "I have a way round this problem. If you have a contract with the client that says *I will erect the building for cost plus twenty per cent,* then you can't go wrong. You get a good building; you don't get rubbish. I know that I'm going to make a profit, and so I don't try to cut any corners. What's the point of doing that?"

Phuti thought about this. He did not want his builder to cut corners; he wanted a solid house that would last them a lifetime. It seemed to him a very good idea, but he was a businessman and an opening percentage was always just that: the point at which negotiations could begin. "It seems a good approach," he said, "but the percentage . . ."

"Oh, that," said Mr. Putumelo. "That nineteen per cent margin . . ."

"Seventeen," said Phuti.

Mr. Putumelo shook his head. "Nineteen."

"Eighteen?"

"Done," said Mr. Putumelo, extending a hand. "You will not regret this, Rra. I can assure you of that."

Phuti took the builder's hand and shook it. "This is very good," he said.

The builder laughed. "Very good? It's excellent. First class." He reached for a piece of paper that had been lying face down on the desk. "Now all that we have to do is write in the relevant percentage here."

He fumbled in the breast pocket of his shirt for a pair of horn-rimmed spectacles. The effect of these glasses was to make him look erudite; like a teacher, thought Phuti, remembering, with a sudden pang, the teacher whom he had idolised at Gaborone Senior School and who had been killed one weekend by a drunken driver on the Lobatse Road, the young Radiphuti's first real encounter with death and with the realisation, so hard at that age, that immortals, too, can die.

A few scribbles of the pen and the contract was duly executed "according to the laws of Botswana," as its final clause attested. Phuti was pleased, and sealed the bargain again with a handshake, while continuing to fold and tuck the piece of paper with his free hand. That done, Mr. Putumelo reached for a brochure from a shelf behind his head and leafed through it to find an illustration to show his client.

"In my opinion," he said, "we should go for brick rather than for these concrete blocks that everybody is using these days. You can't go wrong with brick."

Phuti looked momentarily confused. "I thought that most houses were built with brick, except for low-cost housing." He pointed out of the window in the direction of the fields of neat, two-room, flat-roofed houses that the Government had built.

Mr. Putumelo shook his head. "No, Rra, you are wrong. Well, you are wrong and right, both at the same time. You see, you are right about that low-cost housing: it is very good for people who do not have much money, and they are happy with the concrete-block construction. And those houses are strong, too! They will not fall down for many years, I can tell you. But when it comes to big houses — the sort of house that a man like you wants to build, then you would think that good materials would be used. You would think that, wouldn't you?"

He waited for Phuti to answer.

"Yes, Rra. You would think that they would use —"

"Good-quality brick," interjected Mr. Putumelo. "Or even stone. You've seen those houses out at Mokolodi? You've seen those good stone walls? Those houses will last forever, my friend. One hundred years — easy. Maybe two hundred years. Who knows how long? How long is a piece of string? That is what I always say."

Phuti began to say something, but was again silenced by Mr. Putumelo.

"Now you'd think that a good-quality

house would be built of brick or stone, but is that what is happening today? I can tell you, Rra Radiphuti, that there are builders in this town who are making those high-class houses with concrete blocks and then just putting lots of fancy plaster on the outside and making people think there are solid things inside. That's what they are doing, those people, but we are not. We are still making good houses out of good building materials." He paused. "So you see this brochure, Rra? You see these bricks? They are top-quality bricks. I would recommend one outer layer and one inner layer, with good metal ties in between. Then we will put ventilation grilles to allow the house to breathe. That will keep you cool in the hot months. That is very important."

Phuti studied the picture of the brick. It seemed like an ordinary brick to him, but it had several lines of explanation printed below, setting out its superior properties. He handed the brochure back to the builder. "That is very good," he said. "I think that we should have those bricks, Rra."

Mr. Putumelo took off his glasses and deftly folded in the arms. "Done," he said. "I will order everything we need and then we can start . . ." He looked at an annotated calendar on the wall. "We can start in four days. Maybe three." Then he added: "Payment for work done will be due every ten days, for work done during those ten days, until completion of the contract. Agreed? Good."

Phuti had not been prepared for this: beginning a house was a major step, he thought, and it seemed now to be happening so quickly.

"There are some details that my wife has raised with me," he said. "I think that perhaps we might . . ."

Mr. Putumelo fixed him with an intense stare. "Your wife? She knows about houses?"

For a few moments, Phuti was at a loss. "She thinks that . . ."

Mr. Putumelo frowned. "Building a house is a very complicated matter, Rra. There are not many women in the building trade."

"But women know about houses, Rra," Phuti protested. "They are the ones who look after them."

Mr. Putumelo burst out laughing. "That is not the point, Rra. Women are very good at cleaning houses, but that does not mean that they know how to make them." He reached for a handkerchief from his pocket and dabbed at the corner of his mouth; a curious, rather fussy gesture. "But I must not stop you from telling me what your wife thinks, Rra. I am sure it is very interesting." The last remark was heavy with sarcasm.

Phuti told the builder of Grace's requirements. Mr. Putumelo reached for a pen and made a few notes; he looked sceptical as he wrote, as an unhelpful bank manager might look as he entertained a risky client's request for a loan. "I have written that down," he said, once Phuti had finished. "We shall see what can be done." He examined his own note. "There are some requests here that are not very practical, of course. And this business of two cookers: Where does that nonsense come from? Has your wife seen some picture in a magazine? Two cookers! Have we each got two mouths, Rra, so that we need to have two dinners at the same time?"

Phuti winced. It had been his suggestion, even if Grace had readily agreed to it, and he should have the courage to say as much to Mr. Putumelo. He should say: "No, that was not my wife's idea, Rra — it was mine, and I am the client. If I want two cookers, then I can have them. You are only the builder and I am paying you to do what *I* want. Understand?" That is what he should have said, he knew; but he did not say it. Instead, he said, "Two cookers are not an important element of the design, Rra. One will do quite well."

Mr. Putumelo appeared to take no notice of the concession. "And as for this business about floor tiles," the builder said. "All floor tiles are of much the same composition. I shall choose the right ones, and do not need to be reminded of what is necessary."

Again, Phuti did not protest. Mr. Putumelo knew what he was talking about — the horn-rimmed spectacles spoke to that, as did the pile of brochures and the certificate on the wall informing the public at large that Mr. Clarkson Putumelo was a member in good standing of the Botswana Federation of Master Builders. One could not argue with that, and if such a person said that one only needed one cooker, and that any floor tile he chose would most certainly not be too slippery, then such assurances should be accepted. Phuti realised that Mr. Putumelo was not perhaps the most charming of men, but did one necessarily want a charming builder? What one needed of a builder was an understanding of technical matters — it was clear that Mr. Putumelo had that. One expected, too, a sense of organisation and logistical skill — and it was equally clear from his orderly yard that Mr. Putumelo was endowed with these qualities. If he was also arrogant and dismissive of women, then these failings were to be regretted, but did not necessarily affect his ability as a builder. Or so Phuti told himself as he left the premises of the This Way Up Building Company, although he somehow felt guilty about this concession. It was as if he had failed in some way to stand up for his wife, as if he had been cowardly. *Perhaps I am a coward, perhaps that is what I am.* The bitter thought brought back something that had not troubled him for many months — his stammer. *C . . . c . . . c . . . coward,* he muttered in unhappy self-reproach. *F . . . f . . . frightened of a b . . . b . . . builder. You should be a . . . a . . . ashamed of yourself, Ph . . . ph . . . ph . . . uti R . . . r . . . r . . . r . . . adiphuti.*

CHAPTER EIGHT:
MMA RAMOTSWE DRIVES CLOVIS ANDERSEN TO MOCHUDI, AND THINKS

Mr. Clovis Andersen, author of *The Principles of Private Detection,* the great work of detection theory that had guided the No. 1 Ladies' Detective Agency since that momentous day on which it had opened its doors — the book now so familiar to Mma Ramotswe and Mma Makutsi that they could quote whole paragraphs without reference to the text itself — that same Clovis Andersen, who had so unexpectedly and impossibly stepped through the front door of the agency, was now due to meet Mma Ramotswe on the verandah of the President Hotel. It was mid-morning on the day following their first encounter, and Mma Ramotswe had arranged the meeting there because she was due to go out to Mochudi that morning and she wanted to show him the village where she was born and where she went to school. It would also be an opportunity for her to talk to the great detective without Mma Makutsi interrupting every second minute. It was clear to Mma Ramotswe that her assistant was starstruck, as she had gone on for some time about Clovis Andersen after he had left the office, her eyes flashing with excitement behind those large round glasses of hers. No, Mma Makutsi should not be allowed to monopolise Clovis Andersen just yet; she would have her fair share of the distinguished visitor's time, but it would be important not to create the impression at this early stage that *everybody* in Botswana wore large round glasses, made rather firm pronouncements on a wide range of subjects, and reminded others of the marks they had achieved in their final examinations in whatever it was they had studied. But even as she thought this, even as she heard Mma Makutsi's voice say *ninety-seven per cent,* she stopped herself. That was unkind, and she should not think it; that ninety-seven per cent was important to Mma Makutsi because she had started off with so little and had worked so hard to escape from a life of poverty and drudgery. She had worked hard to make something of her life when there were so many who simply sat about and took what life offered them. No, she would make sure that Mma Makutsi had ample time to spend in the company of Clovis Andersen, but not just yet . . .

The verandah of the President Hotel is not a place in which a great deal happens. This is not in any way to disparage it: it is important that there should be places where not a great deal happens because such places remind us that life is not entirely and exclusively made up of exciting or significant events. Every life needs spells of calm, every life needs expanses of time when nothing much occurs, when one may sit for several hours in the same place and gaze upon static things, upon some waxen-leafed desert plant, perhaps, or a patch of dry grass. Or a group of cattle standing under a tree for the shade, the slow, flicking movement of their tails the only indication that they are animate beasts, not rocks; or a sky across which no clouds, or perhaps only the merest wisp of white, move. Now, seated at her table on the verandah of the President Hotel, Mma Ramotswe had nothing much to look at while she waited. Down below, beyond the parapet, there were people in the square: sellers of clothes and dried herbs, carvers of wooden ornaments, sunglasses merchants, purveyors of potions to put on one's hair. All these were there, as were their customers, but Mma Ramotswe chose not to watch this market scene; rather, she looked up at the sky and wondered what it would be like not to have a sky above one's head — to be a prisoner, perhaps, or one who could not take the sun and had to remain indoors. She had known one such person when she was at school in Mochudi; a girl afflicted by albinism, whose pale, patchy skin, as brittle and translucent, it seemed, as the bark of what they called the paper tree, was so sensitive to the rays of the sun that she would burn painfully if she spent more than a few minutes outside. And that poor girl had been unable to go to school as she could not walk those miles from the family's village outside Mochudi, and they could not afford the creams that could protect her skin from the sun. And the other children had stared at her on the occasions that they saw her and had whispered among themselves. Mma Ramotswe felt the shame still that she had not done anything for that girl, and now she had heard that she was late, having died giving birth to her first child, and there had been no husband. There were so many lives, she thought, that could only be led with difficulty, with pain, and because we were so bound up in our own lives, so many of these were invisible to us until suddenly we saw, and knew, and felt that sudden pang of human sympathy that comes with knowing.

It was strange that the girl should come into her mind, the memory triggered by no more than looking up at the sky. But that, she told herself, was how memory worked; one would see something and then it would make one think of one thing and then of another; snatches of conversation would come back, images of things one had seen, memories that one thought one had forgotten, but that had been filed away in the back of the head, in those recesses where such things are tucked away. Clovis Andersen and his *Principles of Private Detection . . .* When had she first seen that book? Right at the beginning of her life as a private detective; and she had held it in her hand and opened it at the title page with all the excitement that you feel when opening a new book and there are the words on the page, ready for you, as if the author himself is standing in front of you, clearing his throat, ready to engage you in conversation. And she had seen the name Clovis Andersen little thinking that years later, after so much had happened, she would be meeting the very man, that he would address her as Mma Ramotswe; that she would, for a short time, have the attention of the world's greatest authority on private detection . . . Such a miracle, such an extraordinary development . . . such a privilege.

"Mma Ramotswe?"

She gave a start, and turned in her seat to see Clovis Andersen standing behind her. He was dressed in rather baggy khaki trousers with an olive-green shirt on to which far too many pockets had been stitched — the sort of outfit that people thought was standard dress for Botswana but was really only worn by visitors. It was a practical enough outfit, she supposed, but she wondered what people could possibly do with so many pockets. Did they imagine that one needed to carry penknives and compasses and the like, even when going to Mochudi?

"This is a very fine view you get from here," said Clovis Andersen as he sat down.

Mma Ramotswe glanced at the square and remembered how, long ago, she had once asked the dress-seller down below for information because she knew that such people missed very little of what happened around them. And Clovis Andersen himself had said . . .

"You see that woman," said Mma Ramotswe as Clovis Andersen settled himself into his chair. "I asked her for information once. She knows everything, I think. And you say in your book *Always ask somebody who knows*. That is what you wrote, Rra, and I have always followed that advice."

Clovis Andersen smiled. "I remember writing that. And I suppose it's true, isn't it? If you ask somebody who doesn't know anything, then you won't get much of an answer. At least, that's the way I look at it."

"But you're so right, Rra," said Mma Ramotswe. "And I have always wondered how you know all these things. It must be experience, I think."

Clovis Andersen looked away. "Experience and common sense," he said. "There are so many jobs that are just a matter of common sense. Most jobs, in fact. They look complicated, but when you look closely you'll see that all you really need is common sense."

Mma Ramotswe considered this. It was true that private detection involved a great deal of common sense, and undoubtedly there were many other professions in which common sense would get you by, but surely there were those where the limits of common sense would very soon be revealed — being a dentist, for example, or an airline pilot . . .

She toyed with the idea of pointing this out to him, but decided not to. The traditional ways of Botswana were clear about correcting a person who was senior to you, or a stranger, and on both of these counts she should not directly contradict Clovis Andersen. You did not have to remain silent, of course, if such a person was wrong, but you should be careful how you voiced your disagreement. So she simply said, "Common sense is very useful. Yes."

There was a brief silence. Then she said, "You must have seen so many things, Rra. In your career as a detective, you must have seen so many things."

Clovis Andersen nodded. "There are many things to be seen in this life, Mma. All one has to do is keep one's eyes open."

Mma Ramotswe voiced her agreement. "Oh, you are so right, Rra. The big mistake is to close your eyes. There are so many who have closed eyes. You look at them, of course, and you think that they have open eyes, but then you look more closely and you realise that although their eyes are open, there is nothing going in."

"That's because they aren't looking," said Clovis Andersen. "If you do not look, you do not see."

"That is so true, Rra," enthused Mma Ramotswe. "That is so true."

He went on. "There are some people who have their eyes open and are looking, but do not see anything because they are looking for something that is not there. That can happen, I believe."

"Oh, I believe that too, Rra," said Mma Ramotswe. "I have always believed that — all along."

"That is not to say there's nothing there," continued Clovis Andersen. "There may be something there, but because nobody's looking for it, it won't be seen. So we should always ask ourselves: are we looking for the right thing?"

Mma Ramotswe agreed again. "That is definitely the thing to do," she said.

The waitress appeared, notebook at the ready, to take their order. Clovis Andersen ordered coffee, which made Mma Ramotswe smile; she had heard about the American weakness for coffee, but again she said nothing; people cannot help liking the things that are liked where they are born. At some point in the future she would introduce him to the pleasures of tea; there would be plenty of time for that.

The waitress moved off, and their conversation continued.

"Your cases must be much bigger ones than mine," said Mma Ramotswe. "I am always dealing with very small things. Is that man cheating on this woman; is that woman cheating on this man? Who is stealing cattle here, or taking money there? Who is using the company truck for private business when the rule is that it must not be used for such things? That sort of thing — very different from the big cases you must have every day. Who has shot this person? Who has shot that person? Who has taken the million-dollar necklace from the neck of this big film star? Big things like that."

Clovis Andersen looked at the floor. "Not really," he muttered.

"And one day I can see them making a big film about your life," Mma Ramotswe continued. "It will be very popular through-out the world, and I will say to Mma Ma-kutsi, 'That is our friend, Mma — that is all about our friend.' "

Clovis Andersen shook his head. "Oh, I don't think so, Mma Ramotswe. I don't think I'll be of sufficient interest for that."

Sensing his reluctance to talk about it — an admirable modesty, she thought — she changed the subject. She asked him about his plans to see the country, and he told her that he had organised a trip to Ghanzi over the next few days. For now, though, he was keen to see the area around Gaborone. "Mochudi, then," said Mma Ramotswe. "That is the place, Rra." They should start the drive up to the village immediately after their tea — or tea and coffee — as it would be better to arrive there before the noonday heat made it uncomfortable to sit in the van, in spite of its ancient, if valiant, fan.

"I am looking forward to seeing it, Mma Ramotswe," said Clovis Andersen. "I come from a similar place, you know — a small town in the Midwest. And my wife too, she comes . . . came from such a place. She always said . . ."

He faltered, and she watched him.

"It is good to talk about late people, Rra," she said quietly. "It is what they want us to do. Late people would be happy if they knew we were talking about them."

He looked up, as if he had heard some important piece of news.

"Do you think that's true, Mma Ramotswe? Do you think they can hear us?"

She wanted to say yes. She wanted to reassure this man who was obviously still so full of grief. But could she? She did not know — not in her heart of hearts — whether her father, the late Obed Ramotswe, could hear her. She addressed him often enough, drawing his attention to some unusual sight she encountered along the road; she addressed him as if he were sitting there in the van with her, but she thought that it was just wishful thinking, nothing more than that. She did not think that he had altogether ceased to exist, but of where exactly he was, where that place to which he had gone was located, she had no idea, other than it was somewhere above Botswana, or on the same level as Botswana but around some corner that one day we all must turn. Beyond that, she could not be certain. All she knew was that it would be a place of cattle bells and gentle, life-giving rain; a place in which all our tears would be wiped tenderly away.

"I am not sure about these things, Rra," she said quietly. "But I think that they are watching over us somehow — the people who have gone before." She fixed him with a gaze; the poor man in his sorrow. "Your late wife will know that you still love her, Rra. She will know that."

Chapter Nine:
The Government Does Not Own the Air

Mma Ramotswe had planned to spend the following day carrying out a number of minor tasks that for one reason or another she had been putting off. There were bills to be paid — a painful process for both her and Mma Makutsi, who had a special expression she adopted as she folded the cheques and placed them in their envelopes. "You have your bill-paying face on," Mma Ramotswe remarked. "It is as if you were swallowing some bitter medicine, Mma. Or eating an aloe, maybe."

Mma Makutsi acknowledged that she found the whole business of paying bills a difficult one. "There are just too many bills," she complained. "If there were only one or two, then I could pay them without looking as if I had vinegar on my tongue. But look at them, Mma . . . electricity bills, the book-keeper's bill, the stationery bill, the water bill . . . How much water do we use here, Mma? How can they charge us this much when all we do is take a little bit of water to make tea? And a little bit of water for the bathroom? That is all. But they charge us as if we're the Victoria Falls. Look at that bill! Just look at it."

"Water is very precious," said Mma Ramotswe. "It is not cheap."

Mma Makutsi was unimpressed. "And soon there will be a bill for air," said Mma Makutsi. "They will be saying: you have used so much of the Government's oxygen this month — please pay us. Terms: thirty days net."

Mma Ramotswe laughed. "I do not think so, Mma —"

Mma Makutsi, sticking down an envelope flap with perhaps slightly more force than was strictly necessary, cut her short. "And who says the air belongs to the Government, anyway?"

"I don't think the Government says that, Mma."

"Oh, don't they? I think they do, Mma. If they didn't say that the air belongs to them, then why do they say that you need their permission to fly through it? Phuti knows a pilot, and he told him that he has to speak on the radio to some government people called Air Traffic Control and ask their permission to fly through the air above Gaborone. That means that they think they own it — as if it's their own yard, or something like that."

Mma Ramotswe shook her head. "They do not say they own the air, Mma. All that those people are doing is making sure that planes don't fly into one another. If you've got one plane going this way and another plane flying from the other direction and they meet, then that would not be very good, would it?"

Mma Makutsi hesitated for a moment; but no, she was not convinced. "They are just interfering," she said. "The pilots can see exactly where they're going. They're not asleep."

"It happens very quickly," said Mma Ramotswe. "And there are clouds, Mma. You cannot see what is happening in a cloud."

"Then you shouldn't fly through them," snapped Mma Makutsi. "You see a cloud and you go round it. That is all you need to do. Phuti says that it's not a good thing to fly through clouds. You can get struck by lightning and then that will be the end."

Mma Ramotswe was silent. She had great admiration for Mma Makutsi, but not when she was in one of these contrary moods.

When that happened, she would dig in over some matter and become quite unreasonable, even if it was plain that she was arguing a lost cause. There were so many examples of her doing this, and Mma Ramotswe had learned that the best response was to change the subject.

"Lightning is very dangerous," she said. "Not just in the air. That poor man in Molepolole — did you read about him, Mma? He was struck by lightning when he was walking home across a field. He is late now."

"It was very sad," said Mma Makutsi. "I read that the lightning hit his hat. Perhaps he should have had a lightning conductor on the top of it, with a wire going down his back to the earth. Do you think that would work, Mma?"

"I do not think so, Mma Makutsi," said Mma Ramotswe. "It is safer to stay indoors."

"Oh no, it isn't," came the quick rebuttal. "One of the men who worked for Phuti — one of the men who loaded furniture — he fell over in his own house and broke his leg. They took him to hospital, but that stuff you have in the middle of your bones . . ."

"Bone marrow."

"Yes, that stuff. It leaked into his blood and blocked one of his pipes . . ."

"Blood vessels."

Mma Makutsi shook her head solemnly. "Exactly. It blocked it up and now he is late too."

There was a silence. Mma Ramotswe looked at the clock. She had things to do outside the office, and she thought that it was a good time, perhaps, to get out and about and leave Mma Makutsi to attend to the office tasks. By the time she got back, Mma Makutsi might be in a less difficult mood.

"I have to go and see Mma Potokwane," Mma Ramotswe announced, rising from her chair. "This business with Mr. Ditso. I must get some more details from her."

"That one's not going to end well," said Mma Makutsi. "We'll never find out anything about that man, Mma. He's far too clever for us . . ." She looked across the room at Mma Ramotswe. "I'll tell you something, Mma. You know how they say *money talks?* Well, I say the opposite is true: *money doesn't talk.* And I say that because money never tells you where it has come from. Never. So if Mma Potokwane thinks that she will find out that this rich man of hers has got his money from some bad place, she is going to be very disappointed.

Money has no mouth, Mma. It cannot speak."

Mma Ramotswe shook her head. "Don't give up before we've started, Mma." She paused. "And remember: we have a secret weapon."

Mma Makutsi frowned. "And what would that be, Mma?"

Mma Ramotswe waited for a few moments before she answered. "Clovis Andersen," she said simply.

The large round glasses caught the light; flashed. The contrariness evaporated — at least to an extent. Yes. Clovis Andersen. Oh yes!

She drove out to Tlokweng along one of the back roads — a roundabout way that gave her time to get over the tension that Mma Makutsi's odd mood had injected into the day. Driving, she found, always helped her to unwind, and as she made her way slowly along the winding dirt road she found herself smiling again. The one thing you could not say about Mma Makutsi was that she was dull; far from it — Mma Makutsi was what her friend Mma Moffat would have described as *a character.* And it was better to be a character, she felt, than to be one of those people who spoke about nothing at all, and probably thought about nothing too; such people were soporific and could be marketed by some enterprising person as *walking sleeping pills.* Yes, that was a good idea: if you had difficulty sleeping you could phone up one of these people and, for a small charge, they would come to your house and sit and look at you, and you would gradually nod off to sleep. You would have to pay them first, though, as otherwise they would have to wake you up to collect their fee, and that would defeat the purpose of calling them in the first place . . . And there could be another service for people who felt sleepy but for some reason needed to keep awake. They could phone for Mma Makutsi, and she would come and talk about this and that and make the sort of remarks that would keep people on their toes, puzzling over what she meant, or getting irritated and hot under the collar because they disagreed with what she was saying. Makutsi Wake-up Services would be a good name for such a concern. There were so many possible businesses . . .

She turned a corner, and there was another small business, set back from the road — one she had not seen before. The Minor Adjustment Beauty Salon. She slowed down. The premises was a tin shed — not much more than a shack — topped with a freshly painted notice announcing the name of the concern and laying claim to national pre-eminence in the field. *Famous throughout Botswana,* the notice claimed. *First consultation free. No appointment necessary.*

She stopped on impulse. Mma Ramotswe did not patronise beauty salons, although she knew many who did, including, she suspected, Mma Makutsi. There was something about this salon that intrigued her, though, and she had time on her hands. Mma Potokwane was not expecting her, and so it did not matter when she arrived at the orphan farm. If the initial consultation was free, then it would be interesting to see what they suggested. And there was another reason for stopping: as a private detective, Mma Ramotswe was acutely aware of the importance of contacts, who might provide information at some point in the future. The people who ran beauty salons were known to be repositories of gossip, and the owner of the Minor Adjustment Beauty Salon would probably be no exception to that general rule. There would be no harm, she thought, in making a new acquaintance who was so placed.

As she parked the van, she became aware of a face and then a pair of eyes peering out at her from the dark interior of the building. She stepped out of the van and closed the door behind her, which was the signal for the face and eyes to emerge too; now she saw a woman in a blue dress, rather like a nurse's tunic, standing in the doorway watching her. The woman greeted her as she approached.

"*Dumela,* Mma." An outstretched hand.

The greetings over, the woman gave her name. "I am Mma Soleti. I am the owner here."

Mma Ramotswe inclined her head. "I am Precious Ramotswe." There was a moment's hesitation; it did not always help to say that one was a detective, but honesty, she felt, required it. "I have a small business, the No. 1 Ladies' Detective Agency."

Mma Soleti smiled, exposing strikingly white teeth. "I know that place. I sometimes drive past it. There is a garage too."

"That is Tlokweng Road Speedy Motors. The mechanic is my husband."

Mma Soleti nodded. "I hear he is very good."

Mma Ramotswe beamed with pleasure. She never tired of hearing compliments paid to her husband. "I am very lucky to be married to such a man," she said. "He is kind."

"That is very good, Mma."

A brief silence ensued before Mma Ramotswe spoke again. "A consultation . . . I was wondering . . ."

Mma Soleti clapped her hands together. "And I was hoping! I said to myself, 'This is a lady who will do very well with a bit of guidance and adjustment.' You have made a very good decision, Mma."

Mma Ramotswe drew back involuntarily. "Just an initial consultation, Mma. I don't know if I want to do too much. I am traditionally built, you see, and I am not normally one who bothers too much about these matters of fashion."

Mma Soleti considered this for a moment, turning her head slightly as if to assess Mma Ramotswe from a different angle. "Really, Mma? But being traditionally built is a positive advantage, in my view. You see, if a lady is one of these modern . . ."

"Stick insects," Mma Ramotswe supplied.

Mma Soleti burst out laughing. "Yes, that is what they are, Mma. Stick insects. It's very difficult to do much with those ladies because . . . well, there's so little of them. But with a traditionally built lady like yourself, it's like painting a big wall — there's much more room for the artist." She paused. "And I do think of myself as an artist, Mma."

Mma Ramotswe found herself warming to this woman. Following her into the tin building, she saw that there was a plastic-covered couch, rather like those used by doctors to examine their patients, a desk, and a glass-fronted cupboard full of bottles and jars. Mma Soleti gestured for her to sit on the edge of the couch. "There is no need to lie down, Mma. Not at this stage. I shall be mostly concerned with the face in this consultation. We can deal with the rest of you some other time."

Mma Ramotswe perched on the edge of the couch. It was of such a height that her feet barely touched the ground, and one of her shoes, her flat walking shoes that were such a contrast to Mma Makutsi's more fashionable footwear, began to slip off. Mma Soleti paid no attention to this. She had picked up a large magnifying glass and had begun to peer closely at her new client's face. It was a disconcerting experience; the beautician's eyes, viewed from the other side of the glass, were large, like the eyes of a fish, Mma Ramotswe thought.

"Mmm," said Mma Soleti, adding: "Aahh."

"You have seen something?" asked Mma Ramotswe.

"Nothing," said Mma Soleti, moving the

focus of her gaze across to the other side of Mma Ramotswe's face. "I have seen nothing that I didn't think I'd see."

Mma Ramotswe wondered what that meant, and was on the point of enquiring when Mma Soleti said, "Oh."

"Is there anything wrong, Mma?"

"There is nothing wrong. This is a very good face, Mma. There can be no arguing about that. This is a good Botswana face."

Mma Ramotswe was not sure what to make of that. She frowned, only to provoke an immediate warning from Mma Soleti. "Try not to frown, Mma. That makes lines on the face, and if you go on frowning, those lines will be there forever, even when you aren't frowning inside."

"I was just wondering about what it meant to say that I have a good Botswana face."

"It means that you have the best sort of face," said Mma Soleti, finishing her examination. "Botswana faces are honest faces. There are some faces that are very different, I'm afraid. Those people have faces that are full of anger or anxiety or all those things — negative things."

"I see."

"Yes, Mma. That is what I meant." She lowered the magnifying glass and sat down opposite Mma Ramotswe. "Now, Mma," she continued, "we need to talk about your skin. There are some big holes in it."

Mma Ramotswe gasped. "Holes in my skin?"

Mma Soleti reached out and took her hand. "Don't worry, my sister. They are just what we call enlarged pores. They are normal. Most people have some enlarged pores. They let grease out. Very greasy people have many of them; people who are not so greasy do not have so many."

"That's a relief, Mma."

"Yes," said Mma Soleti. "You need not worry. Your skin is actually very good. But we can do something to make those enlarged pores go away. There are some cleansers that we can use to get all the impurities out, and then the skin will take care of itself."

The beautician rose from her chair and opened the cupboard behind her. Leaning forward to read the labels, after a few minutes she chose a jar with a white and silver label. "This is very good," she said. "If you apply this at night before you go to bed, it will do its work while you are asleep. Many of my customers have been made very happy by this cream."

Mma Ramotswe took the open jar from Mma Soleti and sniffed at it. She liked the smell. "I suppose there's no harm in trying . . ."

"No harm at all," said Mma Soleti, taking the jar back from her and slipping it into a paper bag. "You are very wise, Mma. That will last you for maybe one month. Then you can get some more."

The cream was less expensive than Mma Ramotswe had feared. She paid, and then accepted Mma Soleti's offer of a cup of tea. Her favourable impression of the beautician had grown stronger, and she did not resent the purchase she had been rather press-ganged into making. But now, she decided, she might get her share of benefit from the encounter.

"You have many clients, Mma?" she asked.

Mma Soleti nodded. "More than ever, Mma. This month was busier than last month, and last month was busier than the month before."

"You must see everything, Mma. In this job of yours you must see everything."

Mma Soleti looked at her sideways. "Are you asking me that as a private detective, Mma? Is that why you are asking?"

She's clever, thought Mma Ramotswe; this woman understands. "As a detective," she confessed.

"You're very honest, Mma. I like that."

Mma Ramotswe waited for her question to be answered.

"So, I see everything? Well, yes, I think I do. I see and hear a lot." She paused. "Is there anything in particular you want to know, Mma?"

Mma Ramotswe was not prepared for this. She had not intended to ask any direct questions — at least not at this stage — and she was not sure what to say. But then she thought: Mr. Ditso.

"There's a man we're interested in at the moment," she said. "He's called Ditso. You will have heard of him, Mma?"

The effect of the question was immediate, and Mma Ramotswe wondered whether she had inadvertently asked about Mma Soleti's cousin. There was a presumption in Botswana, she had discovered, that if you talked to one person about another, then the two persons in question would be cousins, or even brother and sister; she had proved that time and time again. And that meant you had to be very careful.

"Are you related to that man?" she asked Mma Soleti.

The beautician shook her head vigorously. "I have never met him. But I know one thing about him, Mma. I know one thing that maybe I shouldn't talk about."

Mma Ramotswe made a sympathetic noise. "It's generally better to talk, Mma. It's not good to bottle things up."

Mma Soleti seemed only too ready for this advice. "I shall tell you then, Mma. My sister is a beautician too, Mma. Actually, she is my half-sister, and she does sessions at that nail place, you know, near the post office. She is very good. She has a diploma in nail care from Durban. She went down there to get it. It was very expensive going all the way to South Africa, but she said it was worthwhile. Now she does very well."

"Time spent on getting qualifications is never wasted," said Mma Ramotswe.

"You have qualifications in detection, no doubt," said Mma Soleti. "Are they hard to get? I can imagine they would be."

Mma Ramotswe sighed. "I have no qualifications, Mma."

Mma Soleti stared at her in surprise. "You mean any old person can go and put a sign up saying that she is a private detective? Is that true, Mma?"

Mma Ramotswe nodded. "But I have done a lot of studying," she said. "There is a very good book, you see. *The Principles of Private Detection*." She paused; she was not boastful, but there were some temptations that were irresistible, and this, she decided, was one. "I know the author, you see, Mma." Immediately she regretted it, and added: "Not very well, though. I could not really call him a friend."

She need not have worried. If Mma Soleti were to be impressed, then it was not to be by the mention of a mere author. "People write books," she said casually. "I have had people in here who are thinking of writing a book."

Mma Ramotswe gently nudged the conversation back in the direction that she wanted it to follow. "Your sister, Mma . . ."

Mma Soleti remembered. "Of course, yes, my sister: she has that nail place near the post office in town. She is very busy with people's nails, and gets many people coming in to see her. Sometimes it is almost too late to do much for them, as they have neglected their nails." Her gaze moved to Mma Ramotswe's nails, and was noticed. Mma Ramotswe glanced down too: she did not use nail varnish, although there was a bottle of it somewhere, unless Motholeli had been playing with it, which was very likely. But there was nothing essentially wrong with her nails, she believed; they did what they were supposed to do, which was . . . What were nails meant to do?

"So all sorts of people come in," continued

Mma Soleti. "And she says that one of the women who come in to have their nails done is the secret sweetheart of that man, that rich man you mentioned. She is secret because he has a wife, and the wife comes in to have her nails done too! My sister has to make sure that their appointments don't overlap. Can you imagine that, Mma? That would not be very good, I think."

Mma Ramotswe nodded. She wanted to hear more of this story, but she did not want to probe too obviously; in her experience, people could suddenly dry up if you became too insistent in your questioning. "Oh well," she said. "Men are often doing that, Mma."

"They are, my sister," said Mma Soleti. "But I do not always blame men, you know. They are very weak, and there are some women who are prepared to take advantage of that weakness." She looked knowingly at Mma Ramotswe, as if to imply that should she wish it, she could provide a long list of such women.

"That is very true," said Mma Ramotswe. "I have known some bad women in my work." She paused, and looked out of the tin building's small window — a patch of sky, cloudless and innocent, blue. There was no glass between her and that sky; the window must be secured by a shutter that had been opened. There had to be a shutter: you could not leave all those potions and creams unguarded, she thought; greasy people, open-pored, walking past, might seize the opportunity to help themselves to skin cleansers . . . "Who is this woman, Mma? Do you know her?"

Mma Soleti shook her head. "She did not give my sister her name. She just calls herself by some name that my sister thinks she has invented. She actually forgot one time what she had called herself before."

"I do not think you forget your own name," said Mma Ramotswe. "Not normally."

"No."

"Even if you are very busy . . ."

"No. Not even then."

Mma Ramotswe asked a final question. "And you know nothing else about her, Mma?"

Mma Soleti appeared to consider this for a few moments. "The only thing my sister said is that she is one of those women who are always looking out for men. You know the type? She is not interested in talking to women."

Mma Ramotswe knew exactly what Mma Soleti meant. There was a certain sort of woman who was always aware of which men

164

were in the vicinity and was always very attentive to them, but who would neither notice women nor bother to speak to them. Women like Violet Sephotho, for instance . . .

CHAPTER TEN:
SHE WAS LIKE
A DEFLATED BALLOON

Mma Potokwane was not in her office when Mma Ramotswe arrived at the orphan farm. This was not unusual: the matron was often to be found in one of the outlying buildings, attending to one of the numerous minor, or sometimes major, problems that might be expected to crop up in the day-to-day life of an orphanage. Most of these she resolved herself, dispensing advice, fixing something, or simply wiping away tears; all of which she did with the same brisk confidence that she applied to any task that confronted her. Not for nothing had Mma Potokwane previously been appointed as matron of a small but well-run hospital, and the skills she had learned in the wards there — dealing with unhappy or nervous patients, keeping nurses and others on their toes — she now applied in the rather different circumstances of the orphan farm.

Mma Ramotswe, still thinking of her

conversation with her new acquaintance, Mma Soleti, parked her tiny white van under the tree that always shaded it on her visits: a towering jacaranda tree on the lower limbs of which the children had climbed, rubbing the bark bare with their legs. We should all have a tree in our childhood, she thought — a tree one might explore, a tree from which one might learn how to fall. She had fallen out of just such a tree as a girl and winded herself, while the children who were with her stood in a circle about her and laughed; they were boys, of course, and found misfortune funny in a way in which girls did not. She had never forgotten the sensation of being winded: of having all the breath knocked out of you and waiting for your lungs to draw it back in — but it was as if your lungs were stunned and were waiting for instructions from you . . .

She made her way to the verandah that lined the building in which Mma Potokwane had her office. The door leading off into the office was open, and she could see that nobody was within. A fan had been left on, though, and was whirring away industriously. That meant that Mma Potokwane would not be far away — a counter of thebes every bit as much as pula, she would not waste electricity for long. Many of the goods supplied to the orphan farm she begged and borrowed from businessmen in the town, but you could not do that with electricity. There was no human face to the electricity board, no manager whom one could negotiate a lower price with or sweet-talk with a promise of some future favour. The electricity board charged a set amount for electricity, and if you used it, you had to pay for it. There was no way round that, as there was with other bills. *You can't be charging the poor orphans that much* was one of Mma Potokwane's favourite lines, regularly invoked against traders who supplied the orphan farm with its needs, and it was often highly successful. But you could not say that to an electricity board that had no shame, no sense of what it was like to be an orphan.

Mma Ramotswe decided to go in search of the matron rather than stay in her office and wait for her to return. She did not like to sit unattended in another's office — even if invited, explicitly or implicitly. There was always the feeling, she thought, that the person whose office it was would think that you had sneaked a look at the papers on the desk, which was what some inquisitive people did, no matter how hard it was to read upside down. And that notion reminded her of Clovis Andersen, who had written — had he not? — in *The Principles of Private Detection,* something about learning to read upside down. It came back to her now, from that section of the book that dealt with the skills that a good detective should try to master. "Being able to read in a poor light puts one at a great advantage over those who cannot," he wrote. "There have been many occasions when I have been able to glean information from a document which would be too poorly lit to be legible to most. And the same ability has seen me safely through a number of tricky, not to say perilous, situations." And what, she wondered, were those? Now she could ask him, of course, although he would only be able to tell her about them as long as disclosure on his part would not compromise the strict rules of confidentiality that he set out elsewhere in the book.

Then had come the section on reading upside down. "Now there can be no doubt," he wrote — and how she loved that phrase, *there can be no doubt;* how assured it was, how definitive — "Now there can be no doubt but that being able to read upside down is extremely useful and is, in fact, a skill well worth mastering. It enables you to read a document that lies before the person on the other side of the desk from you. They may think that you cannot read it; they may think that they can tell you what is in the document without your being able to verify their version. But they reckon without your ability to read upside down!"

Indeed they do, thought Mma Ramotswe.

"And it also enables you," Clovis Andersen continued, "to read papers lying about on a suspect's desk. These are usually facing the wrong way, and you cannot necessarily turn them round. Nor will it do to turn your head."

Mma Ramotswe had imagined the contortions such a manoeuvre would entail and had decided that it was impossible to angle one's head and neck in such a way as to be able to read satisfactorily. It could not be done, she decided, unless one were somehow to upend oneself — to do a handstand, so to speak — which would be difficult and self-defeating, as one's dress would drop down over one's head and eyes and effectively prevent one from seeing anything, let alone reading. And it would be difficult to explain what was happening if the suspect returned to his office and found a visitor with her legs pointing up to the ceiling. Anything you might say in such circumstances would surely sound somewhat weak.

"I was practising my handstands — I hope you don't mind." Nobody would believe that, not even the normally gullible. They would suspect that something untoward was happening — and they would be right about that.

There were few matters on which she disagreed with Clovis Andersen's advice, but this, perhaps, was one of them. She was not sure that it was ever right to read somebody else's letters or private papers unless you were certain that it was the only way of averting some very serious consequence. Or . . . and there were other exceptions. Errant husbands, for instance, could hardly complain if a wife, or somebody acting for the wife, read the letters they might write to their mistresses. That was because a wife has a right to read her husband's letters, in Mma Ramotswe's view, because he agreed to that in the marriage ceremony; not that those exact words were used, but they were surely implied. Perhaps it might be better to spell it out in the wedding service, where it might be put tactfully, along with the general promise to share. *I promise to share all my worldly goods — including letters, parcels, and other items of correspondence, opened or unopened.* Perhaps that sounded a bit too formal, but no doubt there were ways of saying the same thing in a warmer, more romantic way.

No, she would not wait in Mma Potokwane's office but would go in search of her. As she stepped off the verandah into the hot sun, she saw one of the housemothers standing at the door of one of the small buildings that served as home for eight or so children. These were busy women, who cooked and cleaned all day, and made a home that each child could regard as his or her own. They were not necessarily educated women, but that was not the point; what they had was far more valuable than any formal education, and that thing was love, vast wells of it, enough for ten children, for twenty if need be.

This house-mother, who knew Mma Ramotswe well — having come from Mochudi — greeted her warmly as she approached.

"I am not just standing here," she said to Mma Ramotswe after the traditional greetings had been exchanged. "Don't think that I'm being lazy. I'm thinking about what I have to do next."

Mma Ramotswe laughed. "I would never think you lazy, Mma," she said. "I know how hard you work."

The house-mother sighed. "Our work is never done, Mma, but there we are. That is just one of the things that God has said must be. He said: mothers must work hard. That is a firm rule."

Mma Ramotswe nodded. "But he also wants mothers to have a bit of a rest sometimes. That is why he said: men must not be lazy, and must help ladies."

The house-mother grinned. "Were men listening when the Lord said that?"

"I think that some were," said Mma Ramotswe. "But others did not hear too well."

That led to further mirth. Then Mma Ramotswe asked if the house-mother had seen Mma Potokwane. "She has gone over to her house, Mma," came the reply. And then, after a short pause, "She is not happy, I think."

Mma Ramotswe frowned. That was very unlike Mma Potokwane, who had a reputation for a certain breeziness and optimism. "Not happy? Are you sure, Mma?"

The woman nodded. "I spoke to her about my fridge and told her that it was not working very well. I told her that some of the meat I had for the children had turned bad, and that this was a waste. You should not waste good meat, Mma."

"And?" pressed Mma Ramotswe.

"And she said something that was really nothing. You know how it is when a person says something but it is really nothing very much at all?"

"I do, Mma. But, tell me, why should Mma Potokwane be unhappy?"

The house-mother said that she did not know. She agreed that it was unusual; perhaps she was not feeling well — there had been a few cases of flu recently, and when you had flu you did not feel inclined to be cheerful.

"No," said Mma Ramotswe. "It is hard to smile when your head is splitting."

The house-mother nodded. "She was like a balloon with all the air taken out of it," she said. "You know how that looks, Mma?"

Mma Ramotswe did. She exchanged a few more comments with the house-mother, and then took her leave. Mma Potokwane's house was at the far end of the orphan-farm grounds, beyond the vegetable patches that the children worked, beyond the scrap of ground that the smaller boys used as their soccer pitch: a square of dusty, baked earth devoid of so much as a blade of grass, but the scene of many a tiny sporting triumph, a ball sent shooting past the goalkeeper, a clever pass — things that were in their transience quickly forgotten but for a short time meant so much in a young life that had not known much triumph or even, until now, much love.

She stood at the door of the Potokwane house and called out *Ko, ko!* Inside, somewhere within the cool interior of the house, the voice of Radio Botswana broke the silence: a discussion about a new power station and the problems of building it. Was that the sort of thing that Mma Potokwane listened to, or was she dozing somewhere, catching up on lost sleep, having left the radio on? Discussion of power stations could easily send people off to sleep, although some people — mostly men, she imagined — might be woken up by such things.

She repeated the traditional request for admission. "*Ko, ko,* Mma! *Ko, ko!*"

There was no reply. "We must be careful that we have enough power in future," intoned a voice on the radio. "We cannot always buy our power from our neighbours, who have a shortage themselves. What is it they said? Enough's enough: no more power for you, Botswana, or you, Swaziland. You go and buy candles."

Mma Ramotswe was not interested in that. She was thinking of what the house-mother had said: *She was like a balloon with all the air taken out of it.* She felt a tinge of alarm. Sometimes people had a stroke without realising what had happened, and then they became confused and could fail to reply when somebody came to their door and called *Ko, ko!* Could Mma Potokwane be lying unconscious, in the kitchen perhaps, or on the cold floor of the bathroom? Her husband was often away for days, she had said: he had cattle somewhere. If that were so, then it might be a long time before anybody thought to look for her, and by then it could be too late. A floor was no place to lie for very long, even in warm weather.

She pushed the door fully open and entered the house, calling out Mma Potokwane's name as she did so. Her voice seemed so loud; even louder than the voice of the engineer who was expressing a view on coal-fired power stations on Radio Botswana. "These stations are much better than they used to be," he said. "Like so many things."

Like so many things, thought Mma Ramotswe. Like medicines, like supplies of vegetables in the supermarkets, like electric fans, like the road to Lobatse, like . . . She entered the sitting room, and there, on the couch before her, was Mma Potokwane, sitting as motionless as a figure in a painting or a photograph — clearly not dead, but not herself. *Like a balloon that has had the air taken out of it.* Yes, just like that.

Mma Potokwane's eyes registered the arrival of Mma Ramotswe and she moved slightly, as if beginning to get up to welcome her but then thinking better of it.

"Mma, are you all right? You didn't answer. I called out and . . ."

Mma Potokwane raised a hand to point to a chair. "You should sit down, Mma. Yes, I am all right, but not all right really. I'll tell you. You sit down."

Mma Ramotswe did as she was bade. "But you do not look very well, Mma. Are you sure you're not ill?"

Mma Potokwane shook her head. "I'm not ill," she said. "No, that is not the problem."

Mma Ramotswe waited for her to continue, and she did.

"I am shocked, Mma; that is all. I shall be better soon, I think, but now I am shocked."

"You've had bad news?"

"Yes," said Mma Potokwane. "I have had bad news. Not bad news that somebody has become late — not that sort of bad news. No, the bad news is that I have been dismissed. As from the end of this month. Dismissed."

It took Mma Ramotswe some time to

absorb this. You did not dismiss Mma Potokwane. You did not tell her that she was no longer going to be the matron of the orphan farm. You did not do it because it was simply inconceivable. You did not dismiss the sun from the sky. You did not tell the Limpopo River to flow the other way. You did not say to the great Kalahari that it was not wanted; that its winds, its dry, desert winds should blow somewhere else, in another quarter, beneath another sky. You did not do that because it was against the order of things. And it was quite against the order of things that Mma Silvia Potokwane, matron, matriarch, scourge of businessmen slow to open their wallets for charity, defender of children, citizen of Botswana, should be dismissed from her position like some young and incompetent girl. You did not do that. Nobody did that. It was impossible.

"Has this thing really happened?" Mma Ramotswe stuttered.

Mma Potokwane nodded. No words were needed; just a nod was sufficient to signify the end of an era, the end of a world.

CHAPTER ELEVEN:
AN INNOCENT MAN,
A FIRST OFFENDER

It would have been bad enough if that was all that had happened that day, but there was something else. Later, when Mma Ramotswe and Mma Makutsi would survey their list of days — happily few in number — when things appeared to go seriously wrong, then this day would seem egregious.

It was while Mma Ramotswe was on her visit to the orphan farm that Mma Makutsi heard raised voices outside the office. This was not altogether unusual: the apprentices sometimes engaged in rowdy banter with one another — so much so that she had occasionally gone into the garage or the yard to ask them to bear in mind that there were at least some people in the vicinity who needed to concentrate on their work, and that was very difficult, was it not, if there were other people who insisted on shouting at the top of their voices about some matter of no interest to anybody else, namely, which girls were particularly friendly towards boys and which were not, or the prospects of the Zebras in the forthcoming football finals, or semi-finals, or whatever they were.

This time, though, it was a bit different. She recognised the voices of the apprentices but there was another voice too, a deeper, more mature voice, and a woman's voice behind that. And was that Mr. J.L.B. Matekoni joining the fray, saying something about somebody making a big mistake? He at least talked calmly, unlike the others, who seemed to be becoming increasingly shrill in expressing their view about whatever it was that lay behind the argument; for it was now clear that it was an argument, and not just a disagreement about some unimportant matter of girls or soccer.

Mma Makutsi put down the document she was reading and went into the small courtyard that separated the offices of the No. 1 Ladies' Detective Agency from the premises of Tlokweng Road Speedy Motors. She stood in the doorway, quite still, in shock as she realised that the two strangers involved in the row, a man and a woman, were both police officers. As she appeared, everybody turned to look at her, and it was then that she saw the handcuffs that had been placed on Fanwell's wrists.

Mma Makutsi gasped. "What is this? What's happening?"

Charlie pointed at the police officers. "They have arrested Fanwell," he said, his voice breaking with emotion. "This is a very bad mistake."

The male police officer, the older of the two, gave him a glance. "We have a warrant," he said patiently. "It's perfectly in order. All signed. Official. We're arresting him for handling stolen goods."

Mma Makutsi shrieked, "No, no. You cannot do that. That is Fanwell. He is a very honest young man. He is not a thief, Rra!" She looked pleadingly at the policewoman. "Mma, you cannot let this big mistake happen. You cannot take this young man." She moved forward to plead with the police officers. "Listen, Rra. Listen, Mma. I am a detective and I can tell you: this young man would never do anything like that. Guaranteed. Guaranteed. I am a detective. I'm telling you, this is not right."

The policeman looked at her doubtfully. "You're a detective, Mma? CID? Which office — Gaborone? Where is your card?"

"I'm not that sort of detective," said Mma Makutsi. "I'm a private detective. The No. 1 Ladies' Detective Agency."

The policewoman smiled. "Sorry, my sister, but you should keep quiet. This is proper police business. This is not play detectives."

Mma Makutsi looked at Fanwell. "What is all this, Fanwell? Do you know what these people are saying?"

Mr. J.L.B. Matekoni answered the question. "They say that he was repairing a stolen car for resale. Some friend of his had it. That is what they're saying."

"I didn't know it was stolen, Mma," said Fanwell, his voice shaking with fear. "I just did it as a favour for Chobie. He's a friend of mine. I did not know it was stolen."

"That friend," muttered Charlie, and spat, "I'm going to get him."

The policeman threw Charlie a warning glance. "Look, we can't stand here forever," he said. "If this young man has a story, then he can make a statement at the charge office. Then he can go in front of the magistrate, who will look at that statement and decide whether it is true or whether it is all lies. I'm sorry to say this, but sometimes people tell lies, and this young man may well be doing that."

"You cannot say that, Rra," protested Mr. J.L.B. Matekoni. "Surely he is still innocent until the magistrate has decided that he is guilty. This is Botswana, you know."

The policeman turned to face Mr. J.L.B. Matekoni. Out of deference to the mechanic's dignity and bearing, he did not speak roughly, but there was nonetheless an edge to his voice. "Yes," he said, "you're right, Rra. This is Botswana. And in Botswana we do not take kindly to young men who take other people's cars and then sell them to unsuspecting members of the public. We do not like that either."

"What are you going to do with him?" asked Mma Makutsi.

"He will stay in the cells," said the policewoman. "He'll be all right there. He'll get a blanket at night. You needn't worry about him, Mma. I'll see that he's all right."

The policeman now took Fanwell by the arm and began to lead him away.

The young man stumbled, but was kept on his feet by the policeman. "I haven't done anything wrong."

"Did you hear that?" exploded Charlie. "Did you hear what he said?"

"Calm down," said the policeman. "It doesn't help if people shout."

"Just keep quiet, Charlie." Mr. J.L.B. Matekoni put a restraining hand on the young man. "We'll speak to a lawyer."

Charlie shook his head. "These

people . . ."

The policeman gave him another warning glance, and Charlie stopped.

They watched in silence as Fanwell was led to the police car parked outside. The rear door was opened and he was bundled inside; the door slammed and the car moved away. They saw his face briefly as he looked back towards them; then the car pulled out into the traffic on the Tlokweng Road and was gone. In the anxious conference that followed, Charlie said very little, but sat morosely shaking his head, muttering about what he was planning to do to Chobie.

"Do you know this Chobie?" asked Mma Makutsi.

Charlie nodded. "I will find him."

"But maybe the police have found him already," said Mma Makutsi.

"Then he can tell them that Fanwell did not know," said Mr. J.L.B. Matekoni.

Charlie and Mma Makutsi exchanged glances. Mr. J.L.B. Matekoni was decent by nature and the problem with people who were trusting, she had always thought, was that they assumed others were like them, and they were not. They could hope that this Chobie might explain that he alone was answerable for handling stolen property, but they could not rely on it. Nor could they rely on his being believed even if he were to say it. If two young men were standing in the dock together, why should a magistrate believe one of them if he said the other was innocent?

"This is very serious," said Mma Makutsi.

"He's innocent," said Charlie.

"Of course he's innocent," snapped Mma Makutsi. "We know that Fanwell would never do anything wrong. But we're not the ones who will be sitting there in court, are we?"

Charlie stared at her. "If they convict him, what then?"

"They send you to prison for handling stolen property," said Mr. J.L.B. Matekoni. "That man at the bottle store — remember him? He went to prison for two years for selling stolen beer."

"Two years!" Charlie exclaimed.

"He's a first offender," said Mma Makutsi.

This remark, innocently intended though it was, drew Charlie's ire. Pointing a finger at Mma Makutsi, he almost shouted. "You think he's guilty, don't you?"

Mma Makutsi shook her head. "I do not think that."

"Then why do you call him an offender? Isn't an offender somebody who's guilty?"

Mma Makutsi tried to explain what she

185

had meant; Charlie listened resentfully.

"We mustn't argue," said Mr. J.L.B. Matekoni. "Arguing won't help Fanwell."

"Nothing will help Fanwell," said Mma Makutsi.

Mma Ramotswe returned to the office an hour or so after the police and a fearful, almost tearful Fanwell had left. Her heart was heavy with the upsetting encounter she had just had with Mma Potokwane, and so when she came in and saw Mma Makutsi sitting disconsolately at her desk, she assumed that her assistant was merely sharing her own distress over the injustice done to her friend. But then she realised that Mma Makutsi did not know what had happened, and whatever the explanation for her assistant's state of mind, it was not that.

"Is there something wrong, Mma?"

Mma Makutsi reached into the pocket of her blouse and took out a handkerchief. "Oh, Mma Ramotswe, it is very bad, very bad."

Mma Ramotswe froze. Her mind went quickly to those she loved: Which one of them had had some terrible accident, was even at this moment under the surgeon's knife at the Princess Marina Hospital? Had something happened in the garage? Mr.

J.L.B. Matekoni had said that one of the pneumatic jacks was playing up — had it failed altogether and a car come down on him, pinning him to the ground? Puso? Motholeli? They should be safely at home from school by now, but there were always perils, even in that short walk between the house and school — only a few days ago a car driven by a young and inexperienced motorist had mounted the pavement and knocked over a fruit-seller . . .

"Fanwell . . . ," Mma Makutsi began.

Mma Ramotswe gasped. "Oh no, Mma, oh no . . ." Fanwell was dead. He had been under the car when the jack had failed.

Mma Makutsi quickly understood the conclusion that Mma Ramotswe had jumped to, and she corrected the mistake. "No, Mma, he is not late — nothing like that. He has been . . ." She struggled with the word; it was just so unlikely, so impossible. "He has been arrested."

Mma Ramotswe's relief on hearing that the worst had not happened was tempered by shock. "Arrested? Surely not, Mma? Not Fanwell . . ." She tailed off; the unspoken thought was that if Charlie had been arrested it would not be so surprising.

"Yes," said Mma Makutsi. "If they had arrested Charlie, then maybe it would not have been so surprising. But Fanwell? No, Mma, it is a very shocking thing."

Mma Ramotswe nodded. "I know, Mma, I have often thought that Charlie was asking for trouble." She paused. "Do you think that they made a mistake? Do you think they thought that Fanwell was Charlie?"

"It is all a big mistake," replied Mma Makutsi. "But it is not that mistake. No, they knew that Fanwell was Fanwell, and he was the one they were after."

Mma Ramotswe crossed the room to her desk and sat down. "There is other bad news too," she said quietly. "Mma Potokwane has been dismissed from her post. At the end of the month she will no longer be the matron."

Mma Makutsi shrieked. "No, Mma. That cannot be. It cannot."

Mma Ramotswe explained what had happened. She had found Mma Potokwane in her house, she said, and had been given the news directly. Mma Potokwane told her that she had had the news given to her by the secretary to the board of directors of the orphan farm. The directors had decided, she was told, that her attitude to the proposed new buildings had been unhelpful and obstructive. In the circumstances, since she had shown herself unwilling to comply with the properly determined policy of the board, it was thought that she should be replaced with somebody who could embrace the new approach to cost-effectiveness that the board had endorsed. And with that, her regime was brought to an abrupt end.

Mma Ramotswe was slightly surprised by the intensity of Mma Makutsi's reaction to this story. Although her assistant had previously not enjoyed the best of friendships with Mma Potokwane, relations between the two of them had been rather better recently. And now, hearing of Mma Potokwane's misfortune, any past disagreements seemed immediately forgotten. "That is terrible, Mma," wailed Mma Makutsi. "Oh, it is so unfair, so unfair. And on the same day as Fanwell's arrest — and he is innocent, Mma, as we both know. Mma Potokwane too. They are both the victims of some very bad things. Oh, Mma . . ."

And with that, Mma Makutsi began to sob. Mma Ramotswe immediately rose from her desk and went to put an arm around the other woman. "It is very bad," she said consolingly. "It is a very bad day for everybody."

Mma Makutsi's sobbing became louder. "Poor Fanwell," she spluttered. "He is looking after that whole family, and there will be no money now. And Mma Potokwane. What will she eat? It is all so wrong, Mma."

Mma Ramotswe felt the tears begin to roll down her own cheeks. She closed her eyes and saw Mma Potokwane sitting on her sofa, staring so blankly and hopelessly ahead. She had given her working life to those children; she had spent every waking hour, it seemed, battling to give the children a decent start. She was tireless in her efforts on their behalf. And there was her fruit cake too, that she used as a means of ensnaring others to help the orphans; that fruit cake, that tea, those hours spent together talking about anything and everything. And the wisdom that the matron had, the under-standing, the deep wells of kindness under that imposing exterior; all that, it seemed, meant nothing to the juggernaut of reform and efficiency and cost-cutting.

She wiped away the tears with the back of her wrist: salt against skin, our human tears. "Mma Makutsi," she managed to say.

Mma Makutsi looked up. Her voice, when she spoke, was half choked with sorrow. "Yes, Mma?"

"I am going to make some tea. We shall drink a cup of tea."

Mma Makutsi nodded, and sniffed. "It is always the best thing to do, Mma."

It was, of course. The sound of the kettle boiling was in itself the sound of normality, of reason, the sound of a fight back against the sadness of things. And the making of tea — ordinary black tea for Mma Makutsi and red bush for Mma Ramotswe — was the first step in restoring a sense of order and control into their disturbed universe. Then, sitting close together for company, nursing their mugs of tea, they began to discuss what they should do.

"Clovis Andersen," said Mma Ramotswe.

Mma Makutsi nodded. "We must speak to him. He will know what to do."

It gave them both a reassuring feeling that Clovis Andersen was there to help them. If anybody would know what to do, then surely it would be the great Clovis Andersen. "He's bound to have some ideas," said Mma Makutsi. "If you have written a book like that, then you will always have ideas on how to get out of a crisis."

"That is true," said Mma Ramotswe. "One of his rules must surely apply here, or if it doesn't, then . . ."

"Then he can make up a new one," supplied Mma Makutsi.

"Exactly, Mma. He can make a new one. Rule 9b, or something like that."

"That will be a very good rule," said Mma

Makutsi. "I think you should go and see him, Mma."

That settled, they sat in silence for a few minutes. Now the tea began to do its work — as it always did — and the world that only a few minutes previously had seemed so bleak started to seem somewhat less so. There was bound to be some solution to both of the problems they faced. As far as Fanwell was concerned, there could be character references to lay before the court; Mma Ramotswe was already beginning to draft one in her head: *This young man came from a background of poverty. He spends all his wages, every pula, on the needs of his grandmother and his brothers and sisters. He is completely honest and upright . . .* Surely they would pay some heed to her if she wrote on their headed paper. And Mr. J.L.B. Matekoni could write as his employer; they would have to listen to him, because everybody loved and admired him and even the magistrate might be aware of that. If he were not, though, was there anything to stop them getting a character reference from the writer of character references . . . ? And as for Mma Potokwane, they would just fight back. There was no doubt in Mma Ramotswe's mind who was responsible for the dismissal of Mma Potokwane: Mr. Ditso.

Those rich men did not like anybody to contradict them; to stand in the way of their pet schemes. Well, if that was the way he chose to conduct himself, then the gloves could come off. Not that she ever saw herself wearing boxing gloves, of course, but if she did, then now was the time to divest herself of them. Mr. Ditso, she thought, you are engaging with a heavyweight; and that, she said to herself, is true. Do not take on a traditionally built person unless you are prepared for a heavyweight bout. *Do not enter the ring with an opponent above your weight.* That was a good proposition, she decided — almost worthy of Clovis Andersen himself. She would suggest it to him, in case he should ever think of a new edition. For a brief, tantalising moment the title page flashed before her eyes: *The Principles of Private Detection: A new and revised edition by Clovis Andersen, with additions by Mma Precious Ramotswe(Botswana) and* . . . yes, she should be generous in such a matter . . . *and Mma Grace Makutsi (Dip. Sec., Botswana Sec. Coll., 97%).*

CHAPTER TWELVE:
THE EFFECT OF LIME

The next three days were days of anxiety — and inactivity. Fanwell had been released from custody shortly after having been charged, but was told that it might be some time before his case was called in court. Until then, there was not much he could do, although Mr. J.L.B. Matekoni had obtained the services of a lawyer, a rather distracted man who had described the case as "an open and shut one."

"That is very good news," said Mr. J.L.B. Matekoni.

The lawyer looked surprised. "Good news?"

"Yes. You said it was open and shut . . ."

The lawyer laughed. "Yes, open and shut from the prosecution's point of view."

Mr. J.L.B. Matekoni looked incredulous. "But he's not guilty. They cannot convict him if he did not do it."

The lawyer tapped the side of his nose; it

was a curious gesture that Mr. J.L.B. Matekoni could not quite interpret. "Oh, Mr. Mechanic, I'm afraid that they all do it. All these people who appear in court say, 'I did not do it.' But usually they did." He tapped his nose again. "I haven't had anybody come to me and say, 'I did it, Rra.' Not one. So I ask myself: If none of these people did it, then who did? Can you tell me? No, I didn't think you would be able to." He sighed. "But I'll do my best for this young man. I'll try to get them to give him a suspended sentence, although that depends on which magistrate gets the case. Some of those fellows have got very bad tempers. You never know."

Mr. J.L.B. Matekoni did not tell Fanwell of this exchange. All he did was to tell him that he had secured the services of a lawyer, and that the lawyer had assured him that he would do his best. Charlie, who was with Fanwell at the time, clapped his hands together and did one of those impromptu dances that he performed to mark pieces of good news. "Ace!" he exclaimed. "You hear that, Fanwell? A big-shot lawyer. Very smart."

"Good," said Fanwell. "I am very lucky then."

Mr. J.L.B. Matekoni looked away. He

wondered whether he should try to get another lawyer, but he had already paid a substantial amount as a retainer, and he would probably lose that if he tried to change. Perhaps it was best to have a lawyer who was realistic — after all, one would not want one who showed unfounded optimism in the face of bleak prospects.

Mma Ramotswe did her best to comfort Fanwell, telling him of the character reference she was preparing and assuring him that justice was bound to be done. For the most part, though, she left the Fanwell affair to Mr. J.L.B. Matekoni; the apprentice had always been his responsibility, and it seemed that he was doing all that was required to see Fanwell through this. Her mind was more taken up with the issue of Mma Potokwane's dismissal. She made a point of going out to the orphan farm each day to speak to her friend and to encourage her to challenge the dismissal.

"I've already done that," said Mma Potokwane. "I have written to the board, but they say that they cannot consider my letter until the next meeting, which will be in two weeks' time. Until then, there is nothing I can do."

Mma Ramotswe bit her lip. "I have been making enquiries about that man," she said.

"I have been speaking to a friend who writes articles on business matters for the *Botswana Daily News*. I have asked him whether he has any information."

Mma Potokwane shrugged. "Nobody knows anything. Your friend will say the same thing."

This was true. The journalist had promised to see if there was any helpful information in the newspaper's files but had come back with nothing to report. "He seems to be absolutely above board," he said. "The money comes from straightforward businesses. A number of dry-cleaning places, a fleet of buses — that sort of thing."

Mma Ramotswe thanked him for his efforts. She tried to keep up an appearance of cheerfulness, but she now felt quite despondent about the chance of being able to help Mma Potokwane in any way. Had she been able to provide her with ammunition, then she was sure that the redoubtable matron would have been able to stand up to Mr. Ditso and his friends on the board. But without that, then Mma Potokwane, it seemed, was powerless and all that she, like any of them, could do was to wait. So all three of them — Mma Ramotswe, Mr. J.L.B. Matekoni, and Mma Makutsi — found themselves bound up in a shared circle of anxiety, each unable to do anything much to reassure the others or to throw anything but a bleak light on the misfortunes of Fanwell and Mma Potokwane. "It seems as if everything has gone wrong," said Mma Ramotswe. "I know that we should not despair, but everything seems suddenly to have gone wrong."

"The whole world is tumbling down," said Mma Makutsi. "It is surely the end."

That, it seemed to Mma Ramotswe, was possibly overstating it, but she knew how Mma Makutsi felt. In fact, they both felt powerless, and were unable even to seek Clovis Andersen's advice, as he had taken the opportunity to accompany his friend to visit a library being built at Ghanzi, on the other side of the country, and had left word that he could not be contacted for four or five days.

"I'm sure he will have something to suggest when he comes back," said Mma Ramotswe.

"Maybe," said Mma Makutsi, but then added gloomily: "But maybe not."

Phuti Radiphuti had been kept informed, and had shaken his head sadly at the news. He had met Fanwell, and he thought it highly unlikely that he had done anything dishonest, but he knew that sometimes the police could, quite reasonably, believe they had a case against an innocent man. It had happened before to one of his employees, and the poor man had spent nine months in prison for an offence that Phuti Radiphuti was convinced he had not committed. There had been evidence, though, and the conviction had been sustained on appeal, which showed, Phuti decided, that even in a well-run system of criminal justice mistakes could be made.

He was busy, though, and, although sympathetic, he had no time to brood on these matters. He had received a large order to furnish a new hotel to be built on the edge of town, and there was a great deal of paperwork to be completed in that transaction. There was also the matter of his new house, for which the foundations had now been prepared. Concrete had been poured, and the lower parts of the walls were beginning to appear, allowing the layout of the rooms to be envisaged. Like the bones of a developing skeleton, of a creature still in formation, the structure of the house was taking shape. Soon the walls would reach the height where the window spaces could be seen, and not long after that, the first beams of the roof would begin to reach out to one another. After that, it would simply be a matter of finishing, as the tilers and the plasterers, the electricians and the plumbers set about their respective tasks. Mr. Putumelo had promised to finish the whole job in two months, and it looked to Phuti as if he would easily meet that target.

Mr. Putumelo had gone out of his way to discourage visits to the site during construction. "It is best if the client doesn't go tramping about the place," he said. "Building sites are dangerous places, Rra. We had somebody, one of our clients, who put his hand into a cement mixer once — while it was turning." He shook his head sadly; whether over the consequences, or whether over the whole issue of human foolishness, it was not apparent.

Phuti said nothing. He resented the implication that he was the sort of man to put his hand into a cement mixer, but his customary mildness of manner prevented his engaging in dispute with the rather arrogant builder. He thought, though, that if he wanted to visit his house, he would do so, irrespective of what Mr. Putumelo had to say about it. It was his land, after all, and he was surely entitled to walk over it if he wished, taking care, of course, not to insert his hand into any cement mixer.

He decided that it would be best to go

shortly after five one evening. Work would have stopped at that time of day, and he would be able to inspect the work without incurring the displeasure of Mr. Putumelo. So one afternoon, a few days after Fanwell's arrest, he drove down to the road-end opposite his plot, parked his car, and walked up the rough track that the builders' vehicles had made to the house.

It was that time of evening when the sun, although still in the sky, had given clear notice of its intentions. Shadows, lengthening, merged with one another; birds exchanged their late afternoon messages, reporting food here, shelter there, or drawing noisy attention to the presence of some predator, a snake perhaps, lurking in a treetop. The soft light seemed to paint everything with warm gold, and for a moment he imagined the scene that was likely to play out in a few months' time; of him coming up the drive and seeing Mma Makutsi waiting for him on the verandah, a fine stew bubbling away in the kitchen and then, maybe a bit later — but not too late, he hoped — children running out to meet him and him holding them up to the sky, as children love to be lifted, to their squeals of delight.

As he approached the house, he felt a sudden rush of excitement. It really was happening; this really was his house — *their* house; the low brick walls were *his,* the expanses of cement, laid where the floor would be, were made up of *his* cement, bought with *his* money. He could not help smiling, and he even said, "Well, well, well," although there was nobody to hear him.

Or so he thought. It was as he was stepping over one of the low walls in order to stand in what would in future be a bathroom that he heard the voice.

"Yes, Rra. Can I help you?"

Phuti Radiphuti spun round. A short man in a set of blue overalls, a battered grey hat atop his head, had appeared as if from nowhere.

"I am Radiphuti," Phuti said. "This is my house."

The man wiped his hands on a piece of grimy towelling. "I have heard of you," he said, switching to English; they had started in Setswana, but the man spoke hesitantly and with an accent. "Mr. Putumelo has told us about you." He folded the piece of towel and put it into his blue overalls. "Have you come to look at the house?"

It seemed to Phuti to be a rather superfluous question. Of course he had come to look at the house. Why else would he be climbing over these little walls and standing in the middle of the future bathroom? But he checked himself and simply nodded.

"We are making good progress," said the man. "I am one of the carpenters, but I also do bricklaying and other things. My name is Thomas."

Phuti reached out to shake the man's hand, which was rough to the touch, like sandpaper. That was the effect of lime; he had heard about how it pitted the skin. Lime and bricks.

"You are not from here," said Phuti.

The man pointed. "Up there."

"The other side?"

"Yes."

There was hardship on the other side of the border; people crossed over to earn a living, to survive. It was not easy for them; those who stayed, or were sent back, had little to look forward to.

The man rubbed his eyes. They were bloodshot. "I have been here for three years now. I have managed to be in work all that time. I have worked every day."

Phuti frowned. "Every day for three years? Even Sundays?"

The man nodded. "Especially Sundays. I have not had one day off. Three years."

Phuti was silent. It was not all that surprising, he supposed. Every thebe this man earned would be doing some important work up there; perhaps even paying for the drugs that kept some relative alive through the illness that stalked Africa, that could be kept at bay but only if you had the money, or somebody had the money, to pay.

"This will be a very good house," said the man. "Lots of room. It is good to see a house with as much room as this."

Phuti acknowledged the compliment. "I designed it myself. There was a draughtsman who drew the plans, but I designed it."

"You have designed it very well," said Thomas. "Everything will be in the right place. Perfect."

They walked into what would be the living room. The walls there were slightly higher — two or three feet by now — and the bricklayer showed Phuti how they were constructed.

"I have asked for very good-quality bricks," said Phuti, examining the outer layer. "These are the ones. They come from South Africa, I think. Mr. Putumelo ordered them specially."

"They are very expensive," said Thomas. "Good bricks always are."

"And I'm very pleased," said Phuti, "that they are being laid by a good tradesman like

204

you, Rra. I'm very pleased."

Thomas looked at him. There was something in his expression that disturbed Phuti, but he was unsure as to what it was. Distrust? But why should this man distrust him, or even feel uneasy? Was he working illegally? That was perfectly possible, but then if it were the case that he did not have a work permit it would have been unlikely that he would have spoken so openly. Those who worked illegally kept to the shadows, claimed to be from the north of the country, protested that they had a Motswana parent; did anything but talk too openly about their necessarily clandestine lives.

Thomas held Phuti's gaze for a few moments, and then looked away.

"Is there something wrong?" asked Phuti.

Thomas again fixed him with an intense stare. It was difficult for Phuti to look directly into his bloodshot eyes — disconcerted, he wanted to pass him something with which to wipe them.

"I cannot always say what I'm thinking," muttered Thomas.

Phuti thought about this. "No, it is not always easy." He paused. A go-away bird — a grey lourie — had perched on one of the acacia trees and uttered its accusing cry; the world, for some birds, was always unfair. As it was for some people too. "But I think you can talk to me, Rra. You can talk to me if you are troubled in some way. I may not be able to help you, but it might help you just to say what you need to say."

Thomas shook his head. "There are some things I cannot speak of. I have a family, you see, Rra, and I am sending money . . ."

Phuti nodded. "I know what you people do. It is a good thing." There was a world of difference between this man's circumstances and his own. Phuti was a citizen, and a secure one at that, of a well-ordered country; this man, he imagined, had known real fear and could not return to a place that was his, his own, the place to which he was entitled. Nobody spoke for him; nobody.

"So I cannot say anything that would put my job at risk. Do you see that?"

Phuti stiffened. There was only one way in which this could be interpreted: this man, this bricklayer from over the border, knew something about Mr. Putumelo that Mr. Putumelo did not want anybody to know. And that could be anything, ranging from not declaring income for tax purposes, to using stolen materials, or building unsafe structures . . . He looked about the site. Was everything being built correctly, or was Mr. Putumelo cutting corners in exactly the way he condemned in others?

He decided to ask directly. "Please tell me, Rra; please tell me man to man, as one brother to another; tell me — is this house being built properly?"

Thomas seemed to be taken aback by the question. "But of course it is, Rra. Mr. Putumelo is a very good builder, and I can promise you that I am taking great care with the work I am doing. I would never build anything that was not solid."

Phuti breathed a sigh of relief. So the disclosure, whatever it was, had nothing to do with his house. If Thomas did not want to make it, then he would not press him; he would not be at all surprised to learn that Mr. Putumelo was up to something, but what that might be was not really his business. Phuti himself was honest — scrupulously so — but one honest man could not make the rest of the world honest, no matter how hard he tried: Where would he start?

Phuti bent down to examine one of the walls. They were in a part of the building where Thomas must have been working that day; the mortar around the bricks was wet to the touch, cool against the skin, soft too. *Our house,* thought Phuti. *Our house.*

And then he thought of something that Mr. Putumelo had said. *Your house has got my name on it.* That was strange, but there were many aspects of the building trade that Phuti found odd, just as he had no doubt others found aspects of the furniture business hard to fathom. He completed his examination of the incipient wall. "This is very well made," he said. "This is very good work." It was: the wall hugged the plumb line, set by a practised and conscientious eye.

He turned round. Thomas, who had been standing immediately behind him only a few moments before, had gone.

Chapter Thirteen:
There are Some Nice People on the Road

Clovis Andersen returned from the far side of the country, exhausted by the journey, to receive the message that Mma Ramotswe had left for him. In this she gave him no news of the awful events that had occurred, but simply proposed that they meet for tea at the President Hotel, suggesting that if he telephoned her they could agree on a time. He did, and they met on the day after his return. It was a hot morning, but even though the air was heavy, it held a hint of what might come; somewhere, still far away, but building up, there were rain clouds. And the rain would bring relief from the heat and the dryness, and the earth would drink it up thirstily and suddenly be touched with the green of new growth.

"So hot," said Clovis Andersen, as he sat down opposite Mma Ramotswe on the hotel verandah. "So awfully hot."

"Then we shall have tea," said Mma Ramotswe. "That will make you feel better."

The tea did not take long to arrive, and as Mma Ramotswe poured it from the stout white pot she began to reveal to Clovis Andersen the troubles they were facing.

"I know these are not your problems, Rra," she began, "but we . . . that is, Mma Makutsi and I, feel that you will have some idea of what to do."

Clovis Andersen stopped her. "Hold on, Mma Ramotswe. I may have written that book, but really I wouldn't hold myself out as . . . as an expert."

Mma Ramotswe could not believe that he was serious. "But, Rra, your book is famous. You have a rule for just about everything. Rule No. 6, for example . . ." She began to quote Rule No. 6; Clovis Andersen, barely concealing his surprise that there should be anybody who remembered that there was a Rule No. 6, let alone anybody who was capable of quoting it verbatim, listened in silence. Then: "Yes, Mma, that is indeed Rule No. 6, but all I'm saying is that I'm not necessarily able to sort everything out." He stared at her, as if willing her to read something into his protestations.

Mma Ramotswe was not deterred. "Let me tell you, Rra," she said. "Let me tell you about a very dreadful thing that has happened. We have a lady here who is the matron of an orphan farm. She is called Mma Potokwane, and she has many fine qualities. She is traditionally built, and she makes very famous fruit cake. She will do anything for those orphans — anything — and for many of them she is their mother. Mma Potokwane has more children than any other woman in Botswana — she is mother to many hundreds of children who are now grown up. That is what she is like, Rra."

Clovis Andersen listened politely. "It sounds as if she must be much appreciated, Mma."

Mma Ramotswe replied that this was true, but it seemed to her that this appreciation did not extend to some members of her board. She told him of the dismissal, and of Mr. Ditso Ditso's suspected role in it. "It must have been him, Rra," she said. "Nobody else would think of such a thing. People like that think they should control *everything* — just because they are a success in business."

"Indeed," said Clovis Andersen, looking vaguely out over the square. He had no idea who Mma Potokwane was, but it seemed to him that to dismiss a woman like that — if she was like that — was not only foolish, but perverse too. When Mma Ramotswe finished, he tapped the table thoughtfully. "This sounds very nasty," he said. "I don't like that sort of thing. It's a form of bullying, isn't it? Hounding somebody out of her job because she sees things differently." He shook his head. "Not nice."

Mma Ramotswe waited for him to say more, but he seemed to be thinking about something else altogether. For a few moments she felt uncertain: Should she really be asking the great Clovis Andersen for advice on something as small, as local — at least in his eyes — as the dismissal of Mma Potokwane? But then he turned to her and said, "Mma Ramotswe, I think you're going to ask me what to do. Is that right?"

She answered him with relief. "Oh yes, Rra. That is quite right. You see, I cannot seem to think of anything that we can do to help Mma Potokwane, and I thought that since you had written that book, and we all know how —"

He held up a hand. "You misjudge me, Mma Ramotswe. I'm not the man you think I am."

She shrugged.

"Anybody can write a book . . ."

She brushed his objections aside. "Rra, you are very modest — and that is good too.

But we do not have to talk about that. The real question is what I should do."

Clovis Andersen sighed. "Somewhere in the book I say something about going to the source of a problem. I forget . . ."

"It is on page one hundred twenty-six," said Mma Ramotswe. "The chapter is called 'Seeing the Wood from the Trees.' "

Clovis Andersen nodded. "Yes, I think it's there. I think I said something about finding out where a problem originates and then going directly there."

"Yes, Rra. That is what you said." She looked at him expectantly. "The source of the problem here is Mr. Ditso."

Clovis Andersen nodded. "Yes. So you ask the question: Why is he doing this?"

Mma Ramotswe looked up at the sky. There were so many reasons for bad behaviour, for meanness and unkindness. Sometimes the explanation of such things was very simple; people caused harm to others because they were of malevolent disposition. That was sheer human wickedness, something that had always existed and always would. Some people, it seemed, derived pleasure from inflicting suffering on others, and any enquiry as to why they did it could stop there. But then there were those other cases where the real explanation lay elsewhere, where there was some quite different motive in play — greed, ambition, a grudge . . . There was so much to choose from.

"He wants to build a new hall at the orphan farm," she said. "He wants the children to eat in one place and save money. It's cheaper, you see, to cook all the meals in one place."

Clovis Andersen considered this. "Is he a frugal man, this Mr. Ditso? Does he live simply?"

Mma Ramotswe smiled. Mr. J.L.B. Matekoni's words were coming back to her. "My husband could answer that, I think, Rra. He says that you can tell what a person is like by looking at his car."

This seemed to interest Clovis Andersen. "He's got something there, Mma Ramotswe. Yes, he's certainly got something there." He paused. "So, what sort of car has our friend got? Something simple?"

"No, Rra. It is very fancy. Fancy and shiny."

Clovis Andersen absorbed this. "So maybe he doesn't want just to save money. Maybe he wants to spend it."

Mma Ramotswe pointed out that it was not Mr. Ditso's money that would be spent: it would be the orphan farm's.

"Sure," said Clovis Andersen. "But who's getting the money? Where's it being spent? Remember what I said in the book. *Follow the money.* It always works, Mma Ramotswe."

She looked at him. Of course he was right. And it had never occurred to her to ask herself this question, not once in the course of all the pondering and worrying of the last few days. And now this man who was so modest, who seemed reluctant to discuss *The Principles of Private Detection* unless pressed to do so, this *nice* man had gone right to the nub of the matter, and had done it effortlessly, as if he had hardly had to think about it at all.

She struggled to contain her excitement. "I think you are right, Rra. That is the very question we should be asking ourselves."

Clovis Andersen made a gesture with his hand — a turning movement that suggested the reframing of the question. "Ask ourselves, or ask him?"

"You think we should speak to him, Rra?"

Clovis Andersen nodded. "Yes. Let's go and talk to him about the building project. And while you're talking to him, I'll watch him."

"You'll watch?"

"Yes. Because in my experience, Mma

215

Ramotswe, people give themselves away. Even if he doesn't say anything, he'll tell us."

They drank their tea. Mma Ramotswe felt almost euphoric. As far as she was concerned, the investigation was now in the hands of one who must, on any view of it, be one of the most highly regarded private detectives in the world. And he was here, in Botswana, with her, working on a case in which they were, without the slightest shadow of doubt, on the right side. If the last few days had been difficult ones, that was now almost completely forgotten. She now felt optimistic that they would come up with something that might bring about a reversal of Mma Potokwane's dismissal. And that had to happen, because if it did not, then there would be no justice left in the country — and that was a thought that Mma Ramotswe was not willing to entertain for anywhere, least of all for the place she loved so much, her Botswana.

It did not prove easy to track down Ditso Ditso, who was not listed under his own name in the telephone directory. It was Mma Makutsi who remembered the name of one of his companies and found a number for that. "It is here," she said proudly, pointing to an entry in the directory. "DD Industries. That is what he calls himself. It is his initials, you see."

They had gone back to the office, where Mma Makutsi, excited by the presence of Clovis Andersen, had made a great show of finding the telephone number. Mma Ramotswe complimented her, and had drawn their guest's attention to Mma Makutsi's framed certificate on the wall. "The Botswana Secretarial College," she had said. "My assistant is one of their most distinguished graduates."

"*The* most distinguished graduate," corrected Mma Makutsi, smiling at Clovis Andersen as she spoke.

"Ninety-seven per cent," said Mma Ramotswe hurriedly, before Mma Makutsi could say it. She did not want Clovis Andersen to think Mma Makutsi boastful.

Clovis Andersen glanced at the certificate. "Very good, Mma Makutsi. It is a very good training for detection, you know. I've come across several people who trained in office administration before they went into the profession. They did well. Very methodical."

Mma Makutsi beamed with pleasure. "Thank you, Rra. They always stressed method at the college. They said that if you follow a method, you'll never get lost. That is what they taught us."

Clovis Andersen nodded his agreement. "There's a lot to be said for that approach."

"And they also taught us a great deal about filing," Mma Makutsi continued. "You see, if you have a good system for filing, then —"

Mma Ramotswe cut her short, looking apologetically at Clovis Andersen. "That number, Mma. That Ditso number, if you don't mind."

At first the number was busy, but at the third try Mma Ramotswe found herself talking to a secretary. "This is not the right number of Rra Ditso," she said. "You will have to phone another number. I'm sorry, Mma. Goodbye."

"But, Mma," Mma Ramotswe blurted out. "That is very sad. Very sad."

There was a moment's silence at the other end of the line.

"I don't have another number for Rra Ditso, and he will be very sorry that we have not been able to speak."

The hesitation was almost audible. "Why so, Mma? What is this in connection with?"

"I cannot tell you, Mma," said Mma Ramotswe. "Other than to say that there is a very important visitor to this country who needs to speak to Mr. Ditso."

"Who is this visitor? I can take a message."

Mma Ramotswe's tone now changed. "Oh, sorry, Mma. This name is too important to give over the telephone. Thank you anyway, it doesn't matter all that much. Not to us."

It was the *not to us* that worked.

"There is a number for his mobile phone," said the secretary. "You can try that."

"Will he answer, though?" asked Mma Ramotswe. "So often I have phoned those things and left a message, and nobody has ever listened to it. It is like talking to yourself. So maybe not, Mma. Some other time — but it's a bit of a pity for Rra Ditso."

"There is another number," said the secretary. "I will give you a number that he will definitely answer, Mma."

The number was provided and the call brought to an end.

"Who is this man?" said Clovis Andersen. "Thinks he's the president, or something?"

"It is because he doesn't want to be asked for money," pronounced Mma Makutsi. "People are always asking other people for money in this country. It happens all the time. And if you're rich, as he is, then every day there must be people who say they are his cousins or something, and want help with doctors' bills or school fees or need new shoes. The cost of shoes these days —"

That's right, blame us! Blame the shoes!

Mma Makutsi stopped midstream. She looked down at her feet, furtively, as did Mma Ramotswe, who also thought she had heard something. It was not clear whether Clovis Andersen had heard anything, but Mma Ramotswe did notice that he frowned slightly and cocked his head, as if straining to pick up something indistinct.

Mma Ramotswe laughed nervously. "Oh, there are many things that people want," she said. "And people try to help, but it is sometimes difficult. So maybe we should understand why he does not want people to be able to phone him up all the time."

"That is what I just said," chipped in Mma Makutsi.

You'd think that —

The small voice from down below — if it really was a voice rather than a figment of the imagination — was cut short by Mma Ramotswe, who cleared her throat loudly and suggested that Mma Makutsi dial the number they had just been given and put her through to Mr. Ditso. Mma Makutsi did this, and Mma Ramotswe soon found herself on the line to Mr. Ditso Ditso himself.

The businessman was abrupt. "Who are

you, Mma?" he enquired.

Mma Ramotswe gave her name.

"So that is who you are," said Ditso. "I have seen your place. It's on the Tlokweng Road, isn't it?"

"That is me, Rra," she said.

There was a brief silence at the other end of the line. Then he said, "So, you want to investigate me. On whose behalf, Mma?"

Mma Ramotswe was momentarily taken aback. It was true that she had been trying to investigate him, but she had got nowhere. And since she was not calling him now as part of that abortive enquiry, then surely she could deny that she was investigating him. She did not have time, though, as Mr. Ditso continued, "If you'd like to see me, Mma, I'm in my office. You can come now, if you wish."

This was even more surprising, but Mma Ramotswe accepted quickly. "That will suit me very well, Rra. May I bring somebody with me? A visitor."

"Yes," said Mr. Ditso. "You can bring anybody you like. I do not mind."

With that he rang off, and Mma Ramotswe turned to face Clovis Andersen. "I had not expected it to be that easy."

"Things that seem easy sometimes are not easy when you get up close to them," chipped in Mma Makutsi. "That is in Mr. Andersen's book. Page seventy-four."

Clovis Andersen looked embarrassed. "I'm not always right, you know," he said mildly.

Mma Makutsi laughed. "You are very modest, Rra. We have always found that you have been right, haven't we, Mma Ramotswe?"

Mma Ramotswe agreed that this was so, but did not press the matter. She had the impression that Clovis Andersen was beginning to feel awkward over these constant references to his book. She would try to avoid mentioning it in future — at least when he was with them — and she would have a quiet word to this effect with Mma Makutsi later on.

The offices of DD Industries proved easy enough to locate. Two large letters had been mounted on the side of an offshoot of the Lobatse Road. The first D was red, the second D a vivid green, and beneath them was a board on which a painted hand obligingly pointed in the direction of a large white building.

Seated on the passenger side of Mma Ramotswe's tiny white van, Clovis Andersen surveyed the sign. "Ego," he said.

"What was that, Rra?"

"I said *ego*, Mma Ramotswe. That man has a large ego. Why else would he choose his initials for the name of his business? And then put them up on great big cut-outs?"

Mma Ramotswe smiled. "There are many businessmen who are a bit like that. They say *look at me*. I have often thought that would be a good name for a business: The Look at Me Company."

Clovis Andersen agreed.

"What is your own business called, Rra?" Mma Ramotswe asked as she steered the van towards a patch of shade afforded by a couple of jacaranda trees.

Clovis Andersen stared out of the window. "It is called Muncie Investigations."

"That is a nice name, Rra. Who is this Muncie? Is he your colleague?"

"Muncie is a place," Clovis Andersen explained. "It is a place in the United States. In Indiana."

"It sounds very nice, Rra. Muncie sounds like Gaborone. Is it like Gaborone at all?"

Clovis Andersen considered this as the van was parked. "Maybe a bit. Some things are different, though. We have a river, and we make glass jars. We make some very famous glass jars for pickling fruit."

"That is very useful," said Mma Ramotswe, turning off the engine. "Rra, I must tell you something. I am a bit nervous of this Ditso Ditso."

"Why is that, Mma Ramotswe? Has he a reputation for violence?"

"No, not that I know of. It's just that these big men — they can make ordinary people seem very small." She paused. "And there is another thing: Why was he so quick to suggest that I come and see him? Why would he do that, Rra?"

Clovis Andersen thought for a moment. "Because he has something to hide," he said. "He knows that you're a detective, doesn't he? He has assumed, then, that you're looking into his affairs. And then he has decided, quite wisely, that the best way of dealing with somebody who is investigating you is to go out to meet them. Make the running yourself, and that will put them off. I've seen this sort of thing before."

She sought reassurance. "Do you think so, Rra?"

"I think so, Mma Ramotswe."

She pointed to the glass door of the building behind which could be made out the figure of a guard slouched on a chair. "We should go in," she said. "And I shall remember what you had to say."

The guard, who was sitting somnolently

staring out across the parched earth at the front of the building, seemed barely to register their arrival. "That way," he muttered, pointing down a corridor behind him. "Second door on the right. That is where he is."

Clovis Andersen exchanged a quizzical glance with Mma Ramotswe.

"That man is very lazy," she whispered, as they made their way in the direction the guard had indicated. "I have always found that guards are not very wide awake. I think it is a good job for a sleepy person."

Clovis Andersen chuckled. "It's probably better for them to be doing that job than driving buses or planes," he said.

"That is very true, Rra," said Mma Ramotswe.

They were now in front of Mr. Ditso's door, which was simply labelled MANAGING DIRECTOR NO ADMISSION.

"No admissions, plural," said Clovis Andersen.

Mma Ramotswe knocked, and they entered when a voice from within called out. Inside, seated behind a large expanse of desk, was Mr. Ditso Ditso, his shirtsleeves rolled up, his left wrist dominated by what seemed an impossibly large wristwatch. A beam of sunlight, slanting in from the wide plateglass window behind him, caught the dial of the watch and flashed rays back across the wall in dancing points of light.

It was the office of a wealthy man and a public citizen: anybody could see that immediately. On the wall to the side of Mr. Ditso's desk there were several framed photographs and letters: Mr. Ditso Ditso shaking hands with a former president; Mr. Ditso Ditso at a charity function, handing over an outsized cheque; Mr. Ditso Ditso presenting the prizes at Gaborone Secondary School. On a shelf there was a series of what looked like business awards: a trophy in the shape of a cash register, an engraved glass bowl.

Mma Ramotswe introduced Clovis Andersen. "Mr. Andersen is a visitor to Botswana," she said. "He is spending some time in my office, seeing how we work."

Mr. Ditso inclined his head politely in the direction of Clovis Andersen. "You are very welcome, sir." Then he turned to Mma Ramotswe. "What is it, Mma? Who is wanting to investigate me? Is this to do with tax? Some people think I do not pay my taxes, but I do. Every pula."

Mma Ramotswe shook her head. "It's nothing to do with tax, Rra. I have come here to speak to you about a friend," she said. "A certain Mma Potokwane."

The effect of this was immediate. Mr. Ditso, who had been tense, appearing to want to be in command of the situation, now visibly relaxed. He had indicated to his visitors that they should sit down; now he stretched out in his own chair, his hands folded loosely on his lap. "Oh yes? That lady. You have come to ask me to give her her job back, I assume. You know her, Mma?"

Mma Ramotswe bit her lip. "I know her, Rra. She is my old friend."

Mr. Ditso reached for a matchstick that was lying on the desk in front of him. Splitting the top with a fingernail, he began to use the stick as a toothpick; a gesture of calculated unconcern. Mma Ramotswe drew in her breath. She was as much embarrassed as angered by this display; what would Clovis Andersen think of people in Botswana if this was how they behaved?

She fixed Ditso with an intense stare. "I am talking to you, Rra," she said. "And this man with me is a visitor."

Mr. Ditso's hand came away from his mouth. The toothpick was held up, as if it were a tiny baton. "So, Mma? If I have something in between my teeth, can I not remove it? In my own office? Or do I need your permission to do that?"

She looked down at her shoes. She knew that she should try to control herself; nothing was to be gained by falling out with the man who held Mma Potokwane's fate in his hands. But I have already fallen out with him, she thought; I have already said too much.

She made a supreme effort. "I beg you to reconsider your decision, Rra. Mma Potokwane has done a wonderful job as matron. Maybe they haven't told you about that. She is a very great lady."

Mr. Ditso lowered the toothpick. "She has certainly done a very good job, Mma. Yes, that is quite true. But . . ." He paused, looking at Clovis Andersen as if for support. "But there comes a time when things must move on. The same person shouldn't run a business forever. That is not good business practice, Mma, as I'm sure our friend here will tell you."

She tried to keep her voice even, but it rose in spite of her efforts. "It is not a business, Rra. It is a home for children. That is not a business."

Mr. Ditso laughed. "Mma Ramotswe, *everything* is a business these days. Even countries. They are businesses too. Churches. Look at how careful churches are with their money. They have accountants running them. Even the Pope — I have heard that he has trained as an accountant."

Clovis Andersen could not let that pass. "That is surely not true, sir," he said.

Ditso Ditso did not look at him as he replied. "What is true?" he said airily. "Who can tell? One man says something is true; another says it is not. How can any of us tell?"

This comment brought silence. Clovis Andersen looked at Mma Ramotswe and frowned. She stared down at her hands. "You won't reconsider, Rra?" she said quietly. "There are many people who would be very happy if you did."

Mr. Ditso shook his head. "Sorry, Mma, but the decision has been taken. I'm sure that Mma Potokwane will find something else. As you say, she has many talents, and there are these hotels looking for good housekeepers. How about that? She'd probably make much more money doing that."

"It is not about money," retorted Mma Ramotswe. "She does not do what she does for money. The children need her."

Mr. Ditso smiled. "The hotels have their needs too, Mma. It is good work. If there were not good hotels, then where would visitors sleep? They need people like Mma

Potokwane."

Mma Ramotswe sighed. "It is such a small thing, Rra: to have an argument over a building. Why is a building that important?"

Mr. Ditso stiffened.

"It is not about a building," he said. "It is not about that." Then he added, "The building contract has been awarded on tender. There is no reason for disagreement there."

For a moment Mma Ramotswe said nothing, and sat quite still. Then she rose to her feet. "What you are doing is wrong, Rra. You do know that, don't you?"

He held her gaze. "That is your view, Mma. But you are the one who is wrong. And please do not be cross with me for saying this, but this has nothing to do with you. I do not wish to be rude to a lady like you, but I have to say that. This is not your business, Mma. That is all there is to it. It is not your business."

The first part of their journey back to the office was completed in silence. Mma Ramotswe felt raw after the encounter with Ditso Ditso, and did not want to speak; but then, almost at the same moment, as Mma Ramotswe negotiated the traffic circle near the automotive trades training centre, they both poured out their feelings over what had happened.

"Who does he think he is?" Mma Ramotswe burst out. "Sitting there and lecturing us on the needs of hotels!"

"I didn't like him," said Clovis Andersen. "Not one bit."

"And what did I say about Mma Potokwane? There was so much I could have said, but the words seemed to go from my head. I let my friend down."

"You did not," said Clovis Andersen. "You put it very well, Mma."

"It was a waste of time."

Clovis Andersen disagreed. "No, it wasn't a waste of time. Not at all."

She glanced at him quizzically. "How can that be?"

"We learned everything we needed to learn," said Clovis Andersen. "First, the reason why he agreed to see you so quickly was that he thought you were investigating him. That tells us something: there are grounds for investigation. And then, when he realised that it was all about Mma Potokwane, he changed. He realised the heat was off, you see."

She saw that, but wondered where it led.

"And then," Clovis Andersen continued, "did you see how he reacted when you mentioned the building? He had been relaxed before that. Then suddenly he was worried. I could see it very clearly from where I was sitting. He clenched his fists — just a little, but I saw. It's the building, Mma. He said it's not about the building, but it is. That's where we have to look."

"I do not see, Rra . . ."

"The obvious question is this, Mma: Who is getting the contract for the building? And why? He volunteered the information that the contract had been put out to tender. Why did he say that? Because even if it's true, you can be sure it wasn't awarded on merit. No, he mentioned it because he has something to hide. He is very transparent, our Mr. Ditso."

"Yes . . ."

"Yes indeed, Mma Ramotswe. And as you know, I don't like to quote myself, but on this occasion may I be permitted to do so? Somewhere in the book — I forget where — I say that if you listen hard enough, people will give themselves away. They will always mention the things that are preying on their mind, the things that they have done wrong. All you have to do is listen: it always comes out."

Mma Ramotswe took her eyes off the road to give Clovis Andersen a look of admiration.

"Be careful, Mma Ramotswe. There is a car coming."

She swerved — just in time to avoid a car approaching from the other direction. The other driver waved; a friendly wave, for some reason, not an ill-tempered one.

"There certainly are nice people on the road in this country," said Clovis Andersen.

"I think that driver was my cousin," said Mma Ramotswe. "It looked like her."

CHAPTER FOURTEEN:
GOLD INSIDE,
NOT JUST OUTSIDE

There was still a general sense that everything was going wrong. It was a strange feeling — shared not only by Mma Ramotswe and Mma Makutsi, but by Mr. J.L.B. Matekoni as well — and it seemed to be there all the time, like ominous background music to some unsettling drama; always playing, filled with foreboding. Mma Ramotswe tried to get things in perspective, tried to project her usual optimism, and to an extent she succeeded — only to find that her efforts at cheering up herself and others would weaken after a while and the memory would return of the sheer bleakness of both Mma Potokwane's and Fanwell's positions: unemployment in Mma Potokwane's case, and the destruction of a world that goes with it, and criminal charges in Fanwell's, and all that such proceedings entail — although the less one thought about the consequences of that the better.

"I hear the food in prison is not too bad," remarked Charlie over tea one morning. Fanwell was not present, having been sent by Mr. J.L.B. Matekoni to collect a part from the spares depot. "I have heard that from a friend who was sent to prison for hitting somebody too hard."

Mma Ramotswe, Mma Makutsi, and Mr. J.L.B. Matekoni all looked at Charlie balefully.

"You should not talk about such things," scolded Mma Makutsi. "Fanwell will not go to prison."

"He might," said Charlie. "I'm only talking about what could happen. What's wrong with that?"

"Sometimes it's better not to think about bad things that are not definitely going to happen," Mma Ramotswe said mildly.

Mma Makutsi looked cross. "And you said that this friend of yours hit somebody too hard. So that means that you can hit people just the right amount? Not too soft but not too hard?"

Charlie defended himself. "I did not say that. I did not say that you could hit people. All I said is that he hit somebody too hard."

Mma Ramotswe sought to end the argument. Mma Makutsi and Charlie rubbed each other up the wrong way even at the best of times; when there was tension in the air, as there was now, it was considerably worse. "I think that we should not talk about prison," she said. "Nor about hitting people. We all know that Fanwell is innocent. What we must do now is hope that the lawyer will do a good job and make sure that the magistrate sees that."

Charlie stared down into his tea. "That is a very useless lawyer, Mma."

Mma Ramotswe frowned. "You should not say that, Charlie."

"No, you shouldn't," snapped Mma Makutsi. "You don't know anything about it."

Charlie looked up. "But I do, Mma. He is the lawyer who defended my friend who hit somebody too . . . who hit somebody."

For a few moments nobody said anything. Mma Ramotswe looked up at the ceiling, her attention seized by a small white gecko that was clinging upside down to the ceiling board. The gecko was stalking a fly that was only a leap away; and as she watched he leaped, bringing the little conflict to a rapid end. It was so unlike our own dramas, she thought: they can drag on and on, can take so long. Fanwell was forced to wait a long, nerve-racking time before he knew his fate; in the world of the fly and the gecko it was seconds. The lawyer . . . She remembered the lawyer's attitude of resignation and the way she had felt about it; and here was Charlie, confirming the fears that she had tried to suppress within her.

She looked at Charlie. "What happened, Charlie? What did your friend tell you?"

"He said that the lawyer came to court late. He said that —"

"Traffic," said Mr. J.L.B. Matekoni. "The traffic can be very bad in the mornings, as we all know. You cannot blame a lawyer for being late at court just because there is too much traffic on the road."

It was a valiant attempt to paint the lawyer in the best light, but Charlie simply shook his head. "He was late because he had left the papers at the office," he said. "He had to go back to collect them. My friend told me that. He said that the magistrate was cross and this made him worried. It is not good to have an angry magistrate dealing with your case. 'That is very bad news,' he said."

"And then?" Mma Makutsi prompted. If there was to be bad news, then she, at least, was in favour of facing it.

"And then he said that he — the lawyer, that is — stood up and my friend realised that he thought he was somebody else."

"The lawyer thought he was somebody

else?" asked Mr. J.L.B. Matekoni. "The lawyer didn't know who he was?" He looked at Mma Ramotswe in dismay. "That doesn't sound like a very good lawyer, Mma."

"No," said Charlie. "It was not like that, Boss. The lawyer knew he was the lawyer. He thought that my friend —"

"The one who hit somebody too hard," interjected Mma Makutsi.

Charlie glanced at her. "Him, yes, him. He thought my friend was another person —"

"Who had not hit anybody at all?" asked Mma Makutsi.

Charlie showed his irritation. "I'm trying to tell the story," he complained. "And she keeps interrupting me."

Mma Ramotswe urged him to go on. "Mma Makutsi is only trying to help," she said. "Carry on, Charlie."

Finishing his tea, Charlie put his mug down on the filing cabinet. "This lawyer — who is also going to be Fanwell's lawyer — had got his clients mixed up. So my friend had to whisper to him that he was not the person he thought he was, but another person. And the lawyer got all flustered and began to mumble all sorts of things. So the magistrate told him to sit down and drink a glass of water."

Charlie paused.

"Go on," said Mma Ramotswe faintly.

"Then he stood up again and asked some questions. My friend said they were stupid questions, and the magistrate eventually said to him that he was to shut up."

"That cannot be true," Mma Makutsi interjected. "Magistrates don't tell people to shut up. It is not how they talk."

"You weren't there, Mma," snorted Charlie.

"Nor were you," countered Mma Makutsi.

"My friend was. And he told me everything that happened. He said that that was why he got three weeks in prison. It was all that lawyer's fault."

Mma Makutsi was not prepared to let this pass. "Excuse me, did the lawyer hit the person? Did I get something wrong? Maybe the lawyer should have gone to prison for hitting somebody too hard."

Mr. J.L.B. Matekoni looked at his watch. "We should get back to work," he said to Charlie. "There are cars out there needing attention. They won't get fixed if we stay in here talking to the ladies."

"You're right, Boss," said Charlie. "Particularly talking to one lady . . ." He glanced at Mma Makutsi, who smiled sweetly in response.

Mma Ramotswe sighed. "All right," she said, "but this business with the lawyer, Charlie, I don't think you should say anything to Fanwell about that. I don't think it will help him to know. And just because the lawyer did not do a very good job with that friend of yours doesn't necessarily mean that he will not do a good job for Fanwell."

"No," said Mma Makutsi. "So don't tell Fanwell about this, Charlie. I know how you talk. Just don't mention it to him. It's much better that he doesn't know."

The door that linked the office of the No. 1 Ladies' Detective Agency to the courtyard of Tlokweng Road Speedy Motors had been slightly ajar during the tea-break. Now it was suddenly pushed fully open, to reveal Fanwell standing on the step, holding in his left hand the car part that he had been sent to collect from the depot.

"Better for me not to know what?" he asked.

There are awkward moments from which one can retreat, and awkward moments from which there is no escape. This was one of the latter, as Mma Makutsi explained to Phuti Radiphuti when she met him that lunch time in his office at the Double Comfort Furniture Store.

"We couldn't lie to him," she said. "He had heard a bit of what was said and so we just had to tell him everything. He's got a no-good lawyer, you see, and Charlie said that . . ."

She narrated the story of Charlie's friend, of his inadequate defence, and of the unfortunate consequences that followed. Phuti Radiphuti listened gravely. "They should get another lawyer," he said. "Surely there are better people around. That man with the big nose — you know the one — they say that he's very good. The judges can't take their eyes off his nose, and so they always decide in his favour."

Mma Makutsi wondered why a large nose should be an advantage in a lawyer, and decided that perhaps it had something to do with authority. Was it more difficult to argue with a large-nosed person? She had not considered the question before, but now it occurred to her that perhaps it was. But it was too late now to look for a lawyer with a more convincing nose, even if one were to be found. Money, she explained, had already been paid to the inadequate lawyer, and Mma Ramotswe and Mr. J.L.B. Matekoni, who were footing the bill for Fanwell's defence, could not afford to pay a second time.

"How did he take it?" asked Phuti.

"He was very worried," she replied. "Mr. J.L.B. Matekoni tried to tell him that it would be all right; that he would speak to the lawyer and make sure that he handled it properly."

"And was Fanwell reassured?"

"No."

Phuti Radiphuti shook his head sadly. "It is a very sad business. And if they send him to prison, you can imagine the men he will mix with there. He is just a young man, and they will corrupt him with their bad talk and their bad stories. It is very worrying."

They looked at one another despairingly, but they had work to do that lunch time, and life, as Phuti Radiphuti pointed out, had to go on. "There are many sad things," he said. "They are all around us, but we have to get on with our lives, don't we? And that means that we must get on with choosing those things, Grace."

Mma Makutsi agreed. The rapid progress with their new house meant that in a couple of months they would have to furnish it. At present Phuti had no furniture of his own, as the house they were occupying, which belonged to the wider Radiphuti family, was filled with family furniture: chairs that had been left in the house by various aunts, tables that had belonged to grandmothers and were now of uncertain ownership, beds that belonged to nobody in particular but had simply always been there.

Of course, to Mma Makutsi and Phuti the task of furnishing a house was considerably less daunting than it would be to most young couples. Not only was money not an issue in the same way that it was for average newlyweds, but Phuti's expertise when it came to choosing items would be invaluable. "Everything we sell," he said, "is of the highest quality and built to last. But some things are of higher quality than others, and also built to last longer."

Mma Makutsi considered this. "That means that some of your things are better than others?"

"You could say that," said Phuti. "Although we do not say that ourselves, or people would then ask us which was the better furniture and they would buy that and leave the stuff that's not so good. That is always a big problem for people who have shops. So you have to say that everything's first class."

"And this is true, isn't it?" asked Mma Makutsi.

"Yes," said Phuti. "Only some first-class items are *more* first class than others."

"I see."

That afternoon they were to look at sofas and beds. They had already identified a dining-room table and a set of eight matching chairs: these had been ordered from a trade catalogue and would arrive from over the border a few weeks later. The sofa and the bed would be chosen from the large stock that the Double Comfort Furniture Store, the largest furniture store in the country, already had in the showroom.

They left Phuti's office and made their way into the cavernous warehouse that was the Double Comfort Furniture Store. As they entered the store itself, they passed one of the employees, a middle-aged woman wearing a smock and carrying a bag of what looked like polishing equipment. The woman stopped, smiled at Phuti, and then turned to Mma Makutsi.

"It is you, Mma," she said. "I'm very happy to see you."

Phuti introduced her. "This is Mma Rosemary. She has worked here for a long, long time."

"Every day," said Mma Rosemary. "Same job."

Mma Makutsi greeted her in the traditional way. She had noticed the courteous way in which Phuti dealt with his employees and had once mentioned the fact to Mma Ramotswe, who had commented that if that was so, then she could be sure that he would make a good husband. "A man who is polite to the people he is in authority over will always be a good man," she said. "Look at Mr. J.L.B. Matekoni; he is always polite to the apprentices. And he is a very fine husband, Mma." She paused. "He is even polite to Charlie, Mma — even when Charlie is being . . . well, you know how Charlie can be."

Mma Makutsi swallowed. She knew that she had to be kinder to Charlie and she was trying, she really was. But how should a woman — any woman — react to a young man who said some of the things that Charlie said? Who had said, for example, that women could not fly aeroplanes because they would always be looking in the mirror to check that their lipstick was all right? Yes, Charlie had said that; those were his exact words, and she had exploded and said that he needed to wake up to the fact that women were flying aeroplanes right over his head at that very moment. Charlie had gone to the window and looked up at the sky and said that he could not see any aeroplanes being flown by women, and was this because they had perhaps already crashed? Mma

Ramotswe had intervened then and politely taken Charlie to task, while Mma Makutsi calmed down. Those occasions were difficult. She knew Charlie would grow up eventually, but what if he grew up from a young man who held opinions like that into an older man who thought exactly the same way? That was the trouble with growing up: people did not always grow up in the way in which you might like them to grow up. And that, as Mma Ramotswe would put it, was a well-known fact.

Now Mma Rosemary reached out and took Mma Makutsi's hand in hers. It was an entirely natural gesture — one of acceptance, one of solidarity. "You are now with us," she said.

Mma Makutsi saw Phuti break into a smile, and she smiled too. "It is very good," she said.

"And you have chosen such a beautiful woman," Mma Rosemary said to Phuti. "You are a lucky man to have a beautiful wife like this. We are all very proud of you, Rra."

Mma Makutsi felt her hands being gently squeezed as this compliment was paid; it showed, she thought, that it was meant. You did not squeeze hands when you lied; it could not be done.

"You are very kind to me, Mma Rose-mary," she said.

The other woman beamed up at her; she was considerably shorter than Mma Makutsi. "That is because you have made our Phuti so happy, Mma Radiphuti," she said. "And that has made us all happy."

They moved off. Mma Makutsi thought: *Mma Radiphuti — that is me; I am Mma Radiphuti. I am the wife of this wonderful, kind man and I am not dreaming. This has happened. I am Mma Radiphuti.*

"She is the best polisher in all Botswana," remarked Phuti as they continued on their way into the store. "She can make tables glow like the sun. People come in, you see, and they touch the tables after they have been eating fat cakes or doughnuts. And so the tables have fingerprints all over them. Mma Rosemary sorts that out with her tins of polish and her rags."

Mma Makutsi listened to this. "People can be very dirty," she said. "They have dirty hands. Not all people, but quite a lot of people do."

Phuti agreed with this. "It must be very difficult if you are a person who has to shake hands with people all day. A president, maybe, or a big film star. All those people come up to you and say, *Please shake my hand,* and you want to ask them if they've washed their hands. But you can't do that, can you — not if you're one of these politicians or film stars. You have to shake hands first and then you must think afterwards: *Have they washed their hands?*"

They passed one of the tables that had been freshly polished by Mma Rosemary. "See that?" said Phuti, pointing at the gleaming hardwood surface. "That is like a mirror. If you had a table like that, you could use it to shave with in the morning. You could look at your face in the surface and shave."

The sofas were next, and there they stopped. Mma Makutsi gazed out over the large array of highly stuffed, opulent-looking couches. Many of them were made of leather, most of it black, but in some cases cream or highly coloured reds and greens. She wondered what it would be like to have a red leather sofa, and for a moment she saw herself seated on such a thing, fanned perhaps by one of those large electric fans, drinking tea and eating some rich morsel. If one had a sofa like that, one might sit on it all day, supported in the utmost comfort, reflecting on one's good fortune though not, she hoped, without a thought for those whose own sofas were less comfortable, or indeed for those who had no sofa at all.

She bent down to examine a large four-seater covered in a gold-coloured material to which a fringe had been attached. She hardly dared look at the price tag, but did so and recoiled in shock. Surely no single sofa could cost anything like that? How many cattle did that represent? She did a quick calculation. Were there people who would actually pay such a price, and if they did, would they not feel permanently uncomfortable knowing that they were sitting on so expensive a piece of furniture? Would one simply admire such an item and not sit on it? Could one perhaps leave the price tag on it after purchase, so that visitors to the house could see what you had paid for it and marvel? An ostentatious person would probably do that, but she, Mma Makutsi, would never want to flaunt her wealth. Or Phuti's wealth, she reminded herself; for I am still Mma Makutsi from Bobonong, and I shall never — *never* — indulge myself in a sofa like that when there are people in villages in the country for whom even a chair, a modest wooden chair, is a luxury, well nigh unaffordable.

Phuti noticed her examining the gold-coloured sofa. "Do you like that one, Grace?" he said. "Why don't you try sitting on it? See if it's comfortable."

Mma Makutsi hesitated. "Oh, I was just looking, Phuti. We do not need a gold-coloured sofa . . ."

"Try it out," he said. "Sit on it."

She moved round to the front of the sofa and very slowly lowered herself onto it. She felt the cushion beneath her, at once firm and soft, supportive but yielding. She leaned back, and it was like giving oneself into the arms of a gentle, comforting lover. "Oh," she muttered, and then, "oh," again.

"You look very good on that," said Phuti. "That sofa is the right colour for you. Gold. That is your colour, Grace."

She felt the fabric with her fingers. It was as smooth as satin. Gold? Was that really her colour? She had always thought that red suited her very well, but perhaps gold was also suitable for people who looked good in red. If they bought this sofa, which of course they would not — not at that price — then she might perhaps buy a pair of gold-coloured shoes that she could wear when she was sitting on her sofa. She had seen a pair in the shoe shop at Riverwalk, and she could go back and see whether they were still available.

"Would you like that one?" Phuti asked. "We can get it if you like."

She sat up and propelled herself off the sofa. "No," she said. "It is very nice, Phuti, but it is not right for us."

He frowned. "Are you sure? You looked so comfortable."

"I am sure. And I can already see one over there — that brown one — that I think might be right for us."

They made their way over to the brown sofa — a much more low-key affair — and she sat down on it. It was considerably less physically comfortable than the gold-coloured sofa, but correspondingly more mentally comfortable. This was a sofa on which one might sit in casual clothes, on which one might eat a doughnut or drink a cup of tea without worrying about crumbs or splashes. This was a sofa *entirely free of guilt.*

"I think that this will be a very good sofa," she said to Phuti. "You try it."

Phuti sat down. "It is well made," he said. "I know the people who make these sofas. They are honest people."

"Then I would like this one," said Mma Makutsi.

Phuti leaned across and whispered in her ear. "I am very happy, Grace. I am very happy that you have chosen this one rather than the gold one. That shows me that you are not one who is impressed with flashy things. You are gold inside, Grace, not just outside."

She turned and kissed him lightly. "That is the kindest thing anybody has ever said to me." *Gold inside, not just outside.*

Phuti called over the floor manager, who had been hovering in the background, and arrangements were made to transfer the sofa to the storage warehouse. Then they returned to the office before Phuti drove Mma Makutsi back to the agency. On the way, they stopped at a petrol station, and Phuti set about filling the car. As he instructed the attendant, a van drew up alongside the neighbouring pump and a man in blue overalls stepped out.

Mma Makutsi watched. Phuti looked up and saw the man, whom he obviously recognised. For a moment or two they looked at one another before Phuti gave a nod of greeting. The other man turned away. Now he hesitated, looked over his shoulder, and then busied himself with the cap of the van's fuel tank. It struck her as strange that the man should have so pointedly failed to respond to Phuti's friendly overture; even a smile would have been polite — a smile or a nod of acknowledgement.

"Who is that rude man?" she asked Phuti

as they drove off a few minutes later.

"He is one of the builder's men," he said. "I met him when I went to look at the house. Now he doesn't seem to want to know me."

Mma Makutsi frowned. "Why?"

"I have no idea," replied Phuti. "There are some people who are very shy. Maybe he is one of those."

Mma Makutsi thought for a moment. "Shy, or rude, maybe. Rude like his boss," she said. "He is rude too. Rude boss; rude men. Sometimes that is the way it happens."

That was possible, he said. His own father had drummed into him the lesson that the way you treat your staff is the way they will treat you. "That is something that some employers just do not understand," Mr. Radiphuti Senior had said. "But in the Double Comfort Furniture Store we will never forget that, will we, Phuti?"

He had not. He had remembered it.

Mma Makutsi was silent for the rest of the brief journey back to the office. Silent; thinking.

CHAPTER FIFTEEN:
HOW MANY CUPS OF TEA . . .

The following day, Mma Ramotswe received a telephone call from the secretary at the orphan farm. This was a woman she knew only slightly — a woman who had been brought up in Lobatse and whose son was a promising athlete, a barefoot runner, whose prowess on the track was occasionally featured in the *Botswana Daily News*. They exchanged the customary greetings, and then Mma Ramotswe, vaguely remembering that there had been something in the papers about the son — what was his nickname? — had asked after the young man.

"I'm sorry, Mma," she said, "I cannot remember your son's name, but I saw something in the papers and I wondered how he's doing. You must be very proud of him."

The woman laughed. "Nobody remembers his real name. That is because they all call him by his nickname. They call him Lightning now, and we even use that at home. Yes, I am proud of him, Mma; I am very proud."

"Lightning is a good name, Mma. Very good."

"As long as it doesn't go to his head," said the secretary. "I heard him call one of the other runners Tortoise the other day. I told him that was very unkind and that one day his own legs would get slow — like mine."

Mma Ramotswe made a sympathetic noise. "Everybody's legs get slow, Mma. That is well known. But it doesn't matter, as long as one can get about a little bit. That is all that is needed."

There was a moment of silence; the point of the call had not yet been revealed, but that was not so unusual. People often took some time to say what they needed to say — to rush a conversation could be considered rude, especially among old-fashioned people, and Mma Ramotswe remembered that the secretary was indeed a somewhat old-fashioned person.

Then the silence was broken. "I am phoning about Mma Potokwane," said the secretary.

Mma Ramotswe felt a momentary stab of alarm. Was Mma Potokwane not well? "Is she ill . . . ?" Mma Ramotswe stuttered.

"I do not know whether or not she is sick," said the secretary. "She never complains about herself, as you know. But I cannot tell because she is not here. She has gone."

"Where has she gone?"

"She has gone somewhere else. I do not know where. All she did was leave a note to say that her deputy, Mma Paloi, is in charge now until the end of the month, when Mma Potokwane is due to go anyway. That is all she said." The secretary paused, allowing this information to be absorbed. "I wondered if she was with you, Mma. You are her great friend. But obviously she is not."

"No, she is not here. And I am very shocked, Mma, to hear this news. Mma Potokwane would normally never leave her post. Never. You know what she's like."

The secretary was quick to agree. "If she was on one of those big ships and it was going down, she would be the last one to jump off, Mma. That is very true."

Mma Ramotswe could not help but picture it: Mma Potokwane standing on the deck of a ship waiting for everybody else to clamber into lifeboats and cast off. And perhaps Mma Makutsi would be beside her, clinging on to her certificate from the

Botswana Secretarial College, anxious to save that from the encroaching waters. And then Mma Potokwane would jump into the last lifeboat and . . . and it would tilt precariously because of her weight and perhaps begin to sink, and again she would make sure that she was the last one to abandon ship, or she would even go down with the lifeboat, dutiful to the last; and the waters would swirl around with odd bits of detritus — spars of broken wood, unoccupied lifebelts, the framed certificate from the Botswana Secretarial College . . .

"Have you spoken to her husband?" she asked.

The secretary explained that Rra Potokwane had gone to spend some time with a cousin who needed help with his cattle. "He has no phone with him," she went on, "and I cannot find the name of the cousin. I do not know how to contact him."

Mma Ramotswe thought out loud. "I do not think she will have gone up to her husband. I do not think so."

"No?"

"No, I do not think that she would do that. She does not like that cousin of her husband's — she has spoken to me about that. She says he is a drunkard."

"I have heard her say that too," said the

secretary. "She says that he eats too much as well. She told me that that cousin eats all the meat in the household and leaves none for his wife. That is what she said, Mma; I am only repeating what she said."

Yes, she thought, there are men like that; men with fat bellies and thin wives and children.

"I have an idea, Mma."

The secretary sounded relieved. "I knew that you would come up with something, Mma. I knew that you would know. You are the detective, you see . . ."

This was not a time for flattery. "Thank you, Mma, but it is only an idea. There is a big difference between an idea and a solution."

"Oh, Mma, that is absolutely true. There is a very big difference." The secretary cleared her throat. "And what is this idea, Mma?"

"The lands," said Mma Ramotswe. "I think that she will be out at her fields."

"Why do you think that, Mma?"

"Because that is where she went once before."

Mma Ramotswe explained how there had been an occasion — not as serious as the current one — when Mma Potokwane had felt rather overburdened by her duties and

258

had arranged to take a short break out at her fields, or lands, as they were called. "It was only for a weekend, but she said that it was the best place to go if one was feeling exhausted. So I think we could see if she's there now."

The conversation came to an end, with Mma Ramotswe promising to contact the secretary as soon as she had any news. She would go out there herself, she said; she knew the way — roughly — and it was a journey of no more than four hours.

The secretary was concerned. "That is a long way, Mma. And I don't think you should go out into the bush by yourself."

Mma Makutsi, on the other side of the room, overheard this. "Tell her you will not be going by yourself," she interjected. "You will be going with me."

Mma Ramotswe relayed this information. She was not sure that it was the best of ideas, but it was a generous offer, and no more than one would expect from Mma Makutsi, who, for all her faults — and they were not very big ones — was loyal and supportive through thick and thin . . . She paused for thought: Would all this be described as thick, or was it thin? She was not at all sure, but whatever it was, it would be good to have Mma Makutsi at her side.

■ ■ ■ ■

Of course there were preparations to be made. A journey out into the Botswana bush was not something that could be undertaken lightly. Those tracks, pitted by use and eroded by rains, were a trial for any vehicle, even one accustomed to such roads, as was the tiny white van. You had to be careful: if you broke down, it could be many miles from help, and so you had to know where you were. You also needed to take water — there would be no supplies of that along the road — and enough fuel to get you to your destination and back, with a little bit left over for emergencies.

At first, Mr. J.L.B. Matekoni was unwilling to allow her to go. "It is the middle of nowhere, that place," he said. "And what if she isn't there? You will have wasted a lot of time looking for somebody who may be at the opposite end of the country, for all you know."

"If she isn't there," countered Mma Ramotswe, "then at least we will have found out that she isn't there. It will not be wasted."

He shook his head in exasperation. "That is no answer, Mma. And what if the van breaks down? That is a very old van, that one, and its engine —"

"Its engine is very good," said Mma Ramotswe. "You serviced it two weeks ago, Rra, and you said that it was in good condition. Have things changed so quickly?"

He sighed. "It is in good condition for a van of its age. But you cannot take an old vehicle like that into the bush without running some risk. I have known many cars that have died . . ." He lowered his eyes as he spoke, as if in respect for the souls of departed cars. "I have known many cars that have died out in the bush. And that has meant a very long walk for their drivers."

"That is a risk we shall take," said Mma Ramotswe. "It is the same with people. People can become late at any time — just like that. But that does not mean that we should not do anything and not go anywhere just because there is a possibility that we may suddenly become late."

Mr. J.L.B. Matekoni sensed that there was no point in his arguing any further; he would never persuade Mma Ramotswe to act otherwise when a friend was in need. And in spite of his anxiety over this trip, he shared her concern for Mma Potokwane, whom he had always admired in spite of her tendency to ask him to fix something whenever she saw him. She had to do that, he understood; it was her job, and the children in her care had benefited a great deal over the years precisely because she took her job so seriously. Rather than waste his energy on trying to stop the expedition, he expended it on making sure that the van was as ready as it could be for the journey. He placed spare cans of fuel in the back and lashed them down for the bumpy ride, and stowed two plastic demijohns of water beside them. Then the oil was checked, the battery tested, and a coil of rope tucked underneath one of the seats. "You never know," said Mr. J.L.B. Matekoni. "You never know, do you?"

"I shall be very careful, Rra," said Mma Ramotswe, adding, "I always am, you know."

And as she said this, she gave him a look that implied that any dangers about which he was concerned were ones that she would be very careful about — whatever they were.

The lands to which Mma Potokwane was suspected of retreating lay to the west of Gaborone, some distance beyond Molepolole, hard against the edge of the Kalahari, the great semi-desert that made up the heart of the country. This was dry land at the limits of the inhabitable, and fields here, if they could be called fields, grew very little: a few melons and patches of sorghum — not much more than that. Yet the families who tilled them, scratching at the parched soil to coax growth out of what sometimes seemed little more than powdered stone, did so by ancient right. This is where their people had been as far back as anybody could remember, and they maintained this link with the land even after they had moved to towns and villages. Each year the women and children would trek off to their lands for weeks at a time, to plant and tend the crops. It was a ritual that survived growing prosperity, even when there was no real need to harvest these small crops; it was a way of showing children who they were and reminding adults of the same thing.

"You do know the way, don't you?" asked Mma Makutsi as they left Molepolole behind them and began to follow the smaller road west.

Mma Ramotswe sounded confident. "Yes," she said. "We follow this road to Takatokwane and then after that we go that way." She pointed vaguely towards the north.

Mma Makutsi glanced at her nervously. "That way, Mma?"

"Yes. There is a road that goes like

this . . ." She made a winding gesture. "We don't follow that one."

"No?"

"No. We follow the one that goes like *this*." The gesture now was more up-and-down. "That's the road we need to look out for. Then, after a while — quite a long time, because you have to go very slowly — there is a place where the road splits in two, or maybe three."

"Which is it, Mma? Two or three?"

Mma Ramotswe shrugged. "I cannot remember everything, Mma. But I will know which way to go, I promise you. I have been taught these things."

Mma Makutsi remained silent while she digested this information. Then she asked what exactly Mma Ramotswe had been taught. The road system of Botswana?

Mma Ramotswe smiled. "You cannot learn all the roads of Botswana, Mma. That would be a lifetime's work because they are always changing roads and adding to them. They look at a map, those people in the Roads Department, and then they draw a line across it and say that is the best place for a new road. Let us build a new road soon. That is what they say."

"And then they have tea," added Mma Makutsi.

They both laughed. "Yes, Mma Makutsi, that is absolutely right. They are always drinking tea in those government offices. When you think of how much the Government must spend on tea . . ." She shook her head in disbelief at the unimaginable figures.

"We spend quite a lot on tea," mused Mma Makutsi. "If you add it up, Mma. You have . . . how many cups of tea do you have, Mma Ramotswe? Ten? Twelve?"

"I haven't counted, Mma Makutsi. And you yourself —"

Mma Makutsi did not let her finish. "Well, let's think, Mma. You have tea when you wake up, don't you? You have told me about that."

"Of course I have tea when I wake up," retorted Mma Ramotswe. "Is there anybody who *doesn't* have tea when they wake up?"

She received no answer to this question, and so she continued, "I sometimes have two cups of tea before breakfast. It depends. There are some days when I seem to drink my tea more quickly than others. Then there are days when I just sip my tea and it takes a bit longer. One cup will do on those days. One cup to start with, that is; there is more tea later on."

"And then?" asked Mma Makutsi.

"And then there is the tea that goes with

breakfast. I make that in a pot and put it on the table and drink maybe two cups of tea . . ."

Mma Makutsi looked at her sideways, and Mma Ramotswe revised her account. "Maybe three, Mma. In fact, three. Always."

Mma Makutsi nodded at the admission. "And then, Mma, there is the office tea. We must not forget that."

"That is correct," said Mma Ramotswe. "Morning tea — one cup only, though, Mma. You have seen that. Then at lunch there are two cups, and then there is afternoon tea." She paused. "How many does that make, Mma?"

"I think that makes eight," said Mma Makutsi. "Call it ten."

"Ten cups," said Mma Ramotswe thoughtfully. "And we haven't counted the evening tea. That must be added. So maybe fourteen cups of tea in all."

"Fourteen cups," intoned Mma Makutsi, making a rapid calculation before continuing. "That means seventy cups between Monday and Friday. What about the weekend?"

"I do not think it is much different over the weekend," said Mma Ramotswe. "I drink that office tea at home over the weekend."

Again Mma Makutsi performed a calculation. "Ninety-eight cups," she said. "Call that one hundred. There is something called reporting error, Mma. I have read about it. It is all over the place. There are many, many reporting errors." She looked out of the window on her side of the van, as if to scan the passing bush, the acacia trees, for reporting errors.

"One hundred cups," repeated Mma Ramotswe. "That will be doing me a lot of good. One hundred cups of red bush tea, Mma. That bush tea is full of good things. It will be making me very strong." She paused. "I am not ashamed of all that tea, Mma."

"Of course not," said Mma Makutsi. "There is nothing to be ashamed of in drinking one hundred cups of tea a week, Mma. Which is . . ." She paused again. "More than five thousand cups of tea a year, Mma. That is very impressive."

"Well, there you are, Mma Makutsi. Those are the figures. You cannot argue with figures, can you?"

Mma Makutsi looked thoughtful. "And ours is just a small business. We use all that red bush tea for you and all that ordinary tea for me, and we are just a tiny business. Imagine how much tea the Standard Bank drinks. Imagine all their tea, Mma. Just think of it. Or the Government. All those government people in their offices drinking tea."

"It is a miracle that there is any tea left for us, Mma," said Mma Ramotswe. "After the Government and the banks and people like that have taken all the tea they need, it is a miracle that there is any tea left for people like you and me, Mma, the tea-drinking public."

"You're right, Mma Ramotswe. It is a miracle. The miracle of the tea."

"A good miracle, Mma Makutsi."

"A very good miracle, Mma Ramotswe."

CHAPTER SIXTEEN:
THE HABITS OF LIONS

Mma Ramotswe seemed to find the turning without any difficulty. "I remember that tree," she said to Mma Makutsi as she swung the van off onto the pitted dirt track. "When I came here with Mma Potokwane four years ago, we turned off at that tree. This is definitely the right place."

Mma Makutsi was impressed. "I could never remember a tree after four years," she said. "Or after four days, really. You are very good at these things, Mma."

"Of course there was the signpost too," said Mma Ramotswe. "That helped. Did you not see it, Mma? There was a small sign that gave the name of the village that we pass through on this track."

Mma Makutsi had missed that. Looking out of the window, she gazed at the feature-less bush. "It all looks the same to me," she said. "All these trees. All the same. And the bushes. Also the same."

Mma Ramotswe gingerly but skilfully manoeuvred the van round a large pothole in the track ahead. "I would not like to drive on this road at night," she said. "All these holes."

"And lions," said Mma Makutsi, shivering at the thought. "We are very close to the Kalahari now, Mma, and there could be lions."

"The lions will keep their distance from Mma Potokwane," said Mma Ramotswe. "It would be a very foolish lion who tried to eat her."

Mma Makutsi smiled. "A very brave lion, perhaps, Mma. But we should not talk about lions like this. It is very bad luck. Talk about lions brings lions — that is what I always say."

Mma Ramotswe considered this. It was true; the contemplation of misfortune undoubtedly attracted misfortune. Why this should be so, she was not sure; perhaps it had something to do with noticing things. If you thought of something, then you noticed it; if you did not think of it, then it might be there but you did not notice it. That was possible, but . . .

She did not finish the thought. They had been travelling painfully slowly but had, for the last couple of hundred yards or so, been on a slightly better section of track, one that did not seem as badly potholed and eroded. Without intending to speed up, she had nonetheless done so, with the result that the tiny white van was now travelling almost at the pace it would have travelled on a much better, official road. That was safe enough, except for the sand, which had slowly been becoming deeper and had begun to encroach on the track itself. Now, with a fair degree of speed behind it, the van hit a section of track in which the sand covered the entire surface. For a four-wheel-drive vehicle, that would not perhaps have presented too much of a challenge; for the van, however, it was too much, and the front wheels, engaging only with sand that shifted and collapsed as the tyres tried to gain a hold, veered sharply and brought the van into a deep bank of fine white earth at the edge of the road.

"We have stopped," said Mma Makutsi, as they shuddered to a halt.

"So it seems," muttered Mma Ramotswe.

"Maybe you can reverse out of this," said Mma Makutsi. "If you reverse, then you can get back on the road. What do you think, Mma?"

"It is the only thing to do," said Mma Ramotswe, through clenched teeth. Sometimes Mma Makutsi's advice was . . . how might one put it? Obvious.

She put in the clutch and engaged reverse gear. The engine responded, but the wheels merely spun in the fine sand, sending up a cloud of dust on either side of the van.

"It's digging in, Mma," said Mma Ramotswe. "The wheels are turning, but they have nothing to grip."

Mma Makutsi sighed. "I think we are stuck in the sand, Mma."

"I think you're right, Mma Makutsi."

Mma Ramotswe turned off the engine. "We should get out and see what has happened," she said. "I was stuck in sand once before. But I got out."

"Oh yes, Mma? How did you do that?"

"I put two sacks under each front wheel. That gave the tyres a surface they could hold on to."

Mma Makutsi clapped her hands together. "That is a very clever idea, Mma. Sacks. We can put sacks under the tyres."

"If we had sacks . . ."

"You don't have any, Mma?"

Mma Ramotswe shook her head. "I thought about it, Mma. I even made a mental note to get some. Mr. J.L.B. Matekoni has a pile of old sacks back at Zebra Drive. If only I had remembered."

They climbed out of the van to inspect the situation, which was worse than Mma Ramotswe had feared. The two front wheels of the van had spun energetically into the sand, effectively burrowing deeper with each revolution. Now the sand came three-quarters of the way up each wheel, and any further movement would undoubtedly sink them further.

"This is very bad," said Mma Makutsi.

Mma Ramotswe looked down the track. "How long will it take us to walk back to the main road, Mma? You are good at calculations."

Mma Makutsi stared in the direction from which they had come. "We've been travelling along here for about thirty minutes," she said. "And we've been doing about fifteen kilometres an hour. That means we have come about seven kilometres. How fast do you think we walk, Mma?"

Mma Ramotswe scratched her head. "Three kilometres an hour?" she ventured. "Maybe less in places where it is very sandy."

"Then we are at least two hours from that road," said Mma Makutsi. She looked at her watch. "And now, Mma, it is almost four o'clock. We would get back to the road at about six o'clock, just as it is becoming dark."

Neither of them said anything. There had been a conversation about lions only a short time ago, and they were both thinking the same thing. Mma Ramotswe looked at Mma Makutsi, who looked first at the ground and then at the sky.

Mma Ramotswe cleared her throat. "People say that you should never leave your vehicle when it breaks down," she said. "If you do, then when the search party arrives, the searchers find the car but they don't find you."

"If there is a search party," said Mma Makutsi.

Mma Ramotswe looked around them. It was often the case that a landscape that appeared to be empty was not; human habitation could be found in unexpected places — a single hut tucked away here, a collection of dwellings there; and there were paths between such places, bringing life to the landscape as arteries do to the body.

"Somebody may come along," she said. "I think that we should stay in case that happens."

Mma Makutsi shook her head. "There will be nobody, Mma. Who is going to come along here this close to sunset? No, we will not see anybody for a long time. Maybe days, Mma."

As Mma Makutsi spoke, her voice faltered slightly, and Mma Ramotswe realised that her assistant was frightened.

"Don't be afraid, Mma Makutsi," she said. "There is nothing that can harm us out here. All we shall have to do is to wait until help comes along." She tried to sound cheerful. "And even if we spend the night out here, we shall be fine. We have water, and we also have food. And we shall be quite safe in the van. Lions cannot open doors, you know. They are not that clever."

Mma Makutsi did not appreciate this mention of lions. "Oh, please don't talk about lions, Mma. I am trying not to think about lions, and you keep talking about them."

Mma Ramotswe laid a calming hand on Mma Makutsi's arm. "I'm sorry, Mma, I should not have mentioned lions. I do not think that there are any lions round here. I shall not mention lions again." She paused. "We could make a fire, Mma. I have some newspaper and some matches. We could get a fire going and then we could have tea. That would help, I think."

"Tea is always a big help," said Mma Makutsi. "I'll get some twigs and some wood and then we can make a fire. Maybe the smoke will attract attention and somebody will come."

"That is a real possibility," said Mma Ramotswe, pleased that Mma Makutsi seemed to be cheering up.

Mma Makutsi wandered off to retrieve a small branch that had fallen off an acacia tree. Part of the wood had been covered by a mud casing painstakingly put in place by termites; this she brushed off as she carried it back to the van. And it was while she was doing this that they heard the creaking sound of an approaching donkey cart.

"You see!" shouted Mma Makutsi. "I told you that somebody would come."

Mma Ramotswe was on the point of reminding her that she had said exactly the opposite, but decided not to spoil the moment. "Well, there we are, Mma. We are no longer alone."

The donkey cart was a rickety affair, cobbled together with ancient painted boards and a chassis that had once belonged to a motor vehicle of some sort — an incongruous union of wood and metal, but serviceable enough. This cart was twenty or thirty years old, and could be expected to last another few decades at least. Out here, where the rainfall was so slight and inconstant, rust was not a problem. More dangerous were the ants, with their appetite for wood, but these could be watched for and dealt with easily enough.

Riding in the cart, on a battered old red-leather seat saved from a car somewhere, was an elderly man. At the end of the reins he held were two donkeys, yoked side by side, pulling the cart with that somnolent acceptance — resignation, even — that marks their breed. Their steps, taken on small black hooves, were sure enough, but slow; they would be faster on the return journey, with the smell of home in their nostrils, but for the moment there was no rush.

Mma Ramotswe stepped out onto the track and raised her hand in greeting. The man riding the cart pulled on the reins, took off his hat and wiped his brow. She caught her breath: the hat was so like the hat that her father, the late Obed Ramotswe, had worn every day of his life after he had returned from Mochudi — or so it had seemed to her. The hat that they had tucked into his coffin to accompany him on that final journey to the grave; the hat that he had once lost on the road and that had been rescued by some stranger and placed on a wall where its owner might see it; that same shapeless hat that she had felt embarrassed about as a small girl, other girls' fathers having more modern hats, but that she had come to love as standing for everything that he, and indeed Botswana, stood for — decency, quiet, courtesy — the things that were slipping away in the world but that were remembered and pined for.

The man replaced his hat, tied up the reins of the cart, and got down from his seat.

"I think you're stuck, Mma," he said to Mma Ramotswe. "This bit of sand is well known for this. Every time anybody comes along here they find that this sand wants them to stay and talk."

Mma Ramotswe laughed. "Maybe it is lonely, Rra."

The man nodded. "That could be, Mma. But maybe it is just thinking that it will remind people that four-wheel-drive trucks are the only way to travel out here — four-wheeled or . . .", and here he pointed to the donkeys, which were eyeing Mma Ramotswe lugubriously, "four-legged."

Mma Ramotswe accepted the implicit censure graciously. "You're right, Rra. My husband would agree with you. But my friend over here and I were very anxious to see Mma Potokwane, and we came anyway. Now I have plenty of time to regret it."

"We always have plenty of time to regret things," said the man. "I have been regretting everything for years and years."

Mma Makutsi, who had been standing to the side, now came forward and introduced herself. "I am this lady's assistant . . . associate. Could you help us, Rra? Soon it will be dark and —"

"My friend here is worried about lions," interjected Mma Ramotswe.

"Lions?" The man chuckled. "There are no lions here, Mma. You ask my donkeys — if they get a smell of a lion, even if the lion is far, far away, they run. No, there are no lions any more — not here. A day's walk over that way — over towards the Kalahari, yes, you get one or two lions. But not here."

"A day or two's walk for us, or for a lion?" asked Mma Makutsi.

Mma Ramotswe made light of the question. "It doesn't matter, Mma. He says there are no lions."

"For us," said the man, turning to Mma Makutsi. "For a lion, two hours, maybe. Lions are very fast runners. Have you seen them running, Mma?"

Mma Makutsi thought for a moment. She had never seen a lion doing anything, not ever having come across one, but somehow she felt she knew how they ran.

"I know how they go," she said. "They lie down on their stomachs and creep along."

The man frowned. "No, that is only when they are stalking their prey, Mma. And that is a lioness. If you are walking through the bush, say, and a lioness sees you and decides that she will eat you, then she goes down like this and she walks on bended legs. That is so that her head doesn't stick up over the top of the grass. It means that nobody can see her. That is what lions like." He paused, and gestured to the bush that stretched out behind the van. "Over there, you see, that is a good place for a lioness to creep. Those little bushes would cover her and we wouldn't know that she was there, while all the time she's getting closer, closer."

He turned back to face Mma Ramotswe. "You said you were here to see Mma Poto-kwane, Mma?"

Mma Ramotswe smiled. "That is so, Rra. She is our old friend, and she has her lands along there."

"Oh, I know that," said the man. "She is my old friend too. In fact, she is the cousin of my brother's cousin, by a different mother. I have known her all my life."

"Is she here, Rra?" asked Mma Makutsi.

The man pointed down the track. "Yes, she is here. She came out yesterday. Nobody had been expecting her, but there she was. There is something wrong, I think, but she won't speak to the other ladies about it. My wife has asked her, and she says that everything is all right. But it isn't."

"No, Rra, you're right," Mma Ramotswe. "There is something very wrong. It's to do with her work."

The man absorbed this. "She can come back here. She has good fields. She could stay. She has many relatives out here, and they will look after her." He turned to look at the van. "But you cannot get to her place in that van, Mma. You will have to leave it here and walk. It is not far to her place now — just half an hour or so along that way."

"But we can't leave the van stuck in the sand," objected Mma Makutsi. "How will we get back to Gaborone? We cannot walk."

"We won't leave it in the sand," said the man. "I will help you pull it out, and then we will leave it here. You can collect it when you have finished visiting Mma Potokwane. It will be perfectly safe."

Mma Ramotswe and Mma Makutsi looked at the donkeys. One of them, clearly older than the other, grey about the muzzle and the eyes, appeared to be asleep on his feet, his head drooping, indifferent to the flies that buzzed about what looked like an open sore on one of his ears.

"They are very strong," said the man, intercepting the glance. "They have pulled bigger vans out of there. You needn't worry, Mma."

"I have some rope," said Mma Ramotswe. "Under the seat there is some rope that my husband put in there. We could use that, Rra."

The man shook his head. "I have my own, Mma. I always carry it because I know that I need it. We can use mine."

He walked round to the back of the cart and extracted a length of rope from a box nailed to the boards. Then he detached the yoke from the front of the cart and began to cajole the two donkeys into position in front of the tilting nose of the tiny white van. Mma Ramotswe was impressed by his businesslike manner — this was a man, she decided, who knew what he was doing. "You get in and steer, Mma," he said to her. "Otherwise the wheels will point in the wrong direction and you'll go further into the sand. Steer back into the middle of the road."

Mma Ramotswe returned to the van and eased herself into the driver's seat. The man now addressed Mma Makutsi, suggesting that she push at the back of the van while he pulled on the yoke at the front and persuaded the donkeys to take the strain. Then they both got into position, and the man started to shout at the donkeys.

Inside the cab, Mma Ramotswe felt the van move — but only slightly. Then, as the man gave a resounding smack to one of the donkeys, it moved again, rolling forwards as the wheels were dragged through the sand; only to stop and then roll back the few precious inches it had just achieved.

"Stop," called out the man, both to the donkeys and to Mma Makutsi.

"I have stopped," shouted Mma Makutsi from the back. "It's too heavy, Rra."

The man was perplexed. "They are very strong . . ." He tailed off. He looked at Mma Ramotswe. "Perhaps, Mma, it might be better if we asked the other lady . . ." He gave a toss of the head in the direction of Mma Makutsi. "Perhaps we could ask that lady to steer while you pushed. It's just that she's quite a bit less . . ."

Mma Ramotswe was polite but firm. "Traditionally built."

"That is right," said the man. "She is a bit thinner, and you are . . ."

"Traditionally built," prompted Mma Ramotswe again. "Don't worry, Rra. I am not ashamed of being who I am."

The man made an elaborate show of rejecting the very thought. "Of course, Mma, of course. It's just that the donkeys are a bit old — that one in particular — and they are finding it a bit difficult to drag a van *and* a . . . a traditionally built lady. With the other lady at the wheel, I think we can do it."

Mma Makutsi, who had been following this exchange, smiled as she made her way round to the door. But she said nothing; that would have been rude, of course, and would have demonstrated a complete lack of feminine loyalty. Men, she knew, did not understand these matters.

"You must be careful not to get *too* thin, Mma," muttered Mma Ramotswe, as she yielded her place in the van.

Mma Makutsi smiled. "Mma, I am already becoming a bit traditionally built. I do not think there is any danger of that."

The man now returned to his position with the donkeys while Mma Ramotswe leaned up against the back of the van, digging her feet into the sand and preparing to apply her weight in the hoped-for direction of travel. Already, as she did so, the van moved slightly, even before the donkeys had engaged.

"I'll count to three," called the man.

"Then we'll pull and you push, Mma. One, two, three!"

This time the reaction of the van was immediate, and Mma Ramotswe had to act quickly to avoid falling over backwards.

"That's it!" shouted the man from the front. "Pula, pula, pula!"

Pula, pula, pula! was the cry of triumph, of joy, that was universal in Botswana. It meant *rain, rain, rain* — just the right cry for a dry country that lived for the day that the first life-giving rains arrived — that day of ominous purple skies, and heat, and the wind that precedes the first drops of water splattering and dancing on the baked ground. *Pula, pula, pula!*

With the van free of the sand, Mma Makutsi decided to start the engine. She did this with her foot pressed down hard on the accelerator pedal — she was no driver, really — and the engine raced in response. For the donkeys, yoked so closely to this unusual burden, this was a source of sudden alarm, and they responded by backing sharply against their restraining straps. One of them, the older one, stumbled, attempted to regain its footing, failed to do so and then collapsed.

The man gave a shout. "Turn the engine off, Mma! Turn it off!"

Mma Makutsi complied, her hands shooting up to her mouth in a gesture of horrified realisation. "Oh, Rra," she cried. "I have killed your donkey."

The man struggled with the straps that held the fallen donkey in the yoke. As he did so, the other donkey brayed suddenly, a mournful, broken sound. It took a few moments, but when the straps were released, the donkey sagged back into the sand, its chest heaving. It moved its head as if trying to get up, but then lowered it again and fixed the sky with a stare of reproach. Mma Makutsi, distraught over what she had done, was now joined by Mma Ramotswe. The donkey's eyes, Mma Ramotswe found herself thinking, were so beautiful; flecked, almost golden, and rimmed with delicate black eyelashes. It was an incongruous thought — this admiration of the beauty of a creature that seemed to be on the point of death.

Mma Makutsi was now in tears. "Oh, Mma, what have I done?"

"It was an accident," said Mma Ramotswe gently. "It was not your fault, Mma. You were not to know."

The man, who had been bending over the donkey, now rose and walked over to his cart. He seemed to be curiously unconcerned by what had happened, simply saying, "He will get up. He will know we are going home now."

He was right. The donkey now suddenly heaved a sigh and staggered to his feet.

"See, Mma," said Mma Ramotswe. "No harm done."

"He is very lazy," snapped the man. "He is always doing this."

"Maybe he is tired," said Mma Ramotswe.

"Maybe," said the man. "But I'm tired too, Mma. We are all tired." He looked about him. "There is so much sand."

She thought about what he said. Perhaps Mma Potokwane was tired too. Perhaps there were just too many orphans, just as there was too much sand. Perhaps she had had enough of helping. If that were true, then she wondered whether she should be seeking her out here, or whether she should leave her in peace. It would be easy to go back now and leave Mma Potokwane at her lands, but then she reminded herself that Mma Potokwane had never once spoken in the past about retiring or giving up. No, the defeatist Mma Potokwane was not the real Mma Potokwane. The real Mma Potokwane was a fighter.

With the donkeys back in harness, Mma Ramotswe reached into her bag to retrieve a fifty-pula note. "You have been very good, Rra. This is a present for you."

The man looked at the money. "You do not have to pay me, Mma. I wouldn't leave anybody here. But since you are so kind . . ." He reached out and took the money, which he quickly tucked into the breast pocket of his shirt. "Since you are so kind, I will take you and this other lady to Mma Poto-kwane's place. You should leave the van here because it gets even sandier later on. You can come back for it when you want to go home."

They collected a few necessities from the van, which Mma Ramotswe had driven on to a piece of firm ground beside the track. Then, climbing onto the back of the cart, they started the journey down the track, the same journey that people had made count-less times over the years, back in the time of their parents, their grandparents; in the same way, in the same quiet, at the same pace, closer to the world than in the metal cocoons in which we now travel. There was birdsong, and the gentlest of breezes; and they heard the donkeys, the noise made by their hooves against the ground, the sound of their breathing, their sighs.

CHAPTER SEVENTEEN: HAVE YOU HAD ANY INJECTIONS RECENTLY?

With Mma Makutsi away, Phuti Radiphuti felt at a loose end. He had very rapidly become accustomed to marriage — so rapidly, in fact, that on this first occasion on which he had been left alone, he found himself unable to settle. Mma Makutsi had left him a stew for his dinner and this required only to be warmed up, but Phuti felt disinclined to eat by himself in a kitchen that he now associated with the presence of his new wife. On impulse rather than on any serious reflection, he telephoned the aunt with whom he had stayed during his recent convalescence. This aunt, who had done her best to discourage his marriage, believing that Mma Makutsi was unworthy of her nephew and motivated, too, by a jealousy that would have prevented her from approving of any prospective wife for Phuti, had not attended the wedding. She had observed it from afar, though, sitting in the brown car with its mean-spirited narrow windows and watching the reception tents through a pair of binoculars. Phuti had seen her car and had started over towards it in the hope of persuading his aunt to bring hostilities to an end and join them at the wedding party; he had not succeeded in speaking to her, though, as she had seen him approaching and had driven off at speed.

This had not prevented him from sending her a piece of wedding cake and a photograph of himself in his wedding suit, inscribed *To my dear aunt, from your faithful nephew, Phuti.* With a more forgiving woman, this might have resulted in a letter of thanks, or at least a message, but neither had been forthcoming. Phuti did not take offence — it was not in his nature to do so — and now, ignoring her previous bad behaviour, he called his aunt and asked her whether he could possibly come for dinner that evening. "Just me," he said quickly. "I shall be alone."

The aunt had been quick to agree to this self-invitation. She had been hoping to see him but had been unable to swallow her pride sufficiently to make the first move. And this reference to being on his own intrigued her: Was it too much to hope that he had tired of the whole business of being married to Mma Makutsi and was keen to revert to bachelor status, preferably living with her and occupying the bedroom in which he had stayed on his last visit? She could feed him up again — as she had done during his convalescence — and make him happy. It would be better, far better, for him to be away from that dreadful woman with her large round glasses and her Bobonong ways.

It was not without trepidation that Phuti parked his car at the aunt's front gate that evening and began his way up the short path to her front door. The last time I was here, he thought, I was a single man. And now I am a married man with a talented and attractive wife. I was a boy back then; now I am a man.

He glanced at the garden in the fading light of evening. There were the paw-paw trees from which his aunt had picked the heavy yellow fruit she had served to him with lumpy custard. There was the tree that he had climbed when he visited his aunt as a twelve-year-old; the branch on which he had strung a swing that had broken at a crucial moment and sent another boy, a friend from school, sailing through the air to a broken leg and three days in hospital.

And there, parked beside the house, in the position it had occupied for so many years, was the unfriendly brown car with its pinched windows and its sign that said *Don't Waste Water.* That sign had always been there, although his aunt, as far as he could make out, had never been particularly abstemious when it came to water. The patch of grass outside her house was always liberally irrigated, and he had noticed that the baths she ran for herself almost reached the rim of the tub.

He knocked at the door and called out, "*Ko, ko,* Auntie!" From somewhere within the house he heard her footsteps approaching and then the door opened. Seeing Phuti on the doorstep, the aunt opened her arms to embrace him. *I am forgiven,* he thought.

"Phuti!" exclaimed the aunt. "Now you have come back to see your auntie."

He stepped into the house and allowed her to give him a hug.

"Let me see you," she said, standing back. "You're looking so handsome, Phuti! Such a waste, such a waste."

He recoiled momentarily at the words. In what way was it a waste for him to look handsome, not that he thought he looked handsome at all?

"You are well, Auntie?"

She made a non-committal gesture. "I am well, and then I am not well."

He looked concerned. "You have been ill?"

"Not exactly ill, Phuti. But then, not well either. It is not easy, being alive these days, what with everything changing. But we must not talk about me, we must talk about you. You are the important one now, not me. Tell me what has happened."

As she asked this question, she led him into the sitting room. In the middle of the room several large armchairs were positioned around a table on which a dictionary, a world atlas and an arrangement of red plastic flowers had been placed. There was a stale smell in the air.

"Sit down, Phuti." It was more of a command than an invitation, but Phuti was used to his aunt's adopting this tone and he obeyed without murmur.

She fixed him with a concerned stare. "You are looking very thin," she began. "Here and here." She pointed to her neck and stomach. "Those are the places where it always shows, Phuti." She narrowed her eyes. "You're not getting enough food, are you?"

Phuti held up his hands in denial. "No, no, Auntie. I am getting too much food, really. I am putting on weight, I think."

She shook her head. "That cannot be, Phuti. Your neck is very thin now, and look at your trousers: they are hanging on you like an empty sack. You are very thin."

Phuti struggled with his feelings of annoyance. It was quite obvious to him what the implication of these comments was: his new wife was no cook — or at least, that is what his aunt was trying to suggest without actually saying it.

"I am eating very well, Auntie," he said. "Grace is a very good cook, and she is giving me plenty to eat."

The aunt affected surprise that she should have thought that Mma Makutsi was anything but an expert cook. "Of course she is," she said. "Of course she . . ." She struggled, as if finding it difficult to remember the name.

"Grace. Grace Makutsi."

"Of course, Grace . . . Grace Ma . . ."

"Makutsi."

"Yes, that woman." She looked down at the floor and frowned. "Makutsi? Where is that name from, I wonder? It is not from anywhere near here, I think. Perhaps it is South African. They have some very odd names over there."

"She is a Motswana, Auntie. She comes from Bobonong."

The aunt transferred her gaze to the window, looking out into the distance in the direction, perhaps, of Bobonong. "That is far away. I do not know any people up there. Maybe they are nice people, but how can you tell when you don't know any of them? There are many people in China, but I cannot say whether they are nice people or not because I do not know any of them."

Phuti felt his cheeks burning. He always felt like that when his aunt said such things. And he knew that if he closed his eyes and counted slowly, he worried less about it. But now he could not do that; Bobonong and China? What had China got to do with it? Nothing, he thought. Nothing at all.

"Bobonong is in Botswana," he said. "The people who live there are all Batswana — the same as you and me, Auntie. They are no different."

"I did not say they were," said the aunt. "All I said is that I do not know any of those people, apart from Gracious . . ."

"Grace."

"Yes, apart from her."

The aunt sniffed. "You must eat more," she said. "It is not good for a man to become too thin."

"I am eating very well, Auntie. You mustn't worry about me."

The aunt looked pained. "How can I stop worrying about you, when you are my own nephew? How can I stop worrying about you when you go off and marry somebody I don't know and whose people we've never heard about?"

Phuti did not answer, and the aunt continued. "And now where is she? Gone away, I believe, and you have nothing to eat. Well, you always have a home to come back to. There is that same room you stayed in — I have changed nothing. And you will get fatter and stronger if you stay here — where you belong."

"But Grace is only away for one night," said Phuti mildly. "She is on business with Mma Ramotswe. They have gone —"

"Oh, that Mma Ramotswe! That fat lady who calls herself a private detective but who sits in her office all day eating doughnuts! That is what they say, you know. You'll have to be careful, Phuti, if Gracious eats doughnuts with that woman all day, then your bed will break. You just remember that."

Phuti closed his eyes. It was easier to talk to his aunt with his eyes closed, he had decided. Not only did this help him to say what he wanted to say, but it also had the effect of disconcerting her, which, he found, was of some help.

"We mustn't talk about Grace too much," he said. "She is a good wife to me and I am very happy. That is what I want you to know, Auntie: I am very happy."

The aunt sniffed. "I'm glad to hear that. But if you ever are unhappy, you know where to come. That is all I will say for the time being." She sniffed again. "And why are your eyes closed, Phuti? Did you not sleep enough last night?"

Phuti opened his eyes. "I slept well, Auntie. But now I'm hungry, and the thought of your delicious cooking is making my stomach jump up and down."

The aunt smiled coquettishly. "You're right to remind me, Phuti. I have some very good stew that I am going to give you." There was a pause — the slightest pause. Then: "Far better than anything you get at your place, I think, but let's not talk too much about that . . ."

The stew, when it was served, proved to be every bit as good as the aunt had claimed. Over the dinner table, watching Phuti tackle his second helping, she seemed to mellow, and the conversation moved on to less controversial subjects. The aunt had been to Lobatse to visit a relative who had been ill; she had found a new pair of shoes in a shop and had bought them because they had been reduced in price by sixty per cent. She had received a telephone call that morning from somebody who had got the wrong number; her neighbour had been bitten by a dog and had been obliged to have anti-rabies injections — "just in case" — but knowing the neighbour as she did, it was almost certainly the neighbour's fault rather than the dog's. "They should give that dog a course of injections, if you ask me, Phuti. You know what that woman is like — I've told you, haven't I?" And then, "Have you had any injections recently, Phuti? I must go to the doctor myself some day and get an injection."

They finished the meal and the aunt made a pot of tea. She served this on the verandah, where it was cooler, and from where they had a good view of the neighbour's house, now a dark shape in the night. "You never know what you're going to see going on in there," said the aunt. "Sometimes they leave a light on and forget that it is on. I have seen some things that I cannot speak about, you know. Even if you ask me, I cannot speak about them."

There was an expectant silence, as if she was waiting for Phuti to ask her. But he did not, and the conversation moved on to the new house.

"I hear that you have that Mr. Putumelo building you a house," said the aunt. "I know his wife. She is a big lady in the church, although you never see him there."

"Maybe that is because he is very busy," said Phuti. "Some people are too busy to go to church."

"That's true," said the aunt. "I myself cannot go every Sunday, because I am so busy." She reached out to refill Phuti's cup. "He is building his own house, you know. It's very close to my butcher's house. The butcher says it is a very fine house."

"That's what you'd expect of a builder," observed Phuti. "I have never known a builder who lived in a not-so-good house. They know what makes a good place. They know those things, Auntie."

The aunt nodded. "That's very true. Yes, they know. The butcher told me that this house is made of very high-class bricks. They are imported, he says."

Phuti was not surprised by this. "He likes bricks, that builder. He recommended that we use bricks, too."

"Mind you," the aunt continued, "I do not know where he finds the money. The butcher says that he has a big bill run up with him, and when he talked to him about it he told him that he is finding things very difficult at the moment. He says that there is not very much work, and that he has a big overdraft with the bank."

This did not sound unfamiliar to Phuti. "People often say that," he remarked. "They say that their business is not doing well when it really is. They do not want to make other people jealous."

The aunt considered this. "Maybe, but not in this case. The reverend at the church said something about them. He said that they were in financial difficulties and we should pray that the Lord brings them some money. The wife must have told him that."

Phuti closed his eyes. Financial difficulties. Bricks. The Lord. Houses. There was so much to think about, and the thoughts came crowding in on him. Then one line of thought, in particular, emerged from the rest. *How could the builder be building a house for himself when he had no money? How did one do that? With the Lord's help?*

While Phuti was wrestling with the question of Mr. Clarkson Putumelo's new house, Mma Makutsi, along with Mma Ramotswe and Mma Potokwane, was sitting around an open fire, under the stars. They had finished the meal Mma Potokwane had prepared for them — a stew of beans, carrots, and tomato soup, all poured over a base of freshly cooked pap. Mma Ramotswe had pronounced it delicious, and Mma Makutsi had enthusiastically concurred. Mma Potokwane had accepted their compliments, but had added a remark to the effect that she would have more time to cook now that "nobody had any use for her." This had been vigorously refuted by Mma Ramotswe, who had insisted that of all the citizens of Botswana — all two million of them — Mma Potokwane was without question one of the most useful. Mma Makutsi, without prompting from Mma Ramotswe, had agreed. "Nobody is useless," she said heatedly, "and you are less useless than nobody else, Mma. Definitely."

This remark was greeted with silence while Mma Ramotswe and Mma Potokwane had tried to work out what it meant. The spirit in which it was made, though, was clear enough, and Mma Potokwane simply thanked her. "You have always been very kind to me, Mma," she said. "Always."

"And you to me," said Mma Makutsi.

Mma Ramotswe knew that this was not entirely true — indeed it was completely false — but was pleased that such good spirit was abroad, and said nothing to contradict what had been expressed. New friendships can be every bit as strong as old friendships, and of course became old friendships in due course. She thought of this in silence, watching the flickering light of the fire play across the faces of the other two women; three friends sitting out in the darkness in the immensity of the surrounding bush, with the Kalahari a stone's throw away and the stars, silver-white fields of them, hanging high above, so dizzying, so humbling to look at.

"No," said Mma Potokwane after a while. "I have made up my mind, you see. I have stopped working, and I am going to do some things for myself — things I've always wanted to do."

Mma Ramotswe understood this. She knew a number of people who had stopped working with the same thing in mind, and they had told her that the decision had been the best decision of their lives. One had opened a poultry farm and now supplied eggs and chickens to many of the major shops in Gaborone; another, a mechanic friend of Mr. J.L.B. Matekoni's, had taken to restoring old cars and had already sold a 1956 Pontiac to a collector over the border. There were so many things that you could do if you simply had the time, but most of us left it too late.

"I can see that," she said. "What will you do, Mma?"

There was a silence. Mma Makutsi looked at Mma Potokwane with interest, as did Mma Ramotswe.

"Well . . . ," Mma Potokwane began. "Well . . ."

"You will be very busy," Mma Makutsi suggested helpfully. "All those things . . ."

Mma Potokwane pursed her lips. "Many things," she began. "There are many things."

They waited. Mma Potokwane poked a stick into the fire, making a few short-lived sparks fly heavenwards. Yes, thought Mma Ramotswe; yes, there are so many other things that might come to mind, but not if you have given your life to orphaned children; not if you have spent every waking hour working out how to advance their interests, how to procure some little benefit, some little treat that would make each of them feel loved, special; not if you had given to those same children all the love that a large — traditionally built — frame could muster; not then, not then was there anything that you wanted to do but to continue with what you had always been doing, which was to look after those children.

Mma Ramotswe decided to break the silence. "But the most important thing to you, Mma, is running the orphan farm. That's what you really like doing, isn't it?"

Mma Potokwane did not answer; she did not need to, as her expression said everything that needed to be said.

"I thought so," said Mma Ramotswe. "And that's why I think you should come back with us."

Mma Potokwane looked up sharply. "No. I have left now. My deputy will run the place until they get somebody else."

"Then he will have won," muttered Mma Makutsi. "That man will have won. Bullies often do."

Mma Potokwane turned to look at her. "Why do you say that, Mma?"

"Because it's true, isn't it? Bullies often win. They know that people are not prepared to stand up to them, and so they win." She looked at Mma Ramotswe for confirmation. "And there are many men who bully women. You agree with that, don't you, Mma Ramotswe."

Mma Ramotswe's reply was cautious. "Well, sometimes . . . But remember, Mma, there are many men who are not bullies."

"Of course," said Mma Makutsi. "Phuti is not like that. Mr. J.L.B. Matekoni is not like that. And your husband, Mma Potokwane, I have heard he is not like that either . . ."

"He is certainly not like that," said Mma Potokwane. "Rra Potokwane is very kind. He does not go around pushing people about."

No, said a small voice, *you do all the pushing, don't you?*

Mma Makutsi shot a glance down in the direction of her shoes.

Sorry, Boss, we couldn't resist that.

She looked at the other two women: Had they heard too? Mma Ramotswe had a slightly puzzled expression on her face — it was possible that she might have heard — but Mma Potokwane seemed unaffected. Of course she would not have heard, Mma Makutsi reminded herself: there was nothing to hear. These apparent interventions by her shoes were nothing but her own imagination: a sort of conversation with herself — that was all.

So you think, Boss!

Mma Ramotswe now continued. "But even if not all men are like that, at least some are. They insist on getting their way on everything, even on the question of whether children should eat at home or in big rooms . . ."

"Horrible big rooms," said Mma Potokwane.

"Yes, horrible big rooms," agreed Mma

Ramotswe. "And how will they get to know each other and their house-mother if they do not eat together, in a kitchen? How will they do that?"

Mma Potokwane became animated. "That's just what I said! And it's just what the house-mothers themselves said. All of them. They said: we want to feed the children in the houses. We want to do the cooking ourselves, in our own kitchen, with our own pots."

"Of course they said that, Mma. And they said that because they knew what they were talking about. And then some man comes along — a man who probably has never cooked so much as a potato in his life — this man comes along and says, *I know best.*"

"Not one potato," fumed Mma Potokwane.

Mma Ramotswe glanced at Mma Makutsi, who was smiling. "Of course, if people — if women — let men like that get away with it, then they'll do it again, and again, and again. Soon they'll have all of us eating in big halls from big kitchens — just to save money."

"That will not be possible," said Mma Makutsi. "People would never agree . . ."

"I do not mean that exactly," said Mma Ramotswe patiently. "I am just pointing out how things could get worse." She turned to Mma Potokwane. "So it's quite important, Mma, that we don't give up too early. Not while there's still a chance."

Mma Potokwane gave Mma Ramotswe a searching look. "Do you think there's still a chance, Mma? Do you really think so?"

Mma Ramotswe had not been able to come up with anything about Mr. Ditso Ditso that could be used to get him off the board, and she was not sure that she would. But of course there was a chance, and there was something that told her that she had already found what it was but just did not realise it. It was a curious feeling, but it was there, and it was enough to make her want to persist.

"I think so," she said.

Mma Potokwane sighed. "So you want me to go back?"

Mma Ramotswe nodded. "Yes, that's what we want, Mma."

Mma Potokwane hesitated before she gave her reply. "If that's what you want, Mma, then . . . then I'll do it."

"Good," said Mma Ramotswe.

"Yes," said Mma Makutsi firmly. "Good."

They sat in silence after that. Later, though, shortly before they retired to bed in Mma Potokwane's large sleeping hut, shared with two young Potokwane nieces who had been helping in the fields, Mma Ramotswe whispered to Mma Makutsi, "She's still not herself, Mma. She says she hasn't given up, but I think she has."

Mma Makutsi was dismayed to hear this; she had been more optimistic. "But she said that she's coming back. She said that . . ."

"People say things," said Mma Ramotswe. "But when they're in that frame of mind, they don't mean them. The lips say one thing, the heart says another. Or says nothing."

The lips say one thing, the heart says another. Those words echoed in Mma Makutsi's mind as she drifted off to sleep that night. Outside, in the night, a dog barked at some shadow, some creature in the night. *The lips say one thing, the heart says another.* She wondered whether that was true, or whether it just *sounded* true. And what did it mean to say that the heart said nothing? Were there people whose heart really did say nothing? And if there were, who exactly were they? The dog gave another bark, followed by a yelp. Then there was silence. She opened her eyes in the darkness. Nothing.

CHAPTER EIGHTEEN:
A LAWYER SPILLS TEA
OVER HIS SHIRT

They returned the next day, a Saturday, arriving back in Gaborone in the middle of the afternoon. On Sunday Mma Ramotswe went to church at the Anglican Cathedral, as she always did, and helped with the tea afterwards, an opportunity for people to chat, to inspect at closer quarters what others were wearing, and to discuss — and if necessary criticise — the day's sermon. One of the members of the congregation, an Indian accountant from Kerala who had lived in Botswana for twenty years or so, was going home to India for a daughter's wedding. He told Mma Ramotswe about the wedding plans, which involved, he revealed with a modicum of pride, several hundred people travelling from all over India, all wanting hotels and feasts and special treatment. She listened to this with sympathy — weddings were rarely simple, and Indian weddings, it seemed to her, were even more complicated and fraught with difficulty than their Botswana counterparts — but she was not really concentrating. Nor did she pay attention when Bishop Mwamba himself came up to speak to her and told her about a book he had been reading that he thought she might enjoy, if she had the time.

"But I know how busy you are, Mma Ramotswe," the Bishop said, "what with your business and all those investigations, and so on."

She nodded politely. He was right, but it was the *so on* that was the trouble now, and in particular that bit of the *so on* that was made up of Mma Potokwane's troubles. And then there was Fanwell, whose trial was due to take place the following day.

"Yes, Bishop. There are many things to worry about in this life. Many things."

The Bishop smiled. "But we must not let those overwhelm us," he said. The smile faded, to be replaced by a look of concern. "You are all right, aren't you, Mma Ramotswe?"

She looked up at the sky. The man to whom she was talking, she reminded herself, had major concerns to think about. He knew the issues of Africa, its sorrows. He knew all about the burdens and difficulties of those who struggled to get by in countries where there was cruelty and oppression. It was all very well for her to stand here drinking tea in a peaceful and well-ordered country, but what about those who did not have that luxury? And should she then worry him with her petty concerns — very small ones, really — when there were many weightier things occupying his attention? No, she thought. No. "Everything is all right, Bishop," she said.

The Bishop was tapped on the shoulder by one of the members of the choir and detached himself from Mma Ramotswe. She helped a few people to tea, poured another cup for herself, and then looked around the group of people who were still talking to one another in the church courtyard. Mma Ramotswe felt that she needed to catch up on local news. There were always the newspapers, of course, but the *real* news, a complete picture of what was really happening, could only be gleaned from actual conversation with people. It was ordinary people who knew what was happening — not official spokesmen or the editors of newspapers. And the closer one got to the grass roots, the nearer one came to the people who actually experienced the effect of what was happening in the public world above them, the more complete one's understanding could become.

She surveyed the faces of the congregation. These were all good people — or they were good people at that hour on a Sunday morning. Some of them, she knew, found it more difficult still to be good as the day wore on, and even more difficult when Monday morning dawned. But they were all human, just as she was, and the real issue was whether they were doing their best. Mma Ramotswe felt that as long as you did your best, then it was not too important if you fell below the standards that others might expect of you. What mattered was doing your best and then, if your best turned out to be not very good, at least admitting it and trying a bit harder next time.

There were some people, of course, who clearly had no intention of doing their best — Violet Sephotho, for instance, but that was another matter . . . . Fanwell's trial: that was the thing she would have to think about now. Poor Fanwell — how would he be feeling now? She imagined that he would not sleep that night — how could one be expected to sleep, knowing that at nine o'clock the next morning one would be standing in the dock facing the full force of the law of Botswana?

She looked down into her cup. If only she could speak to the magistrate, whoever he was, and tell him what sort of young man Fanwell was; of course he would be reading the letter that Mr. J.L.B. Matekoni had so painstakingly drafted that would say much about Fanwell's character — and she had drafted one too — but it was one thing to receive a letter, quite another to have somebody express her feelings to you in person. If she were to be given five minutes — only five minutes — with the magistrate, she would explain to him that it was simply impossible that Fanwell would knowingly fix a stolen car. He was not like that; it was just not in his character. She would say, "Rra, I beg you. Rra, I beg you: listen to what I am saying. I have met many wicked people in my work, Rra — just as you have — and I'm telling you, Rra, from the bottom of my heart I do not think this young man could have done what they say he has done."

She sighed, and took a sip of her tea. Magistrates must hear that sort of thing day in, day out. They could be forgiven if their eyes glazed over, or if they looked out of the window in the face of such pleas. Everyone has a mother who believes in them; everyone has somebody who says that they would never do anything wrong; of course they have. And the job of a magistrate was not to let everybody off just because their mother, or their aunt, or their employer spoke highly of them.

Again her eyes moved over the members of the group. It was interesting, she thought, to see how different people held their teacups: that woman over there, for example — the woman who sometimes arranged the flowers and whose daughter had married that man whose brother was a pilot with Air Botswana — that woman held her cup round the rim, ignoring the handle. And the man she was talking to was balancing the saucer on his palm as if his hand were a table; it was very strange. And the man next to him, the one in the dark suit . . . he was a lawyer. She stopped; a possibility had occurred to her. He was a lawyer.

Putting down her empty teacup, Mma Ramotswe negotiated her way past the milling members of the congregation until she was standing beside the lawyer. He was in the process of bidding farewell to the woman to whom he was talking; having done so, he turned to Mma Ramotswe.

"So, Mma, how are you?"

She might have replied that her world, in various respects, was falling down about her head, but she did not. "Everything is fine, Rra, and you?"

Everything was fine in his world too, he said; indeed, it could not be better — he had recently won a major case and his client had given him a large Brahmin bull as a present. "Your late father would have approved of this bull, Mma Ramotswe. He is a very fine beast, and we will breed many good cattle from him."

Mma Ramotswe expressed her satisfaction at this. "A good bull is better than —"

"A bad bull," the lawyer chipped in, and laughed. "There is no doubt, Mma Ramotswe, that it's worth paying for the best."

She smiled at this, but ruefully. This man was a good lawyer — everybody said that — and his clients obviously paid well for his services. Fanwell's lawyer, by contrast, was reputedly hopeless, and yet Mr. J.L.B. Matekoni had already paid handsomely for him.

"My husband has a young mechanic," she said. "He works in the garage — a very good young man. But unfortunately he has got into a bit of trouble."

The lawyer shook his head. "Young men and trouble — those two things go together, Mma."

"Yes, Rra."

The lawyer gave her a searching look. "Are you wanting me to help him, Mma?"

She looked at him hopefully. "He has a lawyer," she began. "But I am not sure about him."

"Well, in that case there won't be anything I can do, Mma. Lawyers are not allowed to steal clients from other lawyers. I'd get into big trouble if I did that." He took a sip of his tea. "I imagine it's the same with private detectives. You cannot take another detective's clients, can you?"

She wanted to explain to him that there were no other private detectives in Botswana, but he had more to say.

"That can be a good thing, I suppose, but it can also be a bad thing. Particularly if you get a bad lawyer. But I'm sure this person you have is fine. Tell me, who is he? Or she?"

Mma Ramotswe gave him the name just as he was taking another sip of his tea. She was not prepared for his reaction, which was to splutter, almost to choke, sending a spurt of tea down his chin and onto his shirtfront.

"Oh, Rra, I'm sorry. Please let me." She fished for her handkerchief to wipe at the tea stain.

"I'm all right, Mma Ramotswe. Don't

worry. It's just that . . . well, it's just that that man is absolutely useless. I know I shouldn't speak about a fellow member of my profession like that, but I can think of nothing else to say. He knows no law at all, Mma — none. In fact, none of us knows how he ever managed to get his LLB in the first place. Maybe they're putting law degrees in cornflakes boxes these days."

There was little comfort in this conversation. She had been hoping that somehow this man might offer to help, yet he seemed to have precluded the possibility. But then he lowered his voice and said, "Don't tell anybody this, but the young man could fire him. Then, once he has no lawyer, he could contact me and I could see what I could do."

Mma Ramotswe reached for his hand and squeezed it. "Oh, Rra, that is such good news."

"When is he due to appear in court?"

"Tomorrow. Nine o'clock."

The lawyer recoiled. "Tomorrow? Oh dear, Mma, that will not be possible then. He cannot dismiss his lawyer at the last moment, because I won't have time to read the papers in the case, and anyway, I am busy for the next three weeks. I have a big case for the Government."

317

"So he'll have to stick with the lawyer he has?"

"I'm afraid so, Mma. And maybe it won't be too bad. You never know with the law. It's a bit of a lottery, as they say: you win some and you lose some." His tone was sympathetic. "This young man, of course, might be one of the losers."

She thanked him. "You have been very kind, Rra."

"I'm sorry I couldn't do anything, Mma, but I hope all goes well . . . if he's innocent. If he's guilty, well, then he's guilty."

She felt she could not argue with that. Perhaps that was why this lawyer had the reputation he did: because he put things succinctly, in a way that anybody could understand.

Mr. J.L.B. Matekoni drove Fanwell to court the next day in his garage truck, with Mma Ramotswe and Mma Makutsi following in the white van. The magistrate's court was in a handsome new building of an open disposition that in no way spoke of the distressing events which it witnessed daily: the accounts of petty crime, the tears and protests of litigants, the outrage and the untruths — in short, the business of the average court. This court stood on the road to the jail, a fact that both Mma Ramotswe and Mma Makutsi could not help thinking about as they drove there that morning but also secretly hoped would not be relevant to Fanwell.

From behind the wheel of the truck, Mr. J.L.B. Matekoni dispensed a few final bits of advice. "When you speak," he said, "look at the magistrate as you give the answers. Don't look at him cheekily — don't stare — but look at him as you would look at a priest or a headmaster: with respect."

Fanwell nodded miserably. "I will, Boss."

"And here's another thing. The person who's going to be asking you questions is called the prosecutor. He may try to make it look as if you're lying."

"But I'm not lying," protested Fanwell.

"I know that," said Mr. J.L.B. Matekoni. "But you have to remember that the people in the court don't know that. So what I was going to say to you is this: you mustn't lose your temper with that person, whatever he asks you. You just reply very calmly and say, 'I am telling the truth, Rra.' That is what you must say. Understand?"

Mr. J.L.B. Matekoni glanced at his young employee. His heart went out to him — it really did; sitting there in that ill-fitting suit with a white collar and tie, and all the time inside he must be shaking and trembling. Poor, poor boy — and he really was just a boy, this young man; he may have been in his early twenties, but at that moment he looked not much more than fifteen. And he had worked so hard and been so good to his demanding family.

"I want you to know something, Fanwell," he said. "Whatever happens today — whether they listen to you or not — Mma Ramotswe and I both believe you. And we will never lose our faith in you. We will not. You remember that."

Fanwell said nothing.

"Did you hear that, Fanwell?"

The young man nodded. "I'm scared, Boss." His voice was small and timid.

"Of course you're scared. Who wouldn't be? But you be brave now, Fanwell. You do that for me. You be brave. And remember what I said."

They drew up in front of the court, where Mr. J.L.B. Matekoni parked the truck. Mma Ramotswe's van drew up next to the truck, and the four of them walked into the court.

"Charlie's already there," whispered Mma Makutsi as they approached the public seats. "He said he would be here early."

They slid into one of the bench seats, with Mr. J.L.B. Matekoni sitting next to Charlie.

Fanwell had reported to the office and was now in the custody of the police, along with a handful of others awaiting trial. They glimpsed him as he was led away, and Mma Ramotswe's heart lurched. *He's too young for this,* she thought. *He's far too young.*

The next to arrive was the lawyer, who was wearing a black gown over his suit and was carrying a pile of dishevelled papers. Mma Makutsi looked at these papers critically, and Mma Ramotswe, noticing this, realised what lay behind this critical look: it was a filing issue. She closed her eyes. *Cornflakes,* she thought.

The lawyer greeted them absentmindedly. "They have found his fellow-accused," he said, reading a name from the paper at the top of his pile. "One Mr. Chombie."

"Chobie," hissed Mma Makutsi. "You should get the name of your clients right, Rra."

The lawyer looked up in surprise. "But he's not my client, Mma. They have very different interests, you see."

Mma Ramotswe leaned forward to ask the lawyer a question. "Is this Chobie going to tell them that Fanwell did not know that the vehicle was stolen?"

The lawyer looked at his papers. "Not according to his statement," he said. "He is going to say that Fanwell knew that it was stolen and that he, Chombie, did not."

Mma Makutsi exploded. "But that's a lie, Rra! That's a big, big lie."

The lawyer shrugged. "These fellows are always telling lies," he said. "You know, Mma, if this building were a cinema and they had a big board outside saying what was showing, they would have to put LIES in big letters. Then they might add, EVERY DAY ADMISSION FREE." He laughed at his joke, which was greeted with silence from the others.

"This is very serious . . . ," Mma Ramotswe began, but could not finish, as Fanwell and Chobie were now being led into the dock and the court had gone quiet.

"The trial is about to begin," whispered the lawyer helpfully. "You must stop talking now."

The lawyer representing Chobie had now arrived — a small man with a bustling sense of energy. He seemed to be much more in command of the situation than Fanwell's lawyer, whom he acknowledged with only a curt nod of the head.

"That is a real lawyer," whispered Mma Makutsi. "See how different he looks."

It was now the turn of the magistrate to enter, which he did through a door at the back of the court. A policeman indicated that everybody should stand up, and there was shuffling and murmuring as people got to their feet. Unfortunately, Fanwell had been looking down at the floor when this happened, and did not see either the policeman's gesture or the figure of the magistrate entering the court. He remained seated.

"Fanwell!" hissed Mma Ramotswe. "Fanwell, stand up, stand up!"

It was too late. Fanwell heard his name, but being unaware of where the voice came from he looked in the wrong direction. And by that time the magistrate had taken his seat and everybody in the court had sat down too.

The magistrate had noticed. Frowning, he nodded to the policeman who was standing immediately behind Fanwell. The policeman leaned forward and seized Fanwell's arm, pulling him to his feet. Fanwell looked completely dismayed; he had now realised what was going on and glanced desperately in the direction of the lawyer. But the lawyer simply shook a finger at him.

"Young man," the magistrate said. "Do you know what contempt of court is?"

Fanwell looked blank.

The lawyer now rose to his feet. "I represent this man," he said.

"I know you do," snapped the magistrate. "Can your client speak?"

The lawyer nodded. "He can speak, sir."

"Then tell him to answer me. Does he know what contempt of court is?"

The lawyer looked at Fanwell. "Do you know what contempt of court is?"

Fanwell shook his head.

"Well," said the magistrate, "let me tell you. It is the offence that is committed by a person who fails to show proper respect for the court. So not standing up when the magistrate or judge enters is contempt of court, and it can be punished there and then with a fine or imprisonment."

Fanwell groaned. "I'm sorry, sir. I did not hear."

The magistrate looked at him in silence. "Well, remember what I said to you." He looked down at his papers. "Pleas?"

Fanwell's lawyer stood up. "My client is not guilty, sir."

The magistrate looked at him incredulously. "That is not for you to say, don't you think?"

The lawyer looked flustered. "He is not guilty, sir."

The magistrate sighed. "Listen, Mr. . . ." He consulted a piece of paper in front of him. "Listen Mr. Mapoeli, the point I'm making is this: whether or not your client is guilty is a matter for the court to decide — it is not for you to say. What I want from you is his plea. Is he pleading guilty or not guilty?"

The lawyer smoothed the front of his jacket. "He is pleading guilty, sir."

The magistrate nodded. "Very well. Guilty."

Mma Ramotswe gripped Mr. J.L.B. Matekoni's arm. "He's got it wrong," she whispered. "He's pleading not guilty."

Fanwell was now tugging at his lawyer's sleeve. The lawyer, however, was attempting to brush him off. "Not now, Fanwell. You can speak later."

Witnessing this, Mma Ramotswe could not contain herself. "He's pleading not guilty," she said in a loud voice.

The magistrate looked up sharply. "Who is that? Who's speaking?"

Mma Ramotswe raised a hand. "Me, sir."

"The public is not to address the court," said the magistrate. "I will not tolerate any disturbances. Is that quite clear?"

Fanwell's lawyer cleared his throat. "For the avoidance of doubt, your honour, my client is pleading not guilty to the charge."

The magistrate took off his spectacles and polished them with his handkerchief. "He's changing his plea, is he?"

"Not changing it, your honour," said the lawyer. "That is what he is pleading."

"Do you mean that was his original plea?"

"No, sir."

The magistrate's irritation was now very evident. "You mean that he originally pleaded guilty?"

"No. He has always said he is not guilty."

The magistrate tapped his pen on his desk. "So the position is this: your client is pleading not guilty and always has."

"Has what?" asked the lawyer.

"Has always pleaded not guilty."

The lawyer nodded. "Only in this case, your honour. He has not pleaded not guilty any other time. Nor has he pleaded guilty."

The magistrate ignored this. "Not guilty," he said tersely.

The lawyer seemed surprised. Turning to Fanwell, he made a gesture to suggest that it was all over. "Not guilty," he said. "The charges are being dismissed."

The prosecutor now sprang to his feet. "I think the defence misunderstands the situation," he said.

The magistrate stared at Fanwell's lawyer. "What is this about the dismissal of charges, Mr. Mapoeli? Who said anything about that?"

The lawyer started to shake. "You said it, your honour. You said my client was not guilty."

The magistrate grinned. "Did I? I don't think I did, Mr. Mapoeli. I merely said that his plea is one of not guilty. That's what I said."

"Oh," said the lawyer lamely. "I see."

"I hope you do, Mr. Mapoeli," said the magistrate. "Now the other accused? Accused No. 1, Chobie?"

Chobie's lawyer rose to his feet. "He is pleading not guilty, sir."

It was at this point, while the magistrate was making a note of the plea, that Mma Ramotswe noticed that Charlie was staring at Chobie. For his part, the young man in the dock initially seemed to avoid the stare, but then returned it. Charlie had made a gesture, not a very obvious one, but a gesture nonetheless. Chobie watched, and shifted in his seat. Charlie then made another gesture — a small movement of the hand that seemed, to Mma Ramotswe's surprise, to be pointing towards her. Or was it something else altogether?

The magistrate cleared his throat and invited the prosecutor to begin. Chobie and Fanwell were prodded to stand up by the two policemen seated one on either side of them. The charges were then read out. A section of the Botswana Penal Code was mentioned, and there was reference to something having been done *knowingly and willingly* and then there was silence.

Mma Ramotswe was watching Charlie, who was still looking at Chobie. Again there was a surreptitious gesture. Mma Ramotswe shifted her gaze to Chobie and noticed, rather to her surprise, that he was staring at her.

The prosecutor mentioned a police witness, but before he could finish what he was saying, Chobie stood up. "I am guilty, sir."

His lawyer spun round. "He has entered a plea of not guilty, sir."

"No," said Chobie. "I am saying I am guilty now."

The magistrate adjusted his spectacles. "That sounds like a guilty plea," he said.

Chobie, still standing, spoke again, ignoring the policeman who was tugging at his shirt, urging him to sit down. "This one here" — he gestured to Fanwell — "this one didn't know the car was stolen, Rra. I am the one who did it. I am very sorry."

The magistrate sighed. He looked at the prosecutor, who was busily conferring with Chobie's lawyer. "It seems that this is going to need a bit of sorting out," he said. "I shall adjourn the court for fifteen minutes while the State decides what to do. But it seems to me as if it might be an idea to dismiss the charges against accused No. 2." He paused. "A cursory examination of the papers seems to point that way. And if accused No. 1 is saying that accused No. 2 had no knowledge of the fact that the car was stolen, then that rather changes things, doesn't it, Mr. Prosecutor?" He then answered his own question. "Frankly, this is a bit of a mess, and I propose to dismiss the charges against accused No. 2. We can come back to deal with accused No. 1's revised plea in a quarter of an hour. No. 2 is discharged. You can go, young man. You, No. 1, you stay."

They went outside. As she left the building, Mma Makutsi ran out into the sun and uttered the traditional ululation of delight that women contribute to any great Botswana occasion. Mma Ramotswe would have joined her, had she not been busy explaining to a shocked and shivering Fanwell that his ordeal was over.

"I cannot believe it," stuttered Fanwell. "What has happened?"

Fanwell's lawyer shuffled his papers about officiously. "A very satisfactory result," he said. "I am very pleased with this case."

"But what happened, Rra?" asked Fanwell. "How did you get me off?"

Mma Ramotswe watched the lawyer, who hesitated momentarily. She realised that he had no idea, but she did not want to spoil his moment of victory. This, she thought, was probably the first case he had won for a long time — if ever.

"You just thank your lawyer," she said to Fanwell. "The important thing is that he has won your case for you. That is what counts."

"Yes," said Mr. J.L.B. Matekoni, reaching out to shake the lawyer's hand. "Well done, Rra."

The lawyer beamed. "Thank you, Rra. These cases can be difficult, but I am very glad that this young man can return to his work without a spot on his reputation."

They made their way to the vehicles. Mr. J.L.B. Matekoni, Charlie, and Fanwell drove back in the truck, followed by Mma Ramotswe and Mma Makutsi in the tiny white van. It was a small procession, but no great march, no Roman triumph could have matched it for sheer joy, or relief.

Once back at the No. 1 Ladies' Detective Agency and Tlokweng Road Speedy Motors, they tried to get back to work, but it was hard, and eventually Mma Ramotswe simply brought forward the tea-break so that they could all calm down and get back to normal.

"One thing I cannot work out," she said, looking at Charlie, "is why Chobie suddenly changed his story. Why would he decide to take the blame?"

"Because he did it," blurted out Mma Makutsi. "He said he was guilty, and he was."

"But he had been planning to try to shift everything on to Fanwell," said Mr. J.L.B. Matekoni. "And then it all changed."

Mma Ramotswe was still staring at Charlie. "I wonder whether he was frightened of something," she mused. "What do you think, Charlie?"

Charlie shrugged. "I don't know."

She watched him. There was the slightest hint of a smile playing about his lips. Of course he knew. Of course he did.

"I think that he might have been frightened of *you,* Charlie. I don't know why I think that, but I think that's what happened."

Charlie was now clearly struggling not to laugh.

"It's not funny, Charlie," reprimanded Mma Makutsi.

Suddenly Charlie put down his mug of

tea and pulled a piece of paper out of the pocket of his overalls. Now smiling broadly, he passed the paper to Mr. J.L.B. Matekoni.

"What's this, Charlie?"

"It's a newspaper cutting, Rra. Or rather it's a piece of paper that I had somebody make up as a newspaper cutting. You know that printing place at Riverwalk? I have a friend there who can print anything from his computer. Driving licence? No problem. Birth certificate? No problem too. And in this case, an article from a newspaper over in Johannesburg."

Mr. J.L.B. Matekoni, who used reading glasses, took these out of his pocket and unfolded the piece of paper and read out loud. " 'Police search for dangerous hit-woman. The public is warned that the convicted murderess, Bella Dlamini, is on the loose and may be looking for further contracts. This woman is dangerous and has been known to carry out contract killings for as little as one thousand rand.' " He looked up from the paper. "What is all this, Charlie?" He looked down again. "And this . . ." He stopped, and held up the paper. "My goodness, this Bella Dlamini looks exactly like you, Mma Ramotswe."

Charlie let out a hoot of laughter. "But it *is* Mma Ramotswe. It's her photograph."

"Why have you made that rubbish?" asked Mma Makutsi. "This is not funny, Charlie."

Mma Ramotswe, though, was looking at Charlie through narrowed eyes. "Charlie," she said. "Did you show that to Chobie?"

He beamed with self-satisfaction. "Yes. Two days ago. I found him and I showed it to him."

"And?"

"And I told him . . ." Charlie looked about him, as if for support. They were all staring at him intently. "I told him that we had arranged something. If he didn't tell the truth in court, then . . ." He pointed to the cutting. "Then he would be seeing this lady."

There was complete silence.

"And she was there in court," Charlie continued. "So he decided to tell the truth after all. And who wouldn't?"

She took Charlie outside.

"Come for a little walk with me, Charlie."

"I don't see what the fuss is about, Mma Ramotswe."

"Just come with me, Charlie, so we can talk."

He went reluctantly, dragging his heels in the sand like a surly schoolboy. Mma Ramotswe took his arm. She would not be cross with him; she knew that this never worked with Charlie. You had to try to reason with Charlie; you had to be gentle.

"You do know how serious it is?" she asked.

"What?"

"How serious it is to threaten a witness. Especially to threaten to have them killed."

He said nothing.

"You could go to jail if the police found out. You know that, don't you?"

Charlie defended himself. "He wasn't a witness, Mma. He was the one who did it. I just told him to tell the truth."

She increased the pressure on his arm. "You threatened him, Charlie. And you brought me into it. You made him think I was that lady, that . . ."

"Bella Dlamini," he prompted. "It's a good name, isn't it, Mma Ramotswe?"

"Charlie, you have to take this seriously. You have done a very bad thing."

"With a good result."

She had to admit that this was the case. Truth, it seemed, had triumphed — by means of a lie.

"Yes," she said carefully. "It may be a good result, but never forget, Charlie, that you should not try to get good results by doing bad things."

"Why not?"

"Because . . ." She looked up at the sky. She was not sure how she could explain it to this young man, and then she decided that she could not. Not just yet.

"Because it's not right, Charlie. Sometimes we have to see bad things happen because we can't do another bad thing to stop them. Do you see that?"

"No," he said. "I don't."

Mma Ramotswe sighed. "I'm very pleased that Fanwell is back with us, of course."

"So am I. He is like a brother to me, Mma."

"I know, Charlie."

"And you have to help your brother, Mma."

"I understand that, Charlie, but . . . but be careful what you do."

Charlie looked at his watch. "We should get back to work, Mma."

She nodded. "All right, Charlie, let's get back to work."

They retraced their steps, as friends now, or at least as those who have established an understanding, even if the understanding is about just what one of them understands and the other does not.

CHAPTER NINETEEN:
YOU ARE A VISITOR
TO OUR COUNTRY

With the removal of the threat hanging over Fanwell, Mma Ramotswe found herself with more energy to help Mma Potokwane. Clovis Andersen had at least given a lead in suggesting that the contract for the building of the new hall should be investigated, and she felt that this could now be tackled. The great authority had offered to accompany her to Mma Potokwane's office to see what could be uncovered, and now they were approaching the gates and the large, shady tree under which Mma Ramotswe habitually parked her van on these visits.

"This is a very fine place," commented Clovis Andersen, looking about him as the van came to a halt. "We had an orphanage in Muncie, Indiana, back when I was a boy."

"Your place in America, Rra?"

"Yes. Muncie. The orphans' home was a place made of a curious yellow brick and its windows were painted red round the edges.

It's odd how you remember these little details years later."

"We all do that," said Mma Ramotswe. *I remember,* she thought. *I remember my late daddy, and how he took me on his shoulders and we walked along the road outside our house and I was proud, so proud that I thought my heart would burst.*

"The boys and girls from the orphanage went to school — same as us. We had three or four in my class. There was a boy called Lance. He had freckles and ginger hair. I remember asking him what had happened to his parents, and he told me that they had been Arctic explorers and had drifted off on an ice floe. He said that there had been an article about them in the *National Geographic.* He said that he used to have the issue the article was in, but another boy in the orphanage had stolen it."

They were standing outside the van now; standing in the morning sun, which was gentle on them. It seemed to Mma Ramotswe that they were in no particular hurry and that they could talk, if that was what Clovis Andersen wanted. "That is very sad, Rra," she said. "That is stealing that boy's past."

He smiled at the memory. "Of course it wasn't true. A couple of years later I was

337

told by some other kid that his parents had committed suicide together and that the story of the ice floe was all invention. I asked my own parents about that. They never lied to me, and so they had to admit that it was true: the suicide had taken place in the dry-goods store that the boy's parents used to run. The father had shot his wife and then himself."

Mma Ramotswe gasped. "And left that little boy . . ."

"Yes. But they probably weren't thinking straight, poor people. They were in debt, I imagine — a lot of those small storekeepers got into terrible debt."

"And the boy?" asked Mma Ramotswe. "What happened to the boy?"

"He went to college in Bloomington. As I did. He was a great football player. He taught high school, I think. Things went well for him."

"I am pleased to hear that ending," said Mma Ramotswe. "It would have been a very sad story otherwise."

"There are plenty of sad stories, Mma Ramotswe."

"Of course there are." She pointed to the scattered cottages in which the children lived with their house-mothers. "Every one of those houses has sad stories in it."

"I guess that's right," said Clovis Andersen.

"But Mma Potokwane tries to write a happy ending for them," Mma Ramotswe went on. "That is what she does."

She held Clovis Andersen's gaze as she said this, and he knew immediately what she meant: this was not an idle enquiry they were about to embark upon — there was a great deal at stake here.

"I think we should go in," he said softly. "Is that the office over there?"

"Yes. That is where she works."

Mma Potokwane was briefly out of her office, her secretary explained, but she would be back soon; one of the house-mothers had sprained an ankle and she was attending to that. In the meantime they were welcome to sit down in the office, where it was cool.

They had talked in the van earlier about what they should do, and now Mma Ramotswe tackled the secretary. "Are you the secretary, Mma, to the board as well as to Mma Potokwane?"

The secretary nodded. "I do both, Mma. When the board has its meetings I am always there to bring papers and do things like that."

Mma Ramotswe looked about the room, at the array of filing cabinets. "You keep the board papers here, Mma?"

The secretary confirmed that this was the case.

"So that means you have the tenders for the new hall?"

The secretary glanced in the direction of one of the filing cabinets. "They are all there," she said.

"Could you show me something, Mma?"

The reply came quickly. "Certainly not, Mma. The board's papers are confidential. They have that typed on the top of them. I cannot show them even to you, Mma Ramotswe. It would be improper."

"Of course it would be," said Mma Ramotswe hurriedly. "It would be improper. But it's a pity, really."

The secretary looked at her suspiciously. "Why, Mma?"

"I take it that you are fond of Mma Potokwane, Mma?" asked Mma Ramotswe.

"Of course I am, Mma. She is the best matron this place has ever had. She is the best boss I am ever likely to get."

"So you'll miss her?"

"Of course I'll miss her, Mma."

"And I can imagine how the children will miss her," said Mma Ramotswe. "Oh, they'll be so sad, those children. First they lose their parents, and then they lose Mma Potokwane. They will be very sad, I think."

"Yes, they will be."

"And there will be a lot of crying."

The secretary lowered her gaze. "We shall all cry, Mma. All of us."

Mma Ramotswe waited a moment or two. Clovis Andersen, who felt as if he were an intruder into a private family moment, studied his hands.

"Then I take it that you would be very pleased to have her dismissal set aside?"

The secretary's reply was vehement. "I would do anything to make that happen, Mma."

"Anything?" probed Mma Ramotswe.

"Yes, anything at all."

Mma Ramotswe glanced at Clovis Andersen before she next spoke. "Then please show us the tender documents that the board received for the new hall," she said.

The secretary hesitated. "They are confidential," she said.

"Then we can do nothing for Mma Potokwane."

"However, if it is in the interests of the children," went on the secretary, "then I shall overlook the confidentiality issue."

She rose from her chair and unlocked one of the filing cabinets. Thereafter it took a few minutes before she found what she was looking for: a brown manila file on which *Hall* had been inscribed in thick black lettering. She turned to face Mma Ramotswe.

"This has the quotes received from the builders," she said. "And it also has the report that went back from the tender committee to the main board."

Mma Ramotswe was intrigued. "The tender committee?"

The secretary explained. "That was the committee that decided who should get the job of building the hall."

"And who was on that?"

"Only two people, I think," came the reply. "Mr. Ditso Ditso — you know him, Mma? — and that lady from the Ministry, I am always forgetting her name. But she never went to the meetings, I believe. She is a very lazy woman — everybody knows that."

"So the meetings of the tender committee just consisted of Mr. Ditso Ditso?"

"Yes. And he said something to me about it once. He joked that it was very pleasant being on a committee where nobody disagreed with you because there were no other members. He said he wished all committees were like that."

Clovis Andersen now intervened. "I'll bet he does!" he said.

342

The secretary handed the file to Mma Ramotswe, who put it on the table in front of her and began to look through the documents it contained. "Here," she said, passing four stapled pages to Clovis Andersen. "Those are the estimates from the builders."

Clovis Andersen looked at the papers. "They aren't too far apart," he said. "It means that the builders wanted this job. If you get one that's much higher, then it usually means that the builder who put it in didn't really want the job but would take it if his excessive price got it."

"And here's Mr. Ditso's letter of recommendation to the board saying that the job should be awarded to . . ." She looked up. "Kalahari Forward Construction."

Clovis Andersen consulted the papers in front of him and frowned. "They're not on the tender list," he said.

"That is the firm," said the secretary. "They are the ones who are going to do the job. You will find a copy of the letter of appointment from the board in there." She gestured to the file. "I copied it myself. It is all in order."

"All in order, not in order," muttered Clovis Andersen. "Can you find that one, Mma Ramotswe?"

Mma Ramotswe paged through the remaining papers in the file. "Here," she said. "This is the one." She examined it more closely. "It is an agreement to build the hall and kitchen for three million and six hundred thousand pula."

"That's right," said the secretary. "That is a lot of money, Mma."

Clovis Andersen took the letter from Mma Ramotswe and read through it quickly. "Interesting," he said at last. "The highest tender from the list was just over two million."

"So the contract was not awarded to the lowest bid," said Mma Ramotswe.

"No," said Clovis Andersen. "Of course that sometimes happens. There may be some reason why a more expensive contractor is preferred. For example, he may do better quality work. Or . . . or he may be a relative." His tone became more ominous. "Or the contractor may be paying a kickback to the person awarding the contract. There are many possible reasons."

The secretary drew in her breath. "That is very bad," she hissed. "I did not know anything about it, Mma Ramotswe."

Mma Ramotswe reassured her. "Of course you didn't, Mma. Nobody is blaming you."

The secretary looked satisfied. "I know

about those people," she said. "They came round to look at the site."

"Kalahari Forward Construction?" asked Mma Ramotswe. "They came here?"

"Yes, they came here, Mma. Their boss came. My brother knows who he is. He used to drive a taxi for him when he was in the taxi business. Then he became a builder and did quite well. My brother did not like him."

Mma Ramotswe looked interested. "And what was this man's name, Mma? Do you remember?"

"He is called Sephotho," said the secretary. "He is a tall man who has lost a finger on his left hand. It looks like this." She held up a hand with one digit tucked back.

Mma Ramotswe felt her heart pound within her. "Sephotho?" she said. "And has he got a sister, this man?"

"Yes. My brother says she is not a very nice woman . . . ."

"Called Violet?"

"I think so," said the secretary. "Violet, or Rose. Something like that. He said that she should really have a name like Thorn or Cabbage."

Mma Ramotswe shuffled the papers back into the file and handed it to the secretary. "I think we are going to go and look for Mma Potokwane," she said, indicating to

Clovis Andersen that he should follow her. "We have some very interesting news to give her."

They told Mma Potokwane about what they had discovered. She listened carefully, then rushed forward and threw her arms around an astonished Clovis Andersen. "Oh, thank you, Rra! Thank you, thank you!" If, over the last few days, there had been signs of depression in her demeanour, these now disappeared with extraordinary rapidity.

Clovis Andersen extracted himself from the embrace. "It wasn't me, Mma. You should thank Mma Ramotswe. She found this out."

"You did," said Mma Ramotswe. "It was your idea."

He refused to accept the credit. "No, Mma, it was you."

"Does it matter?" said Mma Potokwane. "Maybe it was the two of you."

"It was definitely her," said Clovis Andersen, pointing at Mma Ramotswe. "It was not me."

They returned to Mma Potokwane's office, where tea was poured and accompanied by liberal slices of fruit cake. Then Mma Ramotswe and Clovis Andersen travelled back to the agency.

"Paper," said Clovis Andersen as they turned on to the Tlokweng Road. "You'd be surprised, Mma Ramotswe, by how often people leave a paper trail. It's the undoing of so many malefactors — so many."

Mma Ramotswe repeated the word *malefactors*. "That is a very interesting word, Rra. We do not use it very much here in Botswana. What exactly does it mean?"

Clovis Andersen explained. "It means people who do wrong — any sort of wrong."

Mma Ramotswe repeated the word several times. "It is a good word," she said. "I shall use it more often. Malefactors. Malefactors. There are many malefactors."

"There are," agreed Clovis Andersen.

"Are there many malefactors in Munchie?" asked Mma Ramotswe.

"Muncie. No, no more than anywhere else. In fact, maybe fewer. Muncie, Indiana, is not a bad place."

"Like Gaborone?"

He smiled. "Yes, a bit like Gaborone. The human heart, you see, Mma Ramotswe, is pretty much the same wherever one goes."

She nodded her agreement. "Yes, Rra, that is certainly true. All human hearts are the same, no matter how different we are on the outside."

They travelled in silence for a short while.

Then Clovis Andersen turned to Mma Ramotswe and said, "What now, Mma?"

"I have an idea," she said. "I have an idea why Mr. Ditso gave the contract to that firm."

"And why is that?"

She smiled. "Would you mind, Rra, if I didn't tell you just yet? I think I'm right, but I'm not absolutely certain."

"Not one hundred per cent certain?"

"No, not one hundred per cent. More like . . . more like ninety-seven per cent, I think."

Clovis Andersen frowned. "Where have I heard that figure before? Where has ninety-seven per cent cropped up before?"

"It is just a guess, Rra. Ninety-seven per cent is a figure that I have also heard before. So it just came into my mind."

Mma Makutsi was sitting at her desk drinking a cup of tea when they arrived back at the office. She glanced up at Mma Ramotswe and knew immediately that something important had happened.

"You have found something?" she asked. "You look very happy."

"We sure do," said Clovis Andersen. "We are feeling very happy, Mma Makutsi."

Mma Makutsi gave him an encouraging

smile. *Star-struck,* thought Mma Ramotswe. *You are still star-struck.*

"Mr. Ditso Ditso has not been behaving very well," said Mma Ramotswe. "And this means, I hope, that we shall be able to persuade him to drop his plans."

Mma Makutsi clapped her hands together. "That is very good news, Mma — very good news."

There was still a further step, though, and Mma Ramotswe now made the request that would make it possible for that step to be taken. "Mma Makutsi," she began, "am I right in remembering that you have a picture of your graduation from the Botswana Secretarial College?"

Mma Makutsi seemed surprised, but was obviously pleased by the question. "As it happens, Mma, I do have that photograph in my drawer here. Would you like to see it?"

"It would be very useful, Mma."

Mma Makutsi opened a drawer in her desk and took out a photograph that had been pasted onto a piece of stiff cardboard. "Here it is," she said, dusting it reverentially. "There were fifteen ladies who graduated in my group. Here we all are, sitting with the Principal. And there, you see, is the college crest and the motto." She turned to Clovis

Andersen. "Ninety-seven per cent, Rra. That is what I got in the final examinations."

"Ninety-seven per cent!" he said. "That's almost impossible. Virtually flawless."

She bobbed her head. "That is what some people said. I am very lucky."

"Not luck, Mma Makutsi," he said. "Talent."

Mma Ramotswe took the proffered photograph and examined it. "Yes," she said. "This is what I need." She looked up. "May I borrow this photograph, Mma? Not for very long, and I will take very good care of it, I promise you."

Mma Makutsi sounded puzzled. "Of course you may, Mma. But why do you need it?"

"I need a photograph of Violet Sephotho," said Mma Ramotswe. "And this is the only one we have, I think. This is her in the middle row, isn't it?"

Mma Makutsi wrinkled her nose. "She looked the same then as she looks today. Look at all that lipstick. Look at it."

"And the nails," mused Mma Ramotswe. "Those nails. They have a lot to do with this."

"With what?"

"With this enquiry," said Mma Ramotswe. "Nails, Mma?"

"I shall explain everything very soon, Mma Makutsi. In the meantime, Mr. Andersen and I need to go into town."

There was something in Mma Makutsi's look that made Mma Ramotswe hesitate. It was a look of disappointment, coupled, perhaps, with yearning.

"Unless you would like to come with us, Mma Makutsi?" she said.

Mma Makutsi blurted out her answer. "I think I would, Mma. Thank you very much."

Mma Ramotswe picked up the keys to the van. "Of course, there is a bit of a problem about seats. The van only has two seats in the cab, which means that somebody will need to sit in the back. That will not be very comfortable."

"Me," said Clovis Andersen.

"No," snapped Mma Makutsi. "I will sit in the back, Mma."

"I won't hear of that," said Clovis Andersen.

"But we cannot let you do that, Rra. You are a visitor to our country."

"I insist," said Clovis Andersen.

Mma Ramotswe drew Mma Makutsi aside. "You must let him," she said. "Mr. Andersen is a gentleman, and he is thinking of the comfort of ladies. You must let him."

Mma Makutsi yielded. It was a small

351

thing, she knew, but a small thing that was, in its way, a big thing. And in the van, on the way into town, with Clovis Andersen bumping around in the back and unable to hear them, she said to Mma Ramotswe: "It is good that there are still gentlemen, Mma. Mr. Andersen, Mr. J.L.B. Matekoni, and Phuti. All gentlemen."

"Yes, all of those are gentlemen," said Mma Ramotswe. "And it is good that they are still there. Not only for ladies who want to ride in the front, but for all sorts of other reasons as well."

Mma Makutsi pondered this. "Why are there fewer and fewer gentlemen, Mma Ramotswe?"

"It is our fault, Mma. It is the fault of ladies."

"Why is that?"

"Because we have allowed men to stop behaving as gentlemen, and when you allow people to do what they wish, then that is what they do. They stop doing the things they need to do." She looked at Mma Makutsi across the steering wheel. "That is well known, I think, Mma. That is well known."

Chapter Twenty:
Better Nails, Better Life

"I never worry about my nails," said Mma Makutsi as they passed the Princess Marina Hospital. "We were taught at the Botswana Secretarial College that long nails were not a good thing if you have to do typing. We were told some very alarming stories."

Mma Ramotswe was intrigued. "Alarming stories about nails?"

"Yes, Mma. There was one case, in the days of electric typewriters, of a secretary who got a shock when one of her nails went through the space between the keys. She became late as a result."

Mma Ramotswe swerved the van slightly at the thought. But could you get a shock through a nail? A finger, certainly, but a nail? "Are you sure, Mma? Would electricity go through a fingernail?"

Mma Makutsi pursed her lips before answering. "It is true, Mma. Electricity can go through many things, not just wires. And

353

there's another thing — you can get long nails stuck in a filing cabinet when you close it. I have seen that happen, Mma."

They negotiated the traffic circle at the end of the central square before parking behind the President Hotel. Clovis Andersen appeared to have enjoyed his ride in the back of the van, and jumped down with a smile. "The best way to see a town," he said. "With the sun on your face." He patted down his dishevelled hair. "Now then, Mma Ramotswe, where are you taking us?"

"To a nail parlour," said Mma Ramotswe, leading them past the entrance to the hotel and into the busy open marketplace beyond.

Clovis Andersen laughed. "I'm not sure whether I need —"

"Not as clients," Mma Ramotswe interrupted.

"These people are always good sources of information," said Mma Makutsi. "Hairdressers, barmen, nail ladies — they always know what's going on. As you say, Rra, in your own book: always ask the people who know."

Clovis Andersen looked pensive. "I said that, did I? Well, it sounds reasonable enough to me."

It was a short walk to the Better Nails, Better Life nail parlour. This was a hole-in-the-wall shop advertising its presence with a large picture of a hand sporting long nails painted in various bright colours.

"If you tried to type with a hand like that, you wouldn't get very far," said Mma Makutsi dismissively.

"I don't think it would be much good trying to do *anything* with a hand like that," said Clovis Andersen.

"People who have nails like that usually don't want to do anything," said Mma Makutsi. "That is not a working hand. That is the hand of an idle, useless person."

"I don't think it's meant to be a real hand," suggested Mma Ramotswe. "I think it's intended just to give you an idea of what they can do."

"A bad idea of what they can do," snorted Mma Makutsi.

They entered the shop. In front of them was a table with a box covered in some soft material. That, thought Mma Ramotswe, was where you rested your hand while your nails were being painted. It looked rather comfortable, she decided. There were several chairs, a stack of well-thumbed magazines, and a shelf along which numerous bottles of nail varnish were lined. As they came in, a curtain at the back of the room was pulled aside and a well-dressed young woman came out to greet them.

"Have you made an appointment?" she asked. Her voice was friendly.

Mma Ramotswe greeted her in the traditional way before asking: "Are you Mma Soleti's sister, Mma?"

The woman smiled warmly. "Yes, we are sisters, Mma. I am called Soleti too. They call her Mma Soleti (Face) and me Mma Soleti (Nails). You know her?"

Mma Ramotswe explained that she had only visited the Minor Adjustment Beauty Salon once, but that she had enjoyed a long conversation with Mma Soleti. "I am a private detective, Mma," she went on. "I am looking into a troubling matter and I need some information. It will be very confidential and nobody else will know about it."

Mma Soleti (Nails) looked at Mma Makutsi and Clovis Andersen. "And these people, Mma? What about them? Are they nobody?"

Mma Ramotswe was quick to explain. "Mma Makutsi here is my assistant —"

"Associate," corrected Mma Makutsi.

"Associate," said Mma Ramotswe. "And this is Rra Clovis Andersen, who is one of the most famous detectives in the United States of America. They are both very good at keeping secrets, Mma. Their lips are permanently closed."

"Forever," confirmed Mma Makutsi.

Mma Soleti seemed reassured. "In that case, Mma, what is it you wish to know?"

Mma Ramotswe took the photograph out of the brown envelope in which she had placed it. "There is somebody in this picture who you may know, Mma. Please, will you look at it?"

Mma Soleti (Nails) took the photograph and examined it. She looked up at Mma Makutsi. "Her. Your assistant —"

"Associate," said Mma Makutsi.

"Yes, your associate. It is you, Mma, standing in the centre."

"I was standing in the centre because I had the highest mark, Mma. That is why."

Mma Soleti (Nails) looked at the photograph again. "And . . ." She looked up, a glint in her eye. "And this lady here. Oh yes! There she is. There she is."

"So that is the lady who comes here, is it, Mma?" coaxed Mma Ramotswe. "The lady who is the mistress of a certain man called Ditso Ditso who also has a wife who comes here to have her nails done?"

"Ow!" exclaimed Mma Soleti (Nails). "You know everything, Mma. No wonder you're a detective. Yes, that is all true."

"Her name is Violet Sephotho," said Mma Ramotswe.

There was a silence as the name was mentioned, and it seemed that it hung in the air for some time, a chilling presence in the room. Violet Sephotho.

Eventually Mma Soleti (Nails) spoke. "I shall remember that," she said. "She is a very rude woman. She speaks on her telephone while I am doing her nails and she never says anything to me. She thinks I am just a . . . a nail lady of no importance."

Mma Ramotswe reached forward and touched her gently on the arm. "The work you do is good work, Mma. You help people to feel good about themselves. That is good work, my sister."

Mma Soleti (Nails) patted Mma Ramotswe's hand, casting an eye on her nails as she did so. "Thank you, Mma. And if there's anything I can do . . ." She looked down at Mma Ramotswe's nails again. "I would be very happy to help, Mma."

Intercepting the glance, Mma Ramotswe laughed. "It would be wasted on me, Mma. I am always washing up and doing things like that. Fancy nails would not suit me, I'm afraid."

"Nor me," said Clovis Andersen. "I don't think much about my nails."

Mma Soleti (Nails) looked disapproving. "But that's a great pity, Rra. These days it is quite all right for men to look after their nails. We are living in an equal society, you see, and that means that nails are equal too." She paused. "So I think we could do something with your nails, Rra. In fact, I am sure we can."

"We now have all the information we need," said Mma Ramotswe.

They were standing about the tiny white van, ready to embark on the next stage of the investigation, which was to confront Mr. Ditso Ditso with the truth.

"This is always the best stage of a case," said Clovis Andersen. "I call it the denouement. It's when you reveal who is responsible for whatever it is you're investigating."

"But we know that already," said Mma Makutsi.

Clovis Andersen raised a finger. "But Mr. Ditso doesn't know that we know. Now we tell him. This is the good part."

Mma Ramotswe looked doubtful. "You have to be careful not to count on anything," she said.

Clovis Andersen agreed. "Of course. A case is not closed until it's closed."

They considered the force of this. It was

most impressive to both Mma Ramotswe and Mma Makutsi how Clovis Andersen spoke in short, pithy aphorisms — just like his book. It was, they thought, a great gift.

"I look forward to seeing his face," said Mma Makutsi. "Big Mr. Ditso shown to be a corrupt bully. Should we invite Mma Potokwane to come with us?"

Mma Ramotswe did not think this a good idea. "You should not rub a person's nose in it, Mma. Let him think about what he has done. Let him reach his own conclusion — it is always better that way."

"As long as he reinstates Mma Potokwane," cautioned Clovis Andersen.

"Of course," said Mma Ramotswe. "That is the most important thing of all."

They had not notified Mr. Ditso Ditso of their arrival, but encountered no obstruction at the offices of DD Industries. Yes, Mr. Ditso would see them if they did not mind waiting for ten minutes or so. Would they like tea?

Eventually an assistant showed them into the office of the man himself. He stood up politely as they entered and gestured for them to sit down. "Last time there were two of you," he said. "Now there are three. Am I becoming more important all of a sudden?"

They laughed at the pleasantry. Then Ditso Ditso looked at his watch. "I'm afraid I only have five minutes, Mma Ramotswe. So what is it, Mma?"

"I've come about Mma Potokwane —"

He raised a hand to interrupt her. "Look, Mma, we've discussed that, and I've told you already. Do I need to spell it out again? Mma Potokwane has resigned, and that's the end of that."

"She did not resign," said Mma Ramotswe. "She was dismissed."

Ditso Ditso shrugged. "What's in a word, Mma? Resigned, dismissed, retired; jumped, pushed, shoved out? All the same at the end of the day."

"You can add to that list of words, Rra," said Mma Ramotswe quietly. "Add: betrayed, destroyed, tricked."

Ditso Ditso's manner changed abruptly; gone was the earlier joviality. "Be careful what you say, Mma."

"You be careful what you write, sir," said Clovis Andersen.

Ditso Ditso spun his chair round. "You said something, Rra?"

"I said: be careful what you write. For instance, when you make a list of contractors' estimates, make sure that you put on that list the name of the firm you eventually

361

give the work to — otherwise it looks odd." He paused. "More than that, Rra. It looks criminal."

Ditso Ditso froze.

"So," Clovis Andersen continued. "So you should be careful when you give a contract to your mistress's brother. Especially if there's one million *pula* difference between the prices. That looks like corruption, I'm afraid."

"Yes," chipped in Mma Makutsi. "That looks very like corruption, and corruption is something we don't like in Botswana. Have you noticed that, Rra? Have you read in the papers about what happens to people who practise corruption? There are not many of them around because they are mostly in another place. And that is that place at the edge of the Village. You know that place, Rra? The place with the big fence around it?"

For a few moments Ditso Ditso was silent. He had now shrunk back in his chair and was looking down at his desktop. When he spoke, his voice was barely audible. "What do you want me to do, Mma Ramotswe?"

"I want you to look at me, Rra."

He raised his eyes. It was clearly difficult for him to look directly at her, but she waited until he did so.

"Now, Rra, you have to call a meeting of the board. You have to tell them that you have let them down and you are resigning. You will say that you will be making a generous gift to the orphan farm to mark your time with them. Then you will withdraw your support for the hall project and tell them that it must be cancelled. You will then ask them to reinstate Mma Potokwane with immediate effect."

He nodded. "I will do all that, Mma."

"And there's another thing," Mma Ramotswe went on. "You will also say sorry, Rra. And don't forget to do that — maybe it is the biggest thing of all."

That evening, Clovis Andersen was invited for dinner with Mma Makutsi and Phuti Radiphuti. Mma Makutsi left the office early to complete the preparations. She could barely believe that she would be actually entertaining, at her own table, the author of *The Principles of Private Detection*; such a thing was almost inconceivable, and yet it was happening. Phuti, too, was aware of the significance of the evening, and had bought a new shirt and tie for the occasion.

"You don't have to be too formal," said Mma Makutsi as they prepared for the arrival of their guest. "He's very natural —

just like an ordinary person. You'd never know he had written an important book like that. You'd never know that he was world famous."

Phuti struggled with his new tie. "There are very few world-famous people in Botswana," he said. "There is President Khama and the two former presidents. They are world famous. But who else is there? Can you think of anybody, Grace?"

"I cannot," she said. "So that makes four world-famous people altogether — and one of them, Phuti, is going to be in our place tonight."

The thought made him fumble more. "You'll have to help me with my tie, Grace. I get very nervous when I think of a world-famous person coming to our house."

She helped him with the knot; she held his hand as she did so; his hand warm against hers, loving flesh on loving flesh.

"I am so proud of you, Grace," he said. "I am so proud."

"And I am very proud of you, Phuti."

There was nothing more to be said, but a great deal to be done, in the kitchen at least, where one of Mma Makutsi's tried-and-tested stews was gently simmering on the stove. She had purchased the best cut of meat available — of fine Botswana beef —

and the largest, most succulent vegetables. It would be a meal that Clovis Andersen remembered; or that was what she hoped.

He arrived on time and they sat down at the table almost immediately. Mma Makutsi said grace before they began, invoking blessings on the stew, the vegetables, the house, the Double Comfort Furniture Store, the No. 1 Ladies' Detective Agency and, at the end of this rather full list, on "our famous guest who has come from so far away but whom we have known as a friend for many years, even if we had never met him." Phuti reached for his fork, but quickly realised that Mma Makutsi had not yet finished. "And as we sample these good things," she continued, "we remember those who do not have these good things on their table or do not have a guest to share their meal with them." Phuti nodded his agreement and reached once more for his fork, but again it was premature. "And may our guest take back to America," Mma Makutsi went on, "memories of this country that are good. May he remember us when he has gone home, and may he remember too that our door is always open for him if he wants to come back. Amen."

The *amen* was taken as a safe enough indication that the grace had come to an end and the meal could begin. Clovis Andersen was delighted with the stew and had three helpings, while Phuti had two, and Mma Makutsi had a single helping — although that was a substantial one.

The conversation flowed easily. Mma Makutsi told Phuti of the events of the day, with certain details being filled in by Clovis Andersen as her narrative unfolded. Then the discussion shifted to talk of Muncie, Indiana, and its charms. Phuti Radiphuti was interested to hear about any woodworking industries in the vicinity and whether they made furniture, and, if so, what that furniture was like. Mma Makutsi was keen to hear details of Clovis Andersen's cases: Had he ever been to Los Angeles? Had he had any cases in Hollywood? Were there any colleges in the United States that taught both private detection and secretarial skills? For his part, Clovis Andersen wanted to know when the rains would arrive, how long they would last, and how the water table held up during the dry season. He wanted to find out, too, about the old steam trains that he heard used to come down from Bulawayo; also, had all the diamonds been discovered, or was there a good chance that more would be found?

Then, when a brief silence had descended,

Mma Makutsi made her suggestion. "Wouldn't it be a wonderful idea to have an academy, Rra Andersen — to have a school of private detection? We could set it up here, and you could be one of the directors. We could call it . . ." She turned to Phuti for inspiration.

"How about the Limpopo Academy of Private Detection?"

Mma Makutsi looked at Phuti admiringly. She was the creative one in the marriage, of course — Phuti's concerns being furniture and cattle and things of that nature — but this demonstrated an imaginative ability that might perhaps be coaxed out further. But not too far. "That would be a very good name," she said. "I could be the Principal, and you could be in charge of the courses. Mma Ramotswe could be in charge of making tea. And we'd use your book as the set book."

Clovis Andersen looked wistful. "That would be very good, Mma. But I'm afraid . . ."

It would be so easy to stay. After all, there was nothing to take him back, and he could spend the rest of his days with these agreeable people, listening to Mma Ramotswe, doing the same small, everyday things that he filled his days with at home, but doing them here, in this place that he was gradually discovering he loved. Could one fall in love with a whole country — just like that? He wondered about that.

"We can think about it," said Mma Makutsi. "It's best to think about these things."

"Yes," said Clovis Andersen, a bit reluctantly. Things you thought about — wild, irresponsible things like setting up the Limpopo Academy of Private Detection — and never did. Good sense intervened; good sense and responsibility and perhaps also sheer inertia. Yet you could dream about them; you could keep an idea alive, filed away with all those other wonderful, foolish ideas.

At the end of the meal, Phuti ran Clovis Andersen back to his friend's house. Mma Makutsi came to keep Phuti company on the way home, and it was on this journey, after they had dropped off their guest, that she and Phuti discussed him.

"I like him very much," said Phuti. "He is a kind man, Mma."

"Yes," said Mma Makutsi. "But there is something sad about him, isn't there? He became sadder as the evening wore on, I think."

"Perhaps it is because he writes books," offered Phuti. "There are very sad-looking photographs of authors on the covers of their books. Perhaps they are all sad.

"He is a widower, isn't he?" asked Phuti Radiphuti. "Perhaps he's missing his late wife." He almost said, *As I would miss you, Grace, if you became late.* But he did not say this. They were just starting their life together, and it was premature to reflect on how it would feel if one of them were to go. And he was sure that it would not happen; not for a long time, until they had been married for years and years and their children were married too and they were ready to go. That is what he hoped, as all of us who have found somebody to ease the pain of the world must hope, for ourselves, and for others.

CHAPTER TWENTY-ONE:
MMA RAMOTSWE, I HAVE A CONFESSION TO MAKE

Following, as he did, the progress of his new house with some interest, Phuti Radiphuti had now taken to visiting the site every day on his way home from work at the Double Comfort Furniture Store. Mma Makutsi sometimes accompanied him on these visits, although she was less interested in the technical details than he was. She wanted to see the walls plastered and painted; she wanted to see the tiles in position in the bathroom; she wanted to stand in her new, finished kitchen and savour the cooking smell coming from the oven. That was the prospect to which she looked forward and that she had heard would be achieved on time, just as Mr. Clarkson Putumelo had promised.

Clarkson Putumelo himself was rarely on site when Phuti or Mma Makutsi visited, which was a relief from her point of view. Most of the time, building operations

seemed to be under the control of a fore-
man, a thickset man with a moustache who
had set up a table on which the house plans
were spread out and from which he directed
operations. This man was pleasant enough,
and seemed to take the trouble to explain
what was happening in a way that could be
appreciated by those to whom building was
a closed book.

Thomas, the builder whom Phuti had met
at the beginning of the project and whom
he had glimpsed briefly at the petrol station, was still working on the site, though
he barely acknowledged Phuti when he saw
him. Mma Makutsi had tried to engage him
in conversation on one or two occasions,
and although he had answered her, he had
seemed embarrassed by the contact.

"It is probably because he is working illegally," said Phuti. "Poor man. He will have
a big family back at his place and no work
permit. It's probably life and death for him."

"He's a hard worker," said Mma Makutsi.
"Have you seen him? He never sits about
when the others are having their breaks —
he carries on with what he's doing."

Phuti had seen that. "I feel very sorry for
him," he said. "It cannot be easy, being
him."

The day after the dinner with Clovis

Andersen, Phuti Radiphuti and Mma Makutsi both paid a visit to the building site. The large wooden beams that would bear the roof were now installed on the already completed walls, and in many of the rooms the window frames had been placed in position.

"It is looking very much like a house now," said Mma Makutsi. "It will make all the difference having a roof."

They inspected the bathroom, where a large white bath was already in position. Mma Makutsi stood and admired this for several minutes, dreaming of the almost inconceivable luxury of lying in the embrace of hot water and scented bath salts. She had always had to rely on showers — and weak and dribbling ones at that; she had never owned nor had the use of a bath, let alone a bath as beautiful and enticing as this. And it was such a large bath too — enough room for two . . . She turned away, her ears burning with embarrassment.

"What were you thinking about, Grace?" asked Phuti.

The question caught her unawares. She could not possibly tell him that she had entertained the thought that they might both use the bath; and yet she could hardly lie to him.

"I was thinking of how big the bath is," she said softly.

He stared at the bath. "Room for two," he whispered.

They both laughed, and her embarrassment faded. "It's also a very suitable bath for a traditionally built person," she said. "Even Mma Ramotswe would fit in that bath."

"She will be very welcome to come round to our place and take a bath," said Phuti. "From time to time, that is. You wouldn't want people coming to use your bath every day."

They moved through to the kitchen, where the carpentry was already at an advanced stage. Mma Makutsi thought that she had never seen so many cupboards and shelves, and said as much to Phuti. He smiled and said, "We shall have a lot of food to put in them, Grace." She examined one of the cupboards; the door had been well constructed and opened smoothly, closing again to make a perfect seal.

"There will be no mice in this kitchen," she said. "There are no holes for them to run in and out of."

It was while Phuti was laughing at this observation that Thomas walked into the room. He had been working elsewhere on the site and had clearly not seen them, as he strode in whistling, with a saw in his hand and a large piece of insulation board tucked under his arm. His whistling stopped, and he stood stock-still.

"Well, Thomas," said Phuti. "This is all looking very good. And my wife thinks so too, don't you, Grace?"

Mma Makutsi smiled at the builder. "You have been doing a very good job. Thank you for all your hard work."

For a moment or two it seemed that Thomas was uncertain what to do. Then he put the piece of board down on the floor, at the same time looking over his shoulder.

Phuti was puzzled. "Is there anything wrong, Rra?"

Thomas shook his head. He had been avoiding Phuti's gaze; now he met it directly. "I want to talk to you, Rra. I will be finished in ten minutes. I will meet you down the road. You go first, and I will follow."

"Can we not talk here?" asked Phuti. "If you want to talk in private, my wife can go and look at the outside."

"No, I don't mind talking to the lady too. But not here."

They left the site and drove a short distance down the road before stopping.

"I'm not surprised by this," said Mma Makutsi. "Something has been going on. I noticed how strangely he behaved when we saw him at the petrol station. Remember? He pretended not to know you."

"I thought he was shy," said Phuti. "There are some people like that. And there's that business with his being illegal."

"No, it was more than that. There was something else."

Phuti drummed his fingers on the steering wheel. He looked in the driving mirror. "We'll soon see," he said. "He is coming now. He's walking down the road."

Phuti got out of the car to greet the builder.

Thomas spoke tersely. "Can I show you something, Rra? Can we go in the car?"

Phuti agreed, and Thomas got into the back seat. Mma Makutsi turned round to smile at him, to set him at his ease. "We can take you wherever you want," she said brightly. "We are not in a hurry."

"I'll show you," he said. "It isn't all that far. If you go down to the bottom of this road and turn right it will take us about fifteen minutes."

They set off in silence. Mma Makutsi exchanged glances with Phuti, and then turned to engage Thomas in conversation.

"We are very happy with the work, Thomas. We are very happy."

He nodded. "It is a well-built house, Mma. It is very solid."

She decided to press him. "But you are unhappy about something? Do you want to speak to us about it? We know how difficult it can be for you people, being so far from home. That cannot be easy, Rra."

He looked at her with his bloodshot eyes; it was the dust, she realised — a building site was not easy on the eyes. "Please do not tell anybody that I have shown you this thing," he said. "Please do not say it was me."

"Of course not. We won't say, will we, Phuti?"

Phuti Radiphuti assured him that he would keep the whole matter confidential — whatever it was. But what was it? Could he tell them now?

"I will show you," said Thomas simply. "Then you will understand."

Thomas said nothing else on the brief journey other than to tell them which turning to take. They arrived at a side-road off a residential street, and there, at the end of the road, was another building site.

"We can go in," Thomas said. "There is nobody working here today, and Mr. Putumelo is up in Francistown this week."

They left the car at the entrance and manoeuvred their way past a pile of building equipment — a cement mixer, a cache of planks covered with a tarpaulin, an upturned wheelbarrow.

"This is another fine-looking house," observed Phuti. "It is a bit bigger than ours, I think."

"This is going to be Mr. Putumelo's own house," said Thomas. "We are working on this one at the same time as we are working on yours."

"Builders often do two jobs at the same time," said Mma Makutsi. "I have heard that . . ."

She did not finish.

"Yes," said Thomas, "we are building Mr. Putumelo's house at the same time as we are building yours." He paused. They waited. "And with your bricks."

He pointed at the front wall of the house. "See," he said. "Those good bricks there. Do you see them?"

Phuti looked confused. "They are . . ."

"Yes," said Thomas. "They are the same bricks. But you paid for them, Rra. He has been ordering double quantities for your house and then using half of them to build his own house." He stared at Phuti. "You have been paying all the bills he gives you, Rra?"

Phuti nodded. "I always pay promptly."

Thomas sighed. "Come with me, please."

He took them up to the wall and pointed to one of the bricks. "Look at that brick, Rra. Just look closely at it."

Phuti bent down to examine the surface of the brick. "It has something scratched on it," he said. "I cannot quite make it out."

"It is the letters PR," said Thomas. "Look. That is the P and that is the R. That stands for Phuti Radiphuti. I scratched those letters myself on a few of your bricks to make sure, and here is one of them. There is another one round the side there. There is no doubt: these bricks are yours, Rra. They come from the pile of bricks he ordered for you — I have made quite sure of that."

Phuti straightened up. He was remembering his conversation with his aunt. She had talked about Mr. Putumelo's financial problems; she had commented on how strange it was that in his straitened circumstances he should still be building himself a house. Of course; of course. "We are being cheated," he said.

"Yes," said Thomas. "Mr. Putumelo is a very good builder. He is quick and he has very high standards. But he is a cheat. That is the problem."

Phuti reached out to put a hand on Thomas's shoulder. "You have been very brave, Rra."

Thomas shook his head. "I am not brave . . ."

"Yes, you are," said Mma Makutsi. "You are very brave. It is hard to tell the truth about the person who gives you your job — and who can take it away again."

Thomas sighed. "I have been feeling very bad about this because I know that you are good people. I felt ashamed."

"But it was not your fault, Rra," said Phuti reassuringly. "You just did your job. It is that Mr. Putumelo." He turned to Grace. "We will have to do something."

"Yes," she said. "We'll have to do something." She had no idea, though, of what to do. Perhaps Mma Ramotswe might suggest something.

But it was Thomas who made the suggestion. "I think that it would be best not to do anything just yet," he said. "If you went to the police, you would not have any real proof, and even if they charged him, then what would happen to all of us — the men who work for him? Let us finish your house. If you have a row with him now, then he will pull all the men off the site and you will have a house with no roof."

"That would not be good," said Mma Makutsi.

Thomas smiled. It was the first time they had seen him do this. "No. You need a roof."

"And then?"

"You will have a final bill to pay at the end. Cut it in half and say that this is for the bricks that he borrowed from you. Tell him that you can easily see how he forgot to take that into account with the bill, and so you have corrected the error. Tell him that you have seen the bricks in his new house — you were just passing by — and you real-ised that this had happened when you saw your initials on one of them. Say that you had put the initials there when you had called in at his yard and he was not there. Tell him that you were keen that the bricks should not be stolen by some passer-by. Tell him where to look for the bricks with the initials."

Phuti listened to this gravely. "I think I shall do all that, Rra," he said. "You know, I'm remembering something. When we first agreed to do this job, he said that my house had his name written all over it. Well . . ."

"His house has *your* name written all over it," said Grace.

The builder reflected on this for a few mo-

380

ments. "That is true," he said.

They walked back to the car. "I'm very grateful to you, Thomas," said Phuti. "You didn't have to do this."

"I did," said Thomas. "I did have to do it, Rra."

Phuti looked thoughtful. "You're a carpenter, aren't you?"

"That, and other things," said Thomas. "But that is my first trade."

Phuti looked at Mma Makutsi, who was watching him with interest. "We have a small workshop," he said slowly. "We have it for repairs and for some contract work. We have been able to get work permits for one or two men we take on because we make quite a lot of furniture for schools. Desks and things like that. We could get you one if you came to work for us."

Thomas stood quite still. "That is not why I did this, Rra."

"I know," said Phuti. "And that is why I want to offer you that job."

"You will like working for my husband," said Mma Makutsi.

"I will," said Thomas. "Yes, Mma, I will."

They got into the car and drove off down the road.

Clovis Andersen came to see Mma Ramotswe on the day before his departure. It was early on a Saturday morning, and she was at home, walking about her garden, when he called. She offered him a cup of tea, which she said they could drink as she showed him her plants and Mr. J.L.B. Matekoni's vegetables. He had expressed an interest in hearing the Setswana names of some of the plants, and she had promised to tell him these — or at least to try to. "The trouble is that we are losing many of those words, Rra. We're forgetting what these plants are called. They are lovely names, but we are losing them."

"We're losing words too," he said. "People are forgetting about the land."

"Even in your place, Rra?"

"Yes," he said. "Even in my place."

Mma Ramotswe looked up into the branches of her favourite acacia tree. "So, we'll all soon be living in towns and cities and will forget where we came from. We'll forget who feeds us. That is the earth, I think. And yet we'll forget her."

"I hope not," said Clovis Andersen. "At least I won't forget it. Nor you, Mma . . ."

"No, I won't forget it."

"I meant: I won't forget you, Mma Ramotswe."

She smiled at him. It was a kind thing for

him to say, but of course he would forget her. He was an important, busy man from far away: Why should he remember a woman who lived in a place that was small by comparison with his own country; a woman who had only a tiny business and not very important things to do? Why should he remember?

She made tea and brought it out to him, and together they started to walk about the garden. She showed him her mopipi tree, which had been making good progress but had to be protected from the ravages of ants. She showed him her bed of aloes that were producing intense red flowers on spiky shafts. She showed him the beans that Mr. J.L.B. Matekoni irrigated in the dry-land way, with drips of precious water tracking down a suspended thread.

And then, quite suddenly, he turned to her and said, "Mma Ramotswe, I have a confession to make. I cannot leave without saying something to you."

She looked up at him; he was much taller than she was. "What is it, Rra?"

"You have been so kind to me, Mma Ramotswe. You and Mma Makutsi. You have made my stay such a good one."

"But we have enjoyed it, Rra, and you have helped us so much. We've been honoured to have you. Mma Makutsi in particular. Your visit has been a very, very big thing for her. She comes from Bobonong, you see, and —"

"It's not that," Clovis Andersen interrupted. "It's just that . . . well, I'm not who you think I am."

She looked him with astonishment. "You're not Clovis Andersen?"

"No, of course I'm Clovis Andersen. But Clovis Andersen is not the great detective you think he is. He's a failed detective from Muncie, Indiana. He's a man who has hardly any clients and never really solves any cases. He's a nobody, Mma Ramotswe."

She laughed. "But that is nonsense, Rra. You are the author of that great book, *The Principles of Private Detection.* That book is world famous. It's very important."

He shook his head — sadly. "No, Mma Ramotswe. The book's not well known at all. I wrote it, yes, but I couldn't even get it properly published. So I had it printed privately — just two hundred copies. Eighty of those are still in boxes in my garage. We sold about thirty copies, that's all. I gave away the rest, but somehow one of those seems to have got into your hands. I have no idea how it happened, but it did. The book's nothing, Mma. Nothing."

She stood in front of him, the sun in her eyes now, preventing her from seeing him properly. She lifted a hand to shade her brow. She saw his face, which seemed to her to be racked with pain, with regret.

"Rra," she said. "You mustn't say that. You must never, never say that. Even if you had printed only ten copies — five copies, maybe — it would still be a very important book. It has helped us so much, Rra, and in turn we've been able to help so many people in our work. Every one of those people, Rra, is happier now because of what you did. Think of that — just think of that."

He stared at her. "Do you think . . . ," he began.

"Of course I think that, Rra. I *know* it, and Mma Makutsi knows it too. And Mr. J.L.B. Matekoni. We all know it."

He was at a loss for words. Mma Ramotswe could see that, and so she continued. "I could tell, Rra Andersen, that you were unhappy when you came here. I could tell that it was because you were thinking of your late wife."

"I was. Yes."

"Of course you were. We must think of late people because I believe they're still with us — in a way. And so a late person

385

can stay with you all your life, until it is your turn to become late too. And the late person doesn't want you to be miserable. A late person doesn't want you to think that your work is no use. A late person wants you to get on with life, to do things, to make good use of your time. That is well known, Rra. It is very well known."

He said nothing, but she knew that he had heard her words.

"So, let's finish our tea, Rra. Then we can look at that tree over there. Its leaves are very fine, Rra, and I want to show them to you."

They walked to the far side of her garden. "We have a lot to be grateful for, Rra," Mma Ramotswe said. She gestured to the small patch of her country that made up her garden. Her gesture took in her fence, and beyond that the road, and beyond that all Botswana and the world. "All that," she said. "That is what we have to be grateful for."

She did not look at him, because she sensed that he needed privacy, and a man may be embarrassed by his tears. So she simply touched him lightly on the arm and waited until he was ready to walk back.

He thought: *The Limpopo Academy of*

Private Detection. Then he thought: *Not really.* But he smiled nonetheless.

africa
africa africa
africa africa africa
africa africa
africa

ABOUT THE AUTHOR

Alexander McCall Smith is the author of the No. 1 Ladies' Detective Agency series, the Isabel Dalhousie series, the Portuguese Irregular Verbs series, the 44 Scotland Street series, and the Corduroy Mansions series. He is professor emeritus of medical law at the University of Edinburgh and has served on many national and international organizations concerned with bioethics. He was born in what is now known as Zimbabwe and taught law at the University of Botswana. He lives in Scotland.

Alice
Bliss

Laura Harrington's award-winning plays, musicals, operas, and radio plays have been widely produced in the US, Canada, and elsewhere. *Alice Bliss* is her first novel.

Alice Bliss

Laura Harrington

PICADOR

First published 2011 by Pamela Dorman Books,
an imprint of Viking, a division of Penguin Group (USA)

First published in Great Britain in paperback 2011 by Picador

This edition published 2012 by Picador
an imprint of Pan Macmillan, a division of Macmillan Publishers Limited
Pan Macmillan, 20 New Wharf Road, London N1 9RR
Basingstoke and Oxford
Associated companies throughout the world
www.panmacmillan.com

ISBN 978-0-330-54411-5

Printed and bound by CPI Group (UK) Ltd, Croydon, CR0 4YY

For Patrick

Alice Bliss

Prologue: August 20th

This is the first time Alice has been allowed to walk back to their campsite from the Kelp Shed alone. She is fourteen, barefoot, her sneakers tied together by the laces and slung across her shoulder so she can feel the soft, sandy dust of the single-track road between her toes. Her sister fell asleep halfway through the square dance, dropping from hyperexcited to unconscious in a flash. Her father carries Ellie draped over his shoulder, and casually, or so it seems, her mother says, "Come home when the dance is done."

She can hardly believe it. The dance is still in her feet, still in her bones, the steps like an intricate game. She danced with everyone and anyone at all, old and young, men and women, just to stay on the floor and moving. The caller was a blind man with two fingers missing from his left hand. His face was wrinkled and brown from the sun, his body heavy and the voice that called the steps strangely high and sweet. A boy's voice in a man's body. A boy's wildness, as though he had no awareness of himself in his body.

She gave in, finally, and danced with her father—embarrassed to be asked by him, worried that everyone would be watching and judging and thinking her still a child. But he surprises her. He is a good dancer. Precise. His hands firm on her back or her hand or her arm. She is suddenly dancing better than she has ever danced before, suddenly experiencing the freedom inside the squares. She can let go because he is so confident. She is tasting something adult, grown-up, or almost tasting it. It is just beyond her reach, this feeling, what it is, how to name it and understand it. Now it is pure sensation, unadulterated fun. Years later she will remember his touch on her back, pulling her in, letting her go, her own helpless laughter, the way he guided her, his touch steady and strong, and how he held her close and let her go, over and over again.

The dust beneath her feet now is cool, the day's heat long gone. It is mid-August and already you can feel fall coming with the way night rushes in. She pulls on her sweater and as she crests the first hill she can see almost all of Small Point, the shape of the island dark against the water. She can hear the waves on the beach below her. There are fires still burning at a few campsites, but mostly it is true dark. Alone on the road, she stops. What is she feeling? Intensely awake. Aware. A bit scared. She senses everything, her body open to the sky and the night, the smell of salt and pine and wood smoke, the wind, the scratchy wool of her old sweater, her hips loose in her jeans, her feet cool and tough and sure on the road.

In the distance she sees what look like stars on the water. Following the dip in the road, she loses sight of them, but cresting the next hill she sees them again. She breaks into a jog and takes the turn down to the ocean, away from her campsite. There it is again. Another curve and she can see where it is: the Devil's Bathtub. She is on the beach now, walking toward the outlying rock formation, a wide cleft in the rocks that becomes an eight foot pool at high tide and empties to sand at low tide.

There are fires on the water. How can that be? And now she sees them: a group of boys lighting small wooden rafts on fire and setting them afloat in this natural pool. They are quiet, intent. Why are they doing this? It's so beautiful, the small rafts floating, in flames, and then gone.

The boys have run out of boats; the last fire winks out. Now they strip off their clothes, daring one another to dive in. She crouches where she is, watching them, their pale bodies against the dark rock. She has never seen a naked boy before. She is not close enough to see much, but their nakedness is loud in the dark. Her eyes pass over each boy as though she could run a hand across a face or a chest, along a thigh.

She turns and lies in the sand, listening to their shouts as they dive and splash, listening as the cold and the search for their clothes quiets them. And the sky overhead is raining stars. These are the Perseids her father has told her about. She wants to get up and go and find him, she wants to tell the boys, Look up! Look up! But she can't move; there is magic occurring in front of her eyes. The heavens are throwing jewels at her feet. It is impossible, as impossible as fire on the water, as impossible as her hand on the chest of a naked boy, and yet here she is, seeing it with her own eyes.

January 29th

Matt Bliss is somebody who knows how to be happy. A former engineer, he's now a carpenter, doing what he loves, a craftsman, meticulous. He likes to say he escaped from his career and got himself a job. He coaches Little League even though neither of his daughters shows any aptitude for baseball. He was a pitcher on the local farm team right out of college, until his father told him to get serious and he went to grad school for his engineering degree. He still pitches for a local team.

Matt grows vegetables. Alice helps. They grow the best corn and the best tomatoes in town, not like there's much competition anymore. Ever since Mr. Hendrickson down the road died, the old time guys who put in vegetables every year have really dwindled. Matt says, "You just wait, the hippie kids will bring it all back again; all that poison in our food now, people are waking up. You can do it yourself. Good food. Cheap." And they've got this black dirt he loves to go on and on about. Topsoil eighteen inches deep. "Beautiful stuff!" He keeps trying to get Angie interested in canning or preserving or freezing their bounty, but this is not Angie's bailiwick.

So Alice and Ellie and Matt are the ones to snap beans, make tomato sauce and tomato juice and salsa, grape jelly and grape juice. Matt wants to plant three more apple trees in the side yard where Angie would like to have a nice patio. Two more cherry trees, too, right next to his grape arbor. Apple butter, he tells her, apple pies, cherry pies. Angie rolls her eyes and says: "Matt Bliss, you did not marry a farm girl." He laughs and picks her up and kisses her. Times like this the two of them head off for a "nap" hand in hand. Eventually figuring out just what this euphemism means makes Alice a little queasy. Here it is, right in front of her face, the power of opposites to attract.

Angie would love to stay in a nice hotel; Matt likes to camp. Angie is upwardly mobile, a striver if ever there was one; Matt likes things just the way they are. Angie thinks they're living in a starter house; Matt thinks they're home. Angie likes French perfume; Matt likes to get his hands dirty. The fact that Angie might like those workman's hands on her perfumed skin is a thought Alice vigorously chases from her mind.

The army reserve was a bone of contention, too. Angie all hung up on what's fair, why should Matt have to do it, what about his own family. Matt talking about doing what's right, not letting somebody else do what he should do: serving his country, an example to his girls. Finally they agree to disagree and Angie seems reconciled to it, even seems to enjoy the additional income, the occasional dinner in a nice restaurant, all dolled up in a new dress and high heels. And, oh, there's that perfume again, Matt's laughter, Angie's surrender, and another closed door.

But now, with the war dragging on and on, Matt's unit has been called up. He's heading to Fort Dix. Until recently reservists got six months of specialized instruction. Now they are fast-tracking volunteers through six weeks of supposedly high-quality, hurry up, move 'em out training.

The weeks prior to his leaving are an insane rush. Angie and Matt

4

talk late into the night, every night, sitting at the kitchen table. They argue, Angie tries not to cry again, they pore over health insurance, Matt's will and living will, the power of attorney forms. They try to anticipate what Angie will be facing in the coming months.

They are running out of time. They all know it. It's in the air they breathe.

Alice is so tired her eyes are burning but she can't sleep. As long as her father is still awake and still in the house and still talking or drinking coffee, Alice wants to be near him. So she sits in the dark at the foot of the stairs and listens.

"Why are you insisting—?" Angie's voice pops up a register when she's upset.

"You know why."

"Tell me why the United States Army is more important than your own family."

"It's not an either or equation, Angie."

"You like this. You're actually excited."

"I like the work, I like my crew, I like the challenge, the chance to—"

"But leaving us, Matt—"

"You know I don't want to leave you."

"They'll throw you right in the middle of—"

"I'm going where I'm needed."

"I need you. Doesn't that count anymore?"

"Of course it does."

"I never imagined—never—that you would do something like this. You were going to play baseball for god's sake. *Baseball!* How did we get from baseball to—"

"Angie, it's not just about you and me."

"Okay, so you're the selfless hero and I'm the selfish wife. You think

5

I want this role? I didn't sign up for this. This was not part of the plan."

"I know."

"I hate this, I really hate this."

"Sweetheart . . ." Alice can hear the ache in his voice.

"I want . . ." Angie's voice breaks.

"I don't want to be one of those guys who gets old and says, I wish I had done this, I wish I had done that."

"Oh, Matt . . ."

"I want to contribute, and I don't think we should just send our kids to this war."

"But what if—?"

"Don't you have any faith in me?"

"Of course I do."

"I'm coming home, Angie."

"Promise me."

"I promise."

It's quiet for a moment.

"I want letters, you know," Matt says. "Real letters. With perfume. You can't carry an e-mail around in your pocket."

"You're not so deluded you actually think this is romantic?"

"I do. A little."

"It won't be romantic if—"

"Oh, yeah," he teases her, laughing. "The fallen hero, blah, blah, blah."

"Matt!"

Alice hears the kitchen chairs scrape across the floor and knows it is time to beat a retreat up the stairs to bed. But she waits another moment, and another. She wants to see her dad one more time tonight.

They walk through the kitchen door. The dining room light is nothing more than a warm glow, illuminating them. Matt pulls Angie to him and kisses her, and kisses her some more.

6

Alice backs slowly up the stairs, carefully stepping over the creak-iest step, third from the top. She puts her freezing cold hands under her armpits to try to warm them as she walks down the hall to her room. She waits to duck inside her door until she hears them on the stairs. Matt has his arm around Angie's waist and he has even managed to make her laugh. That soft, musical, surrendering laugh Angie saves just for Matt and his beautiful blue eyes.

Alice closes her door as softly as possible and leans against it, hop-ing they have not heard her. She hears them pass by whispering and giggling like little kids.

Ellie has kicked her covers off as usual. Alice pulls the quilt over Ellie and then climbs into her own bed. She listens to Ellie breathing; she closes her eyes, tight, tight, and tries to breathe through the knot in her chest. She wishes she could call Henry but that would mean waking up Mr. and Mrs. Grover and getting into trouble for calling so late. She wishes they still had their walkie-talkies hooked up. She could ask Henry to leave his on so she could listen to the static and hear him sleeping and breathing the way she did that whole terrible month in fourth grade when her grandfather was dying. What hap-pened to those walkie-talkies she wonders, and what's Henry doing right now? She'll ask him tomorrow. If it doesn't sound too crazy in the cold light of day.

January 31st

Matt is in his workshop puttering around with a cup of forgotten cof-fee sitting on the windowsill. It's a cold day with flurries and a gust-ing wind, so he's got the woodstove going full blast and he's wearing his tan work jacket with the ripped pocket. Alice slips in and sits on a wooden crate near the stove. What is she doing here, exactly? Her English homework lies forgotten in her lap. She is, what? Hanging out? Breathing the air? Daydreaming? Making a nuisance of herself?

All of the above? She brought her dad a toasted muffin as a way of interrupting him and then stuck. Like a burr. She is uninvited, she feels awkward; but this is where she has to be even if Matt would rather be alone.

But Matt would not rather be alone. There are things he wants to say to his daughter before he leaves but they all sound so portentous and ominous that he can't bring himself to begin. There are things she needs to know, things she needs to prepare for, and it's really not fair to leave all the talking and informing and awkwardness to Angie. So he talks about the garden instead. He pulls out last year's plan and asks Alice to come over and take a look. She throws another log in the woodstove and joins him at the workbench.

"So I was thinking less corn because there will only be three of you."

"What about Gram? She can always take the extra."

"Because that way we could squeeze in another row of yellow beans."

"Okay."

"And beets."

"You're the only one who likes beets, Dad."

"Okra?"

"Blech."

"Broccoli?"

"Two plants at most."

He notates the changes as they talk.

"You can do peas spring and fall like we did last year."

"Can we do basil?"

"Sure. And Mom likes arugula."

"Yeah."

Suddenly Alice's hands are clammy and she can't lift her eyes from the plan.

"You don't like it," he says.

"I liked it just fine last year. I thought last year was perfect."

"No changes? No building on our successes and learning from our failures?"

"We didn't have any failures."

"Just way too much yellow squash."

"Okay. Let's take out half the yellow squash."

"But keep the corn?"

"Yes."

"And everything else."

"Just like last year," Alice says, slowly and carefully.

"Because . . . ?"

"Because I want it to be the same."

Alice manages to look him in the eye, which is when he can see how hard she is working to stay in control.

"Okay." He smiles at her. "We'll go with last year's design."

"Good."

"You want gourds even if I'm not here?"

"Yes!"

In the far corner of the garden Matt grows decorative gourds. They are strange things: bumpy and lumpy and misshapen. But they are colorful and surprising and they serve no purpose other than to amaze. Alice has every intention of growing gourds this year and every year for the rest of her life.

Matt labels the plan with the date and tacks it up on the wall.

"You can rototill mid-April if the ground isn't too wet and heavy. You can call Jimmy Rose to do it; or ask Uncle Eddie to help you."

"Got it."

"You might have to pester Jimmy. He gets busy."

Matt looks out the window at the snow covering the garden.

"And I want you to help your mom."

"I know."

"No, Alice. Really help her. Like you're her partner. I want you to

9

help her take care of Ellie and the house and . . . She's gonna need you."

"Okay. But tell her to remember to ask me."

"What?"

"She acts like I'm supposed to know everything she wants and when I don't she gets mad. If she'd just tell me. Or ask me—"

"You tell her."

"She doesn't listen to me."

"Keep trying."

Alice looks at her feet.

"Honey? Keep trying."

"Okay."

"You know where all my papers are."

"Dad! We've been over this!"

She doesn't want to hear about his will and his life insurance again. She doesn't even want those papers to exist.

"I opened up an account for you." He reaches into his back pocket and holds out a bankbook from the local bank. "It's just a basic savings account. But I put five hundred dollars in there for you. In case you need something."

"Dad, it's okay."

"Or there's an emergency."

She's backing away from him. She doesn't want to touch the bankbook.

"Or your mom can't handle things for a few days."

"Dad!"

"Alice, there are things you need to know."

She trips backing away from him and sits down, hard, on her butt. Which is funny. In an awful sort of stupid, annoying way.

He reaches out to help her up and pulls her into a hug. It's a real hug, the kind of hug he used to give her before she started turning into a teenager and growing breasts and getting sweaty and unsure.

He holds her for a long time. She breathes him in. Sawdust. Wood smoke. Cold coffee. Aftershave. Linseed oil. *Dad.*

Matt is trying to stay right here with Alice; he is trying not to let his mind run off with all the *what ifs* that have been keeping him awake at night. He's wishing his parents were still alive. His mom would know how to pick up the slack, or how to step in if Angie and Alice really can't get along. And his dad . . . his dad would plant the garden with Alice, and take her to baseball games and . . .

"I need to show you something."

"Not your will again."

"Come over here."

He leads her to the big wooden tool chest. He pulls out the first three levels of tools, then opens a drawer and slides that out completely. Underneath the socket wrenches there's a plain white envelope with her name on it. He opens the envelope and fans five one hundred dollar bills.

"What's *that* for?"

"It's there if you need it. And in the envelope there are some important numbers. The VA so you can get benefits, my lawyer, my life insurance . . ."

"Dad! You're talking like you're not coming back."

"No, no, no." He grins at her, and his whole face lights up. "This is like carrying an umbrella in case it rains, and then it doesn't rain, so . . ."

"What?"

"It's just insurance. It's just an umbrella. You can't take it too seriously."

She wants to believe him.

"And together, right now, I want the two of us to make a list of who you can call if you need help."

She's looking at the floor and she's thinking, no list, no cash, no strategies. Can he just back out, refuse to go, change his mind? Could they move to Canada? Or Mexico? Could they just get into the car and go? Or could she get violently sick right this minute or have some awful but minor accident that would keep him from leaving?

"C'mon. A list."

"Define help."

"Shoveling the driveway, jumpstarting the car, advice on a repair, moral support, somebody to take you to the movies or the library or out for ice cream."

So they agree on Gram and Uncle Eddie and Henry and his parents and her favorite teacher, Mrs. Cole, and Mrs. Minty, who lives down the road, in a pinch, and her parents' friends the Hoyts, from the old neighborhood, and her dad's baseball buddy Bobby Lester. She adds Mrs. Piantowski, the lady who bakes bread for Gram's restaurant, at the last minute.

Her dad writes all these names down in his perfect block printing and adds the phone numbers from memory or the phone book. And then he adds the family doctor, dentist, banker, and insurance man.

He writes up a second copy to put in the house and tacks the original to the inside lid of his toolbox. He pulls the only chair over to the woodstove next to Alice's crate and opens the door to the stove so they can watch the fire burn. He picks up the muffin and hands a piece to Alice before sitting down and stretching his feet out to the fire. They sit like that, not talking, for what seems like a long time.

Outside the back window Alice can see the outlines of the garden, some of the furrows visible under the snow, stretching away in long thin rows. She can't imagine doing the garden without her dad. It's his thing; she's always thought of herself as his assistant at best. She can't imagine doing anything without her dad and she starts to feel like she can't breathe. And then she looks at him. Just looks at him as he watches the fire with muffin crumbs on his lap.

"I'll write to you."

"I'm counting on it."

"Every day."

"Good."

She takes a breath.

"Dad . . ."

He closes up the woodstove.

"We need to go in, I think."

Not yet, Alice thinks, not yet.

"I wish . . ."

"Me, too, sweetheart. Me, too."

February 1st

Matt is getting on a bus headed to Fort Dix, New Jersey. That's not so bad. Nothing to worry about, really. It's just a bus. It's just New Jersey. And if anybody actually gets to know Matt Bliss on base it's absolutely a foregone conclusion that they will find him so useful, so essential to the running of, well, everything, that his superior officers will choose to keep him stateside. And safe. And alive. Until they send him home. On his own two feet. Much sooner than expected. This is what keeps running through Alice's mind as they go through the motions of saying good-bye.

Henry wanted to come with them, but that idea got nixed. So he and his parents stood out on their front steps to wave at them as they drove along East Oak Street. Henry was waving his baseball mitt over his head, which got a laugh out of Matt. Matt slowed the car way down and cranked his window to wave back before he blasted the horn and sped away.

Now they're standing with the other reservists and their wives and families at the Rochester Greyhound station. The men are in fatigues, the wives are in jeans or stretchy pants, the kids are wearing dirty parkas and have pink cheeks and runny noses from the cold. It's not romantic like all those classic movie scenes of parting at train stations;

13

it's more like being stuck at the mall with a lot of strangers. There's no brass band, no sound track at all, just the tinny annoying bus terminal Muzak and the muffled announcements. There are also no wonderful hats, or handkerchiefs, or stockings with seams. No one is dressed up at all, except Angie, who is wearing high heels, a skirt and a blouse, her dress coat and her favorite silk scarf, the one that Matt gave her. She is not, Alice notices, wearing her glasses. She never wears her glasses when she gets dressed up, which Alice thinks is just plain stupid, because then she can't see anything much past the middle distance. But once Angie gets started with the silk and the perfume and the high heels, the glasses get left behind.

Alice is watching her mom and her dad and holding on to her dad's other hand until Ellie worms her way in and pushes her out of the way. Then she hangs back feeling forgotten.

She wishes she knew what to say, but every phrase that pops into her head sounds stupid or childish. And Matt's not one for big gestures or big speeches, and he's definitely not one for spilling his guts at the Greyhound station surrounded by strangers.

Last night Matt gave Alice a map of the Middle East. They put it up on her wall together and put pins in where he's supposed to be going. Not that anybody knows for sure. Alice wonders how anybody can get things done when nobody knows anything for sure.

And then he's walking away from them, his duffel slung over his shoulder, his too-short hair bristling out the back of his cap. The backs of their necks, she thinks—the skinny, tense ones and the ones with rolls of fat—they look like kids, like boys, really.

She sprints out of the waiting group and catches up with her dad.

"Dad . . . Dad—"

He stops and lifts her off the ground in a hug. When he sets her down, he slips his watch off his wrist and puts it into her hand. She's working as hard as she can not to cry. It suddenly seems so important to see him, really see him. He turns away and the wind picks up and

14

the grit of the parking lot blows into their eyes, and Alice thinks desert and Alice thinks land mines and Alice thinks will she ever see her dad, this dad, the way he is right now, full of this life, again?

She stands there watching until every last one of them is on board and the bus begins to back out of its bay.

She turns around to see that some of the families are waving little flags, like the ones you get for the Memorial Day parade. It begins to snow, the heavy, quiet snow that blankets the world in stillness and makes the road surfaces treacherous within minutes.

Angie waves her scarf as the bus drives away. She stands there too long, long after the bus is out of sight, long after the other families have piled into their cars and left. She blows her nose and finally crosses the parking lot to join Ellie and Alice at the car.

"Could you unlock the car please?" Alice asks, shivering.

Angie gives Alice a long, unreadable look.

"It's *cold*, Mom."

For once Alice and Ellie do not fight about who gets to sit in the front. The three of them get into the car and it's way too quiet. Angie pulls the seat forward so she can reach the pedals and reaches up to adjust the rearview mirror. Ellie has brought her recorder along and thinks that now might be a good moment to practice.

"Not now, Ellie."

"But Mom—"

"Not now!"

Angie backs up and turns and when she reaches the street she doesn't seem to know which way to go. These hesitations are so unlike her mother, Alice thinks.

Driving down Monroe Avenue, Angie pulls her silk scarf off, rolls down her window, and holds the scarf outside, billowing and snapping in the wind.

"Mom—?"

When Angie lets the scarf go, Alice turns in her seat to watch it float away before it drifts to the snow-covered ground. The car behind them runs over it.

"What did you do that for?"

"I love that scarf! You could have given it to me," Ellie chimes in.

Angie just keeps driving.

"Mom! It's cold back here! Close the window!"

"I think . . ." Angie begins and then trails off.

"Mom!" Alice says. "The window!"

"Who wants frozen custard?" Angie asks.

"In this weather? Are you crazy?"

"I do! I do!" Ellie shouts.

Angie makes a sudden U turn, throwing Alice against the door. Alice feels a jolt in the pit of her stomach. The car fishtails in the snow as she tries to grab the door handle.

"Mom! What are you doing?!"

"Can I get jimmies?" Ellie wants to know. "Extra jimmies? A cup full of jimmies?"

Alice is looking at Angie. She is driving way too fast. Angie never drives too fast. And, Alice registers again, she is not wearing her glasses.

"Mom, do you want me to drive?"

"You don't know how to drive."

"I think you need to pull over."

"Why?"

"You need your glasses."

"I'm *fine.*"

"You're driving really fast and you're scaring me."

"And it's freezing in here!" Ellie adds. "Close the window!"

Angie turns to look at Alice.

"We're going to Don and Bob's. We're getting frozen custard. Then we're going home."

"Okay. Okay. Would you just keep your eyes on the road?"

"I sure could use a scarf back here where it's as cold as the arctic tundra!" Ellie says.

Alice wishes she could laugh.

"Is anybody listening to me? I'm probably catching a terrible cold right this minute. Mom! Earth to Mom! Come in, Mom!"

Angie manages a smile.

"Your window!?"

Angie rolls up her window and turns the heat up high.

"Can I have hot chocolate with my ice cream?" Ellie wants to know.

"You can have whatever you want," Angie answers.

"Onion rings?"

"At the same time?" Alice makes a face.

"No. Onion rings and a vanilla shake. Then hot chocolate. Then ice cream."

"You're gonna be sick."

"Mom said whatever I want."

"You're crazy."

"I don't care. That's what I want."

They pull into Don and Bob's, and Angie nearly clips the SUV at the entrance as their car slides a bit on the snow. She gives the fat guy in the front seat a jaunty wave, like we're all in this crazy weather thing together, aren't we?

Crossing the parking lot, Angie is tiptoeing through the snow trying not to ruin her new heels. She slips and grabs on to Alice to steady herself.

"Wrong shoes," she shrugs.

"Yeah," Alice concedes.

"I was trying to look pretty."

"Yeah."

"For Dad."

"Yeah."

"He likes heels. He likes a woman in heels."

17

"That's about all I want to know about that, Mom."

Ellie has run ahead and grabbed a booth. She's already chatting up the waitress as she shakes the snow from her shoulders and takes off her coat. Alice slides in beside her and picks up the menu.

"I'm ready!" Ellie announces to no one in particular.

"Give me a minute."

"You know what you're going to have. It's what you always, always have."

"I like to look. Just in case."

"Just in case what? You turn into another person?"

"Just in case it's a grilled Reuben kind of day."

"Yeah, yeah, yeah. Stick to the tried and true."

"That could be boring."

"You're already boring, Alice."

"Thanks a lot!"

Alice looks up to see that Angie has her head resting against the back of the booth and her eyes closed. Her long, fine fingers are crossed over her stomach. She looks pale and tired in the fluorescent light. She's sitting in the middle of the booth as if she can cover up Dad's absence. Alice checks to see if Ellie has noticed any of this.

"Can we order, already?" Ellie asks.

"Yup."

Ellie waves to the waitress, who comes right over. Her name tag says "Marge." Her glasses are incredibly thick and her hair looks like it's been teased and shellacked with hair spray. Who wears their hair like that anymore?

"Hi, Marge!" Ellie says. "Can I get started with onion rings and a vanilla shake?"

"You bet."

"I'll have the classic burger and a root beer, please. Mom? What do you want?"

Angie opens her eyes and sits up. Alice holds out a menu, Angie ignores it.

"Do you have soup?"

"Beef barley or chicken vegetable."

"Chicken, please. A cup."

Marge heads off to shout their order to the cooks behind the counter.

"We could play hangman," Ellie says.

"Okay."

"Mom, you got a pen?" Ellie asks.

Angie finds a pen in her purse, and Alice fishes her carefully folded geometry homework out of her back pocket. Ellie, Little Miss Genius, instantly takes the pen and thinks up a nine-letter word, drawing the short lines carefully

"Nine letters?"

"You're never gonna get this one."

"E."

Ellie fills in two blanks.

"A."

Two more blanks.

"Where did you get that?" Angie's voice is maybe a little sharper than she intended. To Alice it's coming at her with enough force to induce whiplash.

"My homework?"

"No. Daddy's watch."

"What? Do you think I took it?"

"I'm just asking."

"No, Mom, you're accusing."

"I am not!"

"Or insinuating."

"Oh, for heaven's sake."

"He gave it to me."

"Why didn't he give it to me?" Ellie wants to know.

"He gave it to you," Angie says, her voice flat and disbelieving.

"Why don't you believe me?"

"He didn't say anything to me about it."

"Why would he? It's not your watch."

"Let's just drop it."

"Do you want the watch, Mom?"

"No."

"Why does Alice always get the good stuff?" Ellie asks.

"Shut up, Ellie."

Which is when, thank you Marge in the Coke-bottle glasses and the Elvis Presley updo, the food arrives.

February 5th

Gram, a.k.a. Penelope Pearl Bird, or Penny to her many friends, owns the last remaining café in Belknap. When Grampa died six years ago, Gram sold her house out on Plank Road, bought one of the old Victorians at the Four Corners, moved into the apartment upstairs, and resurrected Belknap's one and only coffee shop. She roped her sister Charlotte, who was also recently widowed, into helping her. They call it The Bird Sisters and are open for breakfast and lunch, six a.m. to two p.m. Wednesday through Sunday.

Angie was predicting the worst from Day One, thought it would be too much for Gram, thought Gram was throwing her money away. According to Angie, all kinds of dire emergencies were going to crop up, from a leaky roof to poisoning patrons. But Gram would retort that she's got her son Eddie and her son-in-law Matt for the roof and anything else that involves carpentry, plumbing, or electrical, and as for the food poisoning, Gram says nobody ever died from eggs, toast, and coffee.

And what do you know? Gram has the touch: she's a savvy

businesswoman, and she's having fun with The Bird Sisters. There is no one in Belknap she hasn't met. Most people come in at some point or another needing a cup of coffee and someone to listen, which is Gram all over. Some people have taken to calling her the mayor of Belknap.

It was more fun, of course, before Aunt Char died last year. The Bird Sisters closed its doors for a month while Gram worked out whether she could go on without Char. Gram needed time to reassess and recover from that long string of losses: her husband, James; her kid brother, George; her brother-in-law Bobby; and her beloved sister, Char.

Ask Gram about Char and she'll say, "Oh, Char was the pretty one," or "Char was the smart one," like Gram isn't pretty and smart? But Gram has this open-hearted way with the people she loves. Some people focus on your flaws, but Gram focuses on your best feature, or tells you that she actually, honestly *likes* your supposed flaw. Gram's highest forms of praise are "He's a real gentleman," or "She's true blue."

As an example of the loving your flaws thing, Aunt Char was a whistler. She'd even whistle classical music. Drove her husband, Bobby, completely bats, but Gram loved it. She'd brag to customers: "My sister, Charlotte, can whistle Schubert's 'Trout Quintet.'"

"Just try it," she'd challenge anybody who laughed.

When Gram reopened she tried to do it all herself, relying on her two short-order cooks, Ginny and Dave, to carry plates now and then. Luckily, Sally Perkins walked in the door one day, ate the best breakfast of her life, so she says, tied on an apron, and never left. Sally's a divorcée from down by the lake. Her kids are grown but still going through their troubles right in Sally's neighborhood, sometimes right outside Sally's backdoor. Her husband's still in the neighborhood, too. Some people say he's trying to make amends. Sally says, what that man broke cannot be fixed.

Sally's a little short and a little stocky, but curvy, too, and she likes to accentuate the positive. She's also got that bottle blonde, tough broad thing going on. And it's like she does backward flirting, giving guys such a hard time they can't believe it, but they keep coming back for more. People from out of town assume Sally and Gram are sisters. Gram always says, "We're like sisters, but we're not the *original* sisters."

Playing on the Bird theme, Gram has birdbaths and bird feeders galore. There's suet hanging in the oldest apple tree next to the house, hummingbird feeders stuck to all the windows, and supposedly squirrel-proof feeders hanging from most branches. All the bird activity, especially the hummingbirds, keeps little kids occupied while their parents get to talk. It's fair to say it's the most popular place in town, but then again, it's the only place in town.

Mrs. Piantowski makes all the bread for the restaurant, right out of her own kitchen. Mrs. Piantowski is forty-something years old, has eight kids, and wanted to make a little money on the side. She didn't really know anything about bread when she sold Gram on this idea, so she started small, just white, wheat, and rye. But Mrs. Piantowski fell in love with bread: Portuguese sweetbread, Finnish Nisu, Swedish limpa rye with caraway and fennel seed and orange rind, anadama, sticky buns, biscuits and scones and on and on. She got her husband to move the fridge into the pantry and install a second double oven. It is a bread adventure with Mrs. Piantowski, and Gram says she's happy to go along for the ride.

Of course people started asking to buy Mrs. Piantowski's bread. But Gram and Mrs. Piantowski were already pushing it given that a home kitchen was supplying a restaurant. Strictly against board of health rules, and nobody wants to get the board of health involved, with regulations and testing and surprise inspections. Until it turns out the board of health inspector is one of their best customers. In fact, Charlie Prophett eats breakfast at The Bird Sisters five days a week and is often seen knocking on the door and begging them to open up on Monday and Tuesday, too. So far he has managed to control himself and not walk up on Mrs. Piantowski's porch on the days the restaurant is closed. But there are bets on how long it will be before he's knocking on her door to say, "Just a piece of toast, Mrs. Piantowski. Or two or three, if you don't mind."

There are people in Belknap who dream about Mrs. Piantowski's bread. Maybe some people even dream about Mrs. Piantowski. She has dark brown eyes and long reddish hair that she wears pulled back or piled on top of her head, and she has lots of freckles on her nose, chest, and arms. She always wears colors, wonderful rich colors, and skirts and sweaters and sometimes a scarf twisted in her hair. She's not exactly pretty, but she has this bearing; it's almost regal. Maybe it's her height, maybe it's her very straight spine and her very straight nose and her no nonsense way of speaking. Maybe it's that nobody knows her first name.

Gram knows but she's not telling. Some men have tried to flirt with Mrs. Piantowski, and women try to get friendly, but she just sails on by. Maybe she's got everything she needs with eight kids and twenty-two different kinds of bread up her sleeve.

Alice's job is to pick up the bread every Saturday and Sunday morning at quarter of six and then help Gram with whatever prep work still needs to be done at the restaurant. Even though every other teenager in America is still asleep. Even though Alice sometimes wonders how she gets roped into this stuff. On the other hand, Alice has never met anyone who can say no to Gram.

She used to use Ellie's red Radio Flyer wagon until neighbors complained about the noise as she squeaked and bumped her way along the sidewalks in the predawn. Then Gram got her a rubber wheeled grocery basket like the ones old ladies use in metropolitan areas. Alice feels ridiculous, but at least now she's quiet.

It's exactly quarter of six Sunday morning when Alice arrives at the backdoor to Mrs. Piantowski's. She leaves the cart on the porch and knocks softly before turning the knob and walking in. The youngest baby is sitting in a bouncy chair on the kitchen table looking around with her big, dark green, and very grave eyes. There are two dozen loaves wrapped and ready to go and Mrs. Piantowski is pulling twelve more out of the double oven.

"Hi, Alice."

"Hi, Mrs. Piantowski."

"Snowing?"

"Not yet."

Mrs. Piantowski works at the stove. She is brushing the loaves with a blend of sugar and cardamom.

"I'm running a little late. You're going to need to take these right in the pans. Can you bring me the pans on your way home later today?"

"Sure."

Usually all the loaves are stacked and ready to go, and then she and Mrs. Piantowski pack the cart together: coolest loaves on the bottom, warmest ones on top. Alice understands that this is probably about allowing the loaves to cool without getting soggy, but it also creates this heady perfume as she walks down the street. She imagines the fresh bread smells wafting like a banner over her head—the best advertising imaginable.

"What's that spice?"

"Cardamom."

"Smells good."

There's never much chat with Mrs. Piantowski. She's not exactly unfriendly; she just doesn't talk much. Maybe she doesn't know how difficult it is for a fifteen-year-old to initiate a conversation. Maybe with eight kids of her own she cherishes the quiet of these early-morning hours and is not willing to sacrifice the silence to talk to one more child.

But Mrs. Piantowski's quiet today has more to do with the fact that her husband has taken to leaving their bed to wander through the house like a refugee from his own life. Isaac will not say they have too many children, he would never say that. Instead he turns away from her, leaves their bed in the darkest hours, only to return when her alarm sounds at three a.m. It is a new dance they do each night, a dance of sleep and wakefulness and loneliness, instead of the old dance of love.

But these aches recede as she steps into her kitchen, lights the stove, puts an apron and the kettle on, and sets the first batch of dough to rising.

Alice doesn't mind the quiet. It gives her a chance to experience Mrs. Piantowski's kitchen. There's eight of everything: eight hooks on the wall for coats, eight hooks above for hats, eight stools around the table, which is set for eight for breakfast. Everything is spotless; nothing is out of place. Alice thinks Mrs. Piantowski must either be a drill sergeant or the most persuasive person on the planet.

The baby starts to fuss.

"Can I pick up the baby?"

"She's fine."

Alice crosses to the baby.

"I never met anyone named Inga before," she says, extending a finger, which the baby grabs.

"My grandmother's name."

"Hi, Inga," Alice whispers, and lays her hand against Inga's cheek.

Eyes closed, Alice inhales the baby smells and the baking smells; the yeast and the sugar and. . . .

"Go ahead."

"What?"

"You've held a baby before?"

"Sure."

She releases the Velcro holding Inga in place and scoops her up in her hands, remembering to support her head as she pulls her close against her body. Alice and Inga engage in a long staring contest until Inga's nose wrinkles and she sneezes. Laughing, Alice is rewarded with one of Inga's smiles. Alice sways with the baby, her weight transferring from foot to foot, and then she starts to dance with the baby, right there in the kitchen. Not too fast, not too jittery; just a slow swirl and glide, anything to keep Inga smiling.

Mrs. Piantowski starts to sing. In a foreign language. What is that, Polish? The song is halfway between a lullaby and a lament. Why would you sing this song to a baby? It's so sad, Alice thinks, it could make you cry. And then Mrs. Piantowski starts to clap and before you know it she is dancing; hitching up her apron and her skirt and doing something fancy with her feet as she continues to sing. The song changes from a whisper to a shout and Inga loves it; with each change in tone, each surprise, Inga turns her head to watch her mother and smiles her toothless smile.

Alice looks back and forth between the two of them, baby Inga laughing, Mrs. Piantowski's face shining in the warm kitchen, and wonders, did this ever happen in her life, with her mother?

She must be looking famished because Mrs. Piantowski pours her a big glass of milk and sets a cinnamon bun on a plate. Then she hands her a cloth napkin and invites her to sit down. She waves away Alice's worry about being late and takes baby Inga from her. This is too much. Mrs. Piantowski is a completely different species from Alice's own mother.

Alice doesn't realize how fast she's eating until she looks up and catches Mrs. Piantowski grinning.

"Good?" she asks.

"The best ever," Alice replies, before she gulps down her milk and slides off the stool to head out the door into the predawn darkness on her way to deliver bread to The Bird Sisters.

March 13th

"Mom? Mom! Are you up? Get a move on!"

The Monday following Angie's surprise birthday party, which Matt and the girls had carefully pre-planned and executed with help from Gram and Uncle Eddie, Angie does not feel like getting up or going to work. When Alice calls up to her, she's still in bed, still feeling devastated and idiotic that the promised phone call with Matt never came through, even though she waited up almost all night, just in case. And it's ridiculous, really. How many times does she have to be reminded that his time is not his own anymore?

The girls, with Gram's help, gave her a silk scarf to replace the one she tossed out the window. They made her favorite cake, angel food stuffed with strawberries and whipped cream, Gram cooked Angie's favorite dinner, even Uncle Eddie came through with a basket of spring bulbs. Matt had wrapped up the far too expensive French perfume she loves and left it with Alice for safekeeping. Why did it all make her feel so sad and so incredibly angry and so stupidly childish all at the same time? Angie feels like a yo-yo; the simplest things set her off. It's exhausting. And she doesn't even like birthdays.

"Five more minutes!"

Downstairs Ellie is half asleep in her cereal, her braids dragging in the milk. Alice is trying to find her sneakers, air out the armpits of her dad's button-down blue shirt, which she has worn for three solid weeks now and refuses to wash, and scavenging for enough change so Ellie can buy milk at lunch. Oh yes, and packing the sandwiches: sliced bananas on graham crackers.

"Mom, we're out of bread!" Alice shouts up the stairs. "And peanut butter. And jam! Again," she mutters under her breath as she returns to the kitchen.

"Get creative," Angie shouts from the bedroom.

The bananas keep sliding off the graham crackers when Alice tries to fit them into the sandwich bags.

"Don't put that crap in my lunch box."

"You can't say crap."

"It's like big tall letters flashing over my head when I open my lunch box: fucked up family!"

"Ellie!"

"What? You say it!"

"Not when I was in second grade!"

"I want lunch money. Not this stupid excuse for a sandwich!"

"I'll ask Gram."

"Yeah. She could set up a lunch fund. And a clothing fund and she could drive us to the supermarket to stock up on food and—"

"Okay, you ready?" Alice asks, handing Ellie her lunch box.

"You can't go to school in that," Ellie says.

"Let's get a move on."

"Dad's shirt? Again? Does Mom know?"

"What do you care?"

"It doesn't fit."

"So?"

"Aside from the fact you're not cool, I think you're starting to smell, Alice. You could at least wash that stupid shirt."

"I aired it out last night."

"That's not enough."

"It'll be fine."

"You need to burn it."

"Henry's gonna be here any minute."

"Maybe Gram would take you shopping. New jeans, new . . ."

"I'm all set. C'mon."

"Okay, but I'm not walking next to you and I'm definitely not holding hands with you. Not even at the crosswalk."

"Whatever."

"I'm reaching my limit with you, Alice. Just so you know."

God, she sounds just like Angie, Alice thinks.

Matt's been gone almost six weeks. He's in the last days of training at the mobilization center with his army reserve unit. The reservists have been kept pretty much in lockdown conditions at Fort Dix: no time off, no time off the base, and very little contact with home. Supposedly this is all preparation for being deployed. It's very strange for Angie and Alice and Ellie. He's gone but not gone; and there's no coming home at this point, not until his one-year tour of duty is done.

Everything is different with Matt gone. Same house, different air, different space inside the rooms. Angie is impatient and irritable; she's working at the insurance company more than ever, and on top of that, she brings work home. It's like she doesn't really want to be at home at all so she piles on the work and makes the kitchen table a second office. That way she has a good excuse to be distracted and tense all the time. She's pretty much dropped the ball on domestic duties and says she's "not interested in eating right now." So Alice does her best with spaghetti most nights and occasionally macaroni and cheese and lots of tomato soup and grilled cheese sandwiches. Ellie is spending inordinate amounts of time with her friend Janna and even manages to get herself invited for dinner several nights a week. Alice is spending too much time alone in the house every afternoon. She wants to be there in case the phone rings but it never does.

Angie was starting to let herself go for a bit but yanked herself right back from the edge with an iron hand. She got a new haircut and renewed her fitness commitment, swimming half an hour three days a week after work. The housework and the cooking are not so high on her list of priorities, but the personal appearance thing has become very important. Alice thinks her mom secretly likes the fact that stress and worry have finally made it possible for her to drop those last pesky ten pounds. She is slipping back into some pre-Ellie clothes. Okay, so it's natural to think your mother is a total idiot at this age, but when your dad's out of the picture it's hard to have your mother quite so strange and foreign. It's a little disconcerting, the sudden lack of parents. Or, to be honest, when nobody prefers you. When you are not anybody's special somebody. This is when it would be nice to have a dog.

Alice doesn't know, can't know, what Angie is going through. Angie, who can't sleep at night or if she does fall asleep, wakes with a start to the unfamiliar silence that is Matt's absence. They have been together since their sophomore year in college; in eighteen years they have slept apart on very rare occasions. Angie wonders whether it is even possible to sleep without him.

In the middle of the night she haunts the house and the closets, running her hands over his jackets and shirts, feeling inside the pockets of his coats for coins, or keys, or penny nails, or anything at all that he has touched.

She's having trouble concentrating at the office, and she's terrified of losing her job. With Matt gone she's suddenly aware of every bill, every little possible repair. It feels like the Camry might need new brakes, and she knows they're due for two new tires. All the things that Matt would take care of or that they would discuss and decide together now tick through Angie's mind like an endless scroll.

Yesterday Angie drove out to the Holschers' farm and sat at Edna Holscher's kitchen table to go over this year's policy and then broke down crying for long minutes when Edna asked how she's holding up. This is not professional, she thinks, this is not what old man Beeman had in mind when he gave her these accounts.

Angie keeps a pair of tall rubber boots and a slicker in her car for her visits to her farms. Once she's appraised them for insurance purposes, everything from buildings to outbuildings to barns to vehicles and tractors and tools and animals, she feels like she belongs to them or they belong to her.

She knows the cost per head and replacement value of every last animal on every farm that she covers. This is another side of Angie, the flip side of the high heels and silk blouses. It was a surprise when old man Beeman took Angie under his wing and taught her the farm side of the business. Pretty Angie, the least likely adjustor in the office to be chosen by Beeman for farm work. Give her commercial real estate, give her residential, give her life insurance, who could say no to Angie? But farms? Try making sense out of that.

It's the big animals, she'll tell you; she fell in love with cows and horses and fields and farms and the way Route 20 curves through mile after mile of fertile, rolling land. Like stepping into another century.

The farmers and their wives were leery of Angie at first, even with old man Beeman vouching for her. But Angie sits in their linoleum-floored kitchens drinking coffee from percolators, adding sugar and cream until they laugh at her. The year she left her own Thanksgiving dinner to follow the fire trucks out to the Holschers' farm for the worst kind of fire, a barn fire, and stayed until every horse and cow was accounted for—the dead animals named and mourned, the living safely housed in temporary quarters—and sat, again, in the kitchen, her coat scorched, ash in her pretty hair; that was the year they took her in. Edna Holscher held her hand at the kitchen table, whispering in her ear so that Hank, pouring whiskey, couldn't hear: *Don't let this be what ruins us, Angie; don't let this be the last straw.*

And here she is, driving nearly an hour to sit in Edna's kitchen and cry because Edna will understand and because really, where else does she have to go?

Alice found her dad's blue shirt in the hamper the day she decided to do laundry because no one had any clean underpants left in their drawers. She set the shirt aside instead of tossing it into the washer. She laid it out on her bed for an afternoon, then put it under her pillow for a few nights. Now she's wearing it. Every night she airs it out and every day she rolls the cuffs up half a turn. She had to spot clean the left front when she inadvertently got into the middle of a ketchup fight in the cafeteria. She hates the fact that the Dad-ness of the shirt is evaporating. She still likes wearing it, though, no matter what Ellie says. Her mom just rolls her eyes. Alice thinks the two of them are planning an intervention so she's started to get very smart about where she airs it out each night.

Henry slams through the backdoor with a blast of clean, cold air, shouting, "Good morning, Mrs. Bliss!" just like he does every morning, whether she's in the kitchen or not. Henry's energy is just the catalyst they need to grab jackets and backpacks and get out the door.

On the way to the elementary school, Henry teaches Ellie and Alice a new round he has written especially for Ellie. It features about four hundred mentions of the word *fart*. He gets Ellie giggling so hard Alice thinks she's going to wet her pants. Henry grabs Ellie's recorder out of her backpack so he can play the tune and make big, fat *splat* sounds every time they sing the word *fart!* Tears are streaming down Ellie's face and she has to stop walking and cross her legs to keep from peeing.

Henry is the only person Alice knows who would sing, play music, and dance around like a maniac to make a second grader laugh. In public. Henry is also capable of walking to school carrying his clarinet case in front of him—sideways, which is so awkward, you think who carries *anything* like that?—while *at the same time* banging his knees against the case to work out some complicated rhythm for jazz band. This sort of thing used to mortify Alice; now it makes her laugh.

When they reach the grammar school bus circle, Ellie grabs her recorder from Henry and sprints to catch up to Janna. Alice and Henry head off across the playground and up the hill and through the playing fields that separate the schools. Henry pulls out his iPod and offers Alice one earbud.

"Listen to this, Alice."

They listen for a bit, walking shoulder to shoulder.

"Who is it?"

"Art Tatum. You ever hear of him?"

She shakes her head.

"He makes the piano *rock*. Listen to the way he rolls those bass notes."

She listens.

Henry reaches out his left hand, imitating what he hears with his fingers, as though he's playing air piano. It's amazing the way he can do that. He's got his eyes half closed, he's making funny faces, he's lucky he doesn't trip and break a leg. He opens his eyes and glances over at her, a grin on his face.

"Good, huh?"

"Yeah," she says, grinning back at him. "Really good."

March 15th

Two days later Alice is sitting in the kitchen, in the chair closest to the phone hanging on the wall, her homework scattered across the table, untouched. Matt ships out tonight and he will have a chance to call between five and nine. Alice staked out her spot by the phone at three, the minute she got home from school. Angie is coming home from work early, to be here by five, just in case.

Ellie and Janna are in Ellie's room playing dress up. Last week Gram gave Ellie a whole bagful of scarves and belts and hats and purses she's been collecting at yard sales. This is their first chance at the stuff.

For two hours as she tries to read chapters six through nine of *A Separate Peace*, Alice can hear Ellie and Janna laughing and talking. She can tell they've moved on to Angie's closet and are searching for high heels. They creep downstairs barefoot, slide into the heels and clomp their way to the kitchen for a TA DA! moment: two eight-year-olds in polyester old lady dresses, elaborately and multiply belted at the waist, fake fox furs, pillbox hats, high heels, and too much lipstick.

Alice tells them they look lovely.

"We're going on the *Queen Elizabeth!*" Ellie says.

"Around the world! The whole entire world," Janna adds.

"Really!"

"The most marvelous boat in the world, darling!"

"Just the two of you?"

"And Luke Piacci!!!!!"

Ellie sweeps out like an elegant matron, trailing fur and too much perfume. Janna wobbles and then trips making her turn, but tosses a brave smile over her shoulder anyway.

Watching Ellie and Janna reminds Alice of her friend Stephie Larson or, more accurately, her former friend Stephie Larson. They were inseparable all through ninth grade after they both got stuck in crazy Mr. Bartolotto's French class. But over the summer Stephie stopped eating and stopped being a pudgy kid and when tenth grade began she started hanging out with a different crowd at school. Last month, when Alice's dad left for Fort Dix, Stephie was being kind of friendly, actually speaking to her in the girl's room or between classes. Not a lot. Not anything like the way it used to be, not laughing, not making plans, just the occasional word or two, when nobody else was around. Today Alice must have lost her mind because she approached Stephie while she was talking to Jennifer White and Stephie actually pretended she didn't hear her or see her.

She looks up to see Ellie in the front hall daring Janna to kiss the newel post.

"Pretend it's Luke Piacci," she giggles.

Alice wishes the phone would ring right now, with Mom gone and Ellie otherwise engaged. She wants five minutes to talk to her dad without an audience, without anyone telling her to hurry up, without Ellie shouting, "My turn! My turn!" She stares at the phone, willing it to ring, and when it does she nearly jumps out of her seat.

"Dad?"

"No, it's me, Alice. Henry."

"I can't talk right now. We're waiting for my dad."

"I thought that was after five."

"It could be anytime."

"Have you done your math homework?"

"Henry!"

"I can't get number six. Or number five either."

"I haven't looked at it."

"Oh."

"I have to go."

"Alice—"

"What!?"

"Did you—"

"Henry, hurry up!"

"Are you avoiding me?"

"No. But I have to go."

"Really?"

"Really."

"Okay."

She hangs up and sits with her hand on the phone, thinking call now, Dad, right now. She glances at the clock: ten to five. You and I could talk, then Mom gets home and you guys have your time, then Ellie. Just five minutes. Just one minute. Just . . .

She closes her eyes and she can imagine the line at the bank of phones on the base. The lucky guys with their own cell phones, talking as long as they want. The rest of them waiting to call, some poor schmo having to keep the line moving, cut the calls short.

Is he already packed? Is he hungry, is he tired, is he lonely? Is he scared of this phone call? She's scared she's gonna cry and end up not telling him . . . telling him what exactly? How do you take the stupid daily details that don't mean anything at all, like yesterday's math test and the way she just blanked out and couldn't think at all, and the new coffee Gram is trying out in the café, and what's in the news about the war and what's not in the news about the war; how is she supposed to pretend that this is all fine and normal and she can handle it when . . .

Suddenly she's angry; she's so angry so quickly she feels like her head could come off. Why is he doing this? Is there something wrong with her? If she were different, if she were better, smarter, prettier, then would he stay? Why isn't Mom enough? And Ellie and Gram and the garden and his baseball team? Why isn't any one of those things enough anymore?

The phone rings. It's exactly five, she notices, as she picks up the receiver. Mom must be stuck in traffic.

"Dad," she says, and her voice sounds dead.

"Honey? Alice? How are you?"

"Fine."

"Where are you?"

"The kitchen."

"Doing homework?"

"Sort of."

"Where's Mom?"

"Not home yet."

"And Ellie?"

"Upstairs playing dress up with Janna."

"We don't have a lot of time. You want to call Ellie to the phone?"

"No."

"What?"

"I want . . ."

"Alice?"

36

"Don't go," she manages to choke out.

"Alice, honey, listen—"

She hears Mom's car in the driveway.

"Mom's home."

"Okay."

"I'll call Ellie."

"Wait!—Alice, are you still there?"

"Yeah."

"We said our good-byes, remember? Let's just have this be a regular call, like hi, how are you?"

"You want to pretend?"

"What?"

"You want me to *pretend?*"

And then Mom is through the door and standing beside her.

"I just want to hear your voice, honey. To take that with me. Maybe hear you laugh. I don't know."

"Keep talking."

"Is Mom there?"

"Yes. But—"

"You can stay on. Or you could get on the extension."

"That's okay. Here's Mom."

"Sweetheart?" Angie says into the phone.

"Angie. . ."

Even Alice can hear the longing in his voice when he says *Angie* like that. She knows she should leave the room; she should give them their moment, but she can hear his voice faintly, and she can't walk away from that any more than she could talk when she was on the phone.

"Are you okay?" Angie asks.

"Yeah. Fine. We're in good shape."

"Did you get the package we sent?"

"Tell Alice and Ellie I loved the cookies. And your mom."

"I know we don't have much time—"

"What are you wearing?"

"*Matt!*"

"I want to picture you."

"I'm wearing that navy dress you like. With the belt."

"And heels."

"Yes. Heels."

"What's Alice wearing?"

Mom holds out the phone to Alice.

"You want to tell him?"

Alice takes the phone.

"Jeans, high tops, and your blue shirt."

"You're wearing my clothes?"

"Just your shirt."

"Send me pictures. Okay, Alice? Send me pictures."

He sounds so young. It's hard to think of her dad as young, but his voice, there's another note in it now. That upper layer of control that's always there is suddenly gone and he sounds like he feels, she thinks. The realization, he *is* scared, suddenly shoots through her like an adrenaline rush.

"Go get Ellie," Angie says, reaching for the phone.

But Alice won't give up the phone. Now she's ready to pretend, she's ready to do whatever it takes to get her dad's voice back to normal.

"Dad," she says, "Dad—?"

"I'm right here, sweetheart."

Angie shakes her head and walks through the dining room to the stairs where she calls up to Ellie to come to the phone.

"Uncle Eddie is taking us to the movies, and it's only three more weeks until the equinox and the Red Wings home opener, and Henry might flunk math this term even though I keep trying to help him, and ever since you left, it's hard to concentrate, and Mrs. Piantowski might be having another baby or maybe she's just getting fatter, and Gram says . . ."

"It's Ellie's turn," Angie says, taking the phone from Alice.

Alice sinks into a kitchen chair and pretends to listen to her sister chatter on about Janna and Janna's new bunk bed with a desk built right into the side of it, and how Ellie thinks she wants to write and draw pictures for a book about a sleepover where the bunk beds are stacked ten high and go right through the ceiling and reach up to the sky with magic ladders.

"Draw me pictures," she hears her dad say. "Draw me lots of pictures."

Her mom takes the phone and shoos both girls out of the kitchen so she can have a minute alone with Dad.

Alice listens outside the door.

"Did you get your orders?"

"Yeah, we did."

"Where are they putting you?"

"F.O.B. Falcon. For the time being."

"Where's that?"

"Somewhere between Baghdad and Falluja."

"I don't like the sound of that."

"It should be pretty interesting, actually."

"Still reconnaissance and surveillance?"

"And artillery."

"I thought you'd be in engineering."

"It's the surge, Angie. They need boots on the ground."

"Or transport. Or supply. Or security."

"You get assigned."

"What about rebuilding roads and schools and bridges and . . . Do they know you're an engineer?"

"Of course."

"Your CO. Does he know? Can you remind him?"

"It's the *army,* Angie."

"I know, but——"

"Write to me, sweetheart."

"Okay."

"Letters are like . . . You have no idea how important they are. Mail call . . ."

"Every day."

"Promise me."

"I promise."

"You're my girl and I love you."

"Come home to me."

"I will. You know I will."

The doorbell rings; Janna's mother Joyce is at the door. Alice helps find Janna's back pack and sneakers, the Shrek lunch box, and her jacket and sweater, and she even manages to say the right things to Janna's mom, who is on her way home from her job at the cosmetics store at the mall and looks tired and a little frazzled.

"My feet are killing me, my cheeks are killing me, I'm so sick of smiling; I can't wait to get home and have a nice cold beer. I probably shouldn't say that in front of you kids, but a day like today? A beer is my one true reward."

She and Janna head down the walk.

Ellie waves from the door.

"I'm gonna draw Daddy a picture right now."

"Good idea."

"I'm gonna draw Daddy a picture every day."

"He'll like that."

"And send it to him. So I can tell him my story, little by little, day by day, like we're on the installment plan."

Ellie gets out her crayons and markers and paper and starts to draw right there at the dining room table with Alice beside her. Alice digs her math homework out of her back pocket and starts solving problems with one of Ellie's pencils. They sit there, drawing and doing math, like they're not hungry, like it's not time for dinner, like they can't hear their mother sobbing on the other side of the kitchen door.

"You want to take a walk?" Alice asks.

"Now? I'm hungry."

"I know."

"Maybe we shouldn't leave Mom."

"Just for a little while."

"Okay."

In the front hall they pull on jackets. Ellie steps into her pink boots and insists on finding the matching mittens to her pink hat.

Outside it's colder and darker than either of them expected. At the end of their driveway they turn left and head away from their usual route to school on Baird Road. The sidewalks are covered with rutted, frozen slush. Ellie reaches out and takes Alice's hand. They walk for a while, not saying anything, their breath puffing out of their mouths. Alice tries to make rings with her breath but can't. Ellie tries snorting like a dragon to see if she can get steam to come out of her nose.

"Is it winter where Daddy is going?"

"Yeah."

"Winter like this?"

"I don't know. I think so."

"Snow and everything?"

"I'll find out."

"I'm cold."

As they turn toward home, Ellie trips and falls on the ice, hard. Alice picks her up before she can even start crying and feels something warm and wet on her neck.

"Is your nose bleeding?"

Ellie puts one pink mitten up to her nose, it comes away red, and she starts to wail.

"It's okay, Ellie. We'll get you fixed up at home."

"My mittens!"

"They'll be okay."

"No they won't!"

"I'll wash them."

"They're my favorite ones."

"I know."

"Can't you go any faster? Daddy can carry me faster."

"He's bigger than me."

"And stronger. And nicer."

"I'm being pretty nice right now."

"Can I have ice cream for dinner?"

"Not that nice."

Ellie gets heavier and heavier with every step. When Alice finally turns into their yard, she's sweating and breathing hard. They get through the front door and head straight into the kitchen. Mom is long gone. No dinner preparations in sight. Alice sits Ellie right on the sink and starts to assess the damage.

"I think you're gonna live."

"Is it broken?"

"Not a chance."

"You sure?"

"Split your lip, though."

"Really?"

"And you've got a little gash on your chin."

Alice slips off Ellie's jacket and turns it inside out so she can't see the blood. She grabs a paper towel and wipes Ellie's blood from her cheek and chin.

"You're a mess, Alice."

"Thanks a lot."

She tosses her own jacket on top of Ellie's.

"Give me your mittens, too. I'll get them soaking downstairs."

"Will you make dinner?"

"As soon as I put our jackets in the wash. I'm gonna give you some ice for your lip, okay?"

She hands Ellie an ice cube wrapped in a dishcloth.

"Hold that right on your lip. Don't press. I'll be right back."

Alice runs down the basement stairs, turns on the washer, and fills up the sink to soak Ellie's mittens. She's secretly glad to have stuff to do. She charges back up the stairs and checks out the fridge.

"You good with grilled cheese and tomato soup?"

"Again?"

Alice gives her a look.

"Get your book and read in here to keep me company, okay?"

"Should I call Mom?"

"No, let's surprise her."

"I could make her a tray."

"Good idea."

While Alice makes grilled cheese sandwiches, the slow, slow, slow way her dad makes them, Ellie gets the tray off the hall table. She finds a cloth napkin to make a little placemat, then sets the tray with the nice china from the china cabinet.

"I need a flower and a vase."

"You could draw one."

"And then can I stir the soup?"

"Yup."

"And pour the milk?"

"It's really heavy, Ellie."

"I can do it."

Alice pulls the stool over so Ellie can stir the soup. She sets the table for the two of them.

"The tray looks nice."

"You think Mom will like it?" Ellie asks.

"Yup."

"I want ice cream for dessert."

"Okay."

"Neapolitan."

"We'll see what we've got."

Alice pours soup into bowls and cuts the sandwiches in triangles the way Ellie likes them, while Ellie pours the milk.

"I want to carry the tray."

"How about if you carry the plate and I'll carry the tray with the soup."

"I won't spill."

"It's even hard for me not to spill."

"Okay."

Upstairs, neither one of them has a hand free to knock on the door to the bedroom. Ellie gives three little kicks with her foot.

"Mom?"

The room is dark. Angie has kicked off her heels and is lying on top of the bed with a cold cloth over her eyes.

"Mom?"

"Not now."

"We brought you some dinner."

"I'm really not hungry."

"On a tray."

Angie opens her eyes and sits up in bed. She reaches over and turns on the bedside lamp. Alice sets the tray on her lap. Ellie sets the pink scallop-edged plate with the grilled cheese sandwich in the exact center of the tray.

"I split my lip on the ice," Ellie says.

"We just went for a little walk."

"My nose was bleeding, too. I bled all over Alice."

"It's okay. I've got our jackets in the wash already."

"Alice carried me all the way home and fixed me up and made

44

dinner. I helped. I drew you a flower because we didn't have one to put on your tray."

Angie reaches out to touch Ellie's lip. She wants to say thank you but she's not sure she can trust herself to say anything at all.

After dinner, after washing the dishes and locking up the house, Alice climbs upstairs to find that Ellie has fallen asleep with her clothes on right on top of the covers. Ellie should have had a bath, Alice realizes, but it's too late now. She pulls off Ellie's shoes and socks and sweater and manages to slide her under the covers. How can she sleep through all that? Her lip is swelling and her chin has a dark bruise.

Alice sits down at her desk by the window and realizes that none of her homework is done and she is too tired to read about the Revolutionary War now. She looks across the backyard to her dad's workshop sitting squat and dark in the moonlight. That is absolutely too sad to dwell on, so she opens the window and sticks her head out, craning her neck to see Henry's house down the block, but his window is dark, too. She looks at her dad's watch and rights it on her wrist so she can read the dial: ten o'clock.

She listens to Ellie snoring and thinks of hearing her dad's voice coming through the phone, saying: "Angie . . . ?" Did they say good-bye? Did they ever actually say good-bye? She thinks of her mom's untouched tray, Ellie's bloody mittens, she hopes their jackets will be dry in the morning, and somewhere in there—after she gets up and gets her old stuffed bear off the shelf, which feels silly and childish but right now she doesn't care—somewhere in there, she falls asleep.

March 23rd

Alice and Henry walk Ellie to school every morning, and then instead of climbing the hill and crossing the middle school playing fields to

45

get to the high school, they go the long way around, down Belknap Road and past the Four Corners. Alice and Henry could take the bus but they both hate the bus. Nothing good ever happens on that bus. They walk no matter what the weather so they can just *be* for twenty minutes before school. They don't talk much; some days they don't talk at all.

Henry and Alice have known each other, as their parents like to say, since they were in utero. This phraseology has become less and less charming the older they get. They've also been stuck having play dates since they were born because their families are neighbors. This was not such a big deal in grade school. Fifth grade got a little uncomfortable. If they could have gone to different middle and high schools it might've been better. But it is what it is.

The facts include things like Henry coming home from school in second grade and telling his mom, "I'm going to marry Alice. William wants to marry her, too, but he can't." Their mothers repeat this stuff. Still! They also got caught—of course—stealing candy from Mr. Ricci's corner store and playing doctor and locking Ellie in a closet—she had a flashlight!—and whatever else little kids get up to. And just when Alice thinks she can't stand one more day of enforced friendship with Henry, he will do something so amazing that she thinks he's a saint or something.

Henry was always small for his age. So small that his parents worried and his doctors worried and Henry had to go through all these tests and things. But in the last six months, he has grown six inches. Henry is not the same boy. At all.

Sometimes Alice looks into his face and sees that his eyes are grayer and he has these cheekbones that look about as sharp as his ankles and wrists. Everything about Henry is a little angular and over defined, like all that fast growing hasn't given his skin a chance to catch up yet. It's like he's still two people: little kid Henry and growing up

46

Henry, and Alice is watching those two people switch places right in front of her eyes.

Henry's brother, Rob, is a lot older. He's already graduated from college in Boston and is working for a relief organization in Haiti. So his parents are older, too, and Alice's mom is always saying that Henry's the kind of kid who needs to come from a big family. He needs the noise and the friction and the company. Not that the Blisses actually qualify as a big family, but if you add Henry, their numbers start to look a little more substantial.

Today Henry is worried about baseball tryouts. He loves to play baseball, but he pretty much sucks in every position. And Alice, who goes to most of Henry's games, has seen him play just about every position. Coaches move Henry around the field, thinking if they could just harness all that enthusiasm, some talent might emerge.

Alice has spent long spring and summer evenings playing catch with Henry, trying to pitch for Henry, and trying to field for Henry. Occasionally her dad would join them and they'd toss the ball around in the spring twilight, the streetlights coming on one by one, crickets whirring, that damp, green spring smell redolent in the air around them. Something else was in the air as well; something about promise and possibility and another beginning, another summer just around the corner.

But with her dad gone, they have not been tossing the ball around much. In fact, Alice doesn't even know where her mitt is.

The whole tryout thing is one horrible round of humiliation after another for Henry. Alice is about to offer to come with him when Henry says he might not try out for baseball this year after all.

Alice is shocked at this news and possibly also a little bit glad for Henry that he can stop feeling so bad trying to do something he loves so much. But then there's this other reaction, like why the hell does everything have to change all the time?

47

She doesn't say any of this, of course, because what could she say? I'm shocked-sad-mad-disgusted-furious, I want to scream at you, I want to celebrate. She sounds schizophrenic, even inside her own head.

She just keeps walking, keeps her head down. She's chewing her lip and tastes blood—damn! Now that's gonna bug her all day. And then they're passing Mrs. Minty's house.

Mrs. Minty lives alone, and Mrs. Minty always comes out on her porch and waves to Henry and Alice. Mrs. Minty is old. Really old, like from another century. But that doesn't stop her from tutoring at the library, where she runs the literacy program. Teaching adults to read and write two afternoons and two evenings a week.

There she is in her tweed skirt and cardigan sweater and those dark brown tie shoes with a little heel. Her hair is in a bun. Her dad used to say, "Mrs. Minty looks like she just stepped out of a bandbox." Whatever *that* is.

"Good morning, Alice! Good morning, Henry!"

"Good morning, Mrs. Minty!"

Henry gives her a little wave. Henry always gives her a little wave.

"Henry, I wonder if you wouldn't mind stopping by after school. I need some help moving a few boxes."

"Sure thing, Mrs. Minty."

"Alice, you come, too. I'm baking cookies this afternoon."

"Yes, ma'am."

Mrs. Minty is smiling at her, not some sappy, oh you poor thing smile, but just a regular spring morning smile. Alice stops. Henry is shuffling his feet and giving her all the nonverbal *let's go* signals he can think of. But Alice ignores him. She stands still right there on the sidewalk and takes a good long look.

The apple tree in Mrs. Minty's front yard is full of fat buds getting ready to bloom. And it's full of birds, too, and they're all singing. Alice didn't notice the birds before, but now she does. They're making a racket. How could she not notice this? And then she looks down into the green, green grass and Mrs. Minty's whole yard is filled with tiny white and blue flowers.

"Those are pretty flowers, Mrs. Minty."

"Snowbells and scilla. Some of the first to bloom each spring. They'll even bloom in the snow. My husband and I planted a hundred bulbs thirty years ago. Now there are thousands."

Henry actually takes Alice by the arm and pulls her away, giving Mrs. Minty a last wave.

Alice is thinking she'd like to just lie down in Mrs. Minty's front yard and skip school altogether, but Henry has this death grip on her elbow and before she knows it, he is propelling her up the drive to school.

They're early—as usual—so they head to the auditorium, which has the only decent piano in the school. The janitor has given Henry the key so Henry can come in and play whenever he wants. This is strictly against the rules. The janitor, Mr. Herlihy, and Henry have decided, after much wrangling and discussion back and forth, that they don't care about that stupid rule.

Mr. Herlihy, it turns out, loves music. He has a huge collection of old jazz records. LPs he calls them. And whenever he can, he slips inside the auditorium and sits in the last row to listen to that kid Henry Grover playing in the dark.

Henry rigs up his book lamp so it creates a little puddle of light, and Alice climbs up onto the lip of the stage, and angles her book into the one spot where there's almost enough light to read by. Henry plays while Alice finishes her English homework.

Henry likes this arrangement. He gets to improvise and no one makes comments. Alice never tells him to shut up or play something different. Alice lies on the stage and reads, and sometimes she puts her book down and just listens to him. Every once in a while she'll tell him she likes what he's playing, or she'll make him stop and listen while she tells him he's gonna be a great musician one day. Every once in a while he can see the music take her someplace else and he can see the old Alice, the six-year-old or the ten-year-old or even the twelve-year-old Alice.

Alice abandons *The Catcher in the Rye* and looks up into the darkness. The velvet curtain smells old and musty, and everything around them is shrouded in shadow. She's trying not to think about her father, about waiting and waiting for the letters that are taking forever to get to them, about the too quick, too hurried call when he first arrived, with every other word breaking up on them, none of them certain that anything they were saying was actually getting through.

She scoots over until she's lying underneath the piano. Here she can feel the sound reverberating in the floor below her and in the piano above her. She closes her eyes and breathes with Henry's playing, until the notes are inside her heartbeat and the notes are in her breathing and the notes are flowing through her veins.

March 24th

After her last class the following day, American history, Mr. Herman hands Alice a blank piece of paper with her name at the top of it, and wants an explanation as to why Alice didn't even bother to try answering one single question on yesterday's pop quiz. She looks out the window, looking for an answer maybe, and sees the track team lope out onto the track.

"Do I need to call your parents?"

She drags her attention back to Mr. Herman and the blank piece of paper in her hand.

"What?"

"Your parents. Do we need to get them involved?"

"No. No. Definitely not. You don't need to call them. I wasn't feeling well."

"You should have told me."

"I didn't really realize until it was too late."

"You should have come to me after class, then."

"Can I make up the test?"

"I'm afraid not."

She steals a quick look at him. He's being a hard-ass because he thinks she's a good student and maybe he can shock her back into line. She thinks, I used to care about this; I used to be able to care about this, when her attention is drawn back to the runners outside on the track.

"I'm gonna miss my bus, Mr. Herman."

"Don't let this happen again, Alice."

"I won't."

She is released; she is walking out the door, running down the hall, and slamming through the back doors that lead out to the playing fields and the track. Dumping her backpack and jacket on the ground, she jogs over to the coach.

"Can I run?" She asks.

"Can you?"

"I don't know. I want to run."

"What's your name?"

"Alice Bliss."

He makes a note on his clipboard.

"Grade?"

"Tenth."

"You have any shorts? Sneaks?"

"I've got these," indicating her battered Chucks.

"Take it easy, okay? We're just warming up. It's our first day out-doors."

"Okay, okay, but I can run?"

"We'll see about that."

Alice sprints to catch up with the runners who are doing laps and falls in beside a tall redheaded girl who looks like she knows what she's doing. The girl turns her head and gives Alice a half smile. Alice in her jeans feels like a mule next to this gazelle, but it's fun to try to match her stride, to lift her head, the way this girl does, to begin to sweat. She's feeling the cool early-spring air and the clouds crossing the sun, and her body, she's feeling her body, and her legs are starting to ache and feel heavy, but it doesn't matter; she's running, she's breathing, and for a second, for a tantalizing series of seconds, she's feeling free.

That night B.D., the coach, calls her mother and tells her that maybe they should get her a pair of running shoes. And shorts and a T-shirt and a sweatshirt, too. Angie wants to know what this is all about.

Alice just says, "I guess I joined the track team."

March 31st

Alice makes a deal with Henry so he'll pick up Ellie and take her home with him on the days she has practice, which is turning into every day. Henry doesn't seem too happy about this, but Ellie loves it. Ellie and Mrs. Grover have started to play Scrabble. Ellie is memorizing all of the acceptable two letter words. Mrs. Grover is scrambling to keep up. Their scores are going through the roof. They've even ordered competitive Scrabble playing dictionaries via interlibrary loan. Mrs. Grover has set up an extra table in the dining room dedicated to Scrabble. Don't even think about doing your homework at that table. And every day at four thirty she serves tea in real china teacups. With little cakes. And sometimes special sandwiches.

Mrs. Grover is good at doing things that really matter but nobody notices. Like being nice to eight-year-olds, or running the community drive to collect children's books for the nursery at the YMCA, or supplying the local kindergarten with craft supplies after all the budget cuts eliminated just about everything except construction paper and snub-nosed scissors. All the kindergartners love Mrs. Grover's feathers, which she collects all year long on her walks through the Mendon Woods, or around Pond View Reservoir, or out by the lake.

Today, right before practice starts, Stephie and a clutch of older girls pass Alice and the other runners on their way to the student parking lot. Alice knows that Stephie, whose new friends call her Steph, as though two syllables are just too much trouble, would not be caught dead running. Stephie is paler than usual and she's wearing one of those push-up bras and a short skirt. When Jeremy Baskin, a senior, catches up to her and runs his hand over her ass, Stephie looks over her shoulder at Alice. But she's too far away now, and Alice can't tell if that's defiance or fear.

Alice turns back to the track. Ginger, the redhead, tosses her a baton on the fly as she sprints past her. They run, one forward, one backward, tossing the baton back and forth. Ginger's hair is cut almost as short as a boy's, she has strong legs and big feet, and she never looks down when she runs, she only looks up. She plays with the baton like Ellie would, and, with her energy and her quickness, she lifts Alice into a world where running *is* play.

Alice finds herself fantasizing about being the school's top tenth-grade 400-meter runner, not that there are a lot of other tenth-grade girls giving up cheerleading or softball to be on the track team. The idea that she might have talent at such a simple thing is amazing. Henry just rolls his eyes when she talks about running sprints while B.D. screams at her: "Breathe, breathe, *breathe!*"

But nobody needs to scream at Alice to run or to breathe. When she's running she doesn't want to stop, she just wants to keep going. She feels something she's never felt before; she feels powerful and strong, she feels like no one can hurt her. Being outdoors, getting into a groove, the freedom and the repetitiveness of her stride; she doesn't know what it is, exactly, but something settles in her head. Running for time or for distance, on the track, on the roads, through the woods, getting lost, falling, the hard runs, the easy runs, all of it, every minute of it, she's living and breathing in another world. It is an escape so profound she finds herself longing for school to end and running to begin.

Alice arrives home to find Mom and Ellie waiting in the car.

"You're late," Ellie says.

"Late for what?"

"I have a surprise for you girls," Angie says, as she pulls out of the driveway.

"Daddy called!" Ellie crows.

"And I missed it? Are you kidding me?"

"An incredibly quick call," Angie says.

"Like five minutes. Super fast."

"He's moving to a new base. And it's normal for mail to be slow."

"Write me, he said to me; and to Mom and to you, Alice. He wants letters. Lots of letters. I've already written him two times and drawn four pictures."

"Where are we going?" Alice asks.

"You'll see," Angie says.

"Did he say where he is?"

"F.O.B. Falcon," Ellie says.

"For the time being," Angie adds.

"What's F.O.B?"

"Forward Operating Base."

"Everything has an acronym in the army," Ellie says. "Like they've got their own special language. F.O.B. and TNT and HQ and IED."

"What do you know about IEDs?"

"They keep inventing new ones: VBIED: vehicle borne IED; SVBIED: suicide vehicle borne IED; DBIED: dog borne or donkey borne IED."

54

"Where do you get these little tips?" Alice asks.

"Bobby DiFiori in the fourth grade likes to watch CNN."

"And he talks about this stuff?!"

"On the playground. At recess."

"Oh, my God . . ."

Angie pulls up to the Holschers' farmhouse and beeps the horn, like it's a prearranged signal. Edna comes out the front door and Hank walks up from behind the barn. They're both wearing muck boots and barn jackets and grinning from ear to ear.

Mom makes introductions, and Edna walks right up and takes Ellie by the hand.

"Mrs. Holscher . . ." Ellie begins.

"Call me Edna."

"Where are we going?"

"You'll see."

They all follow Edna and Ellie to the barn, all the way down the central aisle to the last stall on the left.

Hank unhooks the door.

"Go ahead."

Inside the stall, in knee deep straw is a mama goat and three brand new baby kids, nursing.

Ellie goes right to her knees, beside them.

"They were born yesterday afternoon," Hank offers. "Triplets. Can you beat that?"

"Can I touch them?" Ellie can barely contain her excitement.

"Sure."

"The mama won't mind?"

"Let her see you. Go slow," Edna says.

"What's her name?" Alice asks.

"Goldie."

"Hi, Goldie," Alice says, stroking her nose.

55

"Can I hold one?" Ellie asks.

"As soon as they're done nursing, they'll be climbing all over you."

Ellie is petting the baby goats and Alice joins her while Angie, Edna, and Hank watch them.

"They're so cute. Can we bring one home?"

"They're gonna get big, Ellie."

"I don't care."

"We've picked out two names for the babies so far," Edna says. "Blondie and Walden. Got any good ideas for the third kid?"

Ellie considers.

"What kind of goats are they?" Alice asks.

"LaManchas. Milk goats from Spain. They're friendly, easy to handle, and great producers. You like goat's milk?" Hank asks.

"I don't know, I've never tried it."

"I like it," Ellie announces.

"You've never had it either!"

"I can just tell."

"Can you tell who's who?" Angie asks.

"The gray one is Walden. The sandy colored one is Blondie. And the one with the white feet needs a name."

"Niblets," Ellie says.

"Niblets it is." Hank laughs.

"Really?"

The kids finish nursing and, just like Edna said, they climb all over the girls, nibbling their fingers, rubbing their heads against them. Ellie is giggling.

"I can't believe how soft they are," Alice says.

"Hi, Niblets," Ellie whispers into the white-footed kid's ear, as she hugs him against her.

"We've got baby lambs and new chicks, too, if you want to see them," Hank says.

"Maybe later," Ellie says, in a dreamy voice.

"C'mon in the house when you're ready. Just be sure to latch the stall door."

Alice looks up and smiles at her mom; just a wide-open uncomplicated happy kid smile. Angie bursts into a laugh.

"They're great, aren't they?"

"Yeah. Really great."

Hank puts his arm around Angie's shoulder as the grown-ups turn to leave the barn.

"I made pineapple upside down cake," Edna calls back to them. "And you can try some goat's milk when you come inside."

April 4th

Matt's letters are finally starting to arrive. Sometimes in a bunch, sometimes just one for Angie. He writes Angie every day he's not out on patrol.

Ellie collects the mail from the mailbox after school and puts everything on the hall table. Alice and Ellie never open anything until Angie gets home, no matter how tempting. After work, Angie pours herself a glass of wine and they all sit in the living room to open the letter, or letters if they're lucky. If there's only one, one for Mom, she'll read the sections she feels she can share or things Dad asks her to tell them.

Tell Ellie we get M&Ms in our ration packets. Some of them are dated 1992.

Tell Eddie there's a 21-year-old kid named Lewis from West Virginia who has a 1982 Ford Mustang. He's planning on going to all the hot-rod shows when he gets home. And there's this new kid named Chad. 19. Hell of a poker player. He's from Wyoming and he loves Texas Hold 'Em. He laughs and laughs every time he takes his buddies' money.

Tell Ellie I saw a blue and green parrot when we were outside the wire yesterday. Perched on a toppled date palm. Where the heck did he come from? Later that day, a dirty, dusty old tabby cat walked out of a building we'd just dropped twenty shells on. Each one big enough to end the world. Tail in the air. Unbelievable.

Tell Alice she will not believe what I have to do to get some coffee when we're out on patrol. There's no electricity and no more water than what we're carrying on our backs. After two hours of sleeping on a cement floor, coffee becomes very important. I collect packets of Taster's Choice instant coffee from the kids who are too young to be hooked on the stuff. And then I beg the powdered-cream and sugar packets we all get in our prefab rations. You open your mouth, pour in all three, toss in some water, and shake your head violently. Instant coffee. Outside the wire. Good morning, sunshine!

The part of the letter Angie won't read, or can't read, or can't trust herself to give voice to, says:

Angie, sweetheart,

I miss you more than I could have ever believed. I knew I was going to miss you but I had no idea how much. And it doesn't go away, it doesn't calm down, it doesn't fit inside my pocket with your letters. It's like an ache, Angie, a constant ache for you.

I can't imagine all the weeks and months ahead of missing you.

I miss our girls, I miss work, the house, the garden. Nothing like being out here to make you appreciate home.

You'll laugh at me, but I love thinking about closing up the house every night. Walking downstairs barefoot, turning out lights, locking the back door. Just that sense of easy quiet, knowing the girls are safe in bed, and that you're in our bed waiting for me. Home. I dream of home, Angie, and you know I dream of you.

    Matt

Later, when Alice slips the letter out of the envelope and reads it as fast as she can, the words, no, the feelings, the impossibly intense feelings burn into her. It's like opening a bedroom door.

April 5th

Three weeks after Matt ships out Ellie gets the stool so she can reach Matt's shelf of favorite books. First up: his leather-bound college dictionary.

She brings this to the breakfast table and announces she's going to read the dictionary while Daddy is gone. Alice is thinking, *yeah, right,* as Ellie opens Webster's Dictionary, Second Edition, reads the inscription from Dad's mom wishing him good luck in college, and begins at the beginning, right there on page one. While eating Cheerios. Ellie gets up and digs a pink notebook out of her school backpack and begins noting down superfascinating words.

Ellie's current teacher is a dictionary nut. She purportedly has hundreds of dictionaries, though this does not sound remotely credible to Alice. Where do you put them? What do you do with them? What, exactly, is the point? She tries to imagine perky Mrs. Baker, who is not even five feet tall, saying to her husband, "I'm just going to curl up with a good dictionary."

But none of this matters to Ellie, the annoying little autodidact. She is eating up the *A*'s like they are the elixir of knowledge, like this is a book with a plot, an action adventure, mystery, crime thriller, page turner, can't-put-it-down-exciting read.

"Ellie," Alice can't resist saying, "Dad *used* the dictionary, he didn't read it."

"How do you know what Daddy did or didn't do in college?"

"If she wants to read the dictionary, let her read the dictionary," Angie chimes in.

"You don't think it's a little—"

"Mrs. Baker says there can be ineffable joy in pursuing the absurd."

Both Alice and Angie turn to stare at Ellie and think, simultaneously—if that's possible—where does she come up with this stuff? and, Ellie and Mrs. Baker were made for each other.

"You want to know my new favorite word?" Ellie asks.

As if they could say no.

"*Sesquipedalian,* which means *'long word.'* I'm collecting them: long, rare words."

Angie is making sandwiches for a change, Alice notices, as she opens the paper to international news. It's just PB & J, but still. And then she sees the headline.

"Gram's taking you two for haircuts after school today."

"Finally!" Ellie says.

Alice closes the paper, folds it in half.

"She'll pick you up here at four thirty."

"I have practice."

"I know exactly what I want. I have a picture," Ellie announces.

"You'll just have to get out of practice a little early, Alice."

"You're gonna be surprised, Mom," Ellie sings.

"I don't need a haircut."

"Just a trim."

"I don't need a trim."

"Do you know how long it took me to get the two of you an appointment when Gram was available?"

"Ellie could still go."

"You're both going. End of discussion."

"But, Mom—"

Henry arrives, shouting, "Good morning, Mrs. Bliss!" As they head out the door, Alice grabs the front section of the paper. She passes up Henry's invitation to come to the auditorium while he plays piano and instead sits on the front steps and watches all the students and

60

teachers arriving at school. Does everyone have a secret life, she wonders? Is everyone carrying an impossible, unbearable secret?

Students stream up the steps and into the building past the army recruiter's table, the baseball bake sale table, and the lone ninth-grade girl passing out fliers for the pep rally. When the stream becomes a trickle she gets up, dusts off the back of her pants, and heads into school, down the hall, past the principal's office, on her way to the stairs to her homeroom. She suddenly notices that everything is worn: the linoleum, the paint on the edges of the doors, the ceiling is cracked and veined. When she glances into the principal's office she can see Mrs. Bradley; even Mrs. Bradley looks worn as she pulls her sky blue sweater over her soft stomach and then leans over to search for a file in the file cabinet. Alice is trying to remember—didn't somebody tell her that one of Mrs. Bradley's kids died of cancer when they were little? Yet here she is every day.

Mr. Fisher, who actually knows every single kid in all four grades in the high school by name, steps out from his office to ask Mrs. Bradley for something and before he speaks, his forehead is creased in a frown. He is pinching the bridge of his nose, as though to relieve pressure or pain. Both of them look pale and drained. And there it is again: worn.

Mr. Fisher straightens his slumped shoulders, leans both fists on Mrs. Bradley's desk, and says something that makes her laugh. You can tell he used to be a football player; he's got that low to the ground swagger to his walk even though he's now too chubby and about fifteen years too old to pull that off particularly well.

Alice's legs are feeling so heavy she's not sure she'll be able to walk up the flight of stairs to her homeroom. Maybe she could just head on down the first floor hall to the nurse's office and ask to lie down. Or back out the door and down the street to Gram's apartment, or all the way home. Suddenly she just wants to lie down on the floor. She crosses to the wall and leans against a locker. She manages to slide along the wall to a seated position before she falls down. She's thinking she should bend her knees; she should fold herself up so no one will notice her, but her legs are ignoring her. She grabs fistfuls of her dad's shirt as she wraps her arms around herself, trying to hold on to something solid. She's having trouble breathing. She thinks she might scream or throw up or pass out. She thinks that not one of these options is a good one.

The National Guard and marine recruiters are folding up their tables, packing their brochures into boxes, chatting and laughing and greeting students they seem to already know by name. Their uniforms, their boots, their bearing, everything about them seems to be shouting at her to pull herself together.

Bells start ringing; she's missed homeroom entirely. How did that happen? Doors are being flung open and she can hear hundreds of feet coming down the hallways above her and all around her. She brings her hands up to her ears to drown out the sound.

A crowd eddies around her, edging closer. No one approaches her, no one kneels down to ask if she's okay. Some kids gawk and move on, others hang on waiting to see how this will play out. Alice keeps her hands clamped over her ears so she can't hear their comments.

The principal has put on his suit jacket and straightened his tie. He is moving down the hallway at the fastest clip he is capable of with the school nurse in tow, the very small, very shy Miss Lambert. They are pushing through the crowds of students, and Mr. Fisher is reminding them to *Keep moving! Get to class!* The students reluctantly break up to let him through, and most of them head off to class. A few just draw back slightly to watch from a safer distance. No one is saying much. Mr. Fisher raises his voice and sends the stragglers on their way.

Somehow Henry is there and he is talking to the principal, gesturing and standing up straight, and even from where she sits on the floor barely daring to look at him through her lashes, Alice can tell he is being very, very convincing.

But this is a fleeting impression when what floods her mind's eye is a road called Highway 10, fifteen miles west of Baghdad, a road she has Googled in the school's computer lab and watched and contemplated, a road her father undoubtedly travels on.

Henry manages to get her to the nurse's office and settled onto a cot. He's about to leave when she hands him the clipping from the *Democrat and Chronicle* that has been burning a hole in her pocket. He bends his head to read the article.

> Four American soldiers, members of the National Guard from New York, were traveling in three Humvees heading west on Highway 10 toward the city of Falluja. The U.S. military reports that they were on combat patrol when their convoy was attacked by improvised explosive devices, small-arms fire, and rocket-propelled grenades. Two soldiers were burned beyond recognition, a third soldier was dragged off. When found, the body was so badly mutilated the military announced it had found the bodies of two men, not one. The body had no head, legs, or arms. Organs were removed. A fourth soldier has been declared missing. There were no survivors. One of the Humvees burned with such intensity that the surrounding trees were incinerated.

He carefully folds the paper into a tiny square and puts it into his back pocket.

"Alice, you've gotta stop reading the papers."

"How else am I gonna find out what's going on?"

"Maybe it's better not to know."

"I don't think so."

"There are guys who—"

"Who what?"

63

"Who survive, who make it back."

"Members of the National Guard from New York. Did you read that part?"

"There are dozens, maybe hundreds of men from—"

"Thousands."

"Okay. Thousands."

"He travels that road, Henry."

"You don't know that for sure."

"It's a good guess."

"Reading about it will not make anything better."

"Not reading about it makes it seem like I don't care."

"No, Alice, that's not the way it works."

"How do you know?"

"I know you're making yourself a little crazy here."

"Just a little?"

"And that Ellie needs you and your mom needs you and—"

"I took the paper so my mom wouldn't see it."

Miss Lambert sticks her head in the door to remind Henry to get to class. She waits, too, while he gets up from the edge of the cot.

"Could we just have a minute?" he asks her.

Lydia Lambert is young and thin and nervous. She is new to this job. She quit the hospital job she took right out of nursing school, then floundered for a while between two local nursing homes. It was distressing to learn, after all that school and all that training, that she didn't actually like being around sick or dying people. They make her anxious, really anxious.

High school kids don't make Lydia anxious; they make her sad, with their cramps and sprains and heartache and heartbreak and above all, with their loneliness. Being young can be so lonely, she thinks; more lonely than anything.

She decides to let them be.

"Do you want to go home? I could take you home."

"That's okay."

"I'll come back after second period. You'll be going stir crazy by then."

"Wait, Henry . . ."

"What?

"Don't go."

Henry sits on the floor next to Alice's cot.

"Tell me he's gonna be okay, Henry."

"He's gonna be okay, Alice."

"Tell me every day, every time you see me."

"Okay."

"Help me believe it."

"If anybody can make it through, your dad—"

"Yeah. Matt Bliss can do anything, right?"

"That's what everybody says."

Alice looks around at the stainless-steel table and the cupboard full of Band-Aids and aspirin and gauze pads and Ace bandages and wishes she still lived in a world where any of these things could make anything better.

"They cut up the bodies, Henry."

"Alice, don't—"

"Why would anybody . . . ? God . . . how do you fight against that?"

"I don't know."

Henry leans his head against the cot and inadvertently against her leg, or perhaps not so inadvertently, and straightens his legs in front of him. If she stretches her arm out, Alice can just barely reach the top of his head. It is nearly, but not quite, touch. She doesn't know why this is so important right now, but it is.

B.D. is not happy with Alice when she leaves practice at four fifteen and sprints for home. Another little checkmark next to her name on B.D.'s clipboard, Alice thinks. She doesn't want any checkmarks next to her name, just improving times.

Gram and Ellie are waiting in the car when she turns into the driveway. Great. Now she gets to go to the hairdressers in her running shorts and sweaty T-shirt. Ellie bamboozled Gram into letting her ride shotgun, so Alice climbs into the backseat and pulls a sweatshirt out of her backpack and over her head.

"Hi, sweetheart," Gram says.

"You stink," Ellie announces.

"Shut up, Ellie!"

Gram puts the car into gear and slowly backs out of the driveway.

"We're just going to make it."

"Don't worry, Gram, they always make us wait."

"Daddy called."

"He did?"

"For two minutes."

"And I missed it?"

"It was a terrible connection," Gram adds. "We were shouting."

"He's okay?"

"He sounded good," Gram says.

"He sounded *great*," Ellie crows.

He's okay floods through Alice and she takes what feels like her first deep breath all day.

At Headlines, Alice's basic trim takes ten minutes. Ellie is furiously flipping through magazines and turning pages down.

"I need glasses," Ellie says as she shrugs out of her coat and climbs onto the stylist's chair.

"What?" Alice asks.

"They tested us at school today. These are the ones I want," she says, tossing Alice a magazine. Then, turning to Patty, she unfolds the picture of the haircut she wants.

"Is your mom okay with this?" Patty asks.

"Oh, yeah," Ellie bluffs.

"You sure?"

"Totally."

Alice gets up to take a look at the picture.

"You want *that?*"

"Yes."

"I could do that at home with a bowl over your head."

"Ha, ha," Ellie says, not laughing.

"Who is that?"

"I don't know. Some film star from the old days."

"Gram? You know who this is?" Alice asks.

"Louise Brooks," Gram says. "I think she's the one who inspired everybody to bob their hair."

"It'll be cute on her," Patty offers.

"You sure you want this haircut?" Alice asks.

"I love it," Ellie says. "Love, love, love it."

"The bangs are really short, Ellie."

"That's the point."

"Okay, then."

Alice sits down to watch as Ellie's braids are cut off. Gram sits down beside her and reaches over to take Alice's hand.

"Your mother is going to kill me," she whispers, as she pulls out a handkerchief and blows her nose.

Patty carefully saves the braids in an envelope, knowing that Angie will probably want them. And if not, Ellie can donate them to Locks of Love. Ellie has her hands over her eyes so she can have the maximum surprise when it's all done.

"You can open your eyes," Patty says.

Ellie takes a look; her expression is dead serious.

"Can I see the back?" she asks.

Patty gets a mirror.

"Okay. Can you take the cape off?"

Ellie hops off the chair. She's wearing a dress with a big skirt and cap sleeves. She twirls around and her skirt bells out around her and her hair flies out from her face and for sure, she will be the only little girl with this hairstyle, the only little girl to wear these kinds of dresses. She looks like she could leave the ground she has so much energy, her skinny arms in a blur as she twirls. And she is grinning from ear to ear.

"Love it, love it, love it," she says, giving Patty a hug.

And then, turning to Gram, "Can we go to the glasses store?"

"Glasses? What kind of glasses?"

"I need glasses, Gram. I told you in the car."

"Well, we probably need to ask your mom."

"Can we just look? I like these," Ellie says, handing Gram a magazine.

At the eyeglass place Ellie is not happy with the selection they have for kids. She pulls out her picture and gives it to the guy behind the counter. He's incredulous, but goes to the locked cabinet with the designer frames and hands her a pair. She tries them on. The lenses are elongated rectangles and the frames are dark green plastic.

"Too big," Gram says, thinking that will be that.

But Ellie studies her reflection in the mirror, turning this way and that, trying to keep the glasses from sliding off her face and not having much luck. Alice suddenly has this stab of fear for Ellie. With this haircut and these glasses she will be teased mercilessly; Alice has already swallowed several choice phrases rather then throw them at Ellie. But now that she's actually looking at her she can see that Ellie is really skinny, maybe even skinnier than usual, and pale, superpale, like maybe she's coming down with the flu or something, or maybe she's not sleeping well or eating well and Alice thinks maybe she hasn't been paying attention to the right things and maybe she should be paying more attention to her sister, and how is she ever going to manage with one more thing to worry about?

"Can you order these in a smaller size?" Ellie asks the clerk.

"Sure. We can have them for you in a week."

"How much are they?" Gram asks.

"Three fifty."

"Three *hundred* and fifty?" Ellie asks.

A tight-lipped smile from the clerk.

"Thanks so much," Gram says, ushering them out the door.

In the car, holding the envelope with her braids in it, Ellie is unusually quiet. Even when Gram gets to talking about the chickens she's thinking about getting and the chicken coop Uncle Eddie has promised to build for her, even though knowing Uncle Eddie, that could take another year, and how Ellie is going to be her right-hand girl in the chicken-and-egg business. Ellie and Gram love chickens. Alice does not really find chickens remotely appealing, let alone lovable, but Gram keeps telling her: "You just wait and see. When we get our first baby chicks . . ."

"eBay," Ellie says out of the blue. "Second-hand stores. We have some options."

"What are you talking about?" Alice asks.

"I'm not giving up on those glasses."

At home, Ellie drops her coat on the floor and twirls her dress and her new haircut for Angie. When Ellie hands her the envelope with her braids inside, Angie sits in the nearest chair and bursts into tears.

"What's the matter, Mom? Don't you like it?" Ellie asks.

"Sure I like it. It's just . . . It's just . . ."

"Don't you think it's pretty?" Ellie asks.

"It's really pretty," Angie says. "And really different."

"Nobody else is gonna have a haircut anything like this. Not in my school. Not even in your school, Alice. It's unique. Unparalleled. Radically distinctive and without equal! Can we take a picture so Daddy can see?"

And Ellie does a wacky herky-jerky dance, her skinny arms pumping up and down over her head, her elbows jutting out; her feet flying. Ellie is taking interpretive dance to new heights, Alice thinks, as she tries to swallow the ache she feels looking at her sister's braids in her mother's lap.

April 8th

"What are you doing?"

Alice is in the front hall closet, surrounded by photo albums and photo boxes, when her mother, wearing one of her dad's old sweatshirts, interrupts.

"And are you ever going to take that shirt off?"

Alice considers which question to answer.

"I'm looking for that picture of me and Dad with the shovel and the pitchfork. The one Uncle Eddie took last October."

"What do you want that for?"

"I'm gonna send it to Dad in the care package."

"What about your school photo?"

"No way."

"Daddy would like that."

"You send it then."

"It's you right now."

"God, I hope not."

Angie gives her a look. Here it comes, Alice thinks. The appearances are not everything speech. The *it's what's inside that counts* speech.

Yup. There she goes. Launches right in. With embellishments even. Alice tunes out the sounds and watches her mother's very pretty mouth forming the familiar words.

Alice does not make the appropriate murmuring noises in response, the oh, mom, thanks so much, you really understand, don't you, and instead just looks at her mother thinking, why do you do this, when we both know it's total garbage?

These silent looks are like a little ticking bomb.

At first Alice can see Angie thinking, in a clenched teeth sort of way, *I'm not going to rise to the bait,* but before you know it, in a nanosecond, she's furious.

"You're making a mess."

"I am not."

"I spent days organizing these photos."

"Days?"

"Any order I had managed to—"

"I'll put it all back."

"The way it was?"

"Yeah. Exactly the way it was."

Just go away, Alice thinks. I was perfectly fine before you walked in here. Angie opens her mouth to say something else, thinks better of it, and turns on her heel and leaves.

Now Alice is thinking maybe it *is* a dumb photo. Now she's thinking about how she's not pretty and how that's probably evident in this photo. It's probably been evident forever, even in her baby pictures. Now she's thinking about this crap when before she was just looking for a photo where she and her dad were having fun and goofing around and it didn't have anything to do with being pretty.

This is why girls hate their mothers, Alice thinks, as she finds the photo.

They're in the garden, standing in the middle of their pumpkin patch. Dad is holding a pitchfork; Alice is holding a shovel. There are

71

two bushel baskets tipped over like cornucopia, full of corn and peppers and zucchini and gourds and tomatoes. They're wearing matching Red Wings T-shirts and baseball hats, and they're both trying—and failing—to look serious.

There's another one and another one—a little series of shots she hadn't remembered. Uncle Eddie caught them laughing and making faces and pretending their biggest pumpkin was too heavy to lift.

She rifles through the box to find the negatives, pockets them, and puts the originals back exactly where she found them. She's going to send her dad the whole series.

She raids the change jar before hopping on her bike to go to the drugstore at the Four Corners to make copies. On her way out the door she tells Ellie she'll be back in half an hour max and then they can seal up the box and take it to the post office.

"Get some batteries," Ellie yells after her. "They all need double As!"

Alice pops back inside.

"Mom! I'm taking five dollars to get Dad batteries!"

And she's out, she's on her bike. Only now does she realize how cold it still is. There's a misting kind of rain and the roads are all slushy. She's gonna get soaked if she rides in the street. She veers off onto the sidewalk, which is marginally better but at least she won't get sprayed by the passing cars. She pedals past Mrs. Piantowski's and Mrs. Minty's and then there's Gram's restaurant, with people waiting outside even in this weather. Happens every Saturday and Sunday, people queuing up around the block.

At the drugstore she marches up to the very tall, very skinny high school boy manning the photo machine, explains what she wants, begs him to make her photos right now, this very minute, *it's urgent,* and then heads off to find batteries.

True to his word, Steven—she reads his badge—has her photos

ready. While checking out, she looks at her dad's watch. Eleven o'clock. They'll just make it.

Outside Henry is standing next to her bike.

"Hey, Alice."

"Hi, Henry."

"You want to go sit at the counter at your Gram's and have breakfast or something?"

"I can't, Henry. I have to get to the post office before it closes."

"After the post office, then."

"I have to ask my mom."

"I'll meet you at the post office. She'll probably say yes, don't you think?"

"Yeah. I gotta go."

"Post office! High noon!" He shouts after her.

At home, Ellie and Angie have the box all ready. Alice tucks the photos into an envelope and slips in the letter she's been writing her dad all week during boring classes at school. It's a dumb letter, she knows that, a rambling, dull letter. She read the guidelines from the army: your soldier wants to hear the news from home. But there is no news in Belknap, there's just the weather and school and Mom and Ellie and Gram and Uncle Eddie and running and not being able to sleep and missing him and wishing . . . But you are strongly advised to keep any and all worries to yourself. All the sleepless nights, and, let's face it, the fights with Mom, all the real stuff, you're supposed to leave that out.

Ellie hugs the box after they seal it up and plants a big kiss right on Dad's name.

They rush into jackets and boots and head to the post office. As if what they're all feeling right now will reach him, as if the hustle and the bustle will somehow cross the miles.

They stop at Gram's, where she has very carefully packed up a loaf

73

of Matt's favorite harvest bread made with pumpkin and walnuts. She has followed the army guidelines to the letter and has real hopes this bread will make it and still taste good by the time it gets there.

Slipping inside the post office at a whisper before twelve, they're giddy because they've made it in time. The two boxes go on the scale: they fill out the customs forms and pay the postman. But then there's the walk from the counter to the door, with the postman following behind to lock up. Just those few yards and the air starts to go out of the balloon. Outside, Angie pulls her coat around her as though she could hug away the loneliness, and reaches out to take Ellie's hand.

"Let's go to Gram's for lunch."

"I meant to ask if I could go to Gram's with Henry."

"That's fine. Ellie and I can have a booth all to ourselves, right sweetheart?"

Alice takes a look at her mother standing on the steps of the post office squinting into the rain. She wants to say, I see it; I notice all the things we are not saying, all the moments we are silently agreeing to ignore. It's like a shadow that follows them and falls between them; this other life full of other feelings, this yawning emptiness where her father belongs.

And then Henry is there, materializing out of thin air, twirling Ellie off her feet and singing something right into her ear that makes her laugh out loud.

"Don't tell," he whispers.

"I won't," she grins back at him.

They walk to Gram's and for some strange reason it's pretty quiet. The line out the door is gone. Ellie and Angie sit at a booth while Henry and Alice settle in at the counter.

Sally, who is trying yet another shade of strawberry blonde, comes over to pour coffee as Gram sticks her head out from the kitchen to say hi.

"Hi, Gram!"

Ellie rushes her for a hug.

"I'll join you for a cup of coffee as soon as I can."

Gram gives Alice a kiss and says to both of them: "If you want to help me clean up, breakfast's on me."

"But I wanted to . . ." Henry begins.

He gets off the stool and whispers to Gram: "I invited Alice, Mrs. Bird."

"Really."

"I've got snow shoveling money."

"You're too young to date."

"This is not a date. And her mother's right there."

"Don't go getting any ideas."

"I wouldn't."

"Yes, you would."

"Not in front of you and Sally and Ellie and her mother I wouldn't."

"I could still use your help with sweeping and washing the floors and the final round of pots and pans. For that you get the employee discount."

"Deal."

"This is not a date, Henry."

"Absolutely not, Mrs. Bird."

Henry slides back onto his stool next to Alice.

"I hope you're hungry," he says. "I'm having the lumberjack special."

"You are not! You can't possibly eat all that."

"Wanna bet? Are you actually drinking coffee?"

"With a lot of milk and sugar. Wanna try it?"

She pushes the mug toward him. He sips. Considers. Hates it.

Sally sits down next to them to take their orders, leans into Henry, with a lot of cleavage, and enjoys his blush.

"You should've seen it in here an hour ago. All morning! A madhouse!

75

We're out of every kind of bread except white and English muffins. No more eggs Benedict, no more Canadian bacon."

"You got the lumberjack special?" Henry asks, looking anywhere but at Sally.

"Bacon or sausage?"

"Bacon."

"How do you want your eggs?"

"Over easy."

"Pancakes or French toast?"

"Get the French toast," Alice says.

"French toast, please."

"Is this a date?" Sally wants to know.

"What?" Alice asks.

"Your Gram's all worried this could be a date or something and you're too young."

"It's not a date," they both say simultaneously, and perhaps too loudly.

"Alice helps me with math all the time. I just wanted to do something nice for her."

"Awwww. . . . The usual for you, Alice?"

"I want my dad's usual."

"Corned beef hash comin' up."

There's an awkward pause as Sally shouts their order into the kitchen. Alice glances up into the long mirror over the counter and catches a glimpse of Ellie snuggled up close to Angie. Angie is stroking Ellie's hair, lost in thought.

"You can't do anything around here without everybody trying to . . ."

"I think it's really nice, Henry."

"You do?"

"Yeah."

"Well, that's good."

"But let's not get weird, okay?"

"No, no, no. Of course."

"Like you're acting nervous and stuff. And you should quit it."

"Okay."

He looks at her. He looks away.

"Listen . . ." and he trails off, uncertain how to proceed.

"What?"

"You know how there's the dance coming up in May?"

"Henry!"

"What?"

"Okay. Wait a minute. Maybe I'm jumping to conclusions. Is there somebody you want to ask?"

"Duh, Alice."

"Julie? Julie Watson?"

"Are you kidding me?"

"Her sidekick, Abby?"

"You, Alice. I want to ask you."

"Henry!"

"What's so wrong with that?"

"We're like almost related."

"We are not!"

"Okay, but—"

"I even asked my mom to teach me how to dance."

"You want to dance with me?"

"Yes."

"I think the dances your mom knows how to dance may not be relevant in this case."

"Well, there's all the stuff about how to hold your partner for a slow dance, and not looking at your feet, and apologizing if you step on her feet, and offering to get punch."

"Manners."

"Dance manners. Yeah."

Alice puts more sugar in her coffee.

"You are full of surprises, Henry."

"Somebody else already asked you."

"No, they didn't."

"Are you saying no?"

"No, I'm not saying no, I'm just saying . . ."

Their food arrives.

"If it's no, tell me quick. I can't stand long drawn out no's."

"I don't know what to say."

"Say yes. It'll be fun."

"Really."

"Yeah!"

"You honestly think so."

"Yeah, I do."

"Have you ever had one minute of fun in that gym before?"

"No, but—"

"Maybe if it was just you and me, Henry, it might be fun. But our classmates will be there. Remember them?"

"I don't care about them."

"Do we have to get dressed up?"

"Yes! That's part of the fun."

"Okay."

"Okay? Is that yes?"

"Yes."

"And we'll get dressed up and everything."

"And we'll send my dad a picture."

"My mom even said she'd drive us."

"Let's walk like we always do."

"Really?"

"Don't you think that would be kind of cool at night?"

"Will your mom let you?"

"Probably. Can I have a bite of your French toast?"

"Sure."

"Gram makes the best French toast in the world."

He passes her the plate.

"We could get Uncle Eddie to pick us up. In one of his retro cars."

"That would be awesome. Maybe a convertible. Maybe he'd wear a chauffeur's hat and be the first car idling at the door when everybody comes out."

"Yeah. Maybe he would."

Henry, relieved, tucks into his food. Gram comes out and sits down in the booth with Angie and Ellie. Sally joins them. Alice is looking at everything. Henry with egg yolk on his upper lip, Gram tired and asking Ellie to rub her shoulders, Sally looking a little haggard, like she's got a headache, maybe left over from Friday night, maybe from more trouble with one of her boys, Angie stretched out with her head resting against the back of the booth, Ellie kneeling behind Gram working on her shoulders with her little hands.

Sally gets up and puts the CLOSED sign in the door and then flips the radio to her favorite country station. A song of lost love fills the room as Sally waltzes across the floor to start wiping down the counters.

"That Teddy Thompson's got a nice voice," Sally says.

"That's not all he's got," Gram adds.

"Gram!"

"I wouldn't kick him out of bed for eating crackers."

"What does *that* mean?" Alice wants to know.

Angie is laughing and covering Ellie's ears.

"Means he's so fine he can break *all* the rules," Gram says.

Henry dips his head so low it's almost in his plate. Alice turns her back on the sight of Gram, Sally, and Angie cracking up over Teddy Thompson and concentrates on composing the perfect bite: hash, egg with some soft yolk, plenty of pepper, and a dab of ketchup. She puts it in her mouth and closes her eyes and tries to let the taste bring her dad into focus inside of her. It doesn't work, not that she was really expecting it to. Mostly she thinks, not bad, but I wish I'd ordered waffles.

April 10th

Alice arrives home from practice to find Angie on the phone with Matt. Angie gives her a quick smile, then turns her back and closes the kitchen door. Alice walks in anyway.

"Is it Dad? Can I talk to him?"

Angie waves her away and closes the door behind her. So Alice stands just outside the closed kitchen door, furious. She can occasionally hear her dad's voice, but very few words. She waits a minute until her mom is distracted again and pushes the door open a crack. Now she can hear the excitement in his voice.

"C'mon, honey. It's what we've trained for."

"You promised me, Matt—"

"It's the army, remember? They make the decisions."

"This is what you *wanted*. Admit it."

"Angie . . ."

There's a pause.

"How are the kids?"

"They're fine."

"Are you getting my checks okay?"

"Two so far."

"I know they're slow, but that's pretty good. It means we're in the system. Are you getting my letters?"

"They take about ten days."

"But they're getting there?"

"Yeah. They're great, Matt."

"Write me. Write me more. You don't know what a letter means."

"I will."

"I wrote to both girls today. Tell them, okay?"

"I will."

"I've gotta go."

"Matt, this is so hard."

"I know. I know it is."

"I wish you could call more."

"Me, too. But we're moving around so much right now."

"Come home to me."

"You know I will."

"Stay safe."

"I love you, Angie. I love you."

Alice lets the door close completely. She can hear Angie hanging up the receiver and then crossing to the sink where she turns on the tap.

Alice retreats to the hall table where, breaking with tradition, she picks up the letter addressed to her and tears it open, not waiting for Angie or Ellie, not waiting for anyone.

Dear Alice,

It was great to get your letter and hear about your running. I'm so proud of you. I want to meet that girl Ginger on your team. And B.D., too.

You asked me to describe Falluja. There's all the stuff you've heard about: the trash, the bombed-out buildings, the piles of white rocks, the dead wires, the burned cars. But there's so much else that doesn't make it into the news. There are kids playing soccer. There are goats, and outhouses, and even beds on rooftops. Date palms, and sand-colored buildings, razor wire, fences, blast walls. From rooftops you can see the river snaking through the city and the network of irrigation canals and the desert in the distance. The dust is so fine it coats every-thing: your hair, your face, your throat, your teeth. The mosques—there are two big ones—are really beautiful—green and cobalt blue domes that you can see from everywhere in the city.

Some of the market places are still thriving and the Andaloos Market, near us, is lively as anything. You can buy everything from sodas to car parts to T-shirts, sandals, scarves, soccer balls, even furniture, all along a crowded street barely wide enough for a HMMWV to pass through.

They sell delicious flatbread that marines call "Muj bread." It looks like a tortilla. Two bucks for 24 pieces. It's a deal. Great with my morning coffee. If only. Ha ha!

Write me. I love your letters. And I love you.
> Dad

April 14th

There is no practice today. B.D. is sick or something. Alice feels lost.

Drifting past the high school playing fields, headed for the cut-through to the elementary school, Alice crosses the track, starts up the hill and steps in dog poop. Shit! All these people who walk their dogs here; they know the leash laws! They know that kids use these paths. Idiots! She's stumbling around trying to wipe the crap off in the grass, and looks up to see John Kimball laughing at her. The cutest guy in school who has never so much as glanced her way ever, not even once, not that she cares; now he takes a moment from doing something spectacular on the baseball field, now he decides to stop and look at her.

"Asshole!" she shouts. Which only makes him laugh louder. "Asshole!" she shouts again and to her amazement, he drops his mitt and heads over to her.

"Hey, I'm sorry."

"Go away."

"Listen—"

"You're just making it worse."

"No, that was stupid. I didn't mean—"

"Didn't mean what? You're so full of shit."

"You're crying."

"No, I'm not!"

"I didn't know you could cry and be mad at the same time."

"You don't know much, do you?"

"Okay, okay," he says, and starts backing off, still looking at her.

She looks down and can't believe her sneaker. This must've been some really big dog.

"Alice, right?" He calls out to her.

"What?"

"Your name's Alice, right?"

She looks past John and sees Stephie and Jeremy Baskin holding hands, standing with a bunch of kids, and realizes they've been watching and of course they're laughing. They're all laughing at crazy Alice Bliss.

Fuck you, Alice thinks, as she heads blindly toward the path through the woods. She's stumbling around like an idiot and tripping over rocks and careening into branches, which are lashing her face. Is that blood? Is her face scratched? Oh, who *cares*, she just wants to get this shit off her sneaker; she's madly scraping away on rocks, on roots, in the leaves and pine needles, and good god—it's almost coming up over her socks! when Henry appears.

"Alice, what are you doing here?"

Why does he sound so mad, she wonders as she grabs the sweatshirt she's got tied around her waist. She can't believe she is wiping her face and blowing her nose on her favorite sweatshirt.

"I thought you had track."

She rolls up the sweatshirt and stuffs it in her backpack.

"It was canceled."

"Why didn't you tell me?"

"What difference does it make?"

"What difference does it make?! I've been leaving band practice early every day for three weeks to pick up Ellie. Not that you've noticed! Not that you care! Not that you've ever even bothered to say thank you!"

"I didn't—"

"What is that *smell?*"

She looks at her shoe.

"Oh, my God, that's gross."

And he turns and heads back to school.

"Where are you going?"

"Maybe if I make it through a whole rehearsal once or twice Mr. Brooks won't drop me from band and take away my clarinet solo."

"Why are you so mad at me?"

"Jeez, Alice! You are not the only person on the planet!"

Well, I know that, Alice thinks, as she watches Henry hurry away from her. She looks at his thin back and narrow shoulders and low-slung pants and too heavy backpack, filled with homework he will actually complete, and those awful black lace-up shoes he wears just to be different. She looks at his shaggy thick hair and his beloved Red Sox hat that his brother gave him. She tries to remember the last time Henry was this mad at her and thinks it might have been her birthday party when she turned seven. The two of them spent weeks planning that party, they even had a theme, the Wizard of Oz, and his mom baked one of her amazing cakes that had the characters all over the top of it, and Henry dressed up as the Cowardly Lion. And then Alice forgot about Henry completely in her excitement over all the other little girls in their Dorothy dresses.

She's late picking up Ellie, even later than she thought. The teacher who got stuck waiting—looks like Mrs. Comstock—glares at Alice as she gets into her car. The school is locked up, Ellie is sitting on the front steps all alone, and it's clear she's been crying, but she's done with that now. Now she's steaming mad. She walks right up to Alice, right up close, and takes a big breath to start yelling at her, when she smells the poop and nearly gags.

This is too much, Ellie thinks, this is insult and injury and grievous and if she were not eight years old she would figure out some way to sue her sister for damages. No, she would figure out how to divorce her sister. She would figure out how to become not-sisters. Un-sisters. Unrelated.

"First you're late! Really late. Later than ever. So late I didn't think you were coming. And now . . . and now—"

Alice looks at her shoes.

"I hate you Alice, I really hate you."

Ellie takes another step back, farther away from the smell.

"Where's Henry?"

"Band practice."

"I am *not* going to walk home with you."

"But—"

"You can walk on the other side of the street. Or you could hide in the woods 'til it's so dark that no one will see you. And *smell* you!"

"Ellie—"

"Do *not!* Do not even *try* to speak to me!"

Ellie turns and walks off, heading for home. She is walking fast, as fast as an eight-year-old can walk. Her head is down and she's swinging her arms, sort of like Mom on a power walk. She's like a little engine. Running on mad.

And she's wearing a hat, Alice notices, even though it's not that cold. A hat that completely covers her hair.

"Hey! How'd everybody like your new haircut?" Alice shouts across the street.

"What do you care?"

"I bet Mrs. Baker likes it."

"Yeah."

"Janna?"

"Pretty much."

"The other kids?"

Ellie is twisting the middle button on her hand-me-down plaid spring coat.

"Luke Piacci?"

The button pops off in her hand.

"Is that why you're wearing that hat?"

Ellie gulps in one of those horrible sobs where it sounds like she's choking and wailing at the same time.

"Can I come over there?" Alice asks.

"No!"

"*I* like it," Alice offers.

"No you don't. And neither does Gram or Mom or—"

"I bet Mrs. Grover likes it."

"What about Daddy?" Ellie asks through a fresh burst of tears.

"Daddy's gonna love it."

"You're just saying that."

"You know what Daddy would say?"

"What?"

"Take off that silly hat and quit worrying about what other people think."

They cross Belknap Road with slightly less distance between them and turn down Baird Road.

"Hey, you want to bake a cake? After I throw these stupid sneakers in the trash?"

"He said I look like an elf."

"Who?"

"Luke Piacci."

"Maybe that was a compliment."

"An *elf.*"

"Well, you're a very, very cute elf, Ellie."

"Shut up!"

They turn into their driveway. Alice carefully keeps to her own side of the drive.

"Could we make a lemon cake?" Ellie asks.

"Sure."

"Caramel frosting?"

"Sounds good."

"Okay!" Ellie shouts, pulling her hat off and skipping along the last twenty yards of their driveway, past Matt's grape arbor and apple trees. A wash of sunlight spills over the trees and dapples her shining cap of hair.

"Okay."

April 16th

They get through the weekend somehow. Alice didn't even tell her mom the truth about her sneaks. She just threw them away wrapped up in dozens of Wegman's bags. She paid Ellie two bucks to keep her mouth shut and told her mom she lost them.

Which made her mom really mad.

"I just bought those sneakers!"

"I'm sorry."

"You're not paying attention, Alice!"

"I'm—"

"How many pairs of sneakers do I have to buy, anyway? In a lifetime of being your mom . . . ? And when are you going to at least *wash* that stupid shirt?!"

So all day Saturday it's mad Mom and a trip to the hated mall and the dreaded shoe store *and* the eyeglasses store to pick up Ellie's new glasses. A compromise pair, yes, but still way too big for Ellie's little face. She loves them.

Now it's Sunday afternoon and everybody is in a bad mood as they play catch up with chores. Alice is stuck in the basement with a mountain of laundry while Ellie is upstairs "dusting" and Angie is what, doing the taxes? Never a good day. Then the washing machine blows a gasket or a hose and floods the basement. Now they've got wet laundry, puddles of water, and that nasty damp basement smell. Nobody wants to pile this stinking, dripping laundry into the car and schlep to the Laundromat. So Angie's terrible mood gets worse. Chores and broken appliances and they can't afford a new washer right now, goddamnit! Which is when Alice calls Uncle Eddie.

"Here comes Uncle Eddie!" Ellie shouts.

Angie can barely contain a groan.

Alice loves Uncle Eddie. Everybody else thinks he's a fuckup.

Eddie was brilliant in school when he bothered to attend, especially math and physics. Could have done anything, won scholarships, the whole nine yards. Instead he got fat and runs a garage. Uncle Eddie can fix anything. It really burns everybody that he does well in his sideline business, too, buying high-end cars at auction for a client base that stretches across the country. Just how much does it bug Angie to see fat Eddie drive up in a vintage Mercedes he's scored for one of his rich clients, smoking a big cigar, with cash in his pockets. Eddie loves cash.

All the pretty girls like Eddie. Even fat he's really handsome, with lashes so dark and thick it looks like he's wearing eyeliner. He's had scores of girlfriends. Angie doesn't like them coming over to the house anymore. What used to be fun and flashy and definitely out of the ordinary is now relegated to the despised favorite phrase of all boring adultdom: "not appropriate."

Uncle Eddie also likes to disappear every few months for a week or so. Nobody knows where he goes. On a drunk, chasing a girl, proving he's still free and unattached and unencumbered. Or maybe he's just tracking down a vintage car he's heard about through the grapevine.

Fastidious little miss Ellie is already starting to turn her nose up at

Uncle Eddie. She's imbibing Angie's attitudes and opinions apparently. But his presents always wow her. Like Uncle Eddie always knows just what you really want, not what your mom thinks you should have, like the fringed cowgirl vest from his trip to Vegas, or the red, glittery Dorothy shoes with straps he bought one time in New York City. You can watch Ellie's ambivalence play out right on her face. First, she's loving the car and then she's hating the cigar, then she's loving Eddie's booming laugh, but hating his big belly and his stubbly face and his grimy fingernails. When he picks her up and calls her pumpkin, she wrinkles her finicky little nose. He's on to her, too. "Don't be a simp," he tells her. "What are you so afraid of, a little dirt?"

Angie is at the front door.

"Eddie, can you lose the cigar?"

"Hi, sweetheart."

"Hi, Eddie. The cigar . . . ?"

"It looks good, though, don't you think?"

"Niiiice set of wheels," Angie says.

Eddie does a little shimmy and shake. Right there on the sidewalk. Angie can't help herself; she smiles at him, covering her mouth with her hands. He's unbuckling his belt in preparation for dropping his pants.

"No! Eddie! It's broad daylight!"

"I just want to get a laugh outta you."

She's laughing and shaking her head—who knows at who? Eddie? Herself? At the fact that she's laughing at all?

"I heard your washer's on the fritz."

He reaches into the backseat and takes out his tool kit.

"So I'm gonna fix your washer and then I'm gonna take you out to dinner, gorgeous. Alice can babysit, right?"

"Why can't we come?" Ellie wants to know.

"Oh, so now you like me?"

"I like you," she says, a little too slowly.

"Your mom needs to put a dress on and go out someplace where she can turn heads and drink a martini. This is my big secret, the reason so many beautiful girls go out with me. I improve their looks. Next to me they look even more gorgeous than they already are."

And then he's inside their little house, bumping into doorjambs, knocking the pictures out of whack on the walls. When Eddie stumps down the basement stairs, the whole house shakes. Angie clucks, she actually clucks, but Alice thinks the house is doing a little happy dance, just like Uncle Eddie.

"I need an assistant!" he shouts from the basement.

Alice looks at Angie who raises her eyebrow, as in, who me? Are you kidding?

So it's Alice who clumps downstairs. It's an act, the clumping. She loves hanging out with Uncle Eddie. Every time she sees him, there's always one shocking thing he tells her and the promise of more revelations to come.

He turns off the water and disconnects the hose. "Pay attention," he tells her. "You could learn something." Alice does not really need to be told to pay attention to Uncle Eddie.

"Okay, that's the intake, that's the outflow. My guess is, it's the outflow. Let's take a look."

He inspects the hoses.

"Hoses look okay. You see anything I'm not seeing?"

It's a rubber gasket that's shot; that's what he figured it would be. He took the liberty of bringing a few basic supplies with him, including a gasket. How does he know these things? He takes the hose and tells Alice to pull off the old gasket.

"It's stuck."

"Yank it! Give it a real tug."

"It's really stuck."

"Yeah, they get corroded."

He zaps it with some WD-40 and it comes right off.

He hands her a new gasket: "Fit that one on."

She slips on the new gasket.

"Like I said, it's not rocket science. Now reconnect it."

When he squats down to test the connection, she wishes he'd wear his pants a little higher. He turns his head, catches her looking at him, and gives his jeans a hoist.

"Sorry about that, kiddo."

"Oh, it's nothing, I . . ."

"Nobody wants to look down an old fart's butt."

This cracks her up.

"Actually nobody wants to look down anybody's butt. Way too much of that these days. It used to be your old man had to tell you to keep your pants on, now they gotta tell you to keep your pants *up*, too. Not that kids are listening. What did your pop tell you?"

"What do you mean?"

"Words of wisdom. Advice. That kind of thing."

She thinks for a minute.

"I don't think we got to that phase, yet."

"Sure you did."

"What, like how to live my life and stuff? I'm in the tenth grade. It's a little early!"

"No. The basics. Like don't kiss a girl if you just ate garlic pizza."

She thinks again. She can't believe she has to think about this! There should be a list, a list that comes trippingly off her tongue, of all the great things her dad told her.

"Marigolds are a natural insect repellent?"

"Apropos of . . . ?"

"How to lay out a garden?"

"Exactly! What else?"

And Uncle Eddie, unlike most adults, is not impatient for her answer. It's okay that she's taking her time. He just hangs in there.

"Let's give her a little test run," he says, and turns the washer on.

So now they've got the snug basement and the friendly washer-filling-up sounds and Uncle Eddie is the first person to ask her a direct question about her dad, to assume, of course they'll talk about her dad, like it's totally natural to talk about her dad, no problem, bring it on.

"He told me, never sell yourself short."

"You'll find yourself thinking of that one even when you're forty."

"Don't let anybody make up your mind for you."

"Yeah."

"You're as good as anybody else."

"Right."

"He gave me a compass when I was twelve."

"Cool."

"He said when I don't know what to do, I should just stop and close my eyes for a minute and see if I can hear my inner voice. And that voice, that's my compass."

"Your dad loves that stuff—maps, compasses . . ."

"Yeah."

"He's a good dad."

God bless Uncle Eddie for talking in the present tense.

"You know how you feel about your mom right now?"

"Yeah."

"Like she's this huge pain in the ass?"

"How do you know these things?"

"She's my big sister. She's been a pain in my ass my whole life! Anyway, you're not gonna feel this way forever."

"I don't believe you."

"Couple years . . . it'll all be different."

"I really don't believe you."

"And right now, you've got a choice about how you want to feel and be around her."

"I do not!"

"You do. I'm not saying it's easy, but you've got a choice."

"Like what, suddenly she's gonna be nice to me?"

"Like maybe you could have a truce. A little cease-fire."

"Did she tell you to do this?"

"Nope."

"'Cause it's really making me mad."

The washer spins to a stop. They both turn to look at it. No leaking.

"Let's load her up."

They both start tossing darks into the washer.

"Uncle Eddie . . ."

"Yeah."

"It's not that I hate her. . . ."

"I know."

"I just don't love her right now."

"That's all I'm trying to tell you, Alice. Right now doesn't go on forever."

"You sure?"

"I'm sure."

"Hey—that's a good piece of advice."

"From me? Hell, no." He grins.

Upstairs Angie has put on a silky dress and red high heels and dangly earrings and lipstick. Uncle Eddie gives Alice a little nudge.

"You look nice, Mom."

Her mom actually smiles, after she gets over the shocked surprise.

"Thanks, honey."

"Your mom's a party girl. I bet she never told you that."

"Eddie!"

"Perfume, too. Wow!"

"Are you going like that?" Angie asks.

"How'd you pack so much disapproval into five little words?"

93

"Thanks for fixing the washer."

"I've got a clean shirt—Ralph Lauren—whoo hoo—and a sports jacket in the car."

"Always ready for a good time."

"That's me. Life is short. Let's go."

Alice watches them walk to the car, their heads close together, laughing at something she can't hear, and she thinks she doesn't really know anything about her mother. She never thinks of her mother as being a sister and that she had this whole other life in her own family, until she sees her link her arm through Eddie's arm and lean into him. Why didn't she ever see this before? She sees that her mom loves Uncle Eddie even though all she ever does is give him a hard time and complain about him. And she's happy to be going out. Putting on some high heels and going out.

"What's for dinner?" Ellie shouts.

"Come into the kitchen and help me figure it out," Alice shouts back at her.

Ellie stomps in.

"I bet there's nothing good," Ellie says.

"You're not helping."

"We could call Gram. She'd come over. She might even take us out."

"We've gotta finish all that laundry."

Alice opens the fridge. Why is she bothering to do this? She knows she's not going to find some yummy leftover casserole, or even fresh sandwich fixings. She slams the door.

"Okay, here's what we're gonna do: Backwards dinner. In front of a movie."

She takes inventory: one tired banana, some ice cream; she knows how to make fudge sauce. She tests the whipped cream canister; it's not full, but it's promising.

"I'll make chocolate sauce."

"Can we make it peppermint?" Ellie asks.

"Yeah. You peel the banana and get it into bowls."

"Can I scoop the ice cream?"

"Sure."

"Make it really chocolaty, Alice."

"Okay."

"Make lots."

"I will."

So Alice melts chocolate chips and stirs in half-and-half while Ellie stands on a chair to scoop ice cream onto banana halves.

"I wish we had a cherry for the top."

"How about walnuts?"

"That's what Daddy likes!"

"I know."

"Okay! Do it like Daddy does."

They sit down in front of *Clueless* for the five hundredth time and eat banana splits and talk back to the movie and say all the lines they know by heart. They pause the movie so Alice can go downstairs and put one load of laundry into the dryer and start the next load.

She gets back upstairs to find Ellie standing on tiptoe on a kitchen chair with the longest wooden spoon in her hand, trying to reach the popcorn maker, and finally managing to pull it toward her by the cord. Alice waits and is rewarded by the sight of Ellie, popcorn maker clutched to her chest, grinning from ear to ear.

She hands the popcorn maker to Alice and says, "I love backwards dinner."

"Me, too."

"Will you make mac and cheese later?"

"If you're still hungry."

"Lots of butter for the popcorn, okay? Not the skinny way Mom does it."

"Okay. You do the butter."

"Yeah?"

"I'll show you."

They manage to fold two loads of laundry in front of the movie before Ellie falls asleep. Ellie was so proud of herself for having given up the baby habit of sucking her thumb in kindergarten, but there's that thumb now, while she's sleeping. Alice brushes the hair off Ellie's sweaty forehead. Ellie is wearing her favorite plaid skirt with pleats. Alice thinks of these clothes as throwback clothes. Maybe her mom wore a skirt like this when she was in second grade. Ellie's bony knees are scraped and scabby, and both kneesocks have scrunched down around her ankles.

When Angie and Uncle Eddie get home, the girls are both sound asleep on the couch. Uncle Eddie picks Ellie up in his arms and carries her upstairs. Angie wakes Alice. Alice was dreaming, she was dreaming about Small Point; she was dreaming about a sliver of moon hanging low over the water; she was dreaming that she and Dad were walking the beach in the moonlight; she's following in his footsteps, and he was just beginning to turn around to say something to her when her mom wakes her up.

"Alice . . . honey . . ."

When she bends over like that, Alice can smell her perfume and the faint scent of her lipstick, and maybe that other smell is a martini or two.

"Time for bed."

"Okay."

Alice sits up and her mom surprises her by sitting down beside her. Close beside her.

"You folded the laundry."

"Yeah."

"Thanks."

"Ellie helped."

"You guys make out okay?"

"Yeah."

"No fighting?"

"Nope. We had backwards dinner."

"Perfect."

"Did you have a good time, Mom?"

"I had a really nice time."

Uncle Eddie clatters downstairs and sticks his head in the doorway.

"We danced," he says.

"You did not!"

"Yeah, we did."

"Where were you?"

"That little roadhouse out by the lake. They've got a dance floor the size of a postage stamp."

"And a piano and this old lady with dyed red frizzy hair who does jazz standards," Angie says.

"How do you dance to *that?*" Alice wants to know.

"Your Uncle Eddie's a good dancer."

"Sure he is," Alice teases.

"He taught me everything I know."

"I thought Dad taught you how to dance."

"That was more like refining what Eddie had already laid down."

"Alice, I'll pick you up tomorrow for your first driving lesson," Uncle Eddie says.

"What?!" Angie can't keep the shock out of her voice.

"Really?" Alice asks.

"She's fifteen! She doesn't have a permit!"

"Relax, Angie. We're gonna drive around in circles in an empty parking lot."

"You're not going to put that child behind the wheel of that Mercedes."

"I don't think that will be a problem for Alice."

"Eddie!"

"Gotta go, kids."

Uncle Eddie heads out the door.

"Thanks, Eddie," her mom shouts, as the door slams. "He's too much sometimes."

"He's great."

"He put the top down."

"Cool."

"We drove out to the park—where the kids go to neck."

"To *what*, Mom?"

"Make out?"

"I'll never understand how you can be so fifties when you grew up in the seventies."

"He put the top down so we could hear the water and look at the stars."

"Nice."

"He had a blanket in the trunk."

"Pretty smooth."

"You need to watch out for boys like your Uncle Eddie."

"I'll keep that in mind."

"I mean it."

"Mom—!"

Angie puts her head back against the couch cushions and reaches for Alice's hand.

"It was so beautiful. We had the radio on . . . And that dumb-ass cigar of his smelled really good outside."

"I love cigars outside."

"He's always surprising me, y'know? Now if he'd just lose twenty-five pounds and find a nice girl—"

"Don't ruin it, Mom."

"It would be good for his health. I worry—"

"Don't you like anybody just the way they already are?"

There's a long pause while Alice disentangles her hand.

"We didn't hear from Dad this weekend."

"He's probably out on patrol or something."

"You think he's okay?"

"I'm sure he's fine."

"How can you be sure?"

"You know Dad; he knows how to take care of himself."

"But what if—"

"Alice, let's not get into this right before bed, okay?"

"I was just wondering."

"I know, honey."

No, you don't, Alice thinks as she heads up the stairs. You have no idea.

Angie walks through the house turning out the lights before she heads upstairs to her bedroom. She reaches under her pillow and pulls out Matt's latest letter:

You've never seen the moon like it is here. Because the base is blacked out for security reasons and there's so little electricity anywhere else, it's truly dark. I don't know if you can experience this kind of darkness in the U.S. anymore. Whenever I'm out walking across the base—for a meeting, for a meal—I'm so aware of the night sky. And looking up, Angie, looking up kind of lifts you up, you know? Almost like praying or wishing or hitching your wagon to a star. That's an old time phrase, something my dad would say. But just sensing that mystery feels like a kind of prayer to me, even though you know I'm not much for prayers and all that.

Angie tries to think of the last time she really paid attention to the night sky. Tonight, maybe, out at the lake in Eddie's convertible. But did she really see it? Or was she all caught up, as usual, in talking or arguing or giving Eddie advice he doesn't want and never heeds? When was the last time she walked beneath the moon, or sang, or danced, or held Matt in her arms under a starlit sky? Here she is, with every freedom and every convenience and she doesn't have time to notice the moon. And there's Matt, doing whatever it is he can't tell her about every day, reveling in the night sky.

My soul lifts up, she thinks. *My soul lifts up* . . . Where did that phrase come from and why is it popping into her head now? The moon, the sky, the possibility of a soul, the miles, the oceans, Matt, trying not to worry, getting through the days believing he'll come home, believing he'll be okay. It's all a prayer, she realizes, every breath, every day. Come home to me. Come home.

April 17th

They are sitting on the bed in Henry's bedroom after track practice, ostensibly working on geometry homework. Alice gets up to open the window because Henry's feet really stink. She can see into the Grovers' side yard where Mrs. Grover is taking the laundry off the line. There are robins on the greening grass and the forsythia is just beginning to bloom. Alice wants to be outside, she wants to lie down in the grass and forget about geometry and school and no news from her father and a million other things.

Mrs. Grover is singing. To herself, really, kind of under her breath but every other phrase or so drifts up to the window and Alice can hear it. She's singing that great Bunny Berrigan song, "Can't Get Started." The only reason Alice knows this song is because it is a very big song at Henry's house. Mrs. Grover has one of the original recordings on a scratchy 78 that she loves to play. She actually has a record player and she changes the spindle and puts this record on and sits down and plays it and listens to it, really leans in and *listens* to it. Alice had never seen anyone listen to music like this, so it was a bit of an event when she was around four and happened to be playing with Henry when his mother took out the old Bunny Berrigan record and put it on. And sat there. And listened.

Here she is, on a spring day, bringing in the wash and singing to herself. Mrs. Grover is no longer young; at least that's how Alice's mother would put it, and Alice's mother would think she was being tactful, not hearing the obvious criticism and condescension in the phrase. Even though Mrs. Grover wears those awful sensible shoes and has gray hair that she wears in a bun, Alice thinks that maybe Mrs. Grover is still young in the ways that are important. Like she's not so serious all the time, and she sings and right now she's teasing a cardinal. Whistling in response to its call and damn if that cardinal doesn't whistle right back. Alice's mother doesn't even have a clothesline, let alone stand outside and lift her face to the sun and sing and whistle to the birds.

Henry works away, oblivious, or so Alice thinks. Henry, of course, has another story to tell and not necessarily one he's ready to tell Alice. For instance, it is impossible to think when Alice is this close to him. The smell of her shampoo, the habit she has of closing her eyes and scratching her nose as she thinks through a math problem, the way he can tell she is miles away from him even though she's in the same room. She's finished her homework, as usual, and Henry is left to try to think his way through the problem on the page when he'd much rather think about, or even just watch, Alice. Which is what he's doing when she turns back from the window.

"Your mom's bringing in the wash."

"Yeah."

"I love the way the sheets smell when they've been dried outside, don't you?"

"Yeah."

"You never thought about it."

"Nope."

"Not a guy thing."

"Nope."

Alice goes back to watching the clouds and the sky and thinking about her dad, but she can't stand this train of thought so she turns back to Henry. Henry on the unmade bed, Henry who is scratching his ankle until it bleeds, Henry who forgot to comb his hair this morning and all of his cowlicks are sticking up.

There are still Transformers on the shelves and the complete set of Harry Potter. She knows if she opened the drawer to her left, Henry's collection of arrowheads would be there, perfectly labeled, right next to the tackle box with all his stuff for tying flies. Henry ties the most beautiful flies. He even has a Web site for selling them. And then there's his iPod—which he earned by mowing lawns—and his collection of jazz CDs. Henry is one of those kind of dorky boys with a lot of interests. But the piano is moving beyond that now; the piano has totally overshadowed the arrowheads; the piano is even starting to move the fly tying aside. Alice thinks that there is always music inside Henry's head, and right now she wishes she could have music inside her head, too.

There are no rules at Henry's house about what Henry and Alice can and can't do, where they can go, what rooms they can be in, what doors have to be open. At Alice's house the rules are probably the same rules her parents lived with. No boys in a bedroom, yours or anyone else's. In fact, no boys on the second floor. Ever. No closed doors. Feet on the floor at all times.

She turns back to the window and wonders what her Dad is listening to. Are there radio stations? Is there rock and roll? R&B? Hip hop? Rap? Does he hear the call to prayer five times a day? Is it just background noise or does he really hear it? What if Alice heard a call to prayer five times a day? And what if, instead of praying, which she only half or one quarter believes in anyway, what if she just stopped and listened five times a day? Could she hear her dad's voice? She can't remember his voice. She can almost see his face sometimes, but she can never hear his voice. And the harder she tries to see him or hear him inside her mind the farther away he recedes. If there were music inside her head could she forget for five minutes, could she ride the sound, the voices of the instruments, just take a ride, fly away from everything she's thinking all the time?

Henry is standing beside her.

"What's so interesting out there?"

"We haven't heard from my dad in three days."

She can feel Henry weighing his words, trying to figure out how to respond, but mostly she can feel his warm, solid presence beside her, and before Alice has time to think about what she's doing, or even know what she's doing, she kisses him. Just leans in and kisses him. Everything slows way down for a few seconds as she bumps into his glasses and stumbles over one foot and wonders, fleetingly, if she should close her eyes or not, but really doesn't have time to worry about that because time flips back to normal mode and Henry recoils in shock— or is that disgust?—she's not sure. Whatever it is, it's not pretty and it's not what she expected, if she expected anything at all and now she can feel a blush blooming from the top of her head and flushing red and hot the whole length of her body. The talking part of her brain is in panic mode: Oh, no! You idiot! Why did you do that? That was so stupid! The feeling/sensing part of her brain is going Wow, not so bad, really, if you were just a little more mellow and relaxed maybe you could get the hang of this. But Henry? What is she doing kissing Henry? From the look on his face, he's wondering the same thing.

Henry has turned away from Alice. His face is flaming hot and he is so acutely embarrassed he doesn't know how he is ever going to be able to face Alice again. He cannot believe that the first time a girl— and not just any girl, but Alice—makes a move, he reacts like one of those supersensitive cats who never let you get within ten feet of them. Why did he do that? What's wrong with him? Surprised. That's it. He was just surprised. Shocked even. Girls like Alice do not just up and kiss boys like Henry. At least not in Henry's very limited experience in which all sorts of girls, in fact, all girls, have handily managed to avoid kissing him. And no fair: It happened too fast. Was that really a kiss? Did he even feel it? Did their lips actually touch? The only person he can ask is Alice, and he can't ask Alice because he still can't look at Alice. Or speak.

Alice is stuffing her books and her notebooks and her jacket into her backpack. He needs to say something. Anything. It sounds like she's crying. Say something, you idiot! But Henry is rooted to the floor like his socks have superglue on them and his legs are made of lead and not one single body part is responding to his urgent, desperate commands.

Alice is at the door.

"We could pretend that never happened, okay? So it doesn't get weird and stuff."

Too late for that! is what Henry would normally say, if Henry could find his voice, if Henry could just turn and look at her. He's thinking this is about the loneliest he's ever felt in his life, this not being able to look at Alice, this business of being glued to the floor when he wants to reach out and touch her hair or her hand or her sleeve even.

And then she's gone, and Henry finds out that loneliest is right now, after she's left the room. Suddenly his feet unfreeze and his legs start to move and he's running down the stairs three, four at a time and throwing open the front door. But Alice is already halfway down the block, jogging steadily, her backpack bouncing on her back.

He watches until she turns in at her driveway and he can't see her anymore. He sits down on the front steps, pops back up, starts down the walk, retreats to the steps. I need to do something; I need to go over there; I can't possibly look her in the face; I have never felt so stupid in my life. But mixed in with the stupid feelings and the indecision and the walking up and down, there's another feeling, a big, welling up feeling in the middle of his chest, this kernel, this diamond—okay, yes, a diamond in the rough—this fact, this incontrovertible fact: *Alice kissed me.* Then he remembers, right, her father.

Three days. No contact. So maybe that wasn't really a kiss. Not a kiss kiss. More like some desperate something that looked like a kiss, that almost felt like a kiss but was not, actually, a kiss.

That would make more sense. But making sense of this turns out not to be comforting in the least. Making sense of this turns out to feel like a direct blow to the solar plexus. Maybe he's wrong, maybe he could talk to her. But what would he say, exactly? Hey, Alice, explain your motives. Hey, Alice, could we try that again? The more he thinks about it the more difficult it is to get up and walk down the block. And just as he's finally getting so uncomfortable he can't really do anything else but head over there, because nothing could make him feel worse, Alice's Uncle Eddie pulls up in an old orange Dodge and blows the horn: three long blasts.

He sees Alice run out to the curb, look up the street at him, watching her. She waves and turns away before he can wave back. She slides into the seat beside Uncle Eddie and they head off. Henry walks out into the street to watch them go. He waves at her, willing her to turn around and see him, which she doesn't do. He waves at her until the old Dodge crests the hill and disappears out of sight.

He turns back and starts trudging up his driveway, staring at the scuff marks and the incipient holes in the toes of his Chucks. Until he is stopped by the sight of the toes of his mother's brown sensible tie shoes. Pointing directly at him.

Don't look up, don't look up, he tells himself! What did she see? Did she see anything? Can he never, not even once in his life do something that his parents don't know about or find out about, or stick their noses into and ruin? Like *splat*, total *splat*. Ruin forever.

"Everything all right, Henry?" his mom asks the top of his head.

"Uh huh," he answers her shoes.

"Alice seemed like she was in a big hurry to get out of here."

"Uh huh."

"Do you need to talk about it?"

"Uh uh." And he shakes his head for emphasis.

"You sure?"

"Uh huh."

"How's the homework coming along?"

"Fine."

"You want a snack?"

"We ate the Oreos."

"All righty, then."

Mrs. Grover heads back inside, the laundry basket resting on her ample hip.

Henry dares to look up only after the front door has closed with its solid *thump*. And then he throws himself on the grass, the cool, damp, early-spring grass. He can feel the wet already seeping into him, but he doesn't care. What if, he's thinking, what if that really *was* a kiss?

The orange Dodge has one of those bench seats in the front. Alice has never seen one of those before. The whole car smells like wax it's so spic and span.

"Nice car, Uncle Eddie."

"Isn't she a beauty? Who knew an old Dodge could have so much style?"

"What's that thing on the steering wheel?"

"Necker's knob."

"What?"

He puts his arm around her and pulls her across the seat until she's snugged right in beside him.

"So you can drive with one hand."

"And . . ."

"Find a country road, open the windows, drive real slow, and give your girl a kiss."

"You ever have a car like this when you were a kid?" she asks as she slides over to her side of the seat and rolls the window down.

"I wish! I had to drive my old man's Ford. Stripped down, strictly utilitarian. Boring, boring car. How are you doing?"

She thought they were talking about cars, now he wants to know how she's doing?

"Where are we headed?"

"I thought we'd go up to the high school parking lot and just get a feel for things."

Alice is thinking that might be a better idea much, much later in the day or in the middle of the night or some weekend when there's no game and no practice going on and really absolutely no people around to watch and make her want to hyperventilate.

"You know how there's that faculty parking lot out by the maintenance shed? I thought we'd head over there."

Uncle Eddie can read her mind.

Next thing she knows she's behind the wheel. When they adjust the bench seat so she can comfortably reach the gas and brake pedals, Eddie is left with both knees jammed against the dash.

"No problem," he reassures her. "Plenty of room."

She puts on her seat belt.

"Okay. You know the difference between the gas and the brake?"

"Gas is right, brake is left."

"Which foot do you use for the brake?"

"Trick question! Right foot for both."

"Smart-ass."

She smiles at him.

"Put your foot on the brake."

He talks her through the gears. The Dodge is automatic but the shift is on the steering column. She's never seen that before. It's cool, though, the way you grab the handle, pull it toward you, and slide the lever to "D" for drive.

"So let's just start real slow in a nice big circle around the parking lot."

"Okay."

"You ready?"

"Yeah."

"Put her in drive and then release the brake nice and slow."

Alice does as she's told and they're moving! She's driving! Okay, so she could walk faster than this, but she's driving!

"Can I give it a little gas?"

"Not yet. Let's just focus on steering."

She misjudges the first turn.

"Straighten out your wheels. You feel that now? You've gotta get a feel for how she handles. Every car is different, different turning radius, different responsiveness to the steering wheel."

The second turn she drives right off the asphalt onto the stony shoulder, but pulls the car back in line a little more smoothly.

"A little more to the left."

The third and the fourth turns are pretty easy. She's proud of herself, but she doesn't dare take her eyes off the macadam in front of her to look at Uncle Eddie and judge his response. By the third time around she's starting to feel pretty good. She actually sits back in the seat a bit and relaxes the death grip she's been keeping on the steering wheel.

"Can we go a little faster?"

"Don't get cocky. You've been driving for five minutes."

"I'm a natural. I take after you."

"Next time. Maybe."

"I think I'm getting dizzy."

"So stop in the middle and start going the other way."

She finds the precise middle of the parking lot, comes to a full stop, puts on her blinker for good measure, and turns right.

"Who taught you to drive, Uncle Eddie?"

"Your mom."

"You're kidding."

"I made my old man crazy in a car. He swore he would never go anywhere with me behind the wheel."

"How come?"

"He thought I was a hothead."

"Were you?"

"Sometimes."

"A lot of times?"

"According to my old man. But as you can see, I've mellowed with the years."

"What kind of a teacher was Mom?"

"Awful. Her knuckles would be white, she'd be holding her breath and grabbing at the dashboard or the door handle for support every other minute."

"How'd you get her to keep getting into the car with you?"

"I paid her."

"You did not!"

"I was desperate. She would even gasp and moan whenever I did something stupid."

"But if she hated it so much—"

"She needed the money."

"For what?"

"College."

"So if she was such a scaredy-cat how'd you get to be such a good driver?"

"I love it. Have you noticed? People tend to be good at the things they love."

"She's not happy about this."

"She's not thinking it through."

"What do you mean?"

"It's just the two of you taking care of things while your dad's away. There could be an emergency where you'd need to be able to drive."

"Like what?"

"To get help."

"For who?"

"Say your mom gets food poisoning or appendicitis."

"Wouldn't I just call an ambulance?"

"Or Ellie falls."

"Ditto."

"Or Gram."

"Same."

"Or something unexpected."

"Like what?"

"I don't know! In my book it's just a good idea to be prepared. In case."

"In case."

"Plus, it's fun."

"Yeah."

"And you'll be the first one—of all your friends."

"Except for Ashley Cooper who lives on a farm and has been driving a tractor since she was twelve."

At which point Alice realizes that she is just cruising around the parking lot. Slower than slow, but making the turns effortlessly, like a real driver. She cranks down her window and sticks her elbow out.

"Both hands on the wheel!"

"Okay, okay."

"Confident is good. Overconfident is not good."

"Got it."

Both hands on the wheel, the cool spring air coming in the window, the nose of the car moving slowly past empty fields, the utility garage, the Dumpster, the crowns of the distant weeping willows gilded by the setting sun.

"There you go, kiddo. There you go."

Alice risks a glance at Uncle Eddie.

"Who was your first girlfriend?"

"Why?"

"Just curious."

"Melissa Pardee. Fourth grade. I followed her around like a puppy."

"First kiss?"

"What is this? Twenty questions?"

"First kiss?"

"Why the sudden interest in kissing?"

"Quit stalling."

"Jessie Simons. Sixth grade. On the bus coming back from a field trip."

Alice tries to picture eleven-year-old Uncle Eddie making his move with little Jessie Simons.

"Did she kiss you back?"

"Who knows? Probably. That was a long time ago. So what about your first kiss?"

"Are you kidding me?"

"'Fess up, Alice."

She laughs and shakes her head.

"I guess I'm one of those late bloomers."

"Sure you are."

"Were you ever in love?" she asks.

"Alice, c'mon—"

"Were you?"

"Lots of times."

"No, I mean, really in love."

Eddie looks out the window.

"Once."

"What happened?"

"That's a long story."

"How come you never got married?"

"What's with all the questions?"

"Well . . . ?"

"I let her get away."

"Why?"

"Couldn't commit I guess."

"Where is she now?"

"Married with four kids, teaching second grade about one hundred miles from here."

"Do you ever see her?"

"No."

"Do you ever get lonely?"

"Geez, Alice, let's move on to brighter things. You're *driving*, did you notice?"

She completes one last circuit before pulling up in the center of the parking lot. She remembers to put the car in park, engages the emergency brake, and relinquishes the wheel to Uncle Eddie. He moves the seat back with a sigh and punches her in the shoulder.

"Good job. I can't believe we need a bigger parking lot already."

"We could go to the mall."

"Next week the mall."

"For real?"

"It's a date."

Uncle Eddie turns the radio on to golden oldies as he pulls onto Five Mile Line Road.

"Crank your window down," he shouts over Van Morrison crooning "Tupelo Honey."

They both start singing along really loud.

She's as sweet as tupelo honey

She's an angel of the first degree

Normally this would embarrass Alice, normally she would be all self-conscious about how her voice sounds while at the same time scanning the streets and the sidewalks to see if anyone is witnessing her craziness. But today, she decides, she doesn't care. Here in the orange Dodge with fat Uncle Eddie, singing at the top of her lungs, she doesn't have to think, she doesn't have to worry, she doesn't have to give a damn. The day has turned to a pink dusk, and just like Henry, she's got music inside her head and all around her.

April 18th

Alice does not like being dragged to the pool with her mother while Ellie takes a knitting class in the Y's paneled, stuffy rec room. After school and track she just wants to go home.

Alice sits in the bleachers. It's hot, it's almost dripping with humidity. She hates the bleachers, she hates the chlorine smell of the pool. Underneath all that bleach there's this nasty, damp rot kind of smell.

This time slot is lap swim only, so it couldn't be more boring. Just a bunch of grown-ups and old people going back and forth, never getting anywhere. How they can put their faces in that slimy water is beyond Alice.

Here comes her mother from the showers. Her Speedo bathing suit and cap on, her goggles in her hand. She stops where Alice is sitting, sweaty and miserable.

"You don't have to sit there like a lump, you know."

"Thanks, Mom."

"You *do* have a bathing suit."

Alice doesn't bother to answer.

"It's healthy."

"Uh huh."

"You get into a different place in your head. It's peaceful."

"Okay, Mom."

"Just once. Will you try it just once?"

"Probably not."

"You love to swim in the summertime."

"That's different."

"How is that different?"

113

"It's outdoors, for one."

"I was thinking this was something we could maybe do together."

"I'll think about it," Alice says.

Angie walks away, hops into an empty lane, pulls her goggles on, gives Alice a little wave, and starts swimming. As she warms up for a few hundred meters with an easy breaststroke, she's trying not to think about Alice and how is she ever going to reach her or even just feel comfortable with her own daughter ever again? She's trying not to think about Matt and where he is and if he's all right; she's trying not to think at all; she's trying to get to that place where she's swimming and *not* thinking, just moving her body, just making her turns, reaching into the backstroke now, her favorite stroke, and letting her mind slow and quiet and then quiet some more until, for a few sweet strokes or lengths or moments, she is nothing but body and breath and motion.

Only it's not working today. She turns and attacks the crawl as though she is attacking her anger, trying to drown it in the pool. No one talks about the anger, the rage, how the love and longing are all mixed up with these other less attractive emotions. How could he leave me? How could he leave us? This was not the deal, this is not where their lives were supposed to be heading. And that shirt, that stupid blue shirt of Matt's hanging out beneath Alice's jacket, looking grubby, looking like hell, looking like a goddamn battle flag waving under her nose: bad mother, bad mother, bad mother.

It's just a shirt, she tries to tell herself. Ignore it. Forget it. Distant daughter. Deployed husband. Another turn, and another turn. Backstroke again, her favorite stroke again. Just breathe, Angie. Just breathe.

Alice grabs her backpack and heads up to the lobby. She rummages in her pockets to see if she has enough change to buy a Coke or a snack from the vending machines. No such luck.

She peeks into the rec room and there's Ellie, sitting in a circle with four other girls. No boys of course. The teacher is this comfy-looking woman with long, scraggly hair, a patchwork skirt, Birkenstocks, and an obviously homemade sweater. She patiently moves from kid to kid, helping them work their big wooden needles, helping them find dropped or lost stitches. Ellie is chatting away like she's found her niche.

Alice closes the door quietly and heads outside. The YMCA is a relatively new building, built on the outskirts of Belknap's Four Corners. Not that there's much left to the Four Corners since they built the stupid mall three miles down Belknap Road. There's just the library, two churches, a gas station, a bar, an upholstery store that always looks like it's on the verge of going out of business, The Bird Sisters, Jansen's Hardware, and the local pharmacy. Ricci's little grocery/ deli is still trying to hang on. It is the dimmest, dustiest store on the block. A 25-watt bulb would be bright in there. Maybe they don't want anybody reading the expiration dates on the canned goods. They've recently updated their penny candy aisle, even though penny candy doesn't cost a penny anymore.

Alice sits on the bench by the bus stop. She'd like to walk the few blocks to the library, but then no one would know where she is. She'd like to be sitting next to Stephie in the library doing their homework just like they used to do, passing notes and sharing M&Ms and giggling and making the librarian come over to tell them to be quiet. *Again.* She'd like to walk the half-mile home. Somehow this stupid trip to the Y is a family outing in her mom's mind. Even though Alice hates it, even though they are all in different parts of the Y. Maybe the family part is when they go out to Don & Bob's afterward for hamburgers and onion rings. Alice is counting on frozen custard for dessert.

She's trying not to think about what happened with Henry yesterday, when she sees Mrs. Minty struggling to get her rolling cart out the door of Ricci's grocery. Alice starts to cross the street to help her when John Kimball maneuvers his way past Mrs. Minty and then not only holds the door for her but picks up her cart and carries it to the sidewalk. He's holding a soda and a package of Devil Dogs in one hand and doing all this maneuvering for Mrs. Minty with his other hand.

She thanks him. She knows his name. He offers to walk her home and help unload her groceries. She declines, says the exercise is good for her heart and her bones. And then she asks him about baseball. Mrs. Minty follows high school baseball? She tells him he's a great shortstop. Mrs. Minty goes to games? Curiouser and curiouser, as another Alice would say.

Alice quickly retreats to the farthest corner of her bench and pulls out *Othello* so that John Kimball won't know she's been eavesdropping and, hopefully, won't even notice her at all. Which is when she hears Mrs. Minty say:

"You remind me of my boy. All you boys do. He was just your age."

"What happened to him?"

"Meningitis. The local doctor didn't realize how serious it was."

"When was this, Mrs. Minty?"

"1963."

"What was his name?"

"His friends called him Pete. We called him Peter. After my father."

"Did he play baseball?"

"Shortstop. Just like you."

"Any good?"

"We thought he was marvelous. So fast."

"Did you have any other—"

"No, no. Just the one."

"And your husband?"

"That was the beginning of a terrible decade. Not the sort of times you can live through with a broken heart."

"You mean the war?"

"And the assassinations. And everything else. Jared found he couldn't keep getting up in the morning. . . . The doctors say he died of heart disease. But I know better."

"I'm so sorry, Mrs. Minty."

"It was his time."

That's what grown-ups always say, Alice thinks. But what does it mean? That every person gets allotted a certain number of days?

"Now how in the world did we get on this topic?" Mrs. Minty continues.

"Baseball."

"Very diverting, baseball."

"I have to be careful it doesn't divert me right into getting C's and D's."

"You following the Red Wings as usual this year, John?"

"Yes, ma'am."

"I'd love to go to the opening game."

"I'll talk to my father, Mrs. Minty. We'll make a date."

"That would be lovely. Tell him I expect the full treatment: beer, peanuts, hot dogs."

"Will do."

"The Boxford High game next week. Is that a home game, John?"

"Sure is."

"See you there. Weather permitting."

Mrs. Minty heads off, with a jaunty little wave, her square purse hanging over one arm, one hand firmly on her rolling basket. She doesn't move quickly, but she's determined. She also, Alice notices, isn't looking down at her feet and the sidewalk, but instead, is looking up at the trees and the birds and the houses, and whatever else there is to see on her six-block walk home.

Alice is watching Mrs. Minty and trying to take in the fact that she lost her son, that she even had a son, and that he was just her age.

Alice has never known anyone who died before except for her grandparents and her great aunt Charlotte. Even though she didn't know him, even though he died before she was even born, suddenly this boy, Peter, who played shortstop, is as real as real can be.

As real as John Kimball, who has materialized in front of her, and not only that, has decided to sit down on the bench beside her and offer her a Devil Dog.

"No, thanks."

"You're not one of these crazy girls who doesn't eat, are you?"

"No."

"Good."

"I just heard, I couldn't help hearing, about Mrs. Minty's son, Peter, and . . ."

"Yeah."

It's really strange, or maybe not so strange, that they just sit there for a minute, thinking about Peter, not saying anything else for a while. Normally this would make Alice squirm and fret: Should I be saying something? Like what? Should he be saying something? But she is not thinking any of these things; she is not, in fact, worrying. This is hard to believe given that it is John Kimball sitting beside her and the last time she saw him she had dog shit all over her shoes. Hard to imagine that that ghastly experience might have been an icebreaker.

"He was only fifteen," Alice ventures.

"Yeah."

"You ever know anyone who died?"

John looks down at the ground.

"My mother."

"Oh my gosh, I'm so sorry."

"Yeah."

"No, I mean, I'm really—"

"Thanks. It's okay."

He opens the package of Devil Dogs.

"I think about it all the time," Alice says.

"What?"

"Dying."

"Really?"

If there were a red light in her brain, it would be flashing. Crazy outcast girl talking to the most popular boy in school. And the topic she chooses: dying. Not a good idea! Cease and desist!

"Why?" he asks, like he really wants to know.

"My dad's in Iraq."

Why is she telling him this? It's not like they're friends, it's not like they know each other at all, really; it's not like this is the person she would choose to confide anything in, about anyone, ever. Ever!

"I didn't know."

There's a big pause here and she expects him to push off and head down the street just like everybody else does whenever the war comes up.

"Is he doing okay?"

She looks at him. He is so not what she thought he was, at least in this moment, that she has to get a visual on him to place herself back in reality.

"From everything I read I don't know how he could possibly be all right," Alice answers.

"I don't follow it as much as I should."

"No, I know, most people—"

"Which kind of makes me a really big jerk, doesn't it?"

"I wouldn't say that."

"I don't know what to say about your dad."

"I know. Nobody does."

"But I wish I could say everything is gonna be all right."

She turns and looks at him again. He has a Devil Dog crumb stuck to his lip. She takes a breath. She tests the waters of this moment with this boy. Could this possibly be real? And before she has a chance to think, to stop herself, she reaches out and brushes the crumb off his upper lip. He pulls away from her, possibly just a startle reflex, possibly total aversion, she notices, as she curls her hands into fists and shoves them under her thighs. Just like Henry, she thinks.

"Hey, Alice!" Ellie yells.

She's running down the steps of the Y, waving her arms wildly, waving her knitting like a flag.

"I've gotta go," she says.

"Yeah."

"Okay. So—"

"I'll see you around, okay?"

He gets up and starts walking away.

She ducks her head; she knows she won't really see him "around," that come tomorrow they will still pass each other in the halls and she will be invisible to him and his friends—which is, of course, better than being the object of their attention and ridicule.

Funny that a bench on Main Street could be neutral territory, kind of floating in a different world with different rules where for a few minutes they could almost talk, almost see each other.

She looks up. Ellie is waiting on the steps.

"Alice, c'mon!"

John stops and turns around. He's coming back to the bench.

"Listen, you want to come to the Red Wings game with me and my dad and Mrs. Minty?"

"Are you joking?"

"No, I'll talk to my dad. It's fun. You like minor league baseball?"

She wonders: Does she like baseball? Does it matter?

"Okay," she finds herself saying. "Okay."

"Great."

And he's off, jogging down the street toward home. John Kimball did not just ask me out. This is not a date, this is probably not even going to happen. This is charity Tuesday with Mrs. Minty and that weird girl whose father is in Iraq. Okay. Good deed for the day. Pull yourself together, Alice.

She joins Ellie on the steps of the Y. Ellie with her new glasses.

"Who was that?"

"Just some guy from school."

"What's his name?"

"John."

"Do you like him?"

"No!"

"Yes, you do."

"I've never even talked to him before today."

"Is he popular?"

"What do you think?"

"I think you like him."

"You're nuts."

"What about Henry?"

"What *about* Henry?"

Ellie gives her one of those all knowing smart-ass teenager kind of looks. Where does she get this stuff?

"C'mon. Let's go find Mom," Alice says.

"Did he ask you out?" Ellie wants to know.

"Did he ask me out? Are you kidding?"

"Did he?"

"To a Red Wings game. With Mrs. Minty."

"See?"

"See what?"

"He asked you out."

"Charity. Strictly charity. He must be getting his Boy Scout Buddha badge in compassion. Or selflessness."

"They don't have Buddha badges in the Boy Scouts. You're making that up. Plus, he must be an Eagle Scout already."

"Right. Eagle Scout Buddha Badge."

"You think Mom will let you go?"

"Who knows?"

"Are you gonna ask her?"

"Maybe."

"He's kind of cute."

"Ellie!"

"What? He *is.*"

"How was knitting?"

"You're changing the subject."

"Yup."

"I'm making a scarf for Dad. I picked double rib stitch."

"What colors?"

"Lots of colors. Mrs. Morris has hundreds of colors."

"Will you show me later?"

Alice takes Ellie by the hand as they head to the parking lot at the rear of the building. She listens while Ellie talks about Mrs. Morris and how she smells like spices and how Dad is gonna love the scarf of many colors even if he gets it in the wrong season and how he could use it as a talisman or a good luck symbol just like the knights of old.

"You want to hear my new favorite word?"

"Sure."

"*Hypergelast.* What do you think *that* means?"

"Sounds like extreme gymnastics to me."

"It means someone who can't stop laughing!"

Ellie doubles over she is laughing so hard. She laughs and laughs. And Alice can't help herself; she joins right in.

April 19th

The alarm didn't go off this morning, or if it did, Alice didn't hear it and now she's late and to top it off she can't find her shirt. It's not under the bed, where she left it, carefully hidden behind her backpack; it's not in the hamper; it's not in the basement in the pile of laundry overflowing the laundry basket. Ellie swears she doesn't know where it is.

"Did you take it?"

"Why would I take your smelly shirt?"

"Did you take it?"

"No, Alice, I did not take your smelly, disgusting shirt!"

"Where's Mom?"

"How should I know?"

"I need my shirt."

"It's just a shirt."

"It is not just a shirt. It's Dad's shirt."

"You are obsessed."

"I am not!"

"How is it I can be so much more mature than you are, Alice, when I'm only eight?"

"Bully for you, Miss Goody Two-Shoes."

Just then she hears the garbage truck screech to a halt at the curb. She looks out the window. There's her mom, *in her bathrobe,* dragging the garbage can down to the curb. Could she be any more embarrassing?

Which is when Alice puts two and two together and speeds through the front door and down the front steps and down the driveway in her bare feet.

"Mom! *Mom!*"

The garbage guy has their garbage can in his hand, he's hoisting it up and pouring it into the open maw of the truck.

"Wait! Wait! *Stop!*"

But it's too late. She doesn't actually see the blue shirt going into the grinder thing in the back of the truck. No, it's probably buried in a bag of trash and used Kleenex and carrot tops.

Angie walks up the driveway. Alice can't even look at her mother she's so furious. She's trying to control her breathing so she'll be able to speak.

"What's going on? . . . Alice?"

"Dad's shirt."

"Oh, don't get started on that again."

"You threw it away, didn't you?"

"You can stand out here and catch your death in bare feet, but I'm going inside."

Angie starts to walk past Alice, but Alice steps in front of her, blocking her way.

"If it's not in the trash, where is it?"

"This is ridiculous. I'm going inside."

But Alice won't move.

"How could you do that? And how could you lie to me?"

"I haven't lied to you."

"You want to know why girls can't stand their mothers? It's shit like this, Mom!"

"Inside!"

"First you steal my clothes, then you lie to me and now you think you can order me around?!"

"Alice!"

Angie tries to walk around her again.

"Couldn't you just ask me, Mom? How hard is that? Just ask me!"

"I am not going to argue with you in the middle of the driveway! We can continue this inside." Angie pushes past Alice. "Or not at all."

"Fine! How about not at all?! That would be just more of the same, wouldn't you say, Mom?"

Alice has the satisfaction of hearing her mother slam the front door. Hard. Which is when she hears the garbage truck shift into second gear as it continues its lumbering journey down the street to Henry's house, where no doubt Henry's father had the trash down at the curb well before six a.m. No mothers running out to the street in bathrobes at Henry's house.

Where is her dad's shirt now? Part of the compost of newspapers, orange rinds, cereal boxes, last night's take out containers. . . . Some of the fight goes out of Alice as her feet begin to ache they're so cold. She starts up the driveway.

Okay. She'll get another one of her dad's shirts, and maybe she'll take one of his jackets, too. And if she can wear both of those things, maybe, just maybe she'll be able to hold it together and walk out the door and go to school like she's supposed to.

As she walks through the front door, her mom pushes past with a cup of coffee.

"Alice, get ready for school. Enough of this nonsense."

Alice does not respond.

"Alice, I mean it. Get a move on."

Alice swallows hard and finds her voice.

"If anything happens to Dad—"

"What?"

"—it's your fault."

"You're being ridiculous."

"Am I?"

"You want to blame me. Fine. Blame me. You know who you're really mad at?"

"I don't want to hear this!"

"You're mad at Dad."

"I am not!"

"Think about it, Alice."

"Dad did not put that shirt in the trash!"

"Dad—"

"—Don't!"

Alice walks up the stairs and into her parents' bedroom where she takes another shirt out of her father's drawer. Angie follows her.

"I'd really rather you didn't take another one of Dad's—"

Alice's hands are shaking as she unbuttons a crisp blue and white striped shirt. Not the same, not the same shirt at all, she thinks in a kind of wild, sad desperation. One of the buttons pops off and skitters across the floor. She looks at the shirt for a moment, the stripes, the missing button, then shoves it back in the drawer, and slams the drawer shut so hard several photos fall off the dresser.

"What are you doing?"

"I'll never forgive you if—"

"Alice. For heaven's sake."

"Can you spare one of these?" Alice asks, as she opens the top drawer and grabs a white T-shirt.

"Take five! Take six! You want them all? Take them all, goddamnit! Take them all!"

"I only wanted one, Mom. The one I had. The one he wore," Alice replies as she slams out the door and down the stairs.

Angie sits on the unmade bed, the broken glass of her favorite picture beneath her fingers. She feels awful, as she always does after a fight. Couldn't she just have *washed* that stupid shirt?

She looks at their wedding photo. Matt is holding her with both hands around her waist, his head thrown back, his whole face lit up with laughter.

Lighten up, she can almost hear him say. *Don't you remember all the shit you put your parents through when you were in high school? She's just a kid, a scared kid.*

Does she have to be so annoying, Angie wonders? Does she have to wave everything right under my nose?

Stop rising to the bait. You're the grown-up here.

Easy for you to say, Matt Bliss, from nine thousand miles away.

April 20th

Alice and Henry catch the bus downtown after school, way downtown, to Pearl Street, to the cool vintage clothing store that specializes in tuxedos. They have twenty dollars to outfit Henry for the dance, and another twenty for Alice. Maybe. For Alice this is all a big maybe. The mothers wanted to take them to the mall; that was a definite no.

Unbeknownst to Alice, Henry also has another fifty dollars in his pocket, given to him by his mother. Henry and his mother have discussed the options; Henry and his mother have outlined a basic game plan; Henry actually knows what he is looking for.

Sitting next to Alice on the city bus, however, Henry feels lost. It's a cold, comfortless day that could belong to any month from October to May. Henry follows Alice's lead and pulls out his history homework, but he can't read. Reading in cars and buses makes him sick. He sneaks a look at her. She appears to actually be reading about the Continental Congress. She does not sense him looking at her and turn toward him and begin to talk, like she usually does.

They have not discussed the kiss. Or the non-kiss. In fact, they haven't really talked at all. They are both pretending that nothing happened, that everything is the same. But of course, nothing is the same. Riding the bus isn't the same, sitting side by side so their legs almost touch is not the same, getting thrown against Alice as the bus makes the long curve up onto I-95 is not the same. Not talking is not the same. Not talking and joking and laughing. Not having to think so much about every single thing it gives you brain cramp is not the same. It's all so overwhelming that Henry falls asleep, right there on the noisy downtown bus, falls sound asleep until Alice wakes him up at their stop on Jane Street at Downtown Crossing.

They walk the two long, dreary blocks to Pearl Street in total silence. Maybe this was a mistake, Henry is thinking. Maybe this whole thing is one big, terrible mistake. Maybe Alice hates him now and maybe he's mad at Alice for ruining everything and maybe they should just go home. But there's Alice throwing open the grimy door and striding inside Rerun like she owns the place.

There are millions of tuxedos at Rerun, crammed into a long, narrow, dusty storefront on a street that has seen better days. Rerun is flanked on either side by empty stores. The middle-aged, potbellied, Hawaiian shirt–wearing guy behind the counter is eyeing them as if they are hardened shoplifters out to rob him blind. Alice starts sneezing. They don't even know what size to look for. Henry walks up to the counter.

"Hi."

"Yeah."

"I need a suit. Or a tuxedo."

"Uh huh."

"For a dance."

"Look around."

"I don't know what size."

The guy whips out a tape measure.

"My name's Henry."

Measuring Henry's waist.

"What's your name?"

Measuring Henry's chest.

"Roger."

Measuring Henry's inseam.

"Nice to meet you, Roger."

"The smaller sizes are on the left. Upper rack."

"What size am I?"

"You're the size that's gonna need alterations."

"Which is—?"

"There might be a couple of thirty-fours in there."

"You got anything for my friend?"

"A tuxedo?"

"Hey, Alice! You want a tuxedo?"

"Maybe," Alice answers from the other side of a rack.

"I was thinking more like a dress," Henry says. And then quietly to Roger: "You know that actress in the movie *Breakfast at Tiffany's?*"

"Audrey Hepburn?"

"A dress like she wore."

"That's a sheath, bud."

"And maybe a hat."

"Does the girl know?"

"No."

"You might ask the girl."

"That's my mom's favorite movie."

Roger gives him a look.

"Do you have anything?" Henry asks.

"I might."

"Is it in a vault or something?"

Roger calls to Alice. "What size are you?"

"I don't know. Small?"

"That's a start."

He walks to the racks of tuxedos, effortlessly extracts four of them, hangs them in a fitting room wallpapered in leopard print, and disappears through a back door.

"Am I supposed to try those on?" Henry asks.

"Yup!"

Alice plops into a lime green swivel chair to wait.

Henry closes the curtain.

"I think you should look at some pearls."

"What?"

"Some long strings of pearls."

"What are you talking about?"

"Are there hats? Have you seen any hats?"

"Henry, have you lost your mind?"

He steps out of the fitting room.

"This one's too big."

Henry is drowning in this tuxedo. The sleeves reach his knees. He'd need stilts to wear the pants.

"Try the next one."

"Look at the pearls."

"What pearls?"

"In the glass case."

"What do I want with pearls?"

"Alice could you just——"

Henry steps back into the fitting room as Roger appears with half a dozen little black dresses draped over his arm. He hangs them one by one across the back wall of a fitting room papered in faded peppermint stripes.

"I think this is what he was looking for," Roger says.

"Those are for me?"

"I'll find you some pearls."

"Henry . . . ?"

"Just try them on. Just for fun," Henry says from behind the curtain.

Alice finds herself in the pink room with the peeling wallpaper taking off her backpack and her clothes and carefully pulling the first dress over her head. There is no mirror inside the fitting room, so she's going to have to step outside to see what it looks like. She hesitates. This could be really embarrassing. It seems like it fits; she can still breathe after she zips the zipper. At least it's not long, and at least it's not full of ruffles and bows, and it definitely doesn't look like anything her mother would pick out for her. It's straight and close fitting but not tight, and the skirt hits just below the knee. Maybe she's gonna look like a fifty-year-old widow in this dress.

She steps outside the fitting room. She still has her socks on, but even so she can see that it's a beautiful dress. And even though she's mostly all covered up, it's also a sexy dress. It hugs her body and her waist looks tiny and it shows off her shoulders and her long neck.

"What size shoe do you wear?" Roger asks.

"Seven and a half."

He hands her a pair of red high heels. She shakes her head.

"Do you have any flats?"

Roger disappears and reappears with a pair of black, pointy-toed flats. Alice pulls her socks off and slips into them.

Henry steps out of his fitting room in a jacket that actually fits and pants that are kind of tight but in a good way. Even just wearing a T-shirt under the jacket, Henry looks good. But Henry is not looking in the mirror, Henry is looking at Alice.

"What?" She laughs.

Roger reappears with an impossibly long string of pearls that he doubles around her neck, and several hairpins.

"Put your hair up," he instructs, handing her the pins.

Alice lifts her hair off the nape of her neck. Roger glances at Henry, raises an eyebrow. Here it is, the simplest gesture in the world: a girl lifts her hair off the nape of her neck and a boy and an old man catch their collective breath.

"There," she says, and turns to them.

She smoothes the front of the dress, looking down at her hands, at her bitten fingernails, at her big feet in the pointy-toed shoes. This is a woman's dress, she thinks, a young woman's dress. It is not a girl's dress. It is solidly on the other side of the line outside of girl-hood. It is a dress that says something big in a very quiet way; it is a dress that is talking to Alice right now, a dress that is making her feel possibilities never before considered, the possibility of perfume and pretty and dancing and boys. This dress is who she might be, only more so.

When she looks up they are both smiling at her.

"You need a shirt," Roger says to Henry, and hustles off to find him one.

Henry almost can't bear looking at Alice. There's something happening in his stomach that could be the flu or could be just plain, pure misery and longing.

"Do you like it?"

He nods his head and closes his eyes to try to contain the intensity of what he is feeling. He closes his eyes and imagines holding Alice on the dance floor, his hands resting on the small of her back; he imagines hearing Duke Ellington and a tenor sax and knowing the tune and knowing the words and knowing the steps, and holding Alice in his arms, Alice in that dress, Alice with that music. . . .

"Henry . . . ?"

He opens his eyes to find Alice grinning at him.

"What?"

"This could be fun."

April 21st

"There are two soldiers at the front door!" Ellie shouts.

"What?!"

"Two soldiers! Knocking on the door."

"What are you talking about?"

"I think you should answer the door."

"Is it Dad?"

"No! It's not Dad!"

"Nobody comes to the front door."

"Alice! I want you to come down here right now!"

"I'm coming!"

Alice is running down the stairs thinking, soldier at the front door, soldier at the front door. Her heart is flip-flopping in her chest, and she's not really sure where her feet are and before she opens the door she has a chance to register Ellie. Ellie who is standing stock still in front of the living room window, a bright blue crayon in her left fist, staring out the window at the soldiers who are improbably standing on the front stoop, patiently waiting for someone to open the door.

She hesitates with her hand on the knob. He knocks again, softly. Do they get training in this? How to knock? What time of day to show up?

She opens the door to a soldier in his twenties who immediately takes off his hat, revealing an extremely new haircut. He is flanked by another soldier twice his size.

"I'm Sergeant Walker Ames. This is Army Chaplain McMurphy. May I speak to your mother?"

"She's not home."

"When will she be back?"

Alice glances at her dad's watch.

"Maybe six thirty, maybe later."

"Can you call her?"

"Is my dad all right?"

"Can you call her?"

"Can you just tell me that?"

"I'll wait while you call her."

He is eerily, almost creepily calm Alice thinks, as her mind races to take in all of the possibilities of what his presence on her front stoop means.

"Do you want to come inside?" Ellie asks.

"No, thank you. Please call your mother."

Twenty minutes later Angie pulls all the way into the driveway and comes in through the kitchen door, the way they always do. As she stoops down to give Ellie a hug, Alice can see that her hands are shaking.

"I just wanted a moment with my girls," she says, as she pulls Alice to her side.

There's that soft knock again.

Angie stands and walks to the front door. The girls are hesitating behind her. She reaches out and opens the door.

"Mrs. Bliss? Mrs. Angie Bliss?"

"Yes."

"Sergeant Walker Ames. May I come in?"

Missing. They have almost no information other than that Matt Bliss is officially MIA.

Here's what they do know, or what the army will tell them, or what they have sanitized to put in the official letter, which is delivered by Sergeant Ames and the very bulky, very bald, and nearly tongue-tied army chaplain McMurphy.

Matt had been patrolling Falluja for six days with his thirteen-man infantry squad. On the day in question, Matt's unit rushed the roof of the tallest building in the northern end of the city. With a nineteen-year-old named Travis Boyd in the lead, the soldiers ran up the building's four flights of stairs. When they stepped out onto the roof, the enemy opened fire. Matt ran past Travis Boyd to the far side of the building where he was shot and wounded. Within seconds, everyone else on the roof was wounded.

In the letter to the family they quote Travis Boyd: "We tried to get to Matt. I could see he was still alive. But the insurgents dragged him away with them." Boyd was hit with shrapnel and suffered a concussion, earning a Purple Heart.

They do not know where Matt is being held or why. Sergeant Ames is talking about hope, telling them of other cases where missing soldiers have been found, or rescued. He advises them to be patient, not to watch the news, to go about their daily life as usual.

The army chaplain is doing considerably less talking. He does manage to ask them to call him, any time of the day or night. He hands Angie his card. Ellie wants one, too.

"Girls, I want you to go to your room."

"But, Mom—" Alice says.

"Alice, take your sister upstairs, please."

Alice turns to Sergeant Ames.

"Did you say he was on a roof?"

"Yes."

"He was ambushed and wounded on a roof?"

"Yes."

"Alice, I'd like you to go upstairs now please," Angie says.

The girls go, reluctantly. Alice sits on the upstairs landing to listen as best she can with Ellie sobbing in their bedroom.

Angie asks to speak to Sergeant Ames alone. McMurphy heaves himself out of Matt's favorite chair and leaves the house, shutting the door very quietly behind him.

"The army recovers her own, ma'am."

"Dead or alive?"

"We always work toward the best possible outcome."

She looks at him.

"Believe me. We are on top of this. We will be the first to know if there is any intelligence."

"Are you actively searching for him?"

"I'm afraid that's classified."

"Is that really all you can tell me?"

"Steps are being taken."

"When will we know more?"

"It is my duty to keep the family informed, ma'am."

"Do you have any idea why they would take Matt like that?"

"It happens occasionally."

"But why?"

"Ma'am—"

"I'm thinking the worst here, Sergeant. Some real information would help."

135

"Intelligence is usually the motive for any capture."

Angie takes a deep breath.

"And how often do you recover soldiers alive?"

"I don't have an exact number, ma'am."

"I don't believe you."

"It's a small number."

"Is it zero?"

"No, ma'am."

"Are you going to make me guess, Sergeant?"

"Less than twenty percent."

"Thank you."

Angie looks out the window at the weak April sunshine shading into evening.

"Is he likely to be tortured?"

"There's no reason to give up hope."

"You didn't answer my question."

"Reports vary widely."

The careful management of information, or lack of information, is making Angie furious.

"My husband has been wounded—we don't know how gravely— and dragged away by insurgents. He is presumably without medical care."

"He's strong, he's fit; he's well trained."

"Do we have any idea how badly wounded he was? Or where he was wounded? Can you contact Travis Boyd with our questions?"

"I will make every effort to do so, ma'am."

"My name is Angie. Please call me Angie."

"We are instructed to—"

"Every time you call me ma'am I feel like a widow."

"Yes, ma'am."

Sergeant Ames with his raw haircut and bad skin ducks his head, embarrassed.

"Is there anyone I can call to find out more? Is there anything I can do for my husband?"

"You have my number. And the number for the chaplain."

"Can I talk to a soldier who was there with him?"

"I'll look into that."

"Where is Travis Boyd now?"

"He's at the army hospital in Landstuhl, Germany."

"Will he recover?"

"Yes, ma'am, he will."

"I'd like to speak to him."

"I'll do my best."

"When, Sergeant? How soon can I speak to him?"

"I'll make it my priority, ma'am. . . . May I make a suggestion?"

"Yes."

"Go to work. Go to school. Go to church. Continue with your daily lives."

"I'm not sure . . ."

"Sitting in your house for days or weeks can be demoralizing. Call your family. Call your priest or your pastor."

"Are you telling me to pray, Sergeant?"

"I don't know what your beliefs are, but most people find it a solace. We can also connect you with another family who has gone through this."

"Thank you."

"Shall I contact someone then?"

"I don't know. Not yet. I don't know . . ."

"With your permission, I'll call on you tomorrow."

"Yes. All right."

Now that he is at the door Angie finds she doesn't want him to go. She doesn't want the next minute and the next to begin.

"Hope is a powerful thing, ma'am."

"Thank you, Sergeant."

Angie stands at the door watching Sergeant Ames as he walks down the driveway and gets into his army-issue Ford sedan. McMurphy is slumped low in the passenger seat, waiting. She notices that Ames is painfully thin and too pale and that he walks with a limp. What has he survived, she wonders? What have we put this boy through? What does he do to prepare himself to bring this news to grieving families? Is this kind of duty something you choose or something you are assigned to? How in the world does he bear it?

Be strong, she hears Matt saying inside her head. *Be strong, Angie.*

If he's still talking to her, if he's still bossing her around, if he's still driving her crazy by holding her to a higher standard, even if it's just inside her own head, then he must still be alive. Matt, she thinks, Matt . . . Be there for me. I need you.

In the sudden quiet after the door closes on Sergeant Ames, Alice sits on the landing and closes her eyes and tries to imagine a rooftop in Falluja.

She's nine years old the first time she goes on a roofing job with her dad. Her mom is at the library studying for her state licensing exams to be an insurance agent and examiner. Ellie is in day care and Alice is on spring break and therefore at loose ends. So Matt enlists her as his helper.

This all sounds like a good idea when they're in the kitchen making sandwiches and pouring strong hot tea into Matt's special work Thermos. Fun project with Dad. Dad and Alice on an outing. No interruptions from baby Ellie.

But then they get to the house in question, with the roof in question, and Alice's stomach takes a nosedive. The house is high on a hill. On top of that, it's a tall house. With a tower. There's an extension ladder and a kind of scaffolding built into the roof. Alice stands at the foot of the extension ladder and looks up. The roof is a million miles above her. And it's really, really steep. She's in the midst of changing her mind and coming up with a plan. She could stay in the car, or near the car, she promises not to be any trouble, not to interrupt him or complain about being bored.

"Okay. Let's go."

"I think I might be afraid of heights."

"I don't think so."

"I didn't think it would be so high."

"It's not that high."

"It looks high."

"Let's go."

"I could stay in the car, I could—"

"Alice—" he says in that tone. That tone that says there's no sense arguing, don't be a wuss, and don't disappoint me. She hates that tone. More than she hates that roof? It's a toss-up.

When she starts up the ladder she's fine, but half way up one of her legs starts to shake. She is not making this up. It's weird.

Matt is right behind her, his hands gripping the rungs on either side of her.

"It's okay. You're not gonna fall."

"But—"

"I've got you. Take a breath. . . ."

She breathes in.

"Don't hold your breath, Alice. Blow it out."

"Okay."

"There's nothing to be afraid of. It's just a ladder."

She climbs two more rungs.

"Daddy—"

She can't move. Her legs are now shaking so badly she can't trust them to hold her up. Matt puts his palm against her lower back.

"Just breathe. You're okay."

She tries that. Her hands are starting to go numb because she's holding the ladder so tightly. She makes the mistake of looking down.

"Dad! I need to go down. I can't do this."

"Yes, you can."

"No, I can't!" I will not cry, I will not cry, she says inside her head.

"You're safe. I won't let you fall."

"I'm so—"

"I know you're scared. It's okay to be scared. You just don't want to give in to it. Don't let it get bigger than you, Alice. It's just a feeling."

She starts to sniffle. She can't help it.

"Crying is not going to help here."

"I know."

"Look up. Four more steps and we're there. You can do it, Alice, I know you can."

She takes another step.

"It's really beautiful up there, Alice. You can see all the way to the lake."

"Really?"

"You're gonna love it."

And another step and another and now there's a new problem, how do you step out onto the roof? That is the scariest step of all.

"Don't think about it. Just reach for the scaffolding and hold on to that."

She closes her eyes.

"You can do it, Alice."

"Are you sure?" she says in a very small voice.

His lips are right next to her ear so she can feel the warmth of his breath as he says: "I'm totally sure. I'm so sure I'll bet you a dollar."

"Dad?"

"Don't think. Just go."

She reaches one hand out and grabs the scaffolding and steps off the top rung of the ladder and onto the roof.

"Now what?" She can feel the breath catch in her throat.

"You see where it looks like a bench? Just step on the braces—there are two—that's all you need to do—and sit right there on the bench."

Her hands are hot and sweaty and slippery and she thinks that sharp tang in the air is her own scared sweat.

"You can do it."

She wants to close her eyes. She wants to be back on the ground. She wants to be home alone. She wants to be anywhere rather than here.

"Two steps. That's all."

She puts her left hand against the roof shingles, as if that could help.

"You've got it."

And she does have it. Two steps and she reaches the bench built into the scaffolding. She sits and grips the edge with both hands. Her stomach is roiling but she is determined not to throw up. When she finally looks up after what feels like a hundred years, her father is grinning at her. He's looking at her like she just hit a home run, which she has never done in her life.

"Way to go, champ."

She tries to smile and feels the bile rise in her throat again. She closes her eyes, her knuckles white.

"Look around," he tells her.

She can't take her eyes off his face. Keeping her eyes glued to her father is what will keep her from falling off this roof.

"I can't."

"Okay. But you're missing the best part."

She closes her eyes, and she can feel her heart pounding and hear her breath rasping in her ears.

"Breathe, Alice. . . . Breathe deep. And then open your eyes and look. Just do it."

They're above the trees; they're above the power lines; they're above everything. She can see the sun shining on the lake and big, puffy cumulus clouds hanging in the sky. She can see more blue sky than she can see from her house or her yard or her street. She can see the curve of the beach at Loudon Pond Park and the old-fashioned bathhouses still closed up for the winter. She lets out a breath and realizes she's been holding her breath for what seems like forever. She dares to turn her head to see where her dad is and Matt Bliss is walking all over the roof like it is a flat surface just above the ground. He looks like he's walking around his own kitchen. She watches him, amazed.

"You'll get the hang of it."

I don't think so, she wants to tell him, but still isn't sure she can safely open her mouth.

"When you're ready, you can start handing me shingles. You see the box? To your left?"

She nods.

"Just one at a time, kiddo."

"If I were a boy, would I be better at this?"

"How many boys do you know who are brave enough to climb up here?"

"I don't know."

"Henry?"

"He's afraid of heights."

"See?"

"Do you wish you'd had a boy instead of me?"

"Never."

"Do you wish I was good at baseball?"

"Yes!"

"Me, too!"

"Okay. You can start with the shingles."

"Now?"

"Yes."

"Already?"

"Now's a good time."

She cautiously reaches for the shingles and just as cautiously reaches out and hands them, one at a time, as he needs them, to her father. At first this takes every ounce of concentration she has, all she can do is look at the roof, and the box and the shingles and his reaching hand. Just as she starts to get used to it, Matt finishes a section. And then he wants her to move to another section of scaffolding and another make-shift bench and another box of shingles. At first these moves reignite the terror inside of her, but by the fourth or fifth time, she's found her roof legs and she is—cautiously—moving a little more freely. And she's able to look up every now and then and take in the new view from a new section of the roof.

"You hungry?"

"We're having lunch up here?"

"You want to go down and come back up?"

"No!"

"Okay, then."

He sits beside her and pulls out the lunch they packed together. Pita pockets and carrot and celery sticks and apples and brownies.

"What if you have to pee?"

He looks at her and raises an eyebrow.

"You do not!"

He shrugs.

"In broad daylight?"

"I face away from the street."

"What about the neighbors?"

Another shrug.

"What am I supposed to do?" Alice asks.

"Skip the apple juice would be my advice."

He lies back against the roof, stretches out like he's at the beach, and closes his eyes.

"You're napping?!"

He hands her his watch.

"Wake me up in ten minutes."

"You have to be kidding me. You could—"

"But I won't. Try it. Just lie back."

"Dad—"

"Try it."

She lies back against the shingles, bracing her hands flat against the roof, her fingernails digging into the asphalt, her feet positioned solidly on the scaffolding. She takes a shaky breath. After the first disorienting moment, it's pretty nice actually. She looks over at her father and he's grinning at her again.

"You're showing off, aren't you, Dad?"

"I might be showing off a little."

"You always tell me not to show off."

"Sometimes I guess it's irresistible."

"You really like it up here."

"I love it up here."

He closes his eyes.

"Ten minutes, okay?"

Alice carefully takes one hand away from where it is trying to grip the roof beside her and brings her arm up to where she can see her dad's watch hanging loosely on her wrist. She notes the time: 12:01. At exactly 12:11 she will wake him up. If he's really asleep. If he's not just faking it. She likes it that he's trying to impress her. She likes it that he cares about her opinion. And now that she's not absolutely slick with fear, she's almost glad he got her up here. On top of the world.

The girls come downstairs slowly, not knowing what to expect. Angie is still at the front door looking out at the street. She wants to get on a plane; she wants to call her senator, her state representative, and her congressman; she wants to call her mother. She wants to fall apart and have someone else take care of things. But that would not be the way Matt would handle this. He would take steps. He would hold it together.

Before he left she was under the illusion that they had talked about everything, every possible scenario; if he were wounded or killed. But this . . . this was never part of the picture. They didn't plan for this.

She can feel the girls waiting behind her, waiting for her to turn around, waiting for her to know what to do, waiting for her to come up with a plan.

"Mom . . . ?" Ellie ventures.

Angie turns away from the street and looks at her girls. When she sees how frightened they are, her own fear threatens to rise up out of her in a howl.

One step at a time, Angie. Don't think about tomorrow. Don't project into the future. Take care of today. Take care of the here and now. Take care of the girls.

"Okay. Here's what we're going to do. We're going to ask ourselves what Daddy would want us to do. And then we're going to do it."

"Will he be all right?" Ellie asks.

"If anybody can come through this, Daddy can."

"Do you believe that?" Alice asks.

"Yes," Angie answers. "Yes, I do."

"I want to help him," Ellie says.

"How? I don't see how," Alice says.

"We can imagine our way to being near him," Angie says. "We can imagine healing him, comforting him. Think about him. Believe in him."

A flash of anger sears through Alice. Does her mother actually *believe* this crap? And then she looks at Ellie. Ellie is soaking this up. Suddenly Alice's anger deflates and she wishes she could be eight again.

"I need something to *do*," Ellie says.

"Go to school. Help at home. Make Daddy proud."

"I don't see how going to school will . . ." Alice trails off, uncertain. Ellie closes her eyes.

"I'm thinking about Daddy right now."

"Good."

"Mom—"

"I'll make dinner," Angie says. "You girls can do your homework."

"You're making dinner?"

"Don't look so surprised."

"And you expect us to do homework?"

"Yes."

"Are you serious? It's Friday night."

"Homework tonight and work and school on Monday."

Ellie obediently gets her backpack and sits at the dining room table. Alice joins her reluctantly, pulls out her planner, opens it, but when she tries to look up today's assignments she has trouble focusing. She finds a pen and opens a notebook so she'll look busy and then just sits there as Ellie actually completes her grammar worksheets and moves on to writing a story about honeybees.

"You're ploitering," Ellie announces.

"I'm what?"

"Ploitering. 'Working to little purpose.'"

"*Loiter* with a *p* in front of it?"

"Yup."

"You made that up."

"Nope."

"Are you sure?"

"Honeybees never ploiter."

"Are you working that into your story?"

"Extra credit vocabulary words."

"What do you need extra credit for? You already get all A's."

"A plus is possible. A plus is within my reach."

"Are you illustrating your story?"

"Of course."

"Hey, maybe you could have one honeybee who ploiters. A renegade. It could add to the drama."

"I'll think about it."

Ellie never incorporates Alice's suggestions into her stories. Ever.

Alice shifts her chair so she can watch her mom in the kitchen, an apron over her dress, going through the motions of making dinner. Shortly afterward, they all go through the motions of eating dinner, washing dishes, giving Ellie her bath, and finally going to bed.

After tossing and turning for what feels like forever, Alice gets up to go downstairs. She wishes she could go for a run. She wishes it were Monday so she could go to the computer lab at school to Google Earth Falluja's streets and houses and, hopefully, find aerial views of rooftops.

She's surprised to find her mom in the kitchen making tea with honey and rum. Angie looks up.

"I couldn't sleep," Angie says.

"Me neither."

"You want some?"

"You're offering me rum?"

"A teaspoon in some tea."

"Sure."

"It'll help you sleep."

Angie gets another mug from the cupboard, pours a second cup of tea.

"Have you told Gram?"

"Tomorrow. Let her have one more good night's sleep."

"And Uncle Eddie?"

"Same."

She adds honey and a small splash of rum.

"I think if I talk about it, if I tell people, that will make it real," Alice says. "Right now, my mind knows it's real, but no other part of me can really . . ."

"That's shock, honey. That's how the body protects us. We can only take it in a little at a time."

"I don't want to take it in."

"I know."

Angie hands Alice her tea.

"Careful—it's hot."

"I need more honey."

"Help yourself."

Alice adds a lot more honey.

"It's pretty good."

"Gram used to make this for me when I had a cold."

"When you were little?"

"Not that little."

Alice gathers her courage.

"Mom . . ."

Angie doesn't answer. She looks away.

"I need to know."

"Let's just drink our tea and slow our minds way, way down so we can get some sleep. We'll talk tomorrow. Okay, Alice? Tomorrow."

And Alice thinks wounded and Alice thinks captured and Alice thinks torture. She sips her tea and feels the slow seep of warmth spreading through her limbs. She feels her body slowing down even while her mind is still racing.

Angie looks at Alice, watches her get lost in her thoughts, sees her chapped lips and her tangled hair and the ancient Grateful Dead T-shirt of Matt's that she wears to bed. It's so old the jersey is disintegrating away from the seams.

"C'mon, honey. Let's go to bed."

Angie puts her arm around Alice's waist. She can feel ribs under her fingers and Alice's cool, smooth skin. Alice lets herself be held, almost, for a brief second, before pulling away.

They walk upstairs, one behind the other now, each carrying her mug of tea like a lantern in the dark.

April 24th

Alice sits in school on Monday and closes her eyes and tries to feel whether her father is still alive. Does the body know before the mind does? Can she feel the connection she has always felt or has it snapped? She wants to know where he was wounded, how badly, could he still walk and talk? What the hell was he wearing all that protective gear for if it couldn't really protect him? And what if his gear did protect him—and he was just stunned, not wounded—does that increase his chances of surviving? What if he was hit in one of the few exquisitely vulnerable places that the gear can't cover? Like his neck or his face and now she imagines a bullet ripping through an artery in his wrist or his thigh.

While waiting in the band room for chorus rehearsal to begin, Alice overhears Jennifer White and Melissa Johnson talking. She's trying to ignore them, but they're loud like they always are, and words and phrases keep hitting her like a punch to the gut.

"How could he do that?"

"I hate my father. I really hate him."

"I can't believe he did that to you."

"He's such an asshole."

"Grounding you for two weeks . . ."

"I wish he'd go away, I wish he'd die, I wish . . ."

Before she can think, Alice shoves Jennifer White. She meant to just give her a little push, but it's like she's so upset she's got this superhuman strength, and that little push hits Jennifer White so hard she stumbles, loses her balance, and falls to the ground. And gets a bloody nose and starts wailing. Alice looks up in time to see Stephie glance at her and then look away, shaking her head. No sympathy from that corner. Melissa Johnson is about to retaliate when Mr. Brooks, the music teacher, pushes his way through the crowd with his immense bulk. And even though Jennifer White gets a bloody nose if you just say boo to her, this looks really bad.

Next thing you know Alice is in the principal's office. Mr. Fisher wants to know what happened, he wants to talk about it; but Alice can't talk about it, she can't answer his questions, she can't tell him her side of the story. She just sits there staring at her hands or out the window. And while the principal is trying to be understanding, the longer she stays silent, the more wound up he gets until he's forgotten all about her father and has convinced himself she's being disrespectful and obstreperous and that she needs a nice little suspension to get her attitude in order.

When he picks up the phone to call her mother at work, Alice gets up to leave the room. He angrily waves her back to her seat just as the lunch bell rings. She knows he will not make himself ridiculous by actually chasing her, so she makes her escape in the general lunchtime melee and walks out the back door of the school and heads for home. Henry follows her for a ways but she can't talk to Henry right now, she can't talk to anybody.

Halfway down Highland Drive, where is she *going* anyway?, B.D. pulls up beside her in his old Chevy. The backseat is filled with orange plastic cones for practice, out-of-date running magazines, and empty coffee cups.

"Alice, where are you going? We've got practice this afternoon."

"I can't come today."

"You want to be on the team, you come every day."

"I'll make it up. Tomorrow. I can make it up tomorrow."

B.D. doesn't say anything. He's just looking at her.

"And I can run tonight. From home. Give me the workout."

"You want to be on this team, or what?"

How can he ask her this? How can he not know?

"*Yes!*" she says too loudly.

"Did something happen, Alice?"

She can't answer.

"You okay, kid?"

Alice is clenching and unclenching her hands. Her legs are so tense that her right knee is vibrating.

"You need somebody to talk to?"

"No."

"You sure?"

"I'll be okay."

"You need a lift somewhere?"

"No, thank you."

"Where are you going? Aren't you supposed to be in school?"

"I couldn't . . . I can't . . ."

He rolls his window all the way down, leans out.

"I'll let it slide this time, Alice. But come and talk to me, okay?"

"Are you gonna give me the workout?"

"Kid, you hardly look like you can stand up, let alone run."

"*I can run!*" bursts out of her with more vehemence than she intended.

B.D. reaches out to touch Alice, her hand or her shoulder, and then thinks better of it. Nothing is simple anymore, he thinks, not even reaching out to a girl who is falling apart in front of your eyes.

"You need me to call somebody? A teacher? Your mom?"

"*No!*"

He thinks about his own kids, lost to him following his divorce, the look they get in their eyes, the faraway look, the fear, the anger, the tough protective layers they build up around their hopes and their losses.

"Alice—"

She looks at him.

"I'm not the enemy, okay?"

She hesitates, then nods and turns away.

B.D. grinds the Chevy into gear.

"Come and see me tomorrow, okay? Alice?"

"Okay."

"I mean it."

B.D. lurches away, tailpipe rattling, looking at Alice in his rearview mirror.

She breaks into a run, and even though she has no idea where to go, she's suddenly like some sort of homing pigeon, and in short order she finds herself at Uncle Eddie's garage. He slides out from underneath the 1979 BMW he's working on.

"Hey, Alice, what are you doing here?"

She looks at her feet. She didn't think she'd have to explain to Uncle Eddie.

He looks at his watch.

"Aren't you supposed to be in school?"

"I . . . It's just . . ."

He grabs a set of keys.

"You want to drive? Take your mind off things?"

"Okay."

"We could head out to the lake. Back roads. Nice and slow."

She nods, uncertain of her voice.

"I'll drive us out to the golf course, then you can take over."

Eddie leads her around back to the little parking lot behind the garage and opens the passenger door of a restored 1966 Mustang. In the back corner of the lot, Matt's truck sits up on blocks, covered with a tarp. Alice hesitates. The tarp looks like a shroud. Don't think like that, runs through her mind. It's just a truck; it's just a tarp.

"C'mon, Alice, let's go."

She turns back to Uncle Eddie and the Mustang.

"Uncle Eddie, I can't drive this car."

"Why not?"

"It's . . . it's . . ."

"Spectacular, isn't it? Hop in."

The seats are deep, buttery leather.

"Don't you feel cool just sitting in this car?"

Alice smiles, she almost laughs.

"If I could afford it . . . man, I'd love to have a car like this."

"Who owns it?"

"Some Kodak CEO. Nice guy. For a CEO. He's got good taste in cars, at least."

"How much longer do you get to play with it?"

"We're done. He's picking it up tomorrow. Lucky us he's busy in Washington right now. This is my good-bye drive. And I'm sharing it with you, you lucky girl."

Uncle Eddie rolls down his window and cranks up the radio.

"Put your window down," he shouts.

She rolls her window down, sticks her arm out, flaps her hand in the wind. Uncle Eddie fiddles with the dial until he finds the classic oldies station and the Rolling Stones: "Satisfaction." Perfect. He turns the volume up so loud the floorboards are vibrating under their feet. Uncle Eddie shouts along with the music.

But I try, and I try and I try and I try-y-y . . .

He drums on the steering wheel.

I can't get no!

More drumming.

No satisfaction!

He looks at her and grins. What can she do? She grins right back.

They change places and moderate the volume just a bit in the parking lot of Silver Lake Golf Course. Alice adjusts the seat and the mirrors under Uncle Eddie's watchful eye.

"You ready?" he asks.

She nods.

"I figure we've had enough practice in parking lots."

"Only three—!"

"That's plenty. You're a natural."

"I am?"

"Time for the open road, girl."

As she eases the Mustang out onto Blossom Road, she thinks, thank God there's no traffic because it sure feels like she is driving down the center of the street.

"A little to the right," Eddie suggests.

She oversteers onto the verge, and then overcorrects, and finally gets the car centered in the lane. It's harder than it looks.

"There you go. You're getting it."

Alice makes it through six miles of open road, she manages the four-way stop at Lakeshore Boulevard, and Uncle Eddie talks her through the tricky intersection right before they get to the lake.

"Hang a left on Seabreeze. Let's get some ice cream."

This is easy, she thinks, until she almost clips the guardrail making her turn into the frozen custard place.

"That was a little close."

And then she hits the brakes too hard as she pulls into a parking spot.

"Sorry! Sorry!"

"You're doing fine. What flavor do you want?"

"Chocolate almond."

"Keep count of how many boys try to pick you up while I'm inside."

"Uncle Eddie!"

"Just keep count. I'm telling you."

"I'm *fifteen!*"

"You're in a Mustang, baby. Count the boys."

Instead she cranks up the radio again and closes her eyes. Driving is almost as good as running, she thinks. Maybe she could just get in a car and drive forever. She could drive from park to park and run at every lake and beach and woods from here to . . . Maine, she thinks. From here to Maine.

She remembers how she would stay awake to keep her dad company on the drive to the campground at Small Point, along the two-lane road that bisects the Phippsburg peninsula, the woods reaching to the sky, the moon shining like a flirtatious girl running in and out of the trees, in and out of sight, making stripes of white on the road ahead of them. She remembers opening the windows, gulping the piney air, breathing in the first hint of salt water. You can almost taste it: the salt and the pine and the cold air exhaling from the woods. She doesn't look behind. There is no need, yet, to look behind, to watch over her shoulder, to shore up moments and memories against future loss. There is only her dad and the car and the road and the turn off to Small Point at the far end of the peninsula. Here it is, the narrow bit of sand that passes for a road at low tide. Mom and Ellie asleep in the back. Alice and Matt awake, the first ones to see the Kelp Shed, the first ones to see the new speed bump, to take the sharp left turning up to the dirt roads and the campsites. Ocean side. They are ocean side, not bay side campers. Number 39. On the bluffs. Over the rocks. Set apart, but not too far to the showers.

There's a knock on her window and Alice nearly jumps out of her skin. There are four teenage boys and two older guys clustered around the Mustang. Wanting to touch it, to run their hands over the bright red curves, pushing each other and their bodies closer and closer. This one guy leans right in her window after she opens her eyes.

"Hey, beautiful."

They jostle each other to get close to the window.

"Goin' my way, honey?"

"Where'd you get this gorgeous car?"

"What's your name, baby?"

Uncle Eddie appears with an ice cream cone in each hand.

"Back off, boys. She's my niece. She's fifteen."

"Just admiring your car."

"No harm meant."

"She's a beauty."

The men and boys disperse as Uncle Eddie hands her the ice cream.

"Six," he says, "I counted six."

"It's the car."

"Of course it's the car. It's also, I'm telling you, every man's fantasy: a beautiful girl in a beautiful car."

They change places so Uncle Eddie can drive them out to the lake. Driving plus eating ice cream is a lesson for another day, apparently, or another car. He parks where they can watch the water and the birds.

"You want to talk?" he asks.

The cooling engine ticks away like a clock running down.

"I don't know."

"How's your mom doing?"

"She's kind of wrapped in cellophane or something."

"What about Ellie?"

"I'm not sure she gets how serious it is."

"Maybe that's good."

"Maybe it is. But she wet the bed last night. And she's sucking her thumb again."

"Wouldn't it be nice if we could press rewind and go backward a couple of years. What about you?"

"I might be suspended."

"Really?"

"I shoved some dimwit girl and she fell over like a . . . she fell over and got a bloody nose."

The ice cream is freezing inside her chest.

"Why'd you hit her?"

"She was talking some dumb shit about hating her father and wishing he were dead. Because he *grounded* her."

"Wow."

"And then the principal was trying to be decent and wanted to give me a chance, wanted to hear my side of the story, only I couldn't talk, so he just sat there getting madder and madder, because it probably seemed like I was doing it on purpose, and then he got so mad he decided to call Mom and suspend me. Which is when I walked out."

"You walked out?"

"Yeah."

"Really?"

"Yeah."

"Go, Alice!"

"Probably not an appropriate response for a grown-up, Uncle Eddie."

"Who cares? That takes guts."

"You're crazy."

"Besides, who says I'm a grown-up?"

Alice looks away.

"It's just . . ." She can't continue.

Eddie waits. He's thinking that ice cream was probably a dumb idea, but what else can you do for a kid?

"The odds aren't good, are they?" she asks.

He looks out at the lake, considers.

"Probably not for most people. But for your dad . . ."

She tries to hold her voice steady.

"Thanks for not lying to me."

Alice shivers as a bank of clouds obscures the sun. Uncle Eddie reaches out and puts his hand on the back of her head. Leaves it there for a moment. And finds himself thinking about his father, so much like Matt in so many ways. The way he could be quiet with you, the way it seemed like nothing frightened him, that he knew his measure as a man, as a husband, as a father, the way some men are just solid, without making a big show of it. All the things I've been running from, Eddie thinks, like it's possible to take a pass on facing up to who or what you want to be, or who you are.

"What do you say we take Lakeshore Boulevard all the way to Sodus Point and then head home? You find some mellow tunes. We'll cruise."

She turns the radio on; there's Van Morrison again: "Brown Eyed Girl."

Do you remember when we used to sing?

"Some smart boy is gonna woo you with that song."

Sha la la la la la la la la la la te da.

"I doubt it, Uncle Eddie."

"You wait and see, girl. It's *classic.*"

"The song or the tactic?" She wants to know.

"Both."

Alice pushes open the door of her dad's workshop. It used to be the garage until Matt went into business for himself. Back then the plan had been to put an addition onto the garage for Matt's workshop, but he was always too busy to work on his own house. So her mom's car sits outside in the driveway. A bone of contention with Angie all winter long; but it's an old bone now so mostly nobody notices it anymore. Except Angie when she's scraping ice off her windshield.

The garage sits directly behind the house on the skinny part of their oddly shaped lot. Beyond the garage the lot opens up to the garden, the three apple trees, two cherry trees, and Matt's grape arbor. Matt installed windows along the back and side walls that look out on the garden. He had plans to put in more windows, too. Capture the view! The second-hand woodstove went in his first winter. A necessity. Can't do much with mittens on, he'd say.

It's four o'clock. Mom's still at work. Ellie's on a play date at Janna's house. It took Alice an hour to decide to come out here, after Uncle Eddie dropped her off, and another ten minutes outside the door gathering the courage to open it. Now she has to walk in.

The late afternoon sun breaks through the thickening clouds to shine through the back windows; dust motes dance in the weak shafts of light. She breathes in. It smells like wood and turpentine and linseed oil. The workshop is cool and a bit damp; it feels as though the room exhales when she opens the door. She closes her eyes; she can almost picture her dad standing at his workbench, sanding the curve on a new piece of wood to make it look old; she can almost hear the rasp of the sandpaper.

She stands in the middle of the space. Her eyes adjust to the dim light. Aside from the dust, the place is as neat as a pin. Every tool has its place to hang, every kind of nail and screw and fastener has its own jar. She crosses to his big wooden tool chest and opens it. This is the chest he built for the tools that never leave the workshop. His father's hammer, his grandfather's awl and plane and C-clamps. The chest is full of ingenious cubbies and sliding doors and drawers opening beneath other drawers. On the inside of the lid there are five photos. Front and center is the four of them the day they brought Ellie home from the hospital. Matt is holding the baby and Mom and Alice are holding on to Matt. The grin on his face is so big it looks like it could lift him off his feet. Then there's Ellie on her trike, Alice on horseback, a romantic picture from their wedding where Matt has lifted Angie off the ground and you can tell he is kissing her like crazy, and an old photograph of Matt's parents.

It starts to rain and the wind kicks up, blowing rain through the open door. She grabs her dad's work jacket, which hangs on a peg behind the door, along with a few baseball caps, overalls, and work boots. Shrugging into his jacket she almost loses it. Listening to the rain tapping out some sort of code on the roof, she closes her eyes and tries to see him. But what she sees is either the family photo in his tool chest or an image of a soldier lying face down in blood-spattered dust. The two impossibilities flash one after the other across her inner eye.

She opens her eyes as the storm begins its crescendo. The rain on the roof has grown loud and the wind is thrashing the lilac bushes outside the south window. She shoves her hands into the pockets of the jacket and finds a stub of pencil and a folded square of paper in the right-hand pocket, a level, a receipt from the paint store, and a pair of keys in the left-hand pocket. She lays them all out on the work-bench.

She unfolds the square of paper. It's a note and a drawing from Ellie, maybe from kindergarten when she was first learning to make her letters. It's a series of colorful squiggles. And on the bottom in block letters, some of them backward:

"ELLIE LOVES DADDY"

She smooths out the creases with her palm and props the note up on the windowsill where he'll be able to see it when he gets home.

Even with the jacket on she's shivering, and she's not really sure if it's shivering or shaking or all the tears she's trying not to cry; so she gets up, grabs a broom, and begins sweeping. The sweeping and the rain and the distant rumble of thunder and the wind sending sheets of rain through the door all feel like they are happening inside of her. Ellie loves Daddy, she thinks. Ellie loves Daddy. And wonders if that will make a difference. If love and caring and needing enter into the equation of what will happen to her father and her family at all.

As she sweeps, she hatches a plan. She'll get one of the air mattresses from the basement and the old Coleman lantern. And she'll bring out her books and her sleeping bag and some old pillows and she'll do her homework out here. Maybe a candle and some CDs, and the rocking chair from her room, and before you know it, Alice is imagining living in the garage and getting some books out of the library so she can learn how to put the windows in that Matt always wanted. She's pretty sure Uncle Eddie would help her. Matt already has the windows, stacked neatly against the far wall. All the windows for the workshop are castoffs he finds in the street. Old windows with lots of panes. The windows for the west wall are long and thin. There is a pair of them, and Matt wanted to install them horizontally. He just thought it would be cool. Alice wonders if there will be instructions for that in a library book; she hopes so.

She knows this is a good plan. She knows her dad would like it. She also knows that her mom won't like it. Especially when Alice starts sleeping out here. Or maybe she'll keep being so busy she won't even notice.

Inside the house she grabs dust cloths, the bucket, the mop, and Mr. Clean. Half an hour later, Alice finishes mopping the workshop floor. She's not sure this floor has ever been mopped before. She had to change the water in the bucket three times, and it was obvious the rafters had never been dusted. She tackles the windows next. Inside first. The outside will have to wait until it stops raining. The stepladder is just tall enough. She starts to imagine what it's going to look like when they install those two long, skinny windows.

It's growing dark by the time she finishes. She knows she should just head indoors and start dinner like her mother asked, but there's something about the busy-ness of working out here that is keeping her going, in spite of both shirtsleeves being soaked, in spite of feeling really cold.

She sits in the lawn chair and makes a list of what she needs to get from the house. Of course there are sharpened pencils in an old peanut butter jar and pads of paper right on the workbench. She uses block printing just the way her dad does:

Air mattress
Sleeping bag
Pillow
Fleece jacket
Milk crate
Bedside lamp
Extension cord

Flashlight
Books
Rocking chair

Maybe she can pop Jiffy Pop on the woodstove. And heat water for instant hot chocolate.

As soon as the rain lets up she will start moving stuff in. She'll fill the wood box next to the woodstove, and the kindling box, and she'll ask Uncle Eddie to find her a wooden pallet or two, so she can keep her air mattress off the floor.

She looks around at Matt's power tools, shrouded in canvas tarps, arranged carefully along the east wall. The way he cleaned up and organized, it's almost like he knew she was going to want to be out here. There's all this space in the middle of the workshop that is usually cluttered with lathes and power saws and sawhorses.

There's something nagging at her, she's not sure what, until she looks up in the rafters she's just dusted and sees a shoebox stuck up there. She gets the stepladder out again, climbs up, and pulls out the box. It has her name on it.

She steps off the ladder and sets the box on the workbench in the watery light coming through the rain slick windows.

What has he left for her? Sand dollars? Shells? Seed packets?

She lifts off the top and looks inside:

Dear Alice,
I wrote you a few letters. They're not really for right now. They're for just in case I have to miss anything important.
I love you, sweetheart. Never forget it.
              Dad

Inside, there's a stack of envelopes, each with his precise writing, each with a date or an event: Graduation from high school, from college, the first time she falls in love, the first time she gets her heart broken, her wedding day, the birth of her first child, the death of her mother.

There's a series of letters with the heading "the little moments that make up the big moments, that might get forgotten." The subheadings in this group are: "the moment you realize you want this boy to kiss you," "the moment you realize you don't love this boy anymore," "the moment you realize you're going to leave home and never really live there again," "the moment you realize you're more like your mother than you want to be."

Alice puts the lid back on the shoebox and centers the box in her lap and puts her hands on top of it. Then she carefully climbs the ladder again and stows the box in the rafters.

There, on the top rung of the ladder, she hears his voice: *Don't look down. Look up, Alice. Look up.* And hope—where does it come from, she wonders, just the sound of his voice?—stirs to life inside of her.

Maybe, she thinks, maybe he'll be home in time for cucumbers, and if not cucumbers, then for tomatoes, and if not tomatoes, then surely in time for corn. Maybe they could go camping in Maine in August, like they always do; maybe, maybe, maybe . . .

She'll take care of the workshop; everything will be ready for him when he gets home. And if he needs help, or needs more time to recover, Alice can be his assistant, she can be his right-hand man, she can be his girl Friday; she can be anything he needs her to be.

April 25th

Taking advantage of her suspension, Alice sleeps in, tries to catch up on some homework, and then shows up at Uncle Eddie's garage for her first lesson in basic car maintenance. Today: the oil change. She has plans to surprise Angie by changing the oil and filters in their Camry.

Uncle Eddie already has somebody else's Camry up on the hydraulic jack.

"Okay, here's what you need for this job," Uncle Eddie says as he gathers the necessary tools. "Socket wrench, oil filter wrench, drain pan, four quarts of oil, car filter, and a drain plug gasket. Your dad will have the wrenches, and I can give you the drain pan, filter, gasket, and oil."

Just as he starts to walk Alice through the job, Janna's mom drops Ellie off. Ellie, who has no interest in cars or car maintenance, waves hi and heads straight to what passes for a waiting area: one bench seat from some old car, a derelict coffee pot, and a mini fridge.

Alice is struggling with the socket wrench and the drain plug and hoping she's not going to have oil pouring down on her head. But Uncle Eddie is right there with a bucket to catch the oil. She pulls out the old gasket with her fingers and watches as Uncle Eddie removes the old filter with the oil filter wrench. Alice installs a new oil filter under Eddie's watchful eye, and replaces the drain plug gasket. All of this is so messy and absorbing that neither of them notice when Ellie leaves the garage.

"Tighten the new filter hand tight. Just use your fingers. That's it. You don't want to overtighten it."

He hands her a rag to wipe up any spilled oil, she puts their tools away, and he returns the car to earth so she can pour in four fresh quarts of oil.

"That was easy." Alice is grinning from ear to ear.

"It's not rocket science."

"Thanks, Uncle Eddie."

"You feel okay doing this on your own at home?"

"Sure."

"Jacking the car up? Sliding under there?"

"Piece of cake."

"Be careful with the jacks. You ever done that before?"

"Dad taught me how to change a tire when I was twelve."

"Figures. I could come by on Saturday if you want. Just to make sure the jacks are safe and everything."

"Sounds good."

"Next time I'll show you how to rotate your tires and check the brake systems."

"Cool."

He tosses her a grimy rag. She wipes her hands.

"You doing okay?"

"Yeah."

"Anything I can do?"

"You're doin' it."

"Ha!"

"Hey, Mom said you might have met somebody."

"Angie and her big mouth!"

"I heard her talking to you on the phone last night."

"It's a long shot."

"She from around here?"

"I'm not ready to share details."

"Oh, c'mon—"

"She's a teacher. That's all I'll say."

"Not at my school—"

"No, not at your school."

"You promise?"

"Absolutely."

"How many dates?"

"Two."

"And she still likes you?"

"No accounting for taste."

Alice looks into the empty waiting room.

"Where's Ellie?" Alice asks.

"She was right there."

"Ellie . . . ?"

"Did she walk home?"

"No, her backpack's still here."

"Ellie . . . !"

"The bathroom?" Eddie suggests.

"You know how Ellie feels about that bathroom."

Alice starts to panic, and then closes her eyes.

"I think I know where she is," she says and heads for the door.

Eddie follows Alice to the parking lot out back where Matt's truck is up on blocks. Sure enough, the tarp has been loosened next to the driver's-side door.

"I'll get her," Alice says.

Crossing the parking lot, just those few feet to her dad's truck, Alice almost can't feel her feet touch the ground. When she opens the door and finds Ellie asleep on the seat, relief washes over her and threatens to spill over into tears. She waves at Eddie to let him know they're all right and climbs up into the cab.

Ellie has a snapshot under her cheek and her thumb in her mouth. Alice looks at the photo: it's a picture from Ellie's birthday party last year, the one with the princess theme. Only Ellie doesn't look like one of those perfect little princesses, she looks slightly possessed. She's wearing a pink tutu and bright yellow tights and her red Dorothy shoes that Uncle Eddie gave her. And a fluffy white sweater and crooked homemade angel wings and long white gloves and a striped ski hat with a long, pointy top and a pom-pom. It's a photo to make you laugh. It must have been in Matt's visor. What else is up there?

Alice pulls the visor down and finds a whole collection of birthday photos. The year he and Angie made the dragon cake, the year they made the volcano cake; the silly hats and the candles and the wishes.

She pulls down the other visor and there's a photo of Matt and Angie in bathing suits, with a Frisbee, laughing. Before kids, it looks like. She opens the glove compartment. A mini road atlas, a first-aid kit, a flashlight, a level, a tape measure, a packet of gum. She pulls out a piece. Not too stale.

Ellie opens her eyes, jerks her thumb out of her mouth, sits up, and grabs the photo from Alice.

"You okay?" Alice asks.

"I like it in here."

"Me, too."

"I wish you could drive it."

"That would be cool."

"Maybe one day."

"When Dad gets back."

"I heard on the radio, in the car, with Janna's mom . . ."

"Don't listen to the radio."

"Car bombs and casualties. They give the numbers but not the names."

"That's in case the families don't know yet."

"Do you know, Alice?"

"Do I know what?"

"Is Daddy still alive?"

"Yes, he is."

"You're just saying that. Like if I asked you is there really a Santa Claus."

"Ellie . . ."

"But you don't really know, do you?"

"Nobody knows. But that's what I believe."

"Honest?"

"Honest."

"Don't lie to me."

"I wouldn't."

"I wish we could just drive over there and pick him up."

"Yeah! A couple of oceans and nine thousand miles, but *yeah* . . ."

"Today. Right now. I wish we could—"

"Me, too."

Alice puts her arm around Ellie.

"Close your eyes."

"Why?"

"Just close your eyes," Alice says, closing her own eyes. "Now breathe in," she says. "What do you smell?"

"Oil."

"Try again."

"That nasty tarp."

"Yeah. What else?"

Ellie wrinkles her nose. Alice waits.

"Daddy."

April 26th

Angie had not been as freaked out by Alice getting suspended as Alice thought she would be. She even talked to the principal, she even defended Alice, and they agreed to reduce her suspension from two days to one. Alice has had to write a lengthy apology to Jennifer White *and* her parents, *and* Mr. Brooks, *and* Mr. Fisher. She is also now a provisional member of the track team. Sort of like being on probation. If she has another infraction, she's off the team.

So she's back in school. Not so great. And back on the team. Much better. Ginger, Alice now knows, is the team's long-distance star, and for some unknown reason she has taken Alice under her wing.

At the start of practice, Ginger hands her a polypro T-shirt.

"This will keep you warmer. And cooler. And *drier.*"

"Wow. Thanks," Alice says, pulling the T-shirt over her head.

Ginger hands her a pair of socks.

"Try these. They're the best I've found."

"Hey, I can't take all this stuff."

"My mother's a little compulsive in the shopping department. I have dozens."

Alice hesitates.

"Really. Try 'em."

Alice sits down in the grass to put on the socks.

"Hurry up!" Ginger is dancing around on the grass.

"Okay!"

"Let's go!"

And Ginger is off with Alice in pursuit.

"Do you know the route?" Alice shouts at Ginger's back.

"Pretty much."

"And if we get lost?"

"It'll be fun."

Keeping up with Ginger is a tall order, but Alice is determined not to lose her as they make their way around the course through the Mendon Woods. Alice's endurance is improving and so are her times. Running is the only place where she can forget what's going on in the rest of her life. She loves falling into a rhythm, starting to know her reserve, and pushing it, the steady driving forward. She sings inside when she runs, sings like an airplane, like a motorcycle, like some kind of powerful engine, humming along.

She gets home after practice to find Gram in the kitchen, standing on the top step of the stepladder.

"Gram, I don't think you should be on that ladder."

"Well, look who's here!"

Alice drops her backpack on the floor.

"What are you doing up there?"

"Where's Ellie?"

"She's coming a little later. They had band practice."

"Band?"

"Yup."

"She plays an instrument now?"

"The recorder. They all have recorders. You remember. You bought it for her."

"I did?"

"In the fall."

Alice hangs her jacket over one of the kitchen chairs.

"Hand me that piece of shelf paper."

"What are you doing?"

"Cleaning out your mother's shelves. They were . . ."

"A big mess. I know."

"Lots of people don't care about cupboards. Close the door, forget about it. I like to know they're fresh. It's a simple thing. A little lift in the spring."

"I'm worried about you up on that ladder."

"I'm fine."

"You could cut the pieces and I could lay them down."

"I am actually very skilled at this. After all these years. Good old Con-Tact paper."

"Are you implying I'd make a mess of things?"

"Not at all. I could show you. Experience, however, is the best guide."

"We were going to bake cookies."

"I know! I'm almost done. I've got the butter softening. Did you pick what kind you want to make?"

"I say molasses; Ellie wants chocolate chip."

"We can do both. Get some more butter out of the fridge."

"Gram!"

"What?"

"You went shopping!"

"I did."

"You cleaned out the fridge."

"I did."

"Have you been here all day?"

"Ginny's covering for me at the cafe. I went to the market at eight, got here by nine, which left me plenty of time to clean out the fridge."

"Wow! And the freezer—you can tell what's in there!"

"A little organization goes a long way. What has your mother been doing?"

"Take out. Breakfast for dinner. If we're lucky. Or I cook."

"Okay, so she's had other things on her mind. Now you can have some real food. It's not so hard. Take some mental notes. These are useful things to know. Not like I could ever get through to your mother."

Gram's got the radio tuned to the country station and every now and then she hums along, or sashays her hips a little. She's wearing slacks and an old denim shirt with the sleeves rolled up and sandals. "Just giving my feet a little vacation," she'd tell you, if you asked.

Alice pours herself a glass of orange juice.

"I had to throw a lot of stuff out," Gram continues.

"Good move. I've been trying—"

"Easier for me, I think. I'm not worried that your mother might really want that two-week-old spring roll."

"Yeah."

"You gonna tell me how things are?"

"Gram, you seem a little hyper."

"Me?"

"Yeah."

"I'm thinking about spending a few nights here each week. I could get things squared away, prepare some meals, do some laundry . . ."

"Gram, you don't have time to run the restaurant and take care of us, too."

Gram gives Alice a look over the top of her glasses, like, *are you kidding me?*

"Okay, let's get the bread started. Then we can make the cookies while the dough rises."

"There's just one thing."

"What?"

"Mom's not big on bread."

"Since when?"

"Since about two months ago."

"The staff of life!"

"I know, Gram."

"It's not normal to be afraid of food!"

"Just one food group."

"I'm telling you, it's not normal."

"Gram . . ."

"Okay. No criticism. But you like bread."

"Yes!"

"And Ellie . . ."

"Loves it."

"Let's see how long your mom can resist toast. Let's make toast till she can't stand it. Hand me that big bowl, would you?"

"Where's the recipe?"

"You don't really need one. This oatmeal bread is very simple and very forgiving. And when we start toasting slices? Your mom is gonna go nuts."

With the yeast proofing, Alice beats butter for the first batch of cookies. Gram chats about this and that and lets her be. Gram knows how to wait for Alice to talk, how to be interested but not too aggressive. She doesn't ask the same old same old questions either—like what's your favorite subject, who's your favorite teacher? She asks where you sit at lunch, what you're reading, what you think about when you're alone.

The bread is fun: the measurements are a "big glub" of molasses, a cup or two of oatmeal, a pinch of salt, "enough" flour to form a soft dough. And the kneading part? Really you just get to beat the dough up. Slap it and punch it and squeeze it and pick it up and throw it down. Alice is making clouds of flour and Gram is laughing and egging her on.

When the dough is a smooth, sweet-smelling bundle Alice almost wants to pick it up and rock it like a baby. But they put it back in the clean, oiled bowl, turn it once, cover it with a dishtowel, and put it to rise on the back of the stove.

Alice goes still for several long moments and stands looking at the floor. When she raises her eyes Gram is there waiting for her, not flinching, not suggesting she get over it, go to her room, start her homework, et cetera. For the first time in she can't remember how long, Alice lets herself get pulled into a hug, and at first, right at the beginning, it feels so good. Gram is wearing Matt's apron and has flour on her nose and smells of the lemon verbena she keeps in her drawers. But then Alice pulls away and stumbles out of the room.

She locks the door in the bathroom and sits on the sink, kicking one heel against the cabinet. She can sense Gram on the other side of the door.

"Alice, you don't need to talk to me. I'll leave you be. If you can just tell me you're safe in there."

"I'm okay."

"You take your time. I'm here if you need me."

"Okay."

"Can you unlock the door?"

"Not yet."

"Ellie can help me punch the bread down and form it into loaves if you don't want to. Or we can leave it another twenty minutes so you can do it."

"Okay."

"Okay, leave it?"

"Yeah."

Turning away from Alice and that locked door would be impossible if Ellie weren't banging through the back door shouting: "Graaaammm!"

Ellie squeals when she finds out they are making *two* kinds of cookies. Alice can hear the fridge and freezer doors opening and closing, she can hear every cabinet door opened and then slammed shut. Ellie is hooting and hollering about how great everything looks. Ellie is little miss neat, Ellie color codes her socks, so this move toward organization is right up her alley. Then there's quiet for a bit, and then there's Ellie, playing her recorder. Must have been a request. Gram is nice like that.

Alice lies down in the tub and listens to Ellie squeaking away. There's a drip coming out of the tap, a very slow drip. Using her foot, she messes with the handle until the cadence of the drip is a little faster. Then she sticks the hole in her left sneaker right under the faucet and feels the steady drip drip of the water filling up her sock and her shoe.

What if, starts to fill her mind. What if I flooded the bathroom and the hallway and it leaked downstairs and flooded the kitchen and the living room and even the porch. What if, what if, what if . . .

She falls asleep. Gram's urgent knocking wakes her up. She actually fell asleep in the bathtub! How weird is that?

"I'm okay, Gram!"

But is she? Her arms and legs feel like lead. Sitting up, her ears are buzzing and she feels dizzy. Maybe she needs something to eat.

"Alice . . . ?"

"I'm coming, Gram."

When she steps out of the tub she feels like she's a hundred years old. Everything hurts and every bit of her, everywhere, inside and out, is tired. Her nose and her eyes and her shins and the backs of her hands. She unlocks the door and can hear Gram's sigh of relief. Stepping out of the bathroom she steps into Gram's waiting arms.

"It's okay, honey. . . . It's gonna be all right."

Just that, her grandmother standing there with her arms open to her. Not asking her anything, not yelling at her, not pushing, pushing, pushing.

"We waited to punch the dough down until you . . ."

"Ellie can do it."

"We need to make three loaves. You can both do it."

"Okay."

"Honey?"

"Yeah."

"Look at me."

She takes Alice's chin in her hands.

"We're gonna be okay."

"Okay, Gram."

"I mean it."

In the kitchen Ellie is standing on a chair with a huge mound of dough in front of her.

"That's our dough?!"

"See what yeast can do?"

"Wow!"

Ellie is dancing on the chair; Ellie is deciding to be magnanimous.

"You can take the first punch, Alice."

"Okay. Stand back!"

Alice lets one fly and then Ellie is pummeling away like a fifty-pound fury. Flour is flying, the dough is elastic and warm in their hands. Ellie starts to laugh. Alice closes her eyes and takes a deep breath. Yeast and molasses and flour and the hot stove and her grandmother's perfume and Ellie's fresh little kid smell. Don't think about anything else. Just this. Right here. Right now.

Gram shows them how to form the dough into loaves. They plop their babies into bread pans and brush them with butter, and put them to rest and rise one more time on the back of the stove. Cookies next. Gram leaves them to it and never once tells them to quit eating the dough while she starts dinner.

Alice knows that Gram is just as scared as she is—well, maybe not just as scared—and that cookies and toast and honey and molasses are not really going to make things right. But they're all we've got. Just the everyday things: the forks and the spoons and the plates and breakfast and lunch and dinner and homework and playing Scrabble with your sister. That's all anybody's got when you get right down to it. Some people not as much, some people lots more. But this is what is right in front of her; this is what she's got right now.

Gram sets out a plate of cookies and two tall glasses of milk. Then she pours herself a nice stiff scotch on the rocks and sits down with her girls. She and Ellie talk about Easter and shopping and will Gram teach her how to play Mah-Jongg after dinner? Gram is saying yes and yes and it's cozy in this corner with the light hanging over the table, the kitchen full of the smell of baking bread, the emptiness and the darkness pushed back, pushed aside. Alice puts her head down on the table and studies Gram's hands. Her rings, the pale skin, nearly translucent. She closes her eyes and she's gone. Gone away, Gram's voice and Ellie's voice fading out like a radio from the house next door. For a moment the tick of the kitchen clock is filling her head and she feels Gram's hand stroking her hair. Another breath and she is fast asleep, blessedly asleep.

Hours later, Alice wakes up, surprised to find herself in bed, stripped down to her underwear. Gram or Mom must have done it. She looks at her dad's watch: almost midnight. She grabs a sweatshirt and pads down the hall to the kitchen to get something to eat. She's slicing a big hunk of bread when she hears voices and realizes Gram hasn't gone home. She slathers the bread with butter and jam and walks back upstairs to her mom's room. The lights are on, the door is closed. She stands there, eating bread and licking jam from her fingers.

"It's not forever," Gram says.

"I know."

"We don't know when Matt . . ."

"I *know*."

"I'm not here to make comments. I'm just here to help."

"You can't help yourself, Mom."

"I'll tone it down."

"Sure you will."

"My comments are the least of your worries!"

"We're doing fine."

"Angie . . ."

"We *are*. I get to work every day, the kids get to school, we eat."

"I'm just saying I could do the marketing and cook ahead so all you have to do on weeknights is reheat. I could teach the girls a few things."

"They love it when you cook with them."

"Sometimes these things skip a generation."

"I can cook!"

"I know."

"I don't want you to move in, Mom."

"For the girls, then—"

"You're just down the street! If I need you I can practically holler out the front door!"

"But—"

"We don't do too well living together, remember?"

"It could be different."

"It won't be different."

Alice slides down the wall into a sitting position.

"You can stay tonight."

"But not on a schedule? Something regular for your girls?"

"We can't need you, Mom; we can't be falling to pieces, because Matt can't be missing."

"That's wishful thinking, honey."

"I don't care! Bring on the magic, bring on the shamans, the charlatans, I can't—"

"I know."

"You don't know!"

"Matt Bliss comes through. He always comes through."

"If one more person says that to me . . ."

"Don't give up on him, Angie."

"Oh, Mom . . ." Angie blows her nose. "Nothing makes sense anymore. Nobody's telling us the truth, there is no way to find out where he is or how hurt he is or what the odds are or if it's even possible to survive."

Alice realizes she's stopped breathing. How do the grown-ups keep taking in this information and walk and talk and act normal? Is she the only one who feels like her skin is going to split apart, her head is going to crack open?

"Sergeant Ames called me at work. They found Matt's ID. *Recovered* is the word they use. Is that good news? Bad news? What does it mean?"

"It means they're looking for him. They're actively looking for him."

Alice curls up on the hallway floor, her toast forgotten. The voices in her mother's room are softer now. She puts her hand into the sliver of light spilling from under the door as if the light could warm her. She closes her eyes and imagines that the murmur of voices is her mom and dad, and Ellie is three and she is ten and none of this has happened, none of it is going to happen. And then she sees him. Clear as day. Sees him traversing a hillside, wearing fatigues, carrying a gun, his boots gray with dust; his face filthy, his hair matted. He looks thin and tired. He is smoking a cigarette and there are soldiers in front of and behind him. It is early dawn and they are moving quickly, or as quickly as they can given the rocky footing. She wants to yell at him to put his helmet on. Is it a vision? A memory? A dream? Is he alive? Is that what this means? If only he would turn and speak to her, if only . . .

The door opens and Angie nearly falls right over her.

"Alice!? What the hell? What are you doing here?"

"I heard you talking and—"

"There's toast and jam all over the carpet! Could you be any more—?!"

Gram pulls Alice to her feet and heads down the hall hand in hand with her.

"I've won the skirmish but not the battle. I can stay the night. Maybe that will give me a little toehold. Think about what you'd like me to make for dinner tomorrow night. Something your mom and Ellie really love, okay?"

Alice slides into her sleeping bag on the floor as Gram climbs into Alice's bed.

"You okay on the floor?"

"Yup."

"This is cozy."

"Yup."

"Ellie can sleep through anything."

"Just about."

"Good night, Alice."

" 'Night, Gram."

Alice stares up into the dark.

"Gram . . . ?"

"What, honey?"

"I saw him."

"Where?"

"In my mind, I think. . . . He was walking across a hillside, smoking a cigarette, other men spread out on the hill around him. How could I see that?"

"I don't know, Alice. You're very connected to your dad."

"That's not rational, Gram."

"Love isn't rational."

"Was it a dream?"

"What do you think?"

"It was so real and so strange. Not like anyplace I've ever seen before. And Dad was different, too. Dirty and thin and . . ."

"He's probably thinking of you just as hard as you're thinking of him."

"But—"

"The mind, Alice, there's still so much we don't know. Think about that. All that mystery, all that unknown territory right between your ears."

"You're funny, Gram."

"He loves you, wherever he is."

Alice finally lets herself cry, the stupid tears falling right into her ears. Gram doesn't say anything, just reaches out and takes her hand. Then Ellie rolls over on her back and starts to snore and they both laugh. Five minutes later—or so it seems—the alarm is ringing.

April 27th

Alice has the woodstove in Matt's workshop going full blast. She's wearing his work jacket and a fleece vest and a hat and a scarf. It's sunny but unseasonably cold with a watery blue sky and a wind fierce enough to rattle the panes of the windows. Will spring never ever come?

First she built a fire, then she refilled the kindling pile and the stack of firewood, and then she hauled her stuff out of the house in two old duffel bags and a milk crate she found in the basement. She blows the air mattress up and hangs her sleeping bag on the clothesline to air out, which shouldn't take long in this wind. She unpacks the milk carton full of books and photographs and sets the crate next to her bed with a small reading lamp on top.

The photographs go on one side of the workbench, so she can see them from her bed. She has collected her favorite framed photos of her dad from all over the house, rearranging desktops and bureaus so her mother won't notice which ones are missing. She adds votive candles in old jelly jars. Three doesn't seem like enough. She'll have to get more.

She lights the candles. They look nice, she thinks, but there should be twelve at least. Maybe dozens and dozens; maybe she should light a new candle for every day that Matt is missing.

The books, which are Matt's books, from his "favorite books" shelf, get stacked neatly inside the milk crate: *The Art of the Stone Wall*, E. B. White's *The Points of My Compass*, Wendell Berry's *A Place on Earth*. These are the books Alice is planning to read every night, if she gets scared staying alone out here. If she can't sleep. If she can't stop thinking about her dad.

Her plan was to get everything set up before Mom gets home from work. A done deal. Not worth arguing about. What she hadn't planned on was Ellie.

Who is now standing in the doorway, her knitting in one hand, her other hand bleeding and held away from her like an accusation, like whatever happened to Ellie, alone in the house, is definitely Alice's fault.

"What happened?"

"Splinter. A big one."

"The kitchen bench again?"

"Yup."

"It's huge."

"It *hurts*, Alice."

"Let's see if I can get it out. Come over to the window where I can see better."

Alice leads Ellie over to the window.

"How can you knit and get splinters at the same time?"

"Hurry up!"

She finds her dad's finest pair of needle-nosed pliers.

"You ready? Hold still."

Alice pulls out the splinter.

"There you go."

Ellie, with her finger in her mouth, takes a moment to survey the workshop.

"What are you doing?"

"I'm moving in."

"You're gonna stay out here?"

"Yeah."

"Alone?"

"Yeah."

"All the time?"

"No, I'll shower and eat and change inside."

"You're gonna *sleep* out here?"

"I was thinking—"

"Every night?"

"Well—"

"You're *leaving* me?"

"No, Ellie—"

"How can you do that?"

"You could stay out here with me sometimes."

"No, I couldn't."

"It'll be fun."

"No, it won't."

"It'll be like camping."

"You and Daddy are the only ones who like camping. I *hate* camping."

Ellie looks at Alice for a long moment.

"What about Mom?"

"What about her?"

"Who's gonna stay with Mom?"

"Ellie, it's just the backyard."

Ellie starts to cry. Alice sits down on the air mattress, pulls Ellie down beside her, and puts her arm around her shoulder.

"Ellie . . . I—"

Ellie cries harder.

"It's one hundred feet away. It's—"

Ellie looks at Alice. Stares at her. Waits.

"Okay, so maybe I could just be out here sometimes."

"Like when?"

"Like in the middle of the night when I can't sleep. Or after school. When you're at Janna's."

"Alice, if you're not in our room at night—"

"I know."

"Right where you always are—"

"I wasn't thinking, Ellie. I'm sorry."

Ellie blows her nose.

"You want to help me set it up? I'm open to suggestions."

"If you make it all wonderful you're gonna want to be here all the time. Besides, it's *Dad's* workshop. I don't think you're supposed to, like, mess it up or make it all yours and stuff. Like, exclusively. Yours."

"You can come out here anytime."

"You're just saying that."

"No, I'm not. I mean it."

Ellie wipes her eyes with the back of her hand.

"Mom's not gonna like it."

"I know."

"Is it secret?"

"It doesn't need to be secret. It's just an air mattress and a sleeping bag and some books."

Ellie gets up and heads for the door.

"Where are you going?"

"I'm not going to help you leave me."

"Ellie—Ellie—! Wait—!"

Which is when Mom drives up from work and Alice thinks, oh, no, here we go, this is all going to fall apart. What a mess. Of course Ellie tells her all about it; Alice can see her making her case right there in the driveway. And then, yup, here comes Mom. Alice braces herself for a shouting match, but Angie steps into the workshop, looks around, and in a normal tone of voice, says:

"I don't really want you sleeping out here."

"But, Mom . . ."

"And no boys, Alice."

"Mom!"

"The deal is, you keep your grades up . . ."

"The whole point of this—"

"Is what, exactly?"

"You know what, Mom."

"No, I don't, Alice."

"The whole point is . . ."

Angie waits.

"I feel like I can . . ." Alice begins.

"What?"

"Hold on to him here."

"That's . . ."

"Or that I can still find him here."

"Oh, honey," Angie softens.

"Do you know what I mean?" Alice pulls Matt's jacket closer around her.

"Yes. I think I do."

"I want it to be perfect when he gets home. I got a book out of the library so I can learn how to clean and oil all his power tools. I mean, I know it's already totally organized, but I thought . . ."

Angie looks at Alice: Her cheeks are flushed and the tip of her nose is bright red. She is swamped in Matt's jacket, it nearly reaches her knees. She looks like a kid again, a little kid.

Angie wishes she could reach out and touch Alice, but with just that thought, just that impulse, she can feel Alice pulling away.

"I didn't think about Ellie. I should have thought about Ellie, but—"

"She needs you."

"I know."

"More than ever."

"What about what I need, Mom?"

"We'll work it out, okay?"

"I don't see how."

"Have a little faith."

"I just want—"

"She'll be at Janna's, there will be sleepovers, there's a week of Nature's Classroom coming up in May."

Alice crosses to her dad's workbench.

"You're not mad that I brought some pictures out here?"

"I'm not mad."

"I want to light a candle for every day he's missing."

"Good idea with the jelly jars."

"Yeah. I don't want to burn the place down or anything."

Angie looks around the workshop again: the clean floor, the sparkling windows, Matt's orderliness echoed in Alice's neat stack of books, clothes hung on pegs, the wood basket, the kindling.

"You cleaned up in here. It looks nice."

"You know how Daddy had plans to put those windows in the west wall? I'm gonna figure out how to do that before he gets back. I'll ask Uncle Eddie to help me."

"Matt was so excited the day he found those windows."

"It'll open things up. More light."

"And a view of his apple trees."

Angie reaches out and straightens Alice's collar.

"You're wearing his jacket."

"It was cold. I—"

"It's okay, Alice."

Angie sits down in the lawn chair near the woodstove. Alice stands nearby, uncertain what to do or say.

"Can I have it?" Angie asks.

"What?"

"The jacket. Just for a bit."

Alice unbuttons the jacket, hands it to her mom. Angie hugs it to her, inhaling its scent.

"Mom . . . ?"

"Throw another log on the fire, would you?"

The fire is blazing, but Alice adds another log anyway.

"Can you open the doors so I can watch it?"

Alice opens the doors of the woodstove, props up the temporary screen.

"That's what Dad likes to do."

She hears her mom take in a quick breath.

"I'd like to stay out here for a little while by myself, if that's okay with you."

"Yeah. Sure."

Alice starts backing toward the door.

"I'll be in soon."

Alice hesitates.

"Don't forget to close up the stove, Mom."

"I won't."

Alice closes the door behind her and wishes she could look through the door to see her mom. Maybe she could replace the solid wood door with a glass one or put windows in on the sides. She's thinking about windows because it is frankly too strange to think about her mom in her dad's space like this, in *her* space, everything turned upside down, Alice outside in the chill wind, her mom by the fire. How did this happen?

But as of right now, right this instant, Alice has a new plan. She has decided to only think positive thoughts, to stop dwelling on all the terrifying *what ifs* that haunt her. She will keep those thoughts to herself and instead prepare for her dad's return. His certain return. She will be the one to believe in him, believe in his strength and his ingenuity, his ability to talk to, to persuade anyone about anything, anywhere, anytime. She thinks about the way he can coach you so you don't even realize he's doing it, whether it's how to throw a better pitch or how to strike a cleaner, stronger hammer blow.

When he comes home, if he's still recovering from his wounds, or so badly hurt that it will take months to recover, then she will be the one to do things for him. She'll drive him to the doctor's because she'll have her permit by then. When he's ready to go back to work she'll be his assistant, handling the things he's not quite ready for, or the things that are too tough by the end of the day when he gets tired. She'll fill his Thermos and pack his lunch. She'll load the tool chest and the truck. She knows how to do these things, she's been watching him and getting in the way her whole life.

It occurs to her that if, no, when, they find him, they'll probably send him home as soon as they can debrief him and stabilize him at the hospital. So the garden has to be perfect. There will not be a weed anywhere, the successive plantings of red and green lettuce will be beautiful, the corn will be knee high, the tomatoes will be staked; she will pick and make him his favorite chopped salad every night. Beets. She should plant some beets.

And if he's too tired to talk about what happened, she promises herself she'll wait until he's ready to tell her the story, the true story that she can hold on to instead of the horror story she plays in her head every night.

Will she tell him about Henry? There's nothing to tell. Or John Kimball? Really nothing to tell. Or Stephie or what it was like to feel so alone the whole time he was gone, the way nobody knew how to talk to her, or how to talk about the war or her father, and it seemed like people just wanted to avoid her. The part about not getting along that great with Mom she can keep secret. Running, she can tell him about running, and B.D. and the way he's fair with everybody, just the way Matt is, and Ginger and her long legs, and how it's looking like Alice might really be a long-distance runner, might have some actual talent in that department. Can she tell him about the miles and miles she runs in practice and learning to believe you've got something left for the end of the race, that believing it is just as important as running it? Will it still be okay to run like that if Matt's legs have been shattered? If only she knew where he'd been wounded, but she's promised herself not to think about that. Just think about him getting out and getting home and being here and being Dad, that's all, just being Dad.

Alice heads inside to see what she can do to start dinner only to discover that her quarterly report card has arrived. Along with a letter from Matt, addressed to Ellie. A letter sent ten days ago. Maybe it's a sign. Maybe it's a good sign.

She hesitates for a nanosecond and then rips open her report card, even though it's not addressed to her, but to her parents. It's bad. No, it's really bad. Every single subject is in the low seventies, having fallen from the nineties. It's not failing. Not yet. But it will be. Each and every teacher makes a note of missing tests and missing assignments and how this just isn't like Alice. There's a special blue slip requesting a conference.

What is she going to do with this? Hide it? Put it in the trash? Hope that Angie is too distracted to notice that it never arrived?

Once again, Alice forgot the Ellie factor, because here's Ellie, having padded into the hall on her little stealth feet to read along right beside her.

"You're in trouble," Ellie says, with a certain gleeful satisfaction. "You're in *big* trouble."

"Want to pretend like this never arrived?"

"Fat chance, Alice."

"Ellie—"

"What are you doing in school? Aren't you even trying?"

"Hey, I don't need you to—"

"What would Daddy say?"

"Listen—"

"You can't just move out of the house and let every single thing go, Alice. That's not what Daddy would do."

"Okay, okay! You can just back off, Ellie!"

Mom walks in the door and takes the report card and strangely, oddly, says nothing. Not now at least. She picks up Ellie's letter and looks at the postmark.

"Oh, this is so strange."

"Maybe it's a good omen," Alice says.

"This was mailed ten days ago."

"There could be more on the way," Ellie says. "Lots more."

Angie holds the letter against her chest for a moment and closes her eyes. A silent wish, or a prayer, Alice thinks, as Angie hands the letter to Ellie.

Ellie rips open the envelope right there in the hallway.

"Wait," Alice says, an edge of panic in her voice. "Let's do it the same way we always do."

So they gather on the couch, where Ellie climbs into Angie's lap and reads her letter to herself, Angie and Alice both pretending they are not trying to read over her shoulder.

"Read it," Alice begs.

Ellie pushes her glasses into place and begins:

Dear Ellie,

You asked me what I miss:

You. Being near you. And Mom and Alice and Uncle Eddie and Gram.

I miss just hanging out with you. To do anything. Or nothing. Sit on the couch. Play chess. Drop you off at school.

I miss your drawings. I miss braiding your hair. I miss your crazy outfits. I miss tickling you. I miss that spot behind your left ear that smells like vanilla.

I miss fresh milk. The stuff here is in little squeezable plastic containers and it always tastes sour to me.

Gram's coffee.

A movie. In a theater. With popcorn!

Libraries. Book stores.

Your laugh.

Walking down a quiet street at dusk with the lights on in the houses and kids doing homework or playing on the lawns. That happy noise. Spring nights when nobody wants to come inside.

Baseball. Playing with my team, playing catch with Alice and Henry, pitching for Henry, trying to get you to play with us.

Trees. Grass. I miss green. I miss mountains and birch trees and evergreens. Let's go for a hike in the Adirondacks when I get home.

My truck. To get in, turn the key, turn on the radio, find some tunes, roll down the windows and just drive. No more body armor. No more Kevlar helmet!

Home cooked food. Hamburgers on the grill. Making sundaes with you and Alice.

A real bathroom. A bathtub. Lots of hot water. A "combat shower" is so fast you blink and you could miss it.

Breakfast at The Bird Sisters, lunch on a roofing job, dinner at home with my three girls.

You. I'll begin and end with you. I miss you, Ellie.

> *Love,*
>> *Daddy*

Ellie, of course, begins to cry as she reads the letter, and when she finishes, she curls into Angie's arms, as though she could burrow inside of her mother, and sobs. Alice can see Angie start to lose it and then pull herself back from the edge so she can take care of Ellie.

"Ellie," Angie says, "Daddy's gonna be okay. He's missing you and loving you—and all of us—right now."

"You promise?" Ellie asks.

Angie meets Alice's glance over Ellie's head.

"I promise."

April 28th

After practice, a long run at Mendon Pond Park, where Alice actually kept up with Ginger for the 3.5 mile course and almost caught her as she made her move up the last hill, Alice helps Uncle Eddie unload the rototiller from the really cool old Ford truck he's driving with wooden running boards and side panels. Red, of course. Eddie muscles the rototiller through the yard, out past her dad's workshop and up the small rise to the garden.

"You sure you want to do all of it?"

"Yup."

"It's pretty big, Alice."

"That's okay. We do corn, remember?"

"What's that smell?"

"Bailey's delivered a load of horse manure."

"Glad I wore my boots."

Uncle Eddie fires up the rototiller and takes off along the outer perimeter of the garden, chewing up and turning the soil. Alice walks behind him picking up and tossing aside any stones that get uncovered. The soil is still pretty heavy and wet, but Eddie and his machine are slicing through it like butter. Every now and then Alice misreads the angle or direction of the rototiller and bends down to grab a stone and gets a faceful or shirtful of dirt for her trouble. Even wearing boots she and Eddie are both getting soaked with water and caked with mud. Halfway through the job Alice is dirtier than she's ever been in her life.

Uncle Eddie's approach is a lot faster and definitely more slapdash than her dad's. He's driving the rototiller, rather than carefully guiding it. He's finding out just what this machine can do, how fast it can turn, what happens when you give it maximum gas. These experiments keep plastering both of them with dirt. Alice has to jog sometimes to keep up. Uncle Eddie's got this thing going top speed and he's whooping and hollering as he slides through the corners, using all his body weight to turn the rototiller, skidding on his heels, and laughing.

This job, which Alice usually hates for its careful, dull, noisy slowness has been transformed into a road race and a mud-pie session all rolled into one. She had dreaded every plodding step as some sort of penitential slog through missing her dad. Instead, Uncle Eddie has turned this task into a game and released her by changing the unwritten rules.

He stops before their last pass around the perimeter and hollers at her over the engine noise:

"You want to drive it?"

"No."

"You scared?"

"No!"

"Yes, you are!"

"I am not!"

"Then come on up here. We'll do it together."

She takes the handles, adjusting the speed. Uncle Eddie walks beside her in case she needs a hand. She's taking it slow, really slow, slow enough to lift her face from looking down at the dirt and take in the whole gentle swath of the garden; the earth turned up, the wet mushroom-y smell of dirt in the spring, full of loam, and promise and possibility. She can do this; she *is* doing this.

Fifteen minutes later she's helping Uncle Eddie drive the rototiller up two planks and into the bed of his truck.

"You want to come in for a beer or something?"

"Like this? Your mom would kill me. She's already gonna kill you."

"I could bring one out to you."

"That's okay, kiddo, I promised to get this baby back to the rental place before five."

"Thanks, Uncle Eddie."

"Anytime."

"I wish I could get a picture of you."

"Wait until you see your own dirty self. We should've made a video. I think it could be a big hit on YouTube. In the farm states."

Uncle Eddie peels out and leans on the horn as Alice turns toward the house. She kicks her boots off outside and goes in the back door and directly down the basement stairs where she strips off all her clothes and throws everything into the washing machine. Every stitch is soaked, even her underwear. She grabs a towel out of the dryer and heads upstairs. Now she can see her dirty footprints on each step. And her path from the back door to the basement is muddy as well. Her big muddy handprints are all over the back door and the basement door. She can't believe it. If it weren't so cold outside she'd go wash down with the garden hose. Now she has to track and drip all the way up to the shower, too. Her mom is gonna kill her. She grabs paper towels and scrubs the bottom of her feet.

She sidesteps her way up the stairs so she won't touch the walls. She turns on the shower and steps in. The water coming off her is black with dirt, her hair is gritty; there's even mud down her back. She leans against the wall of the shower, letting the hot water wash over her. She's feeling better than she's felt in days. They got the job done. She's going to have her garden no matter what her mother says, just the way she planned it with her dad. Exactly like last year. Sunday she'll plant peas and radishes and the earliest lettuce and spinach. Sunday she'll be in the garden, down on her knees with stakes and string and seeds.

"Alice!? Alice! Get down here right this minute!"

Oh, shit, here we go, she thinks, as she steps out of the shower, slips on a pair of jeans and a T-shirt, and heads downstairs.

Her mother has a bottle of Fantastik in one hand and a big pink sponge in the other. She shoves them both at Alice.

"Here. It's your mess. You clean it up."

Without a word, Alice sets to work.

"I thought we discussed this. I thought I made myself perfectly clear."

No answer from Alice.

"Why are you insisting on——?"

"I promised Dad," Alice mumbles into the floor.

"What? I can't hear you."

"I promised Dad," Alice enunciates slowly and clearly.

"Well he's not here now, is he?"

"That's the point, Mom."

"What did we agree on last night?"

"We didn't agree on anything last night. You made some pronouncements, I kept my mouth shut."

"We agreed that *if* you get your grades up where they belong *then* you can do the garden."

"I didn't agree to that."

"That's the deal."

"I can't accept that."

"You're going to have to learn how to accept it. If your father were here——"

"—We wouldn't be having this discussion."

"If your father were here—"

"—Don't go there, Mom."

Alice stands up, puts the Fantastik under the counter, rinses the sponge in the sink, and walks out of the kitchen.

"Just where do you think you're going?"

"To do my homework."

Alice hears a cabinet door slam as she crosses the yard to her dad's workshop, where she will most likely not do her homework, where she will most likely sit there wishing she could write a letter to her dad about fat, fast Uncle Eddie and the garden and the muck and the mud, and the way the machine was roaring under her hands as she guided it through its last pass around the garden.

She closes her eyes and it's a September afternoon. Clear blue sky, bright sun, cool breeze. She and Matt are in the garden picking tomatoes. He finds a flawless Brandywine, wipes it clean with his shirt and passes it to her. He finds another one for himself, polishes it, and takes a bite, like it's an apple. He pulls the kitchen salt shaker out of his pocket, sprinkles on some salt and savors every last bit of it, tomato juice running down his chin. Nothing has ever tasted better. The sun-warmed flesh of the tomato, the sharp, acidic tang of the first bite, the kick of the salt intensifying everything. This is a ritual with them. The finding, the picking, the perfect late summer beefsteak tomato, the salt shaker stolen from the kitchen, the hum of the crickets heralding fall, and the explosion of flavor in their mouths. No words required.

April 29th

It's the Red Wings' home opener against Syracuse. Alice is sitting in the bleachers with John Kimball, his father, his kid brother, Joey, and Mrs. Minty. A very short and very chubby high school girl from Mendon with beautiful long, dark hair has just sung "The Star-Spangled Banner." How is it possible to belt out notes that high? The team sprints out onto the field to take their positions as the announcer introduces them. They get a welcoming standing ovation. Rochester loves its Red Wings. Not that Frontier Field is full; but it's a respectable crowd. Rowdy, too.

It's cool and windy but John and his father know where to sit to get some shelter from the wind and to take full advantage of whatever sun there is. They've got peanuts in the shell and, true to his promise, John has gotten Mrs. Minty a hot dog with all the trimmings.

Mrs. Minty is wearing her usual skirt, blouse, cardigan sweater, and tie shoes, but over this she has layered an extra sweater, her winter coat, and two scarves. She has also brought fuzzy mittens that look homemade, and to top it off she is sporting a well-worn Red Wings baseball cap. They are all wearing Red Wings baseball caps, which makes Alice feel slightly ridiculous.

Mrs. Minty has already purchased her season player roster and she has not one but two sharpened pencils in preparation for keeping up with the box scores. This is more baseball ephemera than Alice and her dad usually indulge in, though her dad reads the box scores every morning in the paper. Or used to.

She leans over to John.

"Do you understand box scores?"

"Yeah."

"My dad explained it to me once, but honestly, I stopped listening after about two minutes."

"I wouldn't worry about it."

Everybody's a little stiff and formal, except for Joey who is happily dashing up and down the bleacher steps following one of the vendors around. Is this because none of them know one another well, or because Mrs. Minty is there and they're all trying their hardest to be polite and not yell and swear, or is it because John is wishing he'd never invited this weird girl to a baseball game and John's father is probably wondering what's going on because he thought John already had a girlfriend? That Melissa Johnson who calls every night and wants to talk on the phone till all hours.

Joey is back, panting.

"Dad! Dad! I want to sell peanuts. Can I sell peanuts?"

"I think you have to be fifteen."

He's crushed. For a moment.

"Dad! Dad! Can I sell peanuts when I'm fifteen?"

"Sure."

"How long 'til then?"

"Eight years."

"You think I could be an assistant before then?"

"Ask him!"

"Ask who?"

"The kid you've been running after."

"He wouldn't have to pay me."

"Don't tell me, tell him."

Joey sprints off, in pursuit of the fifteen-year-old demigod selling peanuts.

Mrs. Minty begins a discussion about the new shortstop, Rich Gelbart, and what the pitching coach is saying about him. John listens carefully but doesn't say much as his dad and Mrs. Minty assess Gelbart and his strengths and weaknesses, until Mr. Kimball turns to John and says:

"You could be there, son. You work hard and you could be there. Right on that field."

"Dad . . ."

"You're quick, you can hit, and you're not afraid to push yourself. Best shortstop Belknap High's seen in fifteen years. Sounds like Peter, doesn't it, Mrs. Minty?"

"Oh, yes. Yes, it does."

There's an awkward pause.

"Thank you for speaking about Peter, Jack. It's a comfort to me to hear his name."

"I know it is."

John turns to Alice.

"Mrs. Minty was my dad's high school English teacher."

"She was not!"

"And she came to his games. Just like she comes to mine."

"Mrs. Minty, I didn't know you were a teacher," Alice says.

"I gave it up for a while when Peter was young. But I went back to it after my husband died."

"I heard you came back to teaching just so you could torture my dad," John teases.

"I wouldn't call it torture," Mr. Kimball says.

"Were you hard on him?" John asks.

"I had high expectations for all my students."

"Even the ones who didn't give a . . . who didn't care?"

"A climate of expectation fosters the possibility, even the near certainty, of achievement. If I believe in you, and I communicate that to you, you will find things in yourself you never knew were there."

"Is this a theory, Mrs. Minty," Alice asks, "or has it been proven?"

"Ask John's father."

"Mr. Kimball?"

"I wouldn't have finished high school without Mrs. Minty. Well, Mrs. Minty and baseball."

"Why not?"

"It's a long story."

Mrs. Minty gives him a look.

"Go ahead, Jack," Mrs. Minty says.

He looks out across the baseball diamond as though he can see into the past and says:

"My father had a massive heart attack my sophomore year in high school."

"He *died?*" bursts out of Alice's mouth.

"At Gleason's. On the factory floor. He was forty-five years old."

Mrs. Minty is completely present; her attention is like a pair of strong hands resting on his shoulders.

"My mom was overwhelmed trying to take care of things and hold on to the house and find a job and feed four kids. I hardly went to school for the rest of sophomore year and barely passed my exams. That summer I worked on Gentle's farm and played on the town baseball team. I was trying to help my mom, but I met older kids on the job and that wasn't good for me."

"Why not?" Alice can't help asking.

"Older kids with licenses, and fake IDs, and money for beer, and nothing better to do."

John and Alice look at each other, taking this in.

"It was a mistake they put me in Mrs. Minty's class. She taught the honors section. I didn't know any of the kids in that class—their parents were the doctors and the lawyers in town—and I was in way, way over my head."

"I asked for you to be in my class," Mrs. Minty says.

"Why would you—?"

"I knew your mother. I knew you were in trouble. And I thought I could reach you."

"So you were my angel, Mrs. Minty," Mr. Kimball smiles.

"Gloria's your angel, Jack."

John's father nods and ducks his head blinking furiously for a moment, as he thinks about his wife.

There's an uncomfortable pause.

"Lovely day to open the season, wouldn't you say, Jack?"

"Yes, ma'am."

"I predict that Gelbart is going to have such a good season we're going to lose him to the majors."

"You could be right, Mrs. Minty."

"I might even wager a small sum on that supposition, if you were inclined to take a gamble."

"Five bucks suit you, Mrs. Minty?"

"Right down to the ground."

John reaches over and takes Alice's hand. She can't stop herself: she turns to look at him in stunned disbelief, but he is not looking at her, he is watching Gelbart, on an 0 and 2 pitch, hit a line drive deep into left field.

She leaves her hand in his. His palm is calloused but his hands are warm, warmer than her hands. But what is he doing? He has a girl-friend. Does this mean he's kind of a bum, seeing what he can get away with far from the prying eyes at school? And what about her? Two weeks ago she kissed Henry. Sort of. If that was really a kiss. Now this. What is this? She looks at him. He won't look at her. She pulls her hand away.

Now John looks at her; he smiles at her, even more confusing, and takes her hand again. She glances over at Mrs. Minty who misses absolutely nothing. She doesn't have the nerve to look at John's father, so she sits there, holding hands with John Kimball and watching the season opener at Frontier Field in the weak but promising April sunshine. Until Joey returns, takes in the hand holding situation, exchanges a glance with his father, and then worms his way between them, laughing and chanting:

"John's got a girlfriend! John's got a girlfriend!"

"Shut up, you little twerp."

John grabs Joey's hat and sails it into the bleachers below. When Joey flies down the steps to retrieve his hat, John does not take Alice's hand again. Which is a relief. Kind of. She shifts away from him.

"I thought you were going out with Melissa Johnson," Alice says quietly, as Mrs. Minty and Mr. Kimball discuss the Red Wings' new outfielder.

John pays extra close attention to the pitcher.

"Well?"

"It's complicated."

"I think that's pretty much a yes or no answer."

It's a full count.

Is this why twelfth-grade boys troll for ninth- and tenth-grade girls, thinking they'll be too wowed to protest or complain about anything as immature as cheating?

"Maybe you're just trying to be nice to me. But I don't really know you because I've never really even talked to you so . . ."

He turns to look at her.

"We've talked."

"Hardly."

"More than I talk to most girls."

"That's not possible. I see you with girls all the time."

"That's not really talking."

"It looks like talking."

"It's *just* talk. It's not anything real."

"But . . ."

Gelbart steals second. Under the cover of the crowd's roar he says:

"I like you, Alice."

"You do not."

"Why is that so hard to believe?"

"It just is, okay?"

"Why?"

"It's impossible."

"Why?"

"For one thing, you're a senior."

"So?"

"It's confusing."

"I thought when you said yes to coming to the game that maybe . . ."

"I figured you were just getting all your good deeds for the year over with in one fell swoop: you know, old lady, sad girl from school," Alice says even more quietly in case Mrs. Minty overhears.

"That's not why I asked you."

"And what about Melissa Johnson?"

"What about her?"

"I heard she spent a lot of money on her dress for the spring dance."

"Which is why I can't break up with her before then."

"Because of a *dress?* That's insane."

"Yeah. But what kind of jerk would I be to break up with her now?"

Gelbart gets to third on a sacrifice bunt.

"I wanted to ask you to go with me," John says.

"You're just saying that."

"No, I'm not."

Alice looks at him, thinking, I don't know you at all, and what I thought I did know about you turns out to be completely, totally wrong.

"I already said yes to Henry anyway."

"Henry Grover?"

"He's my best friend."

"But do you . . . ?"

"Do I what?"

"Do you like him?"

"Of course I like him!"

"You know what I mean."

Sammy Marston hits a double deep into left field, sending Gelbart home.

"Save me a dance, then," he says.

"What?"

"One slow dance."

"Wouldn't that be . . . ?"

"It's just a dance."

"Melissa Johnson won't think it's 'just a dance.'"

"Fair enough."

They go back to watching the game.

"What happened to your mother?" Alice asks.

"Breast cancer."

Alice registers that she has never heard a seventeen-year-old boy say *breast* before.

"I'm sorry. I can't imagine . . ."

"Yeah."

Why is this so hard to talk about?

"You must miss her."

"All the time."

"How old was Joey?"

"Four."

"Does he remember her?"

"Sort of. But I think his memories get mixed up with all the pictures we have."

Alice pulls off her Red Wings hat.

"I can't remember my dad's voice."

"Doesn't he call all the time?"

"He's missing in action."

He looks at her.

"You didn't say anything."

"I never know what to say."

"How long has it been?"

"Eight days."

She looks at her hands.

"Alice . . ."

She can't look up.

"He'll be okay."

She wants to believe that. She wills herself to meet his gaze.

"Let's not talk about it anymore," she says. "Let's just . . ."

He's still looking at her

"Are you close?" he asks.

"Yeah . . . Yeah. We are."

He takes her hand again and Alice thinks, don't ask me if I'm all right or I am going to totally lose it.

After a long pause he says, "I'm thinking of enlisting."

"What?"

"I've been talking to the recruiters at school. I want marines, I think."

"What are you talking about?"

"I'll get all this training. They'll pay for college. And it's really great experience. Plus, with my dad on his own, we can't really afford—"

"What about baseball?"

"That's a one in a million chance, Alice. You know that."

"But you're really good."

"Thanks, but—"

"I don't know what to say."

"I turn eighteen next month. I can enlist on my birthday. And head off to basic training right after I graduate."

"Does your dad know?"

"Yeah."

"I can't believe you're doing this. They'll send you overseas."

"Probably."

"Oh, God . . ."

"I thought . . ."

"Isn't there any other way—?"

"It's an incredible opportunity."

"You can't be all you can be if you're dead," she blurts out and can't believe how much she sounds like her mother.

Mrs. Minty and Mr. Kimball both glance over.

"I thought you'd understand," he says.

"I understand that there are a million things that could happen to you, a million things that could go wrong."

"C'mon, the war could be over by the time I'm done with my training."

"You don't actually believe that, do you?"

He focuses on the game again.

"Don't do it. Don't sign your life away. Don't go," she says, suddenly afraid he's going to laugh at her intensity.

"Are you saying we could start something?"

"What? What do you mean? No—"

"And I could stay in Belknap and live at home and work in a garage, learn how to be a mechanic, or work at Gleason's like my grandfather did, or get my electrician's license and go into business with my dad."

"No, I—"

"Marry my high school sweetheart and have three kids before I'm twenty-five, divorced by thirty."

"That's not what I'm saying."

"I want to get out, Alice. I want something more."

"You sound like my dad."

She has to let go of his hand to steady herself. She's holding on to the bleachers with both hands and looking down trying to quiet the tumult inside of her when Benny Benjamin hits a home run and the hometown crowd is on its feet yelling and cheering.

A home run on opening day, she can hear her dad saying, *that's a good omen, sweetheart. That's a good omen for the season to come.*

April 30th

All day long Alice has been trying to get out to the garden to start planting. In the morning they had a dusting of snow, which melted when the temperature soared to fifty-five and the sun came out. Now it's drizzling.

Her mother keeps piling on the chores and she's suddenly obsessively interested in Alice's homework and is demanding to see her planner. Only Alice's planner is pretty blank because Alice doesn't have many plans when it comes to schoolwork. Somehow her mother wheedled some information out of Henry's mother. Alice can just picture poor Mrs. Grover standing there asking Henry if they do, in fact, have a research paper due tomorrow? Three pages on the Continental Congress. So then it's off to the library. Why is the library even open on Sunday, Alice wants to know, doesn't anybody ever get a day of rest anymore?

Now she's got three books to skim through and three pages to write. She calls Henry.

"I need a topic sentence."

"That's cheating, Alice."

"Give me one of your discarded ones. I know you have at least five topic sentences up your sleeve."

Henry considers.

"Okay."

She can hear him take a piece of paper out of his wastebasket and uncrumple it.

"Was Jefferson the sole author of the Declaration of Independence?"

"That's a question."

"It's a teaser. Here's the rest: While we often think of Jefferson as the sole author of the Declaration of Independence, John Adams edited it, and he defended it to the rest of the Congress and helped get it passed."

"This is a *reject* for you? Geez!"

"I got interested in the role that Franklin played."

"You should quit worrying about math, Henry. You're a genius. Thanks a lot. 'Bye."

"Wait, Alice—"

"Gotta go, Henry."

"Did you—?"

"—What?"

"I heard—"

"—*What?*"

"John Kimball."

There's an uncomfortable silence.

"I need to write this paper, Henry."

"Alice—"

"We just went to a baseball game. With Mrs. Minty. *And* his father. *And* his brother."

"Why didn't you tell me?"

"There's nothing to tell."

"Do you like him?"

"I don't know."

"You do like him."

"I don't even know him."

"Did he kiss you?"

"No!"

"He did, didn't he?"

"*No!*"

"He already has a girlfriend."

"I know that!"

"Can I come over?"

"No. I have to write this paper."

"I'm coming over."

"Don't. I'm having a terrible day."

"I need to talk to you."

"I will be horrible to you if you come over here."

"Alice—"

"Everything is going wrong today, Henry. I don't want to have a fight with you, too."

"Could you just tell me—"

"What?"

"Never mind."

"Henry, you're my best friend."

"Okay."

"See you tomorrow?"

"See you tomorrow."

She hangs up and finds that she is actually grateful to get lost for a few hours in the prickly lifelong relationship between Jefferson and Adams, which turned into this amazing friendship in the last years of their lives with hundreds of letters written back and forth. And then they died on the same day: July 4, 1826. You can't make stuff like that up.

She finishes her paper and looks up to see the rain still falling. Is it ever going to stop?

She heads downstairs only to get roped into helping her mother make dinner. Her mother hasn't cooked in weeks, and today she's making pot roast? So Alice is at the sink peeling carrots to throw in with the roast that is already bubbling away inside the stove, and potatoes for mashed potatoes. Her mom is making a pie. A pie! What is going on? Okay, so it's the Pillsbury roll-out crust, but it's also cherries, real cherries that they freeze every year from their own trees.

"It's Sunday," her mom offers, by way of explanation.

"So . . . ?"

"Uncle Eddie is coming over and so is Gram."

"I need to get out in the garden, Mom."

"I thought it would be nice to have a family dinner. Gram is bringing her green bean casserole."

"It's not like it's Thanksgiving."

"Just some family time."

"Dad and I always plant on this Sunday. Some people go by the equinox, we go by the Red Wings opening game. The Sunday after. It's always the Sunday after the home opener."

Angie carefully unrolls the crust from the package.

"Mom?"

The squeak of the rolling pin.

"Mom? Are you trying to keep me from planting the garden?"

"No."

"Well, good. Because you can't."

"I just thought—"

Angie stops rolling out the crust for a minute and puts the heels of her hands over her eyes. She's wearing Dad's apron, Alice notices. Everybody's wearing Dad's apron lately.

"This is your dad's grandmother's pot roast recipe. And cherry pie is—"

"Daddy's favorite."

"Exactly."

"So?"

"I just want my family here with me."

Okay, Alice can understand all of this and she can even like it that her mom is cooking dinner for a change and that Uncle Eddie and Gram are coming over, but why did this have to happen today?

"Will you set the table when you're finished there? With the good china?"

"Couldn't Ellie do it? And I could at least stake out the first half dozen rows—"

"—Alice—"

She can't exactly slam down the good china plates, though she would like to drop them in a big heap. Her mother pokes her head in the door.

"Not that tablecloth."

"Why not?"

"The other white one."

"What difference does it make? They're both white."

"Thanks, honey. And cloth napkins, please. Can you fold them?"

This is like torture, Alice thinks. Drip, drip, drip. All day long. And there goes the sun, a tiny sliver managing to peek out from the rain clouds, there goes the sun disappearing from the sky. Along with Alice's plans. This is not how today was supposed to go. Dad would not have let this day get away from him, no matter what Angie had planned. He would have known how to work around her or ignore her or tease her into going along with him. Grown-ups have more options in that department, Alice thinks. She would like to just say no to her mother; in fact, she has been trying to do that all day.

"Mom!" she shouts. "I need to plant the garden!"

"That's just going to have to wait for another day, Alice. How many times—?"

"—How many times do I have to tell you this is the day! Today, Mom! Not yesterday! Not tomorrow! Today!"

"I don't understand what the big deal is."

"You're not listening to me. This is the day. Same day. Every year. Tradition. Me and Dad. Tradition."

"I don't see what difference one day more or less makes."

"Mom!"

Alice is so frustrated she is almost crying, which she has vowed never to do in front of her mother ever again.

"Alice, you're just going to have to give in on this one. Can you finish setting the table, please?"

"Why can't Ellie help you? Why can't—?"

"—Alice!"

Uncle Eddie appears, having let himself in the backdoor.

"Would you just lay off the poor kid?"

"Stay out of it, Eddie."

"I'm just saying—"

"What do you know about raising kids?"

"I thought you were talking about the garden."

"What sacrifices have you ever had to make?"

"Is this a contest? You win, Angie. You've made more sacrifices than I have. What does that have to do with anything?"

"This is none of your business, Eddie."

"Angie, c'mon . . . She just wants to plant the garden."

Alice considers stepping into the fray and then thinks better of it when Angie's next tirade turns into tears, and Uncle Eddie takes her in his arms. Angie's sobs are so loud and so ragged Alice would like to put her hands over her ears or turn on the radio to drown out the sounds and the feelings, but she can't move. It's kind of like watching a car wreck, only scarier.

When Angie finally pulls herself together, Alice turns away and very carefully, very quietly finishes setting the table.

And then it's as though they all make a silent pact to pretend that everything is fine, everything is perfectly normal as they navigate the minefield that is dinner.

After dinner, Alice stands next to Gram at the sink drying dishes while Mom and Uncle Eddie smooth things over with a bottle of wine in the living room.

"Good pie, huh?" Gram says.

"Yeah," Alice agrees, looking out the kitchen window through the rain, squinting to see the garden.

"Maybe a bit too much sugar."

Alice hands the pie plate back. "You missed a spot."

"I did not!"

"Right there."

"You remember Grampa?" Gram asks.

"Of course!"

"From before he got sick?"

Alice thinks of the hospital and the blue-striped bathrobe he insisted on bringing from home, but then she remembers sitting on his

lap on the maroon velvet couch in the big old house and Grampa
reading to her, *The Girl of the Limberlost*, she thinks it was.

"He'd do all the voices when he read to me."

"That's right."

"And he always smelled good."

"Bay rum."

Gram hands her a mixing bowl to dry.

"He was a good-looking man."

"Gram!"

"What? He *was*."

"Are you twinkling, Gram?"

"And lovable; he had this sweetness."

"Sweet as pie?"

"Maybe that's why Char always wanted more sugar. If she could've
had Grampa, she'd have been waking up with sweetness every day of
her life."

"Wait a minute—"

"Her whole life that girl loved sugar. Spoonfuls in her coffee, on her
oatmeal. It makes my teeth ache just thinking about it."

"Maybe that's what made her so sweet."

"Ha! My sister was a barracuda!"

"She was not!"

"Get in between Char and what she wanted and watch out!"

"What did she want?"

"Oh, that's ancient history."

"C'mon, Gram."

Gram hands Alice the roasting pan.

"Grampa. Before he was Grampa, of course."

"What?"

"Stopped speaking to me for nearly a year when James fell in love
with me."

"You're kidding me."

"And then she married his brother Bobby. And never, ever stopped flirting with James."

"But you loved her—"

"Of course I loved her. She was my little sister. Doesn't mean we didn't have our issues."

Ellie walks into the kitchen and pulls her recorder out of its case.

"Check this out," Ellie says, unfolding a list of words. "*Cabbaged* and *fabaceae,* each eight letters long, are the longest words that can be played on a musical instrument."

And then she plays them on her recorder.

Alice looks at Gram and bites her lip to keep from laughing.

"What does *fabaceae* mean?" Gram wants to know.

"Of, or consisting of beans," Ellie says as she pushes her glasses up on her nose.

"Who knew?"

"Seven-letter words you can play on a musical instrument include *acceded, baggage, bedface, cabbage, defaced,* and *effaced.*"

"*Bedface?*" Alice asks.

"It's in the dictionary," Ellie says, as she plays the seven-letter words.

"It's not exactly a tune."

"No, it's an oddity, an aberration, an anomaly . . ."

"Okay! Okay!"

"What's your new favorite word?" Gram asks.

"I have two: *Acnestis.* Noun. On an animal, the point of the back that lies between the shoulders and the lower back, which cannot be reached to be scratched. And *pandiculation.* Noun. The stretching that accompanies yawning."

"How about *procrastinate?*" Alice shoots back. "Or *perseverate?* Or *temporize?* Delay! Delay! Delay!"

"What are you talking about?" Gram wants to know.

"I'm supposed to be planting the garden. It should be done. Finished. Put to bed."

"Too late now," Ellie says.

"Thanks a lot, sport."

"Maybe it's just as well," Gram offers. "We're supposed to be getting more sleet tomorrow."

"These are the cold weather crops. Cold weather crops *like* the cold."

Alice finds herself close to tears, yet again. Why is it no one will listen to her today?

"Ellie! Time for bed!" Mom calls from the living room.

"That's my cue," says Gram. "Eddie, I need my coach and four!"

The next thing you know, Gram and Uncle Eddie are on their way home, Ellie's in the bathtub talking a mile a minute to Mom, who is perched on the edge of the tub, and Alice is out the door. In the workshop she puts on her dad's jacket, work gloves, and a hat. She slips into her rubber boots, then gathers what she needs: a hoe, string, stakes, seeds, the Coleman lantern. And finally, finally she is in the garden.

She goes back into the workshop to get the stool for the lantern so that, elevated, it can shed more usable light. In the cold, drizzling rain, in the dark, she stakes her rows one by one. Leaf lettuce, red and green, spinach, beets, radishes, peas, carrots. She hears her dad's voice reminding her to alternate the red and green lettuce. They look so nice like that. *Short rows, Alice. Stagger the planting over two weeks.*

She stops for a moment to listen to the wind in the branches and the steady drip of the rain, and then bends to work with the hoe, making her furrows. Not too deep. The soil is wet and heavy but she takes her time, just the way her dad does, and her rows are true.

She has to take her gloves off to handle the seed packets and the seeds. Her hands are freezing as she tears open the first seed packet.

"Alice?"

It's her mom. In a raincoat and rain boots and holding an umbrella.

"Half an hour, I'll be done."

"Can I help?"

"Not with that stupid umbrella."

Angie closes the umbrella, pulls a hat out of her pocket, and waits for Alice to tell her what to do.

"Dad and I work in from the outside. So we don't get in each other's way."

"Okay."

"Can you see the last row? Beets."

She hands her the seed packet.

"Be patient. Don't over seed."

"Just one row?"

"I'll see how you do and then decide if you get to do another one."

They work in silence except for the slight hiss of the Coleman lantern and the steady drip of the rain.

"It's raining down my neck!" Angie complains.

"You'll live," Alice says.

Alice is down on her hands and knees, carefully mounding soil over the seeds.

"Sweetie, I'm not really dressed for kneeling in the dirt."

"I'll do it. You just do the seeds."

Angie straightens up from the row of beets.

"Good enough?"

Alice checks out her mother's work, as well as she can, given the limited light.

"I guess I'm gonna have to trust you on this one."

"What's next?"

Alice hands her a packet of carrot seeds.

"How do you keep your hands from freezing off?"

"You don't."

Alice finishes the spinach and the radishes and the peas in the time it takes Angie to finish the row of carrots, and then she's on her knees, mounding the soil over the seeds. She is rewarded with her dad's voice again: *Tamp it down a bit. Not too tight.*

The soil is cold and wet and she is thinking of the days to come, the sunny days to come when she will plant peppers and tomatoes and beans and corn and squash and the soil will be warm in her hands. She can hear her dad rattling off his favorite varieties of tomatoes: *Early Girl, Brandywine, Big Rainbow, Mr. Stripey, Nebraska Wedding*. She'll plant them all.

"Is that it?" Angie wants to know.

"That's it."

"Okay. Let's get you into the bathtub."

"I'm gonna stay out here for a bit, Mom."

"Alice . . ."

Alice looks at her mom; she notices that her hair is plastered to her neck. Then she looks out over the dark mass of the garden.

"Sometimes I can hear him," she says. "Not like in a crazy way or anything. I can hear the things he's said to me. How to do things and stuff."

"It's really cold, honey."

"We'd always just sit here for a few minutes when we finished planting."

Alice picks up the lantern and wipes the rain off the stool for her mom. Angie hesitates and then sits. Alice sets the lantern down and then kneels in the dirt. She pulls a Snickers bar out of the jacket pocket, unwraps it, and hands half to her mom.

"Snickers?"

"Dad's favorite."

"Really?"

"You didn't know that?"

"Nope."

They eat the Snickers.

"Normally, when Dad and I would do this the sun would be shining and some birds would be singing and . . ."

"I know, I know . . ."

"And you'd just sort of feel things beginning and things continuing . . . the way some things get to continue . . . because it's the same things that are beginning every spring . . . and it's like . . . so full of hope, you know? To put those seeds in the ground every year."

Alice hasn't said this many words in a row to her mother in a long time. She wonders if it's the dark that is letting her talk like this. Or the fact that Angie has entered Alice's world for a change.

"Can you smell that smell?"

Angie sniffs, skeptical and dubious that there could be something out here she would actually like to smell. Because while she may like big animals and barns and farmers and farmers' wives, she does not, in any way, shape, or form, like dirt.

"Which smell?"

"All of them."

"Honey, the garden isn't really—"

"Ellie told me a new word today. *Petrichor.* The loamy smell that rises from the ground after rain. Isn't it cool that there's a word for that?"

"Ellie and her dictionary."

"It's there. Just like she said. It's there."

Water is now dripping from Angie's neck down Angie's back and she is wishing she could enter into the spirit of all of this with Alice a bit more fully, that she could just inhale *petrichor* like a really good sport, but just as fervently she is wishing she could get inside her nice, dry house.

"So . . . is that enough communing with nature for one night?"

Alice laughs.

"You go in. I'll put the tools away."

Angie picks up her umbrella and heads back to the house. She's washing her hands at the kitchen sink and looks up to see that Alice is still in the garden, still kneeling in the dirt. The light from the lantern barely illuminates her. Angie turns out the kitchen light and returns to the window, thinking she might be able to see a little better. What is she waiting for? Her father's voice? A miracle? Is she praying?

Angie realizes that she has no idea what Alice is thinking and she suddenly sees just how hard it is to know anyone, ever. But is there anything more difficult than trying to know your adolescent daughter? No one warned her that you can go from feeling like a really good mother to a really clueless and crappy mother the minute your daughter turns twelve. Or was it eleven?

Alice stands and stretches and picks up the lantern to walk the six rows, making sure everything is as it should be. Just the way her dad does it.

Alice is taller, Angie realizes, she suddenly looks more like Matt than ever; she has even started to move with Matt's easy grace and confidence.

Angie watches her, sees her care and her competence and the threads that connect her to Matt. Each string stretched tight over each row, each careful furrow, each seed in the dark earth weaving a web of connection and memory.

Alice, satisfied, puts the hoe over one shoulder, picks up the stool and the lantern, and heads to the workshop.

Angie calls out the backdoor.

"I'm drawing you a hot bath."

"Five minutes, Mom. I have to clean the tools."

Just like Matt: meticulous with his tools. In the last thirty minutes Angie has suddenly found herself face-to-face with a whole slew of things Matt has taught Alice. Angie wonders what she has taught her daughter, and feels like that list is woefully short. In this moment she cannot think of one truly valuable thing to put on that list. How to do laundry? Fry an egg? Not in the same league.

How in the world is she going to fill in for Matt? Not that anyone could ever fill Matt's shoes. But for Alice, for Alice . . . she gets a sudden and dizzying glimpse into the size of this loss. If Matt doesn't come home . . . No, she can't go there, she can't think that. He will be found. He will return. She has to believe this. She has to.

Alice walks in the backdoor, soaking wet and muddy, her dark hair dripping down her back.

"C'mere."

Alice visibly recoils.

"Mom, I'm a mess."

"I don't care." And Angie opens her arms. She opens her arms to her daughter, hoping beyond hope that Alice won't turn away.

There's a long moment before Alice can bring herself to walk into them, and when she does she's stiff and cold and uncertain. But for once, Angie is not worrying about getting wet or dirty or what she has to do next. For once, Angie just holds on and holds on, until she can feel Alice melt into her, until she can feel Alice's head sink onto her shoulder, until she can feel Alice's arms go around her.

"I've missed you," she says into Alice's damp hair.

May 4th

Four days later, when Sergeant Ames, accompanied by a second soldier, appears again at their front door there is no need for Angie or Alice or Ellie to say a word. They all know why he is here; they know what the letter he holds in his hand says. They stand in the open doorway and attempt to listen as Sergeant Ames does his duty and recites his script about a grateful nation.

"On behalf of the President and the Commandant of the Army, it is my unfortunate duty to inform you . . ."

It is a beautiful, balmy May day and the air is rich with new earth smells and fresh cut grass. They can hear the Peterson twins down the street as they shoot baskets in their driveway.

How many other screen doors open when Sergeant Ames drives

up the street? How many of their neighbors are looking at his brown Ford sedan and knowing exactly what it means? The distant war suddenly brought close, suddenly right here in their driveway, right here on their front stoop, right here and right now on East Oak Street.

Sergeant Ames seems hesitant to leave. There are details: the return of the body, the return of Matt's effects. These will be handled by the military. Sergeant Ames promises to come back in the morning to guide them through the process and the decisions.

They watch him drive away and then step back inside the house and close the door. They sit on the couch, Angie in the middle, Ellie and Alice on either side of her. Angie holds the letter with the official army seal in her hand. They are not screaming, they are not wailing; they are barely breathing. It is so quiet Alice can hear her dad's watch ticking on her wrist.

The phone starts to ring.

"We need to call Gram," Angie says. "And Uncle Eddie."

The ringing phone is like a crying child; but Angie does not get up to answer it. Angie seems paralyzed.

"I'll call them," Alice says.

Angie can't seem to focus.

"Mom . . . ?"

"Okay."

Alice gets up and heads for the kitchen, the ringing phone getting louder and louder. She turns to look back at her mother. Ellie has climbed into Angie's lap and Angie is rocking her back and forth. In between "I'll call them," and "Okay," Alice has crossed an invisible line. She was expecting Angie to say, "No, no, that's all right, honey; I'll take care of it." She was expecting Angie to hold on to her, to hold on to both of her girls. But here she is on the outside of the circle, steeling herself to break her grandmother's heart. What is this longing to be touched and held and six years old again, to go backward in time, to be smaller than Ellie, to be the only one, to be held by her mother and her father?

She turns to look at her mother once more, thinking: *Call me back. Call my name. Reach out to me.*

But Angie is holding on to Ellie too tight, too tight. She is thinking that her heart is going to burst or stop beating. She wants to sink through the sofa and the floor and into the earth, to be with Matt, nowhere else, not to go on, not to put one foot in front of the other, not to be brave and true, but to let go, to surrender, to join him wherever he is.

The phone stops ringing. Alice picks up the receiver and punches in Gram's number. She notices that her hand is shaking. She notices that the breakfast dishes are still in the sink. She notices that the linoleum floor could use a good scrubbing. There's no answer at the apartment. She calls The Bird Sisters.

"Gram?"

"Alice? Are you all right?"

"It's . . ."

And she can't say "Dad," she can't say his name.

"I'll be right there. And I'll call Uncle Eddie. Is your mom there?"

"Yes."

"I'm on my way."

Alice hangs up the phone and sits in a kitchen chair.

Henry shows up at the back door and lets himself in.

"I saw the car."

She closes her eyes.

"Alice . . . ?"

She nods her head. He pulls a chair up and sits beside her.

"Did you call your Gram?"

She nods.

"And your Uncle Eddie?"

Another nod. That's all she can manage.

"Okay, then."

He takes her hand.

"We'll just wait."

They wait. Wait for the news to sink in, for the tears to begin, for a telegram telling them it was all a mistake. That night Alice waits and waits for sleep to come. She finally gives up and goes downstairs. She finds the photograph album she is looking for and quietly steps outside the back door and crosses the grass to the workshop.

She climbs into her sleeping bag, turns on her flashlight, and opens the cover of the photograph album. It is the summer of 1997; she's six years old. This is the summer she finally learns to swim on top of the water, like the big kids do. There are dozens of photos of their week's vacation camping at Small Point. Ellie hasn't even been born yet. Angie and Matt look so young. There are photos of a dinner—was it a birthday? An anniversary? There's a bottle of wine and a jar full of wildflowers on their picnic table. There's a photo of Matt, grinning at Angie as he holds two live and kicking lobsters over the pot boiling on their propane stove. In the next photo Angie has her hair up and a skirt on and Alice can see in the photo how pretty Angie is as she turns to smile at Matt taking the picture; and she can see how her father is looking at Angie and loving her; she can see right there, in this photograph, right there in that moment, that they are in love.

She turns another page and there she is, in her red and white gingham checked bathing suit. That was her favorite bathing suit of all time. She never wanted to outgrow that suit. She wonders what happened to it, if it is still in her bottom drawer. She doesn't remember Ellie ever wearing it. She can't imagine she would ever, ever let her mother give it away.

It's a long walk for a six-year-old, all the way across the island. Mom is back at the campsite reading her book while Alice hikes with her

222

dad. At first she was dawdling because she was distracted by the trees and the ferns and the sounds of animals in the woods. She has been practicing walking like an Indian, so she doesn't disturb anything: not a pine needle, not the carpet of leaves and hidden stones. It's really hard! And really slow. It is driving Dad nuts. He keeps turning around to find that she is not, in fact, behind him because she has stopped to investigate some new discovery.

"Alice, get a move on!"

"Alice, look up!"

"Alice! You're missing everything while you worry about your feet!"

How did the Indians do this, she wants to know as she trots to catch up with her father.

They're out of the woods now and climbing over a rise along a ridge of granite and moss. At the top of the ridge they can see the other side of the island and their destination: Sand Dollar Beach.

"Race you!" Dad calls out as he takes off down the trail. Of course he lets Alice catch up with him and pass him and then fakes running out of breath and falling behind. When she starts to slow down he runs circles around her.

"Come on, come on, come on! We're almost there."

And then there it is: a perfect crescent of a beach tucked away between the rocks and the trees. Deserted.

"Last one in is a rotten egg!"

He drops their backpack to the sand and pulls off his T-shirt and his hiking boots and pants and sprints into the water, jumping over the waves and then diving headfirst into a big breaker. He surfaces and swims hard for a few minutes before turning back to check on Alice. Who is stuck on the beach, one boot on, one boot off, trying to get a knot out of the lace of her left boot.

"I beat you!" Dad crows.

"There's a knot!" she tosses back. "No fair!"

"Slowpoke!"

He flips over on his back and spouts water like a whale.

She tries wriggling the knot back and forth to loosen it up and finally gets it undone. She kicks her boot off, pulls off her T-shirt and her shorts, and heads down to the water.

She's wearing her new red and white checked bathing suit and wondering if Dad will like it, when she steps into the water. How can it be so cold? Dad is out there lolling around like it's a bathtub and the water is so cold it makes her teeth hurt.

"It's cold!"

"Run. Don't walk. Just go."

She hesitates.

"Alice! Just go!"

She runs through the little waves and dives into the first big wave and swims underwater to her dad. She has her eyes open even though the salt stings, and she's kicking as hard as she can and pulling with her arms with all her might. He picks her up and throws her into the water, over and over. With variations. Backward. Sideways. She stands on his legs and pushes off as he throws her. She stands on his shoulders and jumps in. She's laughing and swallowing water and coughing and sometimes choking but always coming back for more.

That's my girl, Matt thinks. Not afraid, not cold, not complaining, not hesitating. Jumping in.

They leave the water and lie down in the sand. They forgot towels. Mom would not have forgotten towels. But it doesn't matter. They lie down in the sand side by side. Alice looks at the sun through her lashes and half-closed eyes, even though she's not supposed to. It's directly above them in a deep blue sky. She can hear the waves and the fir trees that line the shore moving in the wind. She can see the sun glinting, she can even see the sun when she closes her eyes. How can that be? She can hear her dad's breathing change as he drops into sleep. And as her skin dries she feels it contract with the sun and the salt. She thinks she's gonna get a burn. They forgot sunscreen. Mom would have

*remembered sunscreen, too. Alice thinks it's nice to forget things some-
times. To lie in the sand with nothing but her dad and the sun and the
water and the trees.*

There's a knock at the door, which startles her.

"Alice . . . ? It's me. Henry."

"It's open," she calls out to him.

Henry steps inside the workshop.

"I saw your light. You okay?"

It's two o'clock in the morning and it turns out that Henry has been
sitting up with her. She puts the flashlight on the floor; its beam casts
a light across the workshop.

"Pull up a chair."

Henry grabs the lawn chair, brings it near Alice, sits. He's wearing
old gray sweatpants that are too short, and an ancient sweatshirt that
must have belonged to his brother. His hair is even more shaggy and
rumpled than usual.

"I can't sleep."

"I figured."

"I've been looking at pictures."

She hands him the photo album.

"From when I was six."

He opens it.

"That was my favorite bathing suit," she says.

"I remember it."

"You do?"

"You wore that in the sprinkler and when we went to the high
school pool for our swim lessons."

"I can't believe you remember that."

Henry wants to tell her that he remembers everything, but when
he tries out the phrase inside his head he sounds like an idiot.

"Alice—"

225

"Henry," she interrupts.

"What?"

"Would you—?"

"—What?"

"I don't know how to say this—"

"That's okay."

"I think if you could . . . maybe . . . I don't know . . . hold me . . ." She hesitates.

"I might be able to fall asleep."

Henry has no objection to this idea, and he would like to play it cool, like, oh sure, what the heck, I get this request all the time. Hold you? All casual like. You bet. No problem. But really he is pumped full of the jitters, which is making it especially difficult not to let his hands and his feet sort of do their own nervous dance, and right away he is thinking logistics, like how is this going to work on that skinny little air mattress with a sleeping bag. But Alice has already figured it out. She unzips the sleeping bag so that it can go over them like a quilt.

"I think if we lie on our sides we can both fit."

So Henry finds himself taking off his shoes and his sweatshirt and lying down next to Alice. She lies with her back to his chest. There's a momentary question about what to do with their arms, but they figure it out.

"I'm gonna leave the light on, if that's okay with you."

"Sure."

Her head is tucked beneath his chin, her body curves into him, his arms are around her. He inhales the heady perfume of her hair, mixed with the workshop smells of woodsmoke and linseed oil. He listens to her breathing. He can feel her breathing.

"Henry . . . ?"

"Shhhh . . ."

"Don't let go."

"I won't."

"Promise me."

"I promise."

They are quiet for a while.

"Henry . . . ?"

"Go to sleep, Alice."

"I wish . . ."

"What?"

"I wish we could stay like this forever and ever and tomorrow would never come."

He begins to sing to her, very softly, almost not singing at all, just a whisper of a tune. He spins out the tune like it is a tale he is telling her, until he feels her body relax, until he feels her falling into sleep. He sings to let her know he's there, to stay anchored to the earth, to keep from laughing or crying in amazement that he is lying with Alice in his arms, he sings as if music could keep her alive, as if music could feed her soul, as if music could weave a protective spell around her to survive these days and these weeks and these months and these years, he sings as if he could give her a piece of himself, which will ring inside of her like a bell, like a promise, like hope whenever she needs him; and in his singing, he promises her every single thing he can think of, and more.

Inside the house, Angie falls asleep from sheer physical exhaustion and then wakes into fresh grief as she returns to consciousness and remembers. She swims up from sleep to the knowledge that Matt's death is not a dream, it is not a nightmare, but more real than anything else that has ever happened to her, more real even than the birth of her children. She comes downstairs to make tea or toast or maybe something stronger and looking out the kitchen window she sees the dim, unexpected glow in the workshop.

She checks the clock. Three a.m. What's going on?

When she crosses the lawn and opens the door, her first thought is: What the hell are they doing? They're fifteen years old for God's sake! Now she has to deal with this, too? Alone. Without Matt. Years of this. And then she sees that they both still have their clothes on. And remembers that the door was not locked. And the flashlight is on. Thank God. Henry turns his head to look at her and puts his finger to his lips.

"She couldn't sleep," he whispers.

Angie nods. And frowns. As frowns go, it is a loud frown.

"I promised to stay with her."

He waits for a response.

"Is that okay?"

"Does your mother know where you are?"

"Not exactly."

"I'm not happy about this, Henry."

"It's not what you think."

"Keep it that way."

"Okay."

"No funny stuff."

"No, ma'am. Absolutely not."

"I'm not kidding, Henry."

"I know."

Henry is getting a crick in his neck from trying not to look like he is plastered against Alice.

"When you wake up, get up. Come in for breakfast. No lollygagging in the damn sleeping bag."

"Okay."

"Eight o'clock. I want you in the house."

"Okay."

"Do you have a watch?"

"I can see the clock."

"One minute past eight I'll be out to check on you."

"Okay."

228

Henry attempts a reassuring smile.

"You're way too young to be sleeping with my daughter. No matter what she's going through. Do we understand each other?"

He nods.

"This is special dispensation for one night and one night only."

Another nod.

"You do understand that now *I* will not be able to sleep for the rest of the night?"

"Why not?"

"Because . . . oh my God . . . do I really have to explain this to you?"

"Shhhh . . . shhhh . . . we don't want to wake her up."

"Maybe I should just stay out here with you."

"Mrs. Bliss . . ."

"What?"

"You can trust me."

"Henry, you're an adolescent boy."

"So?"

"There are forces at work here that are bigger than both of us and both of you."

"I don't know what you mean."

"You will," Angie says, as she turns and leaves her daughter in the arms of this boy, in the safe haven of her father's workshop, in a world turned upside down and inside out, as she turns to go back to . . . what? Her empty bed? A stiff drink? To crawl into bed with Ellie, to steal comfort from her eight year old? None of these choices were even a remote part of her life when Matt was alive. Stop thinking, she admonishes herself, just make some tea and curl up on the couch with a blanket to wait for eight a.m. Matt would be beside himself if he knew she was letting Alice sleep with Henry. In the same bed, in a separate building, with no supervision. She can hear Matt hollering, *What are you thinking?!* But Matt hasn't met this moment, Matt hasn't met these nights and these days with this pain and dislocation and the sense that they will, all of them, have to find their comforts and their safe places and their moments of peace and rest and respite wherever and whenever they can.

Henry wakes to find the sun up and Alice gone. It is 7:27, he notes, according to the clock over Matt's workbench, so at least he hasn't broken any promises to her mother yet. The pillow is squashed from Alice's head, the sleeping bag is still warm from her body, but where is she? His mouth feels like sandpaper, which probably means he was snuffling and making strange noises all night long. He would like about a quart of orange juice and a salad bowl full of Cheerios, but what is he supposed to do now? Look for her? Go into the house and have breakfast? Disappear down the street to his own house as though he was never here in the first place?

He throws off the sleeping bag, gets up, and crosses to the window overlooking the garden and what do you know, there she is, in her pajamas and his sweatshirt and a pair of too-big rubber boots, hoeing away. What does she think she is, some kind of farmer? She has braided her hair to keep it out of her face. She is hoeing very carefully, turning over the soil, loosening the clods.

Every row is planted now, except for the tomatoes, which have to wait for Memorial Day, or so he has been told on innumerable occasions. Soon there will be a pale green fuzz to the garden, a green, hopeful, babyish fuzz of barely born, half-baked plantlets all in straight rows. Alice finishes hoeing and heads back to the workshop. She opens the door, hangs the hoe on its hook, and asks:

"Want some breakfast?"

And that seems to be that. Like last night never happened. Like he hasn't been holding her in his arms for hours, watching her and listening to her breathe. He had been determined to stay awake all night, but something, who knows what, happiness maybe, stole him away and took him off to dreamland.

"You coming?"

"Maybe I should go home."

She considers this.

"Okay. If you want."

"Your mom came out here last night."

"She did? Was she mad?"

"Yes and no."

"Did you talk to her?"

"Well, yeah. Sort of."

"And she let you stay?"

"Yeah. Kind of."

"What do you mean, kind of?"

"She established some ground rules."

"Like what?"

"The usual."

Alice turns toward the house.

"You coming in, or what?"

"My parents might be worried."

"Okay."

"But I left a note."

"So they're fine, then."

She starts across the lawn.

"Alice—"

When she turns to look at him, the rising sun catches her square in the jaw and she steps back as though it is a physical blow. And now the birds. As he tries to find words, as he tries to find what to think and what to say he can suddenly hear the birds, dozens of them in the apple trees, dozens more in the lilacs.

"C'mon. Let's go," she says.

He follows her across the lawn and toward the house, like a guilty party, like a hungry man, like a frightened boy, and he is full of words and feelings and confusion and a rumbling belly and somewhere important something hurts and aches and he can't tell if he is aching for Alice or if he breathed in her grief with the smell of her shampoo.

Henry pauses at the kitchen door. Alice is already pouring juice into jelly jars. When he steps into the kitchen it is unnaturally quiet, as though the house itself is holding its breath. And he suddenly knows that the millions of changes no one wants and no one can prevent, the avalanche of change falling down on Alice and her family, is just beginning.

She hands him his glass of juice as her mother steps into the kitchen.

"Right on time," she says, looking at the clock.

"I was just leaving," Henry says, and makes his escape out the door.

He turns to wave at Alice, walking backward, waving at her through the doorway. He wants to make her smile somehow; but she seems lost to him, so he doesn't even dare flash a goofy grin. She raises a hand to him, like a salute, and inside his head he thinks, be strong, Alice, just as inside her head, she hears her father's voice: *courage, Alice, courage.*

May 6th

Within twenty-four hours every neighbor has brought a casserole or a cake or a plateful of cookies. Mrs. Grover arrives with stacks of paper plates and cups, plastic forks and spoons, and a fresh apron. She has quietly installed herself in the kitchen to take care of the food and the family.

Gram has left the restaurant in Sally's hands. Sally, Ginny, and Dave have rearranged their schedules to be there for the duration, as everyone is calling this.

Gram and Uncle Eddie have made all the necessary calls to friends and family. Uncle Eddie is shuttling back and forth between their house and his garage, trying to keep a lid on things. He's installed coolers on the back porch crammed with ice and soda and beer.

Sergeant Ames has called to tell them Matt's body will be arriving stateside, with a military escort, in two days. Do they want to meet the body in Delaware? Do they want to view the body before the autopsy? Which will take two more days. At which point Matt will be placed in a coffin in his military dress uniform, unless they choose cremation. Have they chosen the coffin? Do they want to accompany the body home along with the military escort? Commercial or military plane? Do they want an honor guard at the burial?

Angie doesn't want an autopsy; she won't even allow the word to be spoken in front of Alice and Ellie, but of course, they've both heard it. Angie and Sergeant Ames have been around the block several times on this issue. Angie is furious and adamant and she's even called her senator's office to ask for help. When the senator herself calls back, Angie has a wild moment of hope, but all of the senator's sympathy and gratitude cannot change army policy.

The funeral director, lugging two sample cases, is knocking on the door with his own long list of impossible questions and impossible choices to be made. Only it's not a he, it's a she. It's a beautiful young blonde with a soft voice and soft hands and just why is it so unsettling to think of this lovely young woman dealing with the dead? How can she do it, Alice wonders? And Angie is thinking, isn't it just like Matt to have a beautiful girl taking care of him, even now.

Allison Mahoney, of Mahoney and Sons, suggests that they sit at the dining room table to go over things. Gram whisks Ellie upstairs for a game of Scrabble while Angie and Alice follow Ms. Mahoney into their own dining room.

The sample cases contain very glossy photographs of all kinds of coffins, shown open and shut. There are samples of too-shiny satin in lurid colors, fancy turned brass handles, all of which can be mixed and matched, like picking an outfit. Urns, should they go that way, large

233

and small, plain and fancy, some are blown glass, some are hammered brass. There are pages and pages of choices for the registry book, for cards and prayer cards, and Mass cards, and preprinted thank-you cards.

"Who will be writing the obituary?" Ms. Mahoney asks.

They make their choices and their decisions, one by one. Angie is numb; Alice just wants to get away, to get outside, to go running, to think about, to feel something, *anything* else.

When Ms. Mahoney finally leaves, Mrs. Grover and Gram serve dinner. They all pretend to eat. Uncle Eddie and Henry are pretty successful at it. Afterward, Alice heads to the kitchen to help Mrs. Grover clean up.

Henry is taking out the trash. Mrs. Grover is trying to keep Alice up to date with the food and the leftovers and what they should keep on hand and what they should freeze. Alice wants someone else to keep track of this. But she is trying to help; she is trying to focus on what they should do with the leftover green beans and will anyone want any more of Stephie's mom's Jell-O salad? Which Stephie delivered herself while Alice was out in the garden.

"Mom, you decide," Henry says as he carries another trash bag out the backdoor.

Angie has gone upstairs to lie down, Uncle Eddie has gone to the garage to check on things, and Ellie is giving Gram a foot massage in the living room.

Mrs. Grover fills the sink to wash the dishes. Alice grabs a dish-towel. This she can do.

"Any more trash?" Henry wants to know.

"That's it."

He sits down at the kitchen table and grabs another molasses cookie. Alice pours him a glass of milk.

"You could still go tonight, you know," Mrs. Grover says.

"Go where?" Alice asks.

"To the dance."

Uh oh, Henry thinks, not a good idea.

"It's not a crime or anything. You could ask your mom, Alice."

"But—"

"I don't think your dad would mind."

"I don't feel like—"

"It might do you good."

"I don't—"

"That's okay, Alice. I don't mind, really," Henry says.

"You could still go, Henry."

"Without you? Forget it."

Alice looks out the kitchen window to her dad's workshop and the garden beyond. The last of the sunset is still coloring the sky. The last thing in the world she feels like doing is going to the school gym to see all those people, to know that they all know what's happened, but they don't know, can't know what to say.

"We wouldn't have to go inside, even."

Henry, it seems, can read her mind.

"You know how there's that grassy area outside the gym, where the big maple tree is?"

"Just watch, you mean?"

"Or just listen. Maybe dance a little on the grass."

Alice dries another plate.

"I mean we could go in if you want to, if you change your mind or anything; I'm just saying we don't have to. . . . Not to pressure you or anything."

Alice continues to stare out the window. Mrs. Grover dries her hands on her apron and puts her arm around Alice's shoulder.

"You do what feels right to you, honey. It was just a suggestion."

Alice puts her arm around Mrs. Grover's soft waist in her paisley dress. Mrs. Grover feels so different from Alice's mother.

"I know your dad would like to see you in that dress."

"No, he'd think . . ."

"He'd be wondering how you grew up so fast and got so pretty. He'd be wondering how it is he hadn't noticed all kinds of things about you while you were right under his nose."

Alice, embarrassed, pulls away.

"You go change. I'll help Henry get ready."

"I have to ask my mom."

"I know. I'll pick you up about . . ."

"We wanted to walk."

"That's fine, then. Henry will be back to pick you up in thirty minutes. If all you do is walk to the corner and back, that's fine, too."

"Okay."

"But stop by afterward and let me see you in that dress."

Henry and Mrs. Grover are out the door and Angie has said yes, it doesn't matter, yes, it's all right, and now Alice is slipping into the dress and lifting her hair off her neck and twisting it and using too many bobby pins to try to hold it up. Maybe a ponytail would be easier. And stepping into her pointy-toed flat shoes and asking her mom if she can borrow a sweater and yes, she'll be warm enough.

Angie turns and looks at Alice. And finds herself looking straight into Matt's blue eyes.

There's a pause while Angie tries to get her voice under control.

"Daddy would like that dress."

"Really?"

"Absolutely."

Matt should be here, she is thinking, Matt should see this, Matt would . . . Oh, when did she get to be so lovely?

"I tried to put my hair up, but . . ."

"Let me help."

Angie deftly pins up Alice's hair.

"Ask Mrs. Grover to take some pictures."

"We won't stay too long."

"Who's driving?"

"We wanted to walk."

"Call Uncle Eddie if you want a ride home."

"Mom, we don't have to go, I'm not even sure I really want to go. . . . I could stay here with you, I could . . ."

"Go."

Angie kisses Alice.

"Go."

Gram and Ellie make Henry come inside when he knocks on the door, Henry who has opted to wear a T-shirt with the tuxedo pants and jacket, Henry who has showered in under five minutes, and slicked back his hair, who is looking older and cooler and somehow also even dorkier than he ever has in his life, Henry who, among other things in the last half hour, has learned how to spit polish his shoes to a mirror shine.

Henry stands just inside the door ready to cut and run at the slightest sign of a critical glance. He is feeling hot and nervous until Alice comes down the stairs in that dress and an entirely new mash-up of feelings starts to slosh around inside his stomach. Alice smiles at him, or at least her mouth smiles at him. Her eyes are still wary and desperate. Henry would like to kiss her eyes, but at the same time wonders just what kind of an idiot goes around wanting to kiss other people's eyes?

Which is when he notices that Ellie is staring at him.

"If you must osculate," she says, "please refrain from cataglottism."

"What?"

"Leave Henry alone, Ellie."

"But what did you just say?"

"If you must kiss, please refrain from kissing with the tongue."

"Ellie!"

Gram makes Ellie find the camera, in spite of Alice's protests. After a significant spell of photographic torture by the front door, Gram lets them go and Alice and Henry find themselves walking down the sidewalk in the near dark of late twilight.

"You sure you're okay with this?"

Alice doesn't say anything in response, she just reaches out and takes his hand. Henry thinks if she keeps doing things like this, which make him feel as if his stomach and his heart have changed places, all of his internal organs are likely to get completely mixed up and rearranged.

Lights are starting to come on in the houses they pass. It's the after-dinner pause and the streets are unusually quiet. The breeze kicks up and stirs the new leaves in the trees arching over their heads.

They are going the long way to school, down Baird Road to Martin Street instead of cutting through the playing fields; they are passing Mrs. Minty's house and Mrs. Piantowski's house and The Bird Sisters and the Four Corners. Henry is worried that his hand is probably all sweaty and slick and gross, but if it is, Alice doesn't seem to notice. Alice has closed her eyes against the well of sorrow that is always there, rising and falling like a tide, but with her eyes closed she is suddenly hearing and smelling the world around her; hearing the leaves rustle and the branches scraping against each other, hearing their footsteps on the cement sidewalk, the scuffing sound Henry makes in his unaccustomed fancy tie shoes, the *click, click* of her little flats, and then there it is, yes, there it is, the spring smells layered one by one, of new grass and clean dirt and somewhere in the twilight there are narcissus spilling their perfume into the night.

"Alice?"

"Yeah?"

"I'd really like to dance with you."

"Okay."

"A slow dance."

"Okay."

"And then we can go home. . . . Unless you want to stay."

Alice takes a breath.

"I sort of promised John Kimball I would dance with him."

"What?"

"It seemed so far-fetched at the time that I never really thought—"

"He asked you—?"

"Yeah."

"What about Melissa?"

"That's what I said."

"Do you want to dance with him?"

"I don't know. I mean, no, I mean . . . Henry, it's not like a lot of people have ever asked me to dance."

She looks at him.

"It was nice to be asked."

"When did this happen?"

"At the Red Wings game."

"I figured."

"And then it was awkward and I didn't know how to tell you, or if there was anything to tell. Which there isn't. Okay?"

"Okay."

"Can we just forget it now?"

Approaching the high school they can hear the deep bass notes thumping and vibrating all the way from the gym. The principal is at the entrance to the school, his tie loosened, talking to the police officer whose cruiser is idling in the street. He looks up and sees Alice and Henry heading to the back of the building.

"You two have tickets?"

Henry sprints over and hands him their tickets.

"Come on in."

"We were planning to just hang out on the grass for a while."

"You're supposed to go inside so we know who's who, what's what, and who's where."

"Mr. Fisher," Henry starts to explain—

"Alice, I'm so sorry to hear about your dad."

"Thank you," Alice says to the asphalt in front of her.

"Mr. Fisher, we don't want to go inside, we just—"

"—You just what?"

Henry steps up close and speaks quietly for a moment. Mr. Fisher considers.

"If I make an exception can you stay out of trouble?"

"Yes, sir."

"I mean it, Henry."

"I know you do, Mr. Fisher."

They give the school a wide berth as they walk around to the back. Behind the school the double doors to the gym are propped open, spilling music and light onto the parking lot and the edge of the playing fields. The dance committee has hung disco balls from the basketball hoops at either end of the gym floor. There's a DJ at one end and a table full of cookies and punch at the other.

Alice and Henry skirt the edge of the light as they make their way to the lone maple tree behind the school. There are several boys hanging out at the doors who seem to catch their scent and gather, in a body, to begin some kind of taunt. But then they recognize Alice, or one of them does, and they decide to leave them alone.

It is dark enough now to see the stars, dark enough and late enough for the DJ to start to slow things down. Alice sees John Kimball come to the doorway, talk to the boys who are still there, look her way, and head back inside. He seems so far away. It all seems so far away. The baseball game seems like it happened in another lifetime to another girl.

A slow song begins. Henry turns to Alice and puts his hands on her waist. She puts her hands on his shoulders and then he draws her close and she puts her arms around his neck and suddenly without thinking about it too much or having a chance to mess it up, they are dancing. Henry feels the music like his own heartbeat and moves Alice gently over the rough ground as though they are gliding on a polished floor. Alice had been afraid she would not know how to do this, or that she would do it badly or trip or step on his feet. But Henry relaxes into the music and Alice relaxes into Henry and it is so lovely and so unexpected that she allows herself to rest her head on his shoulder. She closes her eyes and she is floating in space, she is riding the music with Henry; she is trusting her body and her feet and she is not thinking about anything but this.

One part of Henry, the dancing part, is inside the music and wants to stay there because that's what he knows, that's where he can just move and hold Alice. But when she puts her head on his shoulder and he takes one hand from her waist and puts it on her head, his fingers in her soft, soft hair, it takes his breath away. He stumbles in that moment and steps on her toes, but they right themselves, they take a breath, together. Henry inhales the perfume of her skin, Alice feels the delicacy of his neck, the new strength in his shoulder; Alice feels the steps, the music, the letting go, the holding on.

The song ends and they separate. Alice does not want to come back to the world; Alice would like to stay lost in the music and the night sky and Henry's arms for a little while longer, maybe forever.

She looks up to see John Kimball at the gym doors again. He takes a step toward her; she waves to him, and then Melissa Johnson is there to reach out and take him by the hand and pull him back inside. Stephie disentangles herself from Jeremy Baskin and comes to the door. Before she can wave, Alice and Henry retreat farther into the dark beyond the maple tree and decide to cut through the Baldwins' driveway to Martin Street so they don't have to see everyone coming out of the school and laughing and talking and waiting for their rides.

In the dark of Martin Street, holding Alice's hand, Henry wants to kiss her. That rogue thought has been zinging around inside of him for weeks now, waking him at odd or inconvenient moments, startling him at breakfast or in the middle of a math test or at the piano. But this feeling in the dark of Martin Street is like a runaway car careening out of control; his blood is doing a jig in his veins, his heart is pounding, his knees feel all watery and weird, and his feet feel like they've grown six sizes. How in the world will he keep from tripping and falling? He is on the edge of falling every single second.

"Henry, are you okay?"

"What? Yeah. Fine. Why?"

"Well, you're kind of breathing funny."

Breathing, is he actually still breathing?

"Sorry. Sorry."

And he trips. His legs are like Jell-O. This is ridiculous. He goes down on one knee and recovers, kind of bounces back up like his knee is rubber capped or something.

"Henry Grover, if I didn't know better, I'd think you were drunk."

I *am* drunk, he thinks, or this must be what being drunk is like; woozy and hyperaware and clumsy.

"Are you okay? Are you sick?"

Yes, sick, that's it. Sick and in pain and really, do people *want* to feel like this? It's kind of like torture.

"Maybe this was a mistake? And we should have stayed home?"

No, no, not a mistake, he's thinking as he trips again and recovers, but just barely. Not a mistake to walk with you and dance with you and hold you and . . . Oh, boy, this is not getting better, he thinks, this is getting worse and worse.

"Henry, I think you might be hyperventilating."

He trips again but Alice catches him, sort of, or at least manages to ease him down to the curb.

"Henry, it's okay. Just try to take one deep breath."

"Alice," he manages to choke out—

"What?"

"When you kissed me . . ."

242

She looks down at her feet. Not a good sign. He braces himself.

"When you kissed me . . . Was it . . . ?"

"Was it what?"

"A mistake?" he asks.

"No, I mean—"

"—Are you sorry?"

"No. I didn't think—"

"Because I didn't mean—"

"I know."

"No, you don't know," he says. "You startled me and—"

"I'm sorry."

"Don't be sorry. Please don't be sorry. What I mean is—"

"What?"

"I didn't have a chance—"

"A chance to what?"

"A chance to kiss you back . . . And last night, when I was holding you, just holding you—"

"Henry, don't."

"Don't what?"

"Don't ask me."

"I don't want to ask you, I want to kiss you."

"Don't ask me."

"Don't . . . ?"

And she is looking at him with her deep, newly fathomless eyes that are shining with something that is not tears and not joy, but is still urgent and unreadable, and he wants to think about what Alice is feeling but all he can think about is what he is feeling. Is this what her mother was talking about this morning, that lifetime ago? It is not careful or considerate or cautious; it is a rush that's propelling him, terrified that he could lose her forever, terrified that this could be his only chance, terrified that whatever happens in this moment cannot be taken back or erased or made right once it happens, that if he stumbles here, somehow that is who he is and who he will be for-ever and ever.

He looks down at his hands dangling between his knees, and sud-denly it is all quiet inside of him. Too quiet, like all the air has been squeezed out of him and he is nothing but a shell. He can hear the breeze in the trees overhead; he can hear the traffic on Baird Road.

Alice kneels in front of him. She puts her hands on either side of his face.

"I don't want anything else to change, Henry."

"It won't change."

"It will."

"But . . ."

"I can't lose one more thing."

He can't hear her, really; he can't hear anything but this new roar-ing in his ears when she is so close to him, and he pulls her to him, too fiercely, they nearly collide, he pulls her to him and for a second, looks into her eyes, her unreadable eyes. He closes his own eyes and with a prayer, a wish, a pure incantation of fear and desire, he kisses her. And this time there is no mistaking it, their lips actually touch. It is equally shocking as the first time, but they do not stumble and jerk and pull away.

Instead, Alice bursts into tears. These are not girly tears pulled out and turned on for effect, not that Alice is that kind of girl; these are racking, hiccupping, blubbering sobs. Henry has one wild, terrible moment where he thinks his kiss has caused these desperate feelings, before Alice leans into him and holds on to him and sobs and sobs into his shoulder.

He manages to stand up and pull her to her feet and hand her his handkerchief, which his mother had not only thought to provide but had carefully ironed that afternoon.

"It's not you," she chokes out, before burying her face in his hand-kerchief again. "It's everything."

Henry knows that everything is her dad and that her dad is everything, which is not exactly the way he feels about his own dad, and if anything, if it is even possible, this fills him further to the brim with Alice feelings.

And while it is true that Henry is nothing but a gangly fifteen-year-old boy, often sloppy, occasionally rude, with marginal hygiene habits, it is also true that he is still in possession of his own heart, his own inspired, musical, untouched heart, a heart capable of taking on Alice and her sadness and her loss and her love. So, on this night, when Alice pours out her grief for her father and her love for her father, and the ending of her time on earth with her father, it is Henry she chooses, Henry she pours these feelings into, Henry she blesses and burdens with her tears, Henry who has the strength of ten men as he stands up and stands steady beneath this onslaught that has knocked lesser men and boys to their knees.

May 8th

They are waiting on the airport tarmac for Angie and the military escort and the coffin to be unloaded from the plane. There is a special place at the airport for this, away from the main terminal. Alice is sitting in the front seat next to Uncle Eddie. Gram and Ellie are in the back. The hearse from Mahoney and Sons waits behind them. No one is talking. It is gray and cool, threatening rain. Good for the garden, Alice thinks, though we could use some sun.

A uniformed soldier follows Angie down the stairs as the hold of the plane is opened from the inside. She is wearing her glasses, Alice notices, even though she's dressed up. Maybe she wants to hide her eyes.

Six soldiers stand with the coffin on their shoulders. Alice had expected a flag, but the coffin is bare. Angie is directed to a place near the hold. The soldier following her stands nearby. The funeral director appears at Uncle Eddie's window.

"They're waiting for us. Just walk up and stand beside Mrs. Bliss."

They pile out of the car and cross the gritty tarmac to stand beside Angie as Matt's coffin is carried down the stairs. The single soldier turns toward the coffin and executes a very precise, slow-motion salute. Alice steps forward. The funeral director reaches out a hand to pull her back and Alice realizes they were not supposed to stop; they were not going to wait for her to meet her father, to acknowledge his return. Their job is simply to convey the coffin across the parking lot and into the waiting hearse. But they do stop for her, each in his dress uniform, each with his eyes front.

"Are you from my father's unit?"

"No."

"Did any of you know him?"

"No. I'm sorry."

Gram steps forward.

"Come on, honey."

Alice stands her ground. She turns to the single, saluting soldier.

"Did you know my father?"

He shakes his head. She turns back to the coffin.

"Can you put the coffin down, please?"

There is hesitation all around, subtle shifts in the soldier's bodies, as they cannot break rank and look at each other. Alice chooses one soldier to speak to.

"Can you just let him touch the ground, please?"

The wind picks up; sand and dust swirl around their feet. It is possible that the soldier could choose to let the wind blow Alice's words away, but she is standing firm and speaking clearly and looking him in the face even though he cannot meet her eyes.

He speaks a brief command, and then, moving as one, the soldiers lower the coffin to the ground and take a step away. She kneels beside the coffin and lays one hand on the smooth wood. She wants a moment for her father to land on the ground, for his body to arrive here, at home. She does not want her father's soul to be lost in Iraq or in a plane flying above the ocean or somewhere in an army hospital in Delaware. She wants his soul to come home, however briefly, *home*, before it goes on whatever journey a soul must take, and she doesn't believe this is possible if he never actually touches the ground. If she could she would open the coffin and put his feet on the ground, but this is the best she can do.

Angie reaches out to take her hand, pulling Alice to her feet, releasing the soldiers. They lift the coffin to their shoulders, walk the last steps to the hearse, and slide the coffin into the waiting bay.

They all wait where they are until the hearse starts up. The soldiers remain at attention while the family piles back into the car and slowly drives off, following the hearse. Ellie kneels on the seat and watches out the back window. Not one soldier moves a muscle while she can still see them. Uncle Eddie takes the turn onto Columbus Avenue too fast and Ellie slides into a seated position in between Alice and Gram. Angie puts her head back against the headrest and closes her eyes. She is as pale as the moon.

Gram reaches up and strokes Angie's hair. Alice notices that Gram's hand is trembling. Gram, realizing what Alice has seen, shifts to rest her hand on Angie's shoulder.

"We'll get through this," Gram says.

Angie clasps Gram's hand, and Alice sees that she is wearing Matt's wedding ring on her second finger. When did they give that to her? In the morgue? Was it in a small plastic bag or an envelope? Did she slip it off his finger herself? Did they let her touch him? Why did Angie go alone, why didn't she take Gram or Uncle Eddie with her, why did she refuse to let Alice come along?

Why are all of these things happening so quickly? There is too much to do, there are too many steps to take, no, no, there is not enough to do, she sees now; it will all go by too fast, it is out of her hands, it will all happen whether she wants it to or not, and he will be gone, truly gone, dead and buried, and there will not even be this, this strange hollow awkwardness, this unnatural quiet to fill up the emptiness he has left behind.

"Home?" Uncle Eddie asks.

"Mom, where are Dad's dog tags?" Alice asks.

"Home," Angie answers, touching her throat and the metal chain under her shirt collar.

"Can I have them?" Ellie asks. "Alice has his watch."

"Not now, girls."

They ride in silence, a terrible brittle silence. The air of the car is so full of unspoken feelings Alice is surprised the windows don't blow out. She wants to shout or jump on the seat or scream; instead she opens the window to try to release the pressure. If they weren't traveling I-90 at seventy miles an hour, she would stick her head out the window; her head, her torso, her arms, her legs, and suddenly she is fantasizing about jumping out of the car window, landing on the pavement, being hit by a car . . . Jesus! Where the hell did that come from? She can't bear to think about the autopsy. But what about his spirit, Alice wonders? Where is it? Can she touch it, reach it, capture it like a firefly in a bottle? She doesn't believe that. And even if she could believe it, even if his spirit is still alive and even if she could find it somehow, know where to look or what to say, if she could still talk to him; even then, it's not enough. She wants all of him back, his face, his body, his voice, his big feet, his laugh, his patience, his impatience. She even wants him correcting her math tests, making her mad, holding her to a higher standard, holding her to seemingly impossible standards all the time. She wants him back, that's all.

She starts to cry. She looks down at her hands, suddenly wet with tears. She tries to stop, but this silent weeping seems to be beyond her volition. As long as his body was still moving, she thinks, he was somehow still alive.

Ellie releases her seat belt and climb's into Alice's lap. She snuggles under Alice's chin as Alice's arms go around her. She insinuates her little hands right around Alice's neck as she shifts her head to Alice's shoulder.

Alice closes her eyes and breathes in Ellie, her clean hair, her compact little kid body, her clattering runaway heartbeat, her perfect shell ears. She rests her cheek on top of Ellie's head and turns to look out the window. She closes her eyes against the day; she tries to let Ellie anchor her, hold her to the earth, when all of Alice just wants to let go, stop breathing, and float away into the sky, to let go of this life and to find her father, wherever he is.

They have left Matt's body at the funeral parlor, dropped him off like delivering a package, and driven home, where they all scatter to their own corners: Angie to unpack and lie down, Gram to the restaurant, Ellie to visit Janna for the first time in days, Uncle Eddie to the garage. And Alice, where does Alice go?

She is furious that they have to leave Matt in yet another place that is not where he belongs; where he is being taken care of by strangers, or worse, stacked among the dead and left alone.

Alice heads out the back door and past the workshop to the garden. She does not pick up a tool. If she had a tool in her hand, she thinks, she would wipe out every plant in front of her. If she had a tool in her hand, she would knock down the workshop or smash the windows in the car. She briefly thinks of which tool would be best for smashing the car windows. The mattock, probably, or the ax.

She kneels at the first row, the beets, the hell with the mud and the nice khakis her grandmother insisted she wear to the airport, and she begins to weed the row and thin the seedlings. She always hated thinning until her father said fine, and they conducted an experiment.

Two rows of carrots, one thinned, one left alone. And Alice saw for herself the result of overcrowding and lack of nutrients. Now she is an expert at this.

The earth is cool and damp and it has begun to drizzle. The sky is a dull oyster gray, almost the color of a sky threatening to snow, though it is much too mild for snow. Still she is cold, with a chill that seems to come from inside of her.

She puts both hands flat on the ground and leans on them. She wants to find her father here in his garden. She wants to believe something, anything, about an afterlife. She wants him to slam out of the back-door, the way he always does, calling out to her, telling her the plan for the day.

But the door doesn't slam. Her father does not call out to her.

She peels off her jacket, trades her khakis for running shorts, her muck boots for sneakers, and heads out for a run. It begins to rain in earnest. At first Alice listens to the rain, the hiss of the water under the tires of passing cars, and beneath that, the dead silence without her father and his voice in her head. She wants to run until her heart explodes. A funny way to die.

Soon Alice is so drenched that her sneakers and her clothes grow heavy and start to make squishing sounds. But somewhere in the road beneath her feet, or the rain on her face, somewhere in the cadence of her stride, in the rhythm of her breathing there is solace. A moment, a small sliver of light, a pause, a breath.

Sustenato, Henry would say, pressing that pedal at the piano. Sustaining.

May 9th

Angie sends Alice back upstairs to change her clothes for the "hours" at the funeral parlor. Wearing black jeans and one of her dad's polo shirts has been deemed inappropriate, disrespectful, and annoying beyond belief.

She is frantically searching her closet for the black skirt and white blouse she wears for chorus concerts. The skirt is on the highest shelf rolled into a ball. She tries to smooth out the wrinkles as she pulls it on, but she still can't find the white blouse. She tears into her parents' bedroom and grabs her mom's cream silk blouse off its hanger and pulls it on over her head. Shoes, shoes, shoes. Back to her room. Her flats from the dance. A scrunchie goes around her wrist; she'll fix her hair in the car. She doesn't really understand how her body can be moving so fast when her mind is stuck in slow motion, when her mind is still in bed, still dreaming about last year and last spring and the days and the weeks and the hours before all of this happened.

Running downstairs she can see that the front door has been left open and everyone is already in the car. Uncle Eddie, almost unrecognizable in a suit and tie, is at the wheel; Gram and Ellie are in the backseat. Alice thinks, I can't do this, I can't go through the motions, I can't stand in a room with my father in a casket and talk to everyone; I can't do this.

She sees her mom lean over Uncle Eddie in the front seat to give the horn a long blast, and on the wave of that sound, she propels herself through the door, slamming it behind her, running down to the street and the car and her family and the final ritualized steps of letting go of her father.

Another funeral director, one of Allison Mahoney's brothers, meets them at the back door. There is a line of people out the front door, down the sidewalk, and around Middle Street. He ushers them into the room with the coffin and the flowers and the folding chairs and a book to sign on its own stupid, phony stand, and all Alice can see is the coffin. There are so many flowers the smell is taking up all the air in the room. The late-afternoon sun is slanting into sunset outside, while inside the shades are drawn and the lights are on. Alice is ready to bolt, when Uncle Eddie rests his hand on the small of her back. Suddenly she sees the roof and the ladder and remembers her father with his hand on her back telling her to breathe.

The funeral director says that they will have a few moments alone in the room with Matt before they open the doors to the neighbors, to the baseball players and the teachers and the firemen and the wives and the children of the other men in his unit, and all the rest of the world. How did her father know so many people?

Angie walks in first and kneels at the coffin, Ellie beside her. Alice recoils; she turns her back on her mother and her sister and the coffin and all that it contains.

She suddenly wants Henry. Where is Henry? Why isn't he here?

Gram is at her side.

"I'll go up with you."

"I can't."

"Yes, you can."

"Gram—"

"These are hard things."

"I *can't*, Gram."

"You have to think about what you can do for your father now."

Alice begins to back away from her grandmother.

"You'll never forgive yourself if you don't do this."

"Gram—"

"Never."

Alice lets Gram take her hand and lead her up to the coffin. They kneel together. Alice is looking down at her clasped hands; Alice is looking at her grandmother's hands; Alice is looking anywhere but at the figure in the coffin, at the uniform that is not her father, that is something else, someone else, because it is still not possible to believe that her father could be dead and cold and lifeless and gone.

Gram stands and leans over and kisses him. She kisses Matt on the forehead and touches his crossed hands, as though this is normal, as though he will feel her touch and her warmth. When Alice stands up she can smell her mother's perfume as it is released from the cream-colored blouse. She takes hold of the edge of the coffin to keep from falling. She closes her eyes. She feels a reassuring hand again on the small of her back. Gram.

Alice lifts her head and opens her eyes and looks at her father. Now she can't get enough of looking at him. He is not the same; he is not the same at all. But what there is, what there still is, right here in front of her, close enough to touch, is this broken body, this man, this soldier. Her father. Hers.

She reaches out and covers his hands with her own. And with that touch, she knows that she will never see his eyes again, his smile again, she will never see him pick up a hammer, or stake a row of tomatoes, or drive a car, or twine his hand in the hair at the nape of her mother's neck.

She lets herself be led away by Gram. The family is receiving instructions from Allison Mahoney; she is telling them where to find the restrooms, where they can take a break from the receiving line to sit down, how they should arrange themselves in line. She will be standing right behind them, she tells them. She will do what she can to keep the line moving. It looks like it is going to be a long night. They can cut it off whenever they want, if they can't go on. People will understand.

Somehow Alice had not really paid attention to the fact that she would be standing in this room, while friends and neighbors came through to pay their respects and speak to the family. Mom, safely hidden behind her glasses, had instructed Alice and Ellie on shaking hands and saying a simple thank you, but Alice had not imagined facing all of these people.

"Mom," she says.

"Not now, Alice."

"What do I do if I feel sick?"

"Go to the restroom."

"Can I go home?"

"Now?"

"If I get sick—"

"You're not going to get sick. Stop being so dramatic. Mom, can you deal with Alice, please?"

"*Mom.*"

"*What?*"

"I can't handle it."

"This isn't about you, Alice. Pull yourself together."

Gram takes Alice by the hand, which only makes Alice angry. She pulls away and stands in sullen, stubborn silence, looking at the floor, shaking hands without looking up or saying anything, until her mother reaches around behind Gram and pinches her. Then, shivering, with cold, sweaty palms, Alice shakes hand after hand, and thanks friends and neighbors and perfect strangers for their condolences. She keeps glancing at the coffin as if she could draw strength from her father, but there are always people kneeling or standing there, blocking her view.

Mrs. Piantowski comes through the line with baby Inga in her arms. She speaks for some minutes to Alice's mother and when she stands in front of Alice, she does the most unexpected thing; she pulls her into a quick embrace and says:

"Come sit down with us for a minute."

Alice looks to her mother who nods permission. Mrs. Piantowski leads Alice to one of the waiting chairs. Alice sits facing the coffin, and Mrs. Piantowski puts baby Inga in Alice's arms. Inga is a sleepy, yielding bundle. When Alice brings her close she molds her little body against her. Mrs. Piantowski has one hand on Alice's shoulder and one hand on Inga's back. She is sheltering them, making a safe space for Alice to catch her breath, to find herself again. Alice listens to Inga breathe amid the noise and the hush of this room, this odd, nowhere place where they are all suspended between life and death. How strange to have a dead man in their midst; how strange to visit a dead man to say good-bye, how strange to hold a baby in a place like this.

Mrs. Piantowski is humming right into baby Inga's ear, and Mrs. Piantowski's warmth and the baby's warmth is somehow warming Alice. She has stopped shivering finally. Alice looks up at her own mother who meets her glance and smiles at her before someone else moves down the receiving line and blocks her view.

There are people waiting in the anteroom, and there is a line out the door and down the sidewalk. Matt's baseball team is here, spilling through the doorway, nearly unable to contain their physical energy in this room of stillness. B.D. and Ginger are right behind them.

She looks at her family in the receiving line. For the first time she notices what a small group they are. Matt's parents are dead and buried ten years or more. His brother, Mark, who works for the Congo Basin Forest Partnership with U.S. AID, is on site in the rain forest. They don't know if their telegram has reached him. So there's only Angie and Gram and Uncle Eddie and Alice and Ellie to wake and bury Matt. And now she's remembering her great aunt Beryl on the phone from the nursing home, "It's a good thing your Grammy and Grampy didn't live to see this."

Ellie is standing next to Angie now. In her favorite spring green dress, her new haircut, and her new glasses, she is kind and polite and efficient; she is a miniature mom. How can she do that? Is she pretending, playing a part, so she won't feel anything?

Here is Lillian Balfour, just arrived from San Francisco, her mom's best friend. Behind her in the line are the Hoyts, her parents' close friends from the old neighborhood, and oh, God, there's Johnny Mason, Matt's oldest friend, the fancy lawyer all the way up from Virginia, with his wife and his three little kids. And Mr. and Mrs. Holscher. This is too much, Alice thinks; this is unreal.

She can't believe it. Stephie Larson and her parents are in line behind the Holschers. Stephie has her head down, and she is crying so hard her dad has to put his arm around her to steady her. He says something to her and she looks up and sees Alice. She lifts her hand in a wave. Alice tries to smile but can't tell if she actually does or not; it feels like her face is frozen.

Lillian walks right up and puts her arms around Angie, Lillian with her red hair and artsy clothes, and Angie is losing it, Alice can see it from here. Her mother's face has gone bright and blotchy and she is fighting back tears. Only with Lillian here, she can't win this fight, with Lillian here, she can no longer pretend she is just going through the motions, or it's all a bad dream, or somehow, somehow she will wake up tomorrow and find Matt peacefully asleep beside her. All of these people, these caring, lovely people, each one like a hammer blow, each one striking a gong, ringing a bell: he's gone, he's gone, he's gone.

Uncle Eddie stands in front of Angie, shielding her from the people waiting in line, giving her a moment to collect herself. He pulls a flask from his back pocket and hands it to her. Both Lillian and Angie drink from it, Lillian even manages to giggle and snort the way she usually does before Eddie takes a good long pull and they are back in business. Lillian positions herself just behind Ellie, one hand on Ellie's shoulder, one hand on Angie's shoulder. Not in the way, not obtrusive, but there, solidly there beside her friend.

Henry is in front of the coffin now, Alice notices with a start. Henry and his mother and his father. Henry is kneeling for a long time; she can see Mrs. Grover urge him to his feet, but not before Henry places something in the coffin. He can't look up as he goes through the receiving line. He shuffles and shakes hands and hangs his head. He makes his way to a chair in the back of the room with his parents. He is trying to compose himself before he speaks to Alice, and he is having a mighty hard time of it; nothing he can say to himself can change the unalterable facts of this day.

"That's my best friend," she tells Mrs. Piantowski.

"Henry Grover, yes?"

"Can I show him baby Inga? Can I let him hold her?"

"Yes, you can."

Alice crosses to Henry and nods to Mr. and Mrs. Grover, who make room for her to sit across from him. Henry is looking at his hands and weeping. He hasn't cried like this in years. He feels the fool, the total fool, but he can't stop. He is undone by Alice's father lying in the coffin. All of his magical thinking, that somehow this could all come right; all of his hopes and wishes for Alice, for her family, all undone by the simple fact of the coffin and the body within it.

Alice leans in and speaks to him. He tries to tell her that he's sorry but can't find his voice. She places baby Inga in his arms. He has to unclasp his hands to take the baby; he has to pay attention to keep from jostling her or dropping her. He has never held a baby before; he must be doing this all wrong. Alice has one hand on Inga's back and one hand on Henry's arm. They are knee to knee and he is holding the baby, he is actually holding the baby, without disaster. When Henry dares to look up at Alice he is met by her bruised eyes. She is saving me, he thinks. I should be helping her and she is saving me.

"Inga likes it when you sing to her."

Does she remember, he wonders? Did she hear him that night when he thought she was asleep?

Alice leans in close to him: "What were you doing up there? Did you put something in the coffin?"

"A baseball. And a picture of you and me when we were six and you were wearing that bathing suit you like so much."

"I didn't bring anything with me. No one told me."

In a panic she tries to think what she has with her that she can put inside the coffin. But she doesn't carry a purse, or a wallet. She needs time to think about this, to plan. She has no coins in her pocket to weight his eyes, she has no picture to slip into his hands, or a stone

257

from Small Point, or an old, handmade iron hinge, or a roofing shingle, or a drawing of the garden.

"We could go back and get something for you. If you know what you want," Henry offers.

Baby Inga starts to cry. Mrs. Piantowski picks her up and she quiets immediately.

"See you tomorrow," she says, and carries baby Inga away.

Alice turns to Mr. and Mrs. Grover.

"Are you sure you don't mind?"

"Not at all." Mrs. Grover smiles at her.

Two hours later, when everyone has finally left, Angie returns to the coffin. Alice and Ellie kneel on either side of her. They are exhausted and yet it feels like they are living outside of time now, with the minutes speeding up and slowing down, with wanting it to be over, and wishing it would never end.

"Can we see him again tomorrow?" Alice asks.

"No."

"Why not?"

"They'll seal the coffin tonight."

"I wish—"

"I know."

Ellie puts a book of drawings next to Matt's body.

"Why can't I see him one more time?"

"Alice—"

"Why? What difference does it make? I'll ask Ms. Mahoney. You won't have to do anything."

Angie touches Matt's face.

"I'm not ready, Mom."

"No one's ready."

"I'll never be ready."

Ms. Mahoney steps up to them. She doesn't have to say a word. It's late and everyone is waiting for Alice and her family to leave.

"We just need another minute."

Ms. Mahoney is looking at Angie. She is not so nice now. Maybe she's tired, too. But this is just a job to her, Alice realizes; she's ready to kick off her heels and take a bath and be done with the Bliss family for the night.

An old man in a dark suit flips on the overhead lights.

"Could you please . . . ?"

He stands at the light switch, his arms crossed over his stomach. The glare of the lights is cruel. Her father looks less and less like himself and more and more like something that no longer belongs to this world.

In the harsh light Alice can see that the chintzy velvet that surrounds the coffin is attached with Velcro. A stage set, that's all it is. Why do they do it like this? It's supposed to mean something, but does it?

She has packets of marigold and zinnia seeds in one hand, and Matt's father's hammer in the other. How weird is that, she thinks. A hammer in a place like this. She places them in the coffin, the hammer by his side where he can reach it, the seeds in his breast pocket. What had seemed so important a few hours ago, now she wonders what difference it will make. Is it all superstition; is it all just piling up little moments, little stacks of memories against the devastation of the future? As though she will somehow feel better next month when she remembers, *at least I put Grampa's hammer in the coffin?* The hammer and the buttons on his uniform will last longer than his clothes or his body or the coffin itself. This is a horrible train of thought.

She jumps when she realizes that the old man is standing just behind them.

"Your father put a new roof on my house ten years ago. Good man. Good roof, too."

They exchange a glance and then Alice and Angie and Ellie step away from the coffin. He turns to let them pass before him to the doorway.

"We'd like to stay until you close the coffin."

He has to stand on tiptoe to reach and close the lid. The hinges are silent.

Angie takes both of her girls by the hand and walks through the building to the door, to the sidewalk, to the night air, to Gram and Uncle Eddie, heading for home.

May 10th

It's four o'clock in the morning when Alice wakes up to find that Ellie has climbed into bed with her. She crawls over her to get up, sees Ellie's pajamas and underpants discarded on the floor, and realizes she must have wet the bed.

She pads quietly down the hall and pushes the door to her parents' room open. She is startled to see another head on the pillow next to her mom until she remembers that Lillian is staying with them.

"Mom?"

Angie sits up immediately; she has not slept. She grabs her bathrobe and follows Alice down the stairs and into the kitchen. Alice puts the kettle on though she's not sure she really wants anything. Angie finds the Drambuie and pours herself a glass.

"You want to try it?"

"Sure."

She passes Alice her glass.

"Ellie wet the bed."

"Poor kid."

"She got herself into clean PJs and she's in my bed now."

260

"Is that what woke you up?"

"I guess."

Alice tastes the Drambuie.

"Mom . . ."

She hesitates.

"We can't bury him."

"What are you talking about?

"It's not right for Dad. He can't . . . I can't . . ."

"What?"

"Put him in the ground."

"Where do you want to put him? The backyard?"

"No. The ocean, a boat, maybe . . ."

"And never be able to visit him?"

"I don't know."

"Never be able to go to where he is?"

"I just can't think of Dad trapped under the ground. I can imagine scattering his ashes from a rooftop, or by the ocean, or—"

"Daddy thought about cremation," Angie says.

"He did?"

"But I asked him for a burial. I wanted a headstone, somewhere to go."

"Why?"

"I need to know where he is. And I want to be buried beside him."

"But maybe—"

"Do you really want to have your father cremated?"

"I don't know. I just—"

Alice turns to look out the window.

"I don't think I can stand there and let them put him in a hole in the ground and cover him with dirt."

"That's what's going to happen, honey. I can try to help you, but you're going to have to accept this."

"Did you and Daddy talk about it?"

"Some. Not as much as we should have."

"What do you believe, Mom?"

"What do you mean?"

"About heaven or an afterlife or the soul . . ."

"It's hard to say."

Angie pulls her robe close around her.

Alice stands there looking at her, needing her mother to know things. Angie hears Matt's voice inside her head, *Try, Angie.*

"I always thought holy rollers were ridiculous, and I never put my faith in any church."

"And . . ." Alice waits.

There's Matt's voice again: *Keep trying.*

"But now I realize I had a lucky life. I had the luxury of not needing to believe in anything. Now that Daddy's gone I wish I believed in all of it."

"Really?"

"Yes and no. I'm trying to figure that out."

"And Daddy?"

"Oh, honey, you know Daddy . . . He was a pragmatist; he liked facts and figures. But this, this is a whole new ballgame."

Alice pushes the glass away.

"When I wake up," Alice says, "at first I don't remember. Every day I wake up and I have to find out he's gone all over again."

"Me, too."

"Really?"

"That's part of why we go through all of this. It seems so strange and bizarre even, but the rituals—saying the words, touching his body, putting him in the ground, remembering him with friends—all of it starts to make it real for us."

"I don't want it to be real, Mom."

"I know."

There is a pause.

"What have they told you about what happened to Dad?"

"Very little."

"I need to know."

"Alice . . ."

"I have nightmares. I keep seeing him."

"Honey . . ."

"How did they find him? Was there a rescue? What happened, Mom? I need to know what happened."

"I don't have answers to all of your questions."

"Just tell me what you know."

"And we don't have the results of the autopsy yet."

"How hard is it to tell whether he died from his wounds, or further injuries, or pneumonia? That's pretty simple."

"Nothing is simple with the U.S. Army."

"You're stalling."

"All that they've told me so far is that he died from his wounds."

"When?"

"That's what the autopsy is for."

"How did they find him?"

Angie takes a sip of her drink, looks out the kitchen window to the dark shadow of Matt's workshop. She does not want her daughter to hear these words, to be haunted, as she is haunted by this knowledge.

". . . Mom . . . ?"

"His body was dumped on the side of the road."

"Where?"

"Eleven miles from where he was captured."

Alice leans against the counter.

"Was he mutilated?"

"No."

"Don't lie to me."

"I'm not."

"Did they take his organs?"

263

"No."

"Are you sure?"

"Yes."

"Really sure?"

"Yes. Alice—"

"Did they ever give you Travis Boyd's phone number or address?"

"They say they're working on it."

"Was anyone else with Dad?"

"I don't know."

"How bad were his wounds? Have they told you?"

"No, they haven't."

"I keep imagining the worst things."

"So do I."

"It must have been terrifying."

"Yes."

Angie reaches out to Alice just as Alice takes a step away.

"Mom, sometimes I think I can't stand it; I won't be able to . . ."

Alice looks down at her hands, clenching and unclenching her fists.

"Daddy would want you to . . . He would want us all to really live, honey, really live in this world and try to make a difference."

"I know."

"He was so proud of you."

"I don't know why. I never did anything amazing."

"He was proud of the person you are, the person you're becoming."

"I want him back."

"So do I, sweetheart. So do I."

Alice is the last one in the shower later that morning. The hot water runs out before her hair is rinsed so by the time she gets the shampoo out she's chilled to the bone. But that's okay, that's perfect, in fact. She is dog tired and feels like she is hearing and seeing and feeling everything through thick layers of cotton wool. Everything is a little vague, a little removed; cool and distant.

Upstairs, she pulls on her dress from the dance and slips on her flats. She rakes her fingers through her hair and goes into her mom's room to grab a sweater. She tries not to look at all the pictures of her dad on the dresser, but there they are: the early morning sun is streaming into the room and lighting them up.

Ellie is sitting on the top step of the stairs, dressed in a new plaid dress Gram bought her with white socks and brand new black patent leather shoes with straps. Ellie has her stuffed polar bear in her lap and her thumb in her mouth, which she yanks out as soon as Alice sits down.

"I put my sheets in the hamper."

"I'll help you make your bed later, okay?"

"You'll forget."

"No, I won't."

"I don't want to go," Ellie announces.

"Me neither."

"I'm scared he'll be stuck in that stupid cemetery forever," Ellie says.

"Me, too."

"I hate that idea."

"Daddy would hate it, too."

"You're lucky."

"Why?"

"He loved you best."

"He did *not!*"

"And you got to be with him longer than me. Seven years longer. That's almost double."

Angie calls to them to come and get in the car.

"Do you have the passage you're supposed to read?" Alice asks.

"Why are they making us do this?"

"You scared?"

"I'm gonna want to cry and I can't cry up there . . . Alice?"

"Yeah?"

"I don't want this day to happen. Can't you tell somebody? Can't you make it stop?"

"It won't be any easier tomorrow, Ellie."

"How about never, then. Never would be good."

From downstairs they hear:

"Girls! Let's go!"

They stand up. Ellie takes Alice's hand.

"I wish we could absquatulate."

"What's that?"

"Flee."

They get through the service somehow. Little old Sacred Heart is packed to the rafters. There's crying all around them, but the Birds and the Blisses seem to be seated in a no-cry zone. That could be because they are all pretty furious every time the priest opens his mouth. Each of them is sorely tempted to shout: Stop saying those stupid things about Matt! Jesus this and blah-blah better place that. It's enough to make you sick. Matt would have hated it. Absolutely hated it. The only thing that's kind of nice is Ellie's reading of that old standby from Corinthians and Johnny Mason's little speech or eulogy or whatever it was. But really, Johnny's speech would have embarrassed Matt to death. He hated testimonials.

Even the music, which might normally be a weep fest, is so baggy and saggy, Alice wonders if there's something wrong with the organ or maybe it's the four-foot tall crone of an old woman who is playing it. Maybe she can't reach the pedals. That would explain a lot. Henry must be grinding his teeth.

There's a big holdup on the church steps with people wanting to stop and talk. Come on, already. Chat, chat, chat, sorry, sorry, sorry, over and over; it is driving Alice crazy. Perfect strangers some of them, wanting hugs, wanting to be comforted themselves. You just want to give some of these people a good shove.

Then there's the hustle and bustle in the parking lot with the hearse and the cars and who goes where. The family is alone in Uncle Eddie's latest Mercedes. A little respite. Lillian, who has been basically joined at the hip with Angie since she arrived last night, is riding in the car with Johnny Mason and his family. The Birds and the Blisses are directly behind the hearse with Lillian and company directly behind them.

In the pause before they pull out, Eddie passes his flask around. When Alice reaches for it, Angie just rolls her eyes and takes it away.

They take the scenic route to Locust Lawn, avoiding the highway and winding along Plank Road and then out on Blossom. It's a beautiful day, which is what everyone keeps saying in order to have something to say. But it's true. It's a perfect spring day, a perfect baseball day, a perfect garden day. Uncle Eddie rolls the windows down even though Angie and Gram complain about their hair. They're only going a stately fifteen miles per hour, how wrecked can your hair get? And Eddie is right to roll the windows down; the air is soft and sweet and it buoys them all, at least for a moment.

"Would you look at that?" Uncle Eddie says.

Dozens of cars line their route all the way to the cemetery, pulled over on the side of the road, their hazard lights flashing. Some people stand by their cars, their hands on their hearts; others sit quietly, their heads bowed.

On the last hill up to the cemetery, two Boy Scout troops stand at attention, holding flags.

The honor guard is already in place when they arrive. They have arranged Matt's helmet, rifle, boots, and dog tags next to the grave.

Allison Mahoney and her father and both brothers are everywhere at once, escorting old people from their cars, seating people, signaling the priest to begin. These people should plan weddings or maybe warfare. They've got it all down.

The honor guard, just like the detail that escorted Matt's body home, lives in another dimension, a world of precision and perfectibility. It is almost soothing to watch their smooth exact unison motions. Until they present arms and start shooting off their damn guns.

Then it's the priest again. Again?! And the sign of the cross and something about silver cords and broken bowls and the spirit returning to the earth. Okay, Alice gets that part. That's okay.

The soldiers take the flag from the coffin and fold it tightly, timing each fold, each move, the number of steps toward each other, the number of steps to hand the flag to Angie, the number of steps away.

In unison, they execute a slow ceremonial salute.

Angie holds the flag and Alice and Ellie hold each other and Gram as one soldier plays taps and they lower the coffin into the earth.

Normally playing taps would undo her. Alice can hear people quietly crying all around them, followed by all the unsuccessful attempts to discreetly blow noses. But the super quiet winch lowering the coffin into the grave and the fake grass hiding the raw earth and the way everything stops at this point is so jarring that Alice can't even imagine crying. Like it's all done, it's all finished. But it's not. She doesn't get it. They are here to bury her father, not leave him alone in a gaping hole. What is going on? Do they think it's too real to see broken sod and turned earth; too real to actually fill in the grave? As if the family somehow needs to be protected from these gory details? There is no detail worse than the plain fact of Matt's death. The rest of it should be simple and honest and handmade. Not this stage set.

Some people have brought flowers, which they throw into the grave. Alice doesn't like that; she thinks it looks like litter. She manages to stay focused on her anger until Uncle Eddie's surprise makes his appearance: a bagpiper standing on the green grass rise above them. Oh, no, she thinks, there is nothing more mournful than bagpipes.

But what he plays is not mournful. It is a rollicking march; it is joyful and raucous and fast and alive. You could follow this song into battle or through the gates of hell.

As Alice listens to the piper she knows that she wants real dirt and real shovels; as real as this music, as real as the coffin that contains what is left of her father.

In the silence that follows, there's a kind of rush to get out of the cemetery, with friends and relatives leading the way to the cars. Mrs. Grover and Mrs. Piantowski and Mrs. Minty are already back at the house with Sally and Ginny from The Bird Sisters, putting together the collation. The night before, Uncle Eddie and Mr. Grover and Henry supervised the gathering of all the neighborhood picnic tables and folding chairs. Food has been pouring in for days.

The promise of that food, and maybe even a good stiff drink, or simply getting away from the land of the dead and back to the land of the living, has put a spring in the step of most everyone who turns away from the grave to head to their cars.

The piper has left the rise and is walking through the woods that border the graveyard. Now he is playing a dirge, now he is playing an ending, not a beginning, gathering their tears and their sorrow into song.

Alice wants to stay until they fill in the grave, but there is not a shovel in sight. Angie is preoccupied with some family friends who can't come back to the house and are saying their good-byes now. Alice scans the graveyard looking for the actual tools of the trade or even a pair of gravediggers. Instead, she finally spots a small backhoe tucked discreetly out of sight behind some trees and an older man in overalls patiently smoking a cigarette, waiting for them to leave so he can finish his job.

That's when she sees him: a young man in uniform standing too far away to have heard the service, but focused intently on her father's grave. He somehow manages to look ramrod straight and broken at the same time. Before she even has time to think, to formulate words, she is running toward him.

He backs away from her, holding his hands out in front of him to keep her from coming closer.

"Are you Travis Boyd?"

He looks at Alice for a long, uncomfortable moment. Alice is taking in the circles under his eyes, the way his dress uniform hangs too loosely on his frame, the tremor in his hands as he tries to figure out what to do with them.

"You are, aren't you?"

He looks at the ground.

"You knew my dad, didn't you? You were in his unit."

He nods, not lifting his head.

"You were with him when—"

He begins to back away from her, still looking down.

"Wait. Don't go."

He turns and begins to limp up the slope toward the drive where his rental car is parked. Alice runs to catch up with him. He keeps her at bay with a sharp gesture. She stops as he continues toward the car.

"Please. You were the last person to—"

He stops. She can hear that he is struggling for breath from this quick walk and realizes that he is probably in pain.

"We've been trying to reach you. My mother wanted to write to you. Or call you or—"

He straightens his shoulders and turns to face her. He is not crying. Nothing as simple as that. His eyes are hollow and his face is contracted in a grimace of suffering so intense Alice stumbles as she takes a quick step away from him.

"He was a good soldier. He looked after his men."

He pauses. It is not clear he will continue. Alice waits.

"He was like a big brother. . . . That was the worst day for me. . . . Not being able to get Matt out . . . That was the worst day . . ."

"Was he—?" Alice begins.

The car door opens and another soldier emerges to hold open the rear passenger door for Travis Boyd.

"I have to go."

"Would you like to come back to the house? We have so much food. My mother would like to meet you."

"I just wanted to pay my respects."

"I could show you my dad's workshop."

He tilts his head so he can look at her out of the corner of his eye.

"He talked about you."

"And I could show you his garden."

"I saw pictures of you. And your little sister."

The soldier at the car calls out to him. And suddenly Alice realizes that he is a nurse or an orderly.

"Sergeant Boyd."

He turns toward the voice and the car and his escape. And then, with a great effort, he turns to her again, pulls himself upright, stills his hands by pressing them against his thighs.

"I am so sorry for your loss."

Alice waits while Travis Boyd is helped into the backseat of the car. He takes his hat off and leans his head back and closes his eyes. He turns his head to look at her as the car starts up and moves away. She holds his gaze for as long as she can and then watches the car disappear down the grassy drive headed for the main road.

She can't begin to take this in, to process what kind of horror and trauma can destroy a young man like Travis Boyd. She suddenly knows, like a kick to the gut, that what happened to her father is even worse than she has imagined, worse than it is possible to imagine.

271

She turns back when she hears a new motor sound and heads down the hill in time to see the backhoe emerge from the copse of trees and approach her father's grave. The fake grass has been rolled up, the winch taken away. Now there is a hole in the ground and a coffin and dirt.

She waves at the man driving the backhoe. He stops and cuts the engine.

"Do you have a couple of shovels?"

"That's not how we do it anymore, miss. A lot of people, they have the wrong idea."

"I'd just like to be the one to bury my father. If you don't mind."

"You're not exactly dressed for the job."

"I'll manage."

"Aren't you supposed to be with the rest of them?" He indicates the cars pulling out of the cemetery.

"They'll keep."

He reaches behind him and pulls out a pair of shovels, climbs out of the backhoe and hands one to Alice. He turns back to grab a work shirt and a pair of rubber boots.

"That dress is too pretty to mess up."

"Thank you."

Alice buttons the shirt over her dress and steps into the rubber boots.

"My name is Caleb," he offers.

"Alice Bliss," she replies.

The sound of the clods of dirt hitting the wood of the coffin may be the most upsetting sound she has ever heard. But as they continue the sounds become muffled, dirt on dirt, and she can concentrate on the bend, lift, swing of her body and the shovel; the simplicity and rhythm and relief of real work.

She looks up to see Henry and his father walking toward them, carrying the folding snow shovels they keep in the trunk in case of an emergency. They have left their suit jackets in the car. They take a moment to roll up their sleeves and then, without a word, set to work alongside them.

"This is Caleb," she tells them. "And this is my friend Henry and his father, Mr. Grover."

The men nod to each other without breaking stride. Alice breathes in. It smells like the garden, but it's not.

"It doesn't take long," Caleb offers.

"No."

"You appreciate the machine on the other end of this job, I can tell you that."

"I bet."

"Or in bad weather."

"My father worked with his hands."

"Soldier, I thought."

"Carpenter. Engineer."

"Awful young."

"Yes, he was."

The earth is dry and fairly light and they make good progress.

"I have to rake it out now and then seed it."

She hands Caleb her shovel. Mr. Grover takes out his handkerchief and mops his brow.

"You did the right thing, Alice Bliss," Caleb says.

She tries to smile at him as she returns his shirt.

"Anybody tell you that you need to be extra careful these next few weeks?"

"No."

"The body gets accident prone."

"Really?"

"You ask people. Ask people who have lost someone whether they were in a little car crash or a little bike accident or took a fall."

"You want to come back to the house, Caleb?"

"No, thank you, that wouldn't be right, I didn't know your father."

"All right then. Thanks again."

Alice heads up the rise to the dirt road leading out of the cemetery with Henry and his father. The digging has tired them all. Alice thinks it's good to be tired in her body.

The Grovers' ancient Honda is the only car still parked on the verge. It hadn't occurred to Alice to be worried about a ride home. Now she realizes that Henry and his father were patiently waiting for her after everyone else had left.

Mr. Grover tosses their shovels into the trunk. Henry and his dad don't interrogate her like her family would. Henry just opens the door to the front seat for her. But she surprises him and slips into the backseat, where she leans back and rests her head against the upholstery. Just like Travis Boyd, she thinks.

She closes her eyes for a moment before turning in her seat to look back at the road winding behind them, at the green bowl of this section of the graveyard, at the newly turned earth over her father's grave, at Caleb, raking the ground, preparing it for seed. They keep leaving Matt behind, she thinks, in each of these places; they reenact leaving him, over and over until finally they will realize that he has left them and gone where they cannot follow.

There are cars parked in their driveway and all along the street. The backyard almost looks festive and the workshop, which Uncle Eddie set up as the bar, looks like they're having a party. At least anyone old enough to drink is having a party.

One table is stacked high with Mrs. Piantowski's bread and tubs of butter. Other folding tables are nearly groaning under the weight of casseroles and fruit salads, green salads, Jell-O molds, and condiments. Cakes, cookies, pies, and brownies are on the dining room table inside along with two jumbo coffeemakers from church.

Alice walks slowly through the house, taking it all in, the groups of people talking and eating and drinking. Some of them are even laughing. Everyone is here, she thinks, everyone that's left from their life. Were they all sitting behind her in the church and riding behind their car to the cemetery? Her principal, Mr. Fisher; the school secretary, Mrs. Bradley; B.D., her coach; Mrs. Baker, Ellie's teacher; Mr. Herlihy, the high school janitor; Sally and Ginny from The Bird Sisters; the Hoyts and the Holschers; and even Stephie and her parents. Mrs. Minty is sitting at a picnic table with John Kimball and his father and his little brother, Joey. And Melissa Johnson. Janna and her mom are sitting with Ellie, and oh my gosh that's Luke Piacci, the third-grade heartthrob, Ellie must be going out of her mind.

Alice keeps walking, looking for her mom, maybe, or maybe not. She makes one more tour of the house and there, sitting on the stairs, where she did not think to look before, is her mom, a Styrofoam cup of coffee abandoned on the step beside her. She is looking down at her hands and does not notice Alice. She is twisting her wedding ring on her finger, round and around.

"Mom . . . ?" Alice ventures.

Angie looks up, wipes her face with the back of her hand.

"I can't . . . ," she begins. "I should be out there, talking to people . . ."

"It's okay, Mom."

"I just . . . I was on my way upstairs, and . . ."

She looks so lost, Alice thinks.

"That's when I knew . . ." she says. "That's when I really knew."

"I'll get Lillian," Alice offers.

"Just stay for a minute," Angie says, pulling Alice down on the step beside her.

She's twisting the ring again.

"We couldn't afford an engagement ring. Did I ever tell you that? And we saved up for months to buy our wedding rings."

She pulls the ring off her finger.

"Here. Try it on."

"Mom, no," Alice says, as she tries to hand it back.

"Go ahead. I could never wear any of Gram's rings. Her fingers are so tiny."

Alice slips the ring on. It feels strange. Alice can see where the ring has made a ridge on Angie's finger. She wonders if that's permanent.

"I was wondering if I'm still married."

"*Mom!*"

Alice tries to give the ring back.

"Keep it for me. Just for a few days. I'll ask for it when I'm ready."

Angie stands, smoothes her hair and her skirt, and heads down the stairs.

"Wait!" Alice says, a note of panic in her voice.

"Just for a few days," Angie says, before turning toward the kitchen and the backdoor.

"Mom! . . . *Mom!*" Alice follows Angie down the stairs, reaches out to her, the ring in her palm. "Please put your ring back on."

Angie hesitates. She seems a little dazed.

"Okay, okay, let's not make a federal case out of it," Angie says, slipping the ring on her finger. "I just thought . . . Oh, I don't know what I was thinking."

Alice watches her mother head back out to their friends and neighbors, to the voices and the sympathy and the dozens of reminders that life goes on in its brutal and sometimes beautiful way, whether you want it to or not.

Not knowing what else to do, Alice heads outside to the workshop. Uncle Eddie has rolled up her sleeping bag and stood the pallets up against the side wall to make room for the bar. Easily done. One plank on two sawhorses and two coolers full of ice and beer underneath. All the "good stuff" is here; whatever you might want to pour into a glass in honor of Matt Bliss, Eddie's got.

She wants to keep on going. Or find her sneaks and start running and maybe never stop.

She walks past the workshop and up the little rise to the garden, which is hoed and weeded, just the way her dad likes it. Filled with promise. Everything at the beginning, just getting started.

She continues past the end of the garden and through the new neighbors' yard. She can't remember their names. She is not worried about trespassing or upsetting anyone; she doesn't care if someone comes out and yells at her to stay off the new grass. At Baird Road she decides to go left heading out toward the old Barnes estate where maybe she can get lost for five minutes in what's left of the old apple orchard, or maybe she'll find that their old fort inside the lilacs is still there, and she can crawl inside and lie down and disappear for a little while.

The apple trees are in bloom and humming with bees. No one has pruned these trees in a long time, but here they are, still blooming and bearing. She heads past the barn where they used to have two Percheron draft horses and a pair of Chincoteague ponies. Old man Barnes hated tractors and loved horses, even after he got too old to work them. They were a kid magnet for the whole neighborhood and also contributed to the most beautiful roses in all of Belknap.

Alice walks between the curved rose beds to the circle of lilacs. The "entrance" is on the far side. Half a dozen lilacs have grown together, forming a dense wall of foliage, with a circular open space in the center. No one can see you in there. She hesitates and then pushes sideways through two slender trunks and she is inside.

It doesn't look as though other kids have found this spot. There are no beer bottles or cigarette butts, no mangy blankets or milk crates. It was Alice and Henry's secret fort through much of grade school. Alice wonders if her parents knew about it. It would be just like her dad to let her go and explore, even if it made her mom kind of crazy.

When did they stop coming here? Was it a decision? Or did they just stop? She thinks she might remember waiting for Henry in here one day, but he never came. Did that happen to Henry, too? Waiting once more and then once more for Alice to come and play.

The branches stir and John Kimball pushes through into the interior. Alice watches him materialize out of thin air and take shape in the dim, green light of the lilac leaves. He crosses to her, it's not more than a step or two, but when he crashes into her it's as though he has been running toward her from a great distance, and without warning, he is kissing her. In the green light, he is kissing her. He grabs her in a tight embrace, his mouth on hers. There is no hesitation, no talking, no asking. His hands are startling on her skin, his lips and his teeth and his tongue and his body are pushing her and she is pushing back, she is kissing back, she is holding him, she is pushing into him, she is feeling everything and nothing.

Is it the rough cloth of his jacket, or the uneven ground beneath her feet; or is it the sun, coming out from behind a cloud and pouring through the leaves, or is it the sound of a truck, grinding its gears as it crests the hill behind them—when suddenly the truck she hears in the distance is the truck that slows but doesn't stop as a body, her father's body, is pushed from behind the wheel well, to fall, to roll, to lie in the sand and gravel at the side of the road. His uniform filthy, stained with dirt and blood, torn, both boots missing, his feet incongruously bare. His face, she can't see his face; he has landed with one arm flung out, his face turned sideways, turned away, his fingers, his short, strong fingers curled into fists.

She opens her eyes and pulls away. She looks around; she shakes her head, as if she could clear these images from her mind. When her mother told her how they'd found her father she couldn't take it in and now, here, kissing this boy, what is she doing kissing this boy, here it is, in a rush, in a flood.

"I have to go."

"Wait . . . Alice—"

"This isn't right."

"Are you okay?"

"I'm—" And she struggles to find the right words. "I don't know what I'm doing."

"Alice?" Henry calls out . . . "Alice? Are you in there?"

She pushes past John Kimball and slips between the lilac trunks.

"Henry, what are you doing here?"

"I saw you leave. You looked upset."

"Of course I looked upset."

"I was worried about you. I followed you."

"You shouldn't have done that."

John Kimball materializes once again. He reaches out to take Alice's hand; she jerks away from him. She can see Henry jumping to conclusions and she wants to stop him. She wants to explain, but doesn't know how she can explain trying to get away from everything and everyone, coming here, coming to this place, *their* place, looking for, hoping for . . . she doesn't know what, the surprise of John Kimball, the kiss, her father, her childhood, the pictures that are haunting her . . .

Suddenly there is that roaring inside Henry's head that makes it impossible to hear; he can't hear the birds, or the wind, or even his own thoughts. Instead, he sees the lilac leaves quivering in the aftershock of John pushing through them; he remembers the interior green-glass shimmer of that space and imagines Alice and John and without warning, he steps forward and shoves John so hard he falls backward into the lilacs. It looks at first as though the branches will be supple enough to bend under this burden, but then there is a terrible ancient keening sound as branches and an entire trunk groan and then crack and fall under John's weight. As John scrambles to his feet, both Henry and Alice register the gaping hole in the circle of trees.

Henry can see that John is beginning to move toward him, but he doesn't care what John does right now, let him do his worst. Henry is looking at the lilacs and the broken trunk and branches and something shifts inside of him.

"Henry," Alice says, and her voice breaks as she says his name.

He looks at her for a long moment, hurt and betrayal and anger loud in the space between them, before he turns to leave.

"Henry!" Alice calls out to him. And then again, more urgently, *"Henry!"*

She is about to break into a run to follow him, when John reaches out to her.

"I'll walk you back."

"I have to go alone."

"Alice—"

"I'm sorry."

And without another word she heads for home.

She walks through the yard and it's eerie the way no one seems to notice her and no one says anything, like she's invisible. She steps into the workshop, where she realizes she is really angry at Uncle Eddie or whoever the hell it was who messed with her stuff and changed everything around in here without even asking her.

But this could be a good place to test out the invisibility shield. There's a knot of guys from Matt's baseball team sitting on or leaning on her dad's workbench, drinking beer and laughing. She punts a "Hey, how you doin'?" right back at them as she circles the table loaded with liquor. Could she grab something? Where would she put it? No pockets in this dress, and the bottles are mostly jumbo size, too big to hide. Then she sees two possibilities: a small squarish bottle of Southern Comfort and a skinny, dark brown brandy bottle.

She lifts her dad's jacket off its peg on the wall and on her way out the door, grabs both bottles, one for each pocket.

In the house she nabs Uncle Eddie's car keys from the bowl in the foyer and before anyone can say one, two, three, she's out the front door. Uncle Eddie has thoughtfully parked his car down the street a ways, to leave room for all of the guests' cars. She slides in behind the wheel, adjusts the seat, rearview and side mirrors, just like he taught her, starts the engine, and she's off. She doesn't look back.

She pulls up in front of Henry's house and leans on the horn.

When he comes to the door she can see he's so mad he's about to brush her off, but then the fact of the car, the pure physical presence of the car, with Alice behind the wheel, pulls him right out to the curb.

"Get in," she tells him, without looking at him.

"Are you crazy?"

"I'll let you drive it."

"Your uncle's gonna kill you."

"Maybe that's a good thing."

"Alice, I don't know how you think you can just come over here and . . ."

"Get in. Or I'm going without you. And you know that's not a good idea."

Furious, he gets into the car. Puts his seat belt on. Refuses to look at her.

"Relax. We're just going down to the lake."

"And you've driven what? Twice in your life?"

"Four lessons from the master. Think of this as practice."

"You're in no condition to . . ."

She pulls out, the big sedan purring quietly. There's a hush inside the car as they glide along East Oak Street.

"Look in my jacket."

He grabs the jacket; the liquor bottles clank together.

"Jesus Christ, Alice!"

"I could have taken anything I wanted. If I had pockets big enough."

"Driving. Plus alcohol. Does this sound like a good idea to you?"

"Don't be a priss."

"I don't want to be a statistic, if you don't mind."

"So what, you want to go to your room or something?"

"What are you talking about? With you?"

"Yeah, with me."

"Right now?"

She takes her eyes off the road and looks at him.

"Watch what you're doing!"

Eyes front.

She drives like a little old grandmother all the way out to the lake, speedometer hovering right around thirty-five. She can tell it's driving Henry crazy, but he's still too mad to say anything. She heads straight to the parking lot for the town beach and pulls into the last possible spot, car pointed toward the water, next to a huge willow tree, relatively secluded, nice view.

"This is where kids come to make out," Henry ventures, and a blush instantly suffuses his face.

"So I hear."

Alice pulls out both bottles, opens them.

"You ever had this kind before?" she asks.

"A taste. Maybe."

She tries the brandy and nearly gags.

"That's disgusting!"

Then she tries the Southern Comfort. The cloying sweetness helps the alcohol slide down a little easier.

"This one's not so bad."

She passes it to Henry.

"Alice, what do you think you're doing?"

She takes another taste.

"Not thinking for five minutes."

He grabs the bottle.

"Is that what you were doing with John Kimball? Not thinking?"

"Definitely not thinking."

"Longer than five minutes."

"One kiss."

"I don't believe you."

"It's true."

"I don't get you, Alice."

"I don't get me, either."

Henry stashes the bottle between his knees. When Alice reaches for it he jerks away from her.

"What, do you think I'm going to attack you?"

"No!"

She takes the bottle.

"How could you . . . with John Kimball and—"

"I didn't know he was following me."

"Ha!"

"I didn't. I was just trying to get away."

"Why did you go *there*, Alice?"

"I don't know. . . . It's a safe place."

"It's more than that."

"I know."

"Do you? Do you even care anymore?"

"I do. You know I do."

She can't look at him. She offers him the bottle; he shakes his head. She takes another taste. There's a long, uncomfortable silence.

"You're not helping," she tells him.

"What do you want me to do?"

"I want you to get drunk with me and . . . and—"

"And what?"

"And do whatever it is that people come here to do."

Alice is starting to make a pretty good dent in the bottle with all her little tastes.

"You're kidding, right?"

Of course she's kidding, she has to be kidding, he says to himself.

"There's a blanket in the trunk."

"How do you know *that?*"

"My mother told me. She also told me to watch out for boys like Uncle Eddie."

"I'm not like Uncle Eddie."

"I know."

Henry's brain is running on high-octane fuel as he calculates what's about to happen. Alice is going to drink herself silly, possibly drink herself right into puking. There could be kissing. Hopefully before the puking. But is that even what he wants anymore? And what is she doing? What is she out to prove and just what the hell was she doing with John Kimball? He's really furious but it's hard to be angry, or stay angry on the day your best friend buries her father. So maybe he's just supposed to stay with her and try to keep her safe and try not to worry too much about, well . . . everything. But by then, the sun will be going down and here they are all the way out at the lake and Alice won't be able to drive and Henry has driven like once in his life for maybe twenty minutes and this is a nice car, a really nice car, that Henry does not want to crack up or dent, or even mess with.

So how the hell is he supposed to get her home?

Alice exits the car, bottle in hand, and heads for the beach. Henry grabs the keys and follows her. She takes off her shoes—for a moment he thinks she's going to take off her dress, too—drops the bottle, and starts running down the beach. He picks up the bottle, thinks maybe he should pour it out, realizes she'd be purely pissed at him then, puts it back, and heads over to the car to get the blanket out of the trunk, which is a good thing, because by the time he returns, Alice has finished off the Southern Comfort, taken her dress off, and gone swimming. And is now, of course, freezing.

He wraps the blanket around her. She presses into him, he tries backing up, she follows; it might be funny if he weren't so mad at her, she keeps pushing against him until he has no choice but to hold her.

"You could have drowned."

"Shut up. You sound like my mother."

"Sobered you up a bit."

"I'm really dizzy."

She tries to kiss him. It's sloppy and none too smooth with her arms trapped inside the blanket. Henry thinks, she's had too much to drink, she's got her dress off; they've got the blanket from the trunk of Uncle Eddie's car. How is it that this turn of events, minus Alice being crazy with grief and drunk, is the stuff of fantasy, only it's all wrong, it's confusing as hell, he can't trust one single thing Alice is doing or saying.

Next thing you know Alice is spewing all over the sand. Thank God she turned her head fast enough. It's disgusting. She's on her knees now, wiping her mouth with her hand and spitting and, oh, God, there she goes again. And then she just passes out, sprawled on the sand right next to the guck. In her underwear. Which Henry has never seen before, and certainly never expected to see in quite this context.

Henry tries to pick her up to move her. Can't. Gets hold of her under the armpits and drags her several feet away. Kicks sand over the mess and the smell, covers her with the blanket, and sits down beside her. Lies back in the cool sand, sudden sorrow washing over him as he listens to Alice snuffling, almost snoring, as he listens to the waves lapping the beach.

She's sound asleep, her mouth is a little bit open and she's kind of drooling. He realizes she probably wouldn't want to be seen like that so he closes his eyes and before he knows it, he falls asleep right there, right beside her, like all this heartache and craziness and anxiety is more exhausting than running ten miles or something.

When he wakes up, Alice is lying in the crook of his arm, her head on his chest, the blanket covering both of them. He can't believe it. He is lying on the beach with Alice in her *underwear*. And the sun is going down. And she has her eyes open and she's looking right at him.

"Henry," she says, her voice thick, her throat scratchy.

"What?"

"I'm sorry."

How can she do this? Why does she always do this to him? Why does he let her?

"You don't believe me," she says.

"Not right now I don't."

She leans over and kisses him. He pulls away from her.

"You just *puked!*"

"That was hours ago."

"So?"

She cups her hand to her mouth and tries to smell her own breath.

"I don't smell anything."

"I think you're immune to your own smell."

"I don't taste anything."

"You were almost passed out when you puked. You didn't see it; you didn't smell it."

Alice grabs the foul tasting brandy. Henry tries to grab it away from her.

"Not again."

She takes a swig, swishes it around in her mouth like mouthwash, turns away and spits it into the sand. Does the breath test again. Henry is trying not to smile, Henry is trying not to laugh, but he is not, he notices, trying to get up.

When she leans over him again he wants to look in her eyes, but her eyes are closed, she is already far away on the Ferris wheel of this hoped-for kiss.

She moves closer to him, if that is possible, she moves closer and presses against him. She puts her hand inside his shirt, her cool hand on his warm skin. She's never done anything like this before. He doesn't know what to do with his hands; he doesn't know what to do

with the confounding fact of her, the body and breath and near nakedness of her.

She takes his hand and pulls it under the blanket.

"What are you doing?" Henry can't keep the alarm out of his voice.

"Touch me . . ."

"Wait." He can feel his heart smashing against his ribs. "Alice . . ."

"Shhhh . . ."

"I don't know . . ."

"It's all right."

"Is this what you really want?"

"Henry . . ."

"You've had a lot to drink—"

"I puked, I napped, I'm pretty sure I'm back to normal."

"But how would you *know?* For sure?"

She laughs.

"I wouldn't want you to change your mind or something tomorrow," he adds.

"I won't," she promises.

Touching her is overwhelming; it is like trying to read a symphonic
score. It is, in fact, so overwhelming it is nearly impossible, but there
are glimpses of comprehension, like something inside of him understands this; the way clusters of notes combine, make melody and
counter melody and he is reading something with his fingers, with
his body, he has never read before.

The hollow beneath her throat; her clavicle, he thinks, and his mind
flashes on an ivory key and a clavichord and he remembers why he
loves that word and that fragile bone. There are the bones in her
shoulders, the hard knobs of her spine and then there is the elastic of
her underpants. He stops. His hand stops.

"Will you take your shirt off?" she asks.

He is looking at the singular, hollow-eyed, broken beauty of her as he starts to unbutton his shirt and then pulls it over his head, and he wants to tell her he can see the broken places, he can see where she is blasted by grief. He somehow knows that what she wants is to obliterate her anguish with their bodies, with their longing, with the whole symphony of sensation that is washing over each of them right now. And he knows it might work, for a minute or two or ten, it might work long enough to gulp down a few clear, pain-free breaths. But he also knows that she will still be brokenhearted when this moment ends, and that she could even blame him for that, for coming back to earth, for not being able to truly rescue her or comfort her at all.

Still, there is no chance that he will refuse her; that he will refuse her anything.

This is what no one tells you, Henry thinks. The nearness of her, the unguarded nearness of her, the wonder and simplicity, now, of what had seemed so complicated and impossible just moments before. He will remember everything, he tells himself, every single thing. Alice lying on the blanket and wriggling away from an ant, which is funny and he has never seen her like this and he is relaxed enough and safe enough and close enough to laugh. He helps her find her shoes; he brushes the sand from between her shoulder blades, from the backs of her thighs. This kind of easy closeness, this is what he wants for the rest of his life. Here is the surprise of it, the simple surprise of intimacy, the deep secret at the center of things, as clear as a glass of water dipped from a well.

There is grace in this, a blessing, a still, quiet pool for each of them.

Alice stands there looking at him as he straightens his clothes and brushes the sand out of his hair and finds his glasses; then she looks at the sky and the sand and the lake. Standing up she takes on the weight of knowing again, the weight of the death of her father, which has been hurtling toward them like a comet falling to earth from the day he got on the bus to go to Fort Dix.

And Alice knows, suddenly, that his death can only hurt her more, not less, as time passes. It is as if the grief is growing inside of her, larger than the shell of her fifteen-year-old self. The burden of this grief makes her feel that she is not a kid anymore; that the most essential part of growing up has happened overnight. And if she must suffer adult loss she wants her own life beyond the borders of her family, beyond the borders of her own body. This is why she is reaching for something of her own, for something as large as this pain and emptiness inside of her. This is why she is reaching for Henry.

They are in so much trouble when they get home it could almost be comic. Every single person in both their lives is angry and upset with them. From Uncle Eddie and the car: Do you have any idea what that car is *worth?!* To Mom and the standard: *How could you?!*

The general themes that are touched on, or pounded on, by anyone even tangentially aware of their multiple misdemeanors are trust, responsibility, trust, danger, stupid choices, trust, et cetera, et cetera, et cetera.

No one seems to have picked up on the personal part of the story, the beach and the blanket part of the story, except for maybe Uncle Eddie who is watching them with a very quizzical expression on his face. He might actually be able to follow that train of thought if he weren't pretty drunk and pretty consumed and distracted with rage about his car.

Alice and Henry listen to the harangues as best they can, trying to remain straight-faced, trying to maintain the proper contrite demeanor, trying not to look at each other. They both feel that they are floating above this moment, deliciously immune to it. Something so much more important has happened to them today, they can't believe that people can't actually read about it right on their faces. But everyone seems oblivious to the warmth radiating off the two of them. This only makes Alice and Henry feel more closely aligned, as though they are, once again, coconspirators, just like when they were kids.

Gram, of course, wants to feed them. They are released to the kitchen where Gram and Mrs. Grover pile food on plates and watch them carefully, each of them beginning to sense something, they don't know what, perhaps picking up on the fact that these two young bodies are vibrating in new and disturbing ways.

"Henry?"

"What, Mom?" he says without looking up from his food.

"Henry—?"

He looks up, startled by her tone. Mrs. Grover tilts her head, looking at her son. Alice watches as Henry meets his mother's eyes and in the next instant blushes so furiously he has to take his glasses off and shade his face with one hand. Mrs. Grover's glance travels from Henry to Alice, then to Gram. Gram shakes her head. Alice is biting her lip to keep from laughing.

"You're too young! Do you hear me, Alice?" Gram says.

"Yes, Gram, I hear you," Alice manages to say quietly, looking down at her lap.

She hopes this looks like remorse rather than an attempt to contain hysterical laughter.

"It's all about trust, Henry," Mrs. Grover says.

"I know, Mom."

"Trust you earn every day."

"Yes, Mom."

Henry's head is bending lower and lower over his plate.

"We didn't . . ." Alice begins.

"Good!" Gram finishes for her.

"You're too young!" Mrs. Grover adds, picking up on Gram's perennial theme.

"Can we go now?" Henry asks.

"Go where?"

"Just for a walk," Alice says in her most innocent voice, like, remember how we were in diapers together?

Miraculously, they let them go. Everyone is so distracted and overwhelmed and exhausted, eating and drinking too much, or not at all, relieved that Henry and Alice and the car are safe and sound, that they return to their conversations and refill their glasses, as Henry and Alice walk out the kitchen door and head off through the backyards.

Gram and Mrs. Grover watch them go and even though Henry and Alice are very careful not to touch each other, Gram and Mrs. Grover can see in their bodies, the way they yearn and turn toward each other, that something has happened. Mrs. Grover sits down suddenly in one of the kitchen chairs, a dishtowel in one hand, a serving platter in the other, feeling an overwhelming urge to cry. Gram sits down beside her and takes her hand.

"He's loved her all his life," Mrs. Grover manages to say.

They ponder this a moment as Henry and Alice pass out of sight into the deepening twilight.

"Maybe that's a good thing," Gram says.

May 31st

The Memorial Day parade passes right by their house, as it always does. Uncle Eddie is driving the newest Miss Belknap in a bright yellow Corvette like he does every year. Different car, different Miss Belknap, same old Uncle Eddie. But Uncle Eddie looks a little different, too, Alice notices, a little uncomfortable, or distracted, like his heart's not really in it. Maybe this is the last year for a lot of things.

Alice and Henry have set up chairs on the sidewalk. Ellie, Angie, and Gram are marching with the local Veterans' Association. This year the Greater Belknap VA invited all the families of men and women serving in Iraq to join them in the parade.

Alice and Ellie made Angie a sign to carry:

MATT BLISS
1968–2006
New York National Guard
42nd Infantry, Iraq

Alice joins Henry, bringing lemonade, though she refuses to sit down. It is too soon to be out here, too soon to rejoin their friends and neighbors like this. Alice still feels raw, as though her emotions are constantly on the verge of being out of control. Some days she can pretend to be normal, some days she can't; so she stays on her feet, ready to clear out if necessary.

She has been drawn to the curb almost against her will, to hear the school bands and see the old soldiers and the young soldiers, to see the policemen in cruisers and on horseback, to see the teams marching, and the Boy Scouts and the Girl Scouts. She is not with her team; in fact, she is off the team. She has promised B.D. that she will run all summer and rejoin them for cross country in the fall. Right now, though, Alice still can't predict what she can and can't do each day. She is only now beginning to think that she could ever go back to school.

She waves at Mrs. Minty across the street and down a ways, and Mrs. Piantowski, a bit farther down, surrounded by her children. And there's John Kimball and his father and his brother, Joey; and Stephie, with her mom and dad.

Here comes the Folding Lawn Chair Brigade. Their annual comic routine of synchronized and choreographed moves with lawn chairs and music is always a big hit. This is Ellie and Henry's favorite part of the parade. Next are the politicians in convertibles, the fire trucks, and the high school band.

The World War II vets and the Korean War vets, in their faded uniforms, their numbers dwindling each year, follow the band, walking a bit slowly, some with pinned up sleeves, some with canes. Next come the Vietnam vets wearing bits and pieces of jungle fatigues, some with ponytails, or bald, with pot bellies or green berets. And finally, bringing up the rear, the Iraq veterans' group in their desert fatigues. People fall silent as they pass. You can hear the hush rolling up the street, the same way you could hear the bands approaching. It's eerie to hear the crowds go quiet.

As they get closer Alice can see that Mrs. Grover is walking with Ellie and Gram. Ellie walks between them, holding their hands. And there's Angie with her sign. Mrs. Piantowski steps off the curb to join them, and so does Mrs. Minty, who is carrying a homemade flag over her shoulder that reads **PEACE**.

Alice surprises herself and walks into the street to join her mother. As if this is what she had planned all along, though in all of the confusion she has been feeling, this is the one thing she was sure she would not do. But here is her mother, carrying a sign with the name of her husband on it, her husband and the father of her children.

There are two other young widows carrying their husband's names, and a few other Iraq vets and their families. There's a young man in a wheelchair, missing both legs, another on crutches, another with part of his jaw gone. A smaller group of men and women march under the banner: Veterans Against the War.

At first Alice just walks beside Angie. Henry joins his mother, and he and Mrs. Grover walk right behind them. Alice links arms with her mother, and finally, Angie hands her the sign. Alice carries her father's name; she holds it high. Angie rests her hand on the small of Alice's back, and Alice thinks of Matt and the roof and his voice in her ear telling her: *You can do it, Alice.* She carries her father's name through the streets of her town, past the houses and yards and faces of her neighbors.

She can hear the band playing up ahead of them. She looks back to get a glimpse of Henry and can see that more and more people have joined them. Not a movement, exactly, but a dozen more people publicly standing with the veterans and their families.

Angie leans over to whisper in Alice's ear before she puts her arm around her waist and draws her close. They walk in unison, more together than they have been in months, possibly years, until Alice hands Angie the sign and peels off from the group and sprints the few blocks home.

She walks through the house. Past the six black boxes that arrived a week ago and that none of them can bear to unpack. Each pair of socks, each T-shirt, each letter, each photograph is inventoried on twenty sheets of paper. Everything has been washed, so when you breathe in the scent of a shirt, it doesn't smell like him. Only his pillow, Alice has found, has any trace of his scent. Maybe they don't know how to wash feather pillows.

It's strange but there is really nothing left of her father in these boxes, in these sheets and towels and uniforms. These things are not Matt, they are just things.

She heads out to the garden and sets to work picking baby green beans, peas, radishes, greens. The gourds are going crazy, the tendrils of their vines fanning out across the low fence Alice and Matt built last year. Looks like it's going to be a bumper crop come fall.

It's quiet in the garden aside from the buzz of insects and the occasional birdsong. She stops for a moment to really listen: she can hear cars on Belknap Road and poplar leaves stirring like soft coins in the breeze. She closes her eyes and listens again. The moments when she hears her father's voice in her head are less and less frequent as each day passes. Alice wonders if his voice has gone silent and if this silence will last for the rest of her life.

She heads for the workshop, leaving her basket of produce in the shade. Inside, she stands for a moment, trying to find him. She runs her hands over the workbench, feeling the nicks and dings in the old wood. She trails her fingers over the tools hung along the wall and opens his tool chest, touching everything inside.

She stands looking at the box of letters stored up in the rafters. She desperately wants to read every single one and just as desperately wants to wait as long as possible to read the first sentence. She can feel the promise of his voice in those letters and she also feels a terrible foreboding that reading them will be the end of something; that reading them now, too soon, will diminish the power she is sure they hold.

Finally, she climbs up to get them. She grabs a folding chair and sits quietly for a long time. Her father is trapped inside boxes everywhere right now, except here in his workshop and in the house, in his closet. How soon before her mother cleans out the closet and gives away his clothes? How soon until Angie wants to turn the workshop back into a garage? Maybe Alice is going to have to learn how to use all of these power tools, learn how to make things and repair things, to justify keeping this workshop just the way it is. Who can teach her, she wonders? Maybe she could work with a carpenter this summer, like an apprentice, like being on the roof with her dad. And in that thought, she thinks, there is the echo of Matt's voice.

She lifts off the top of the box, flips through the letters. The big events he wrote about haven't happened yet, graduations and a wedding and losing her mother. So she looks through the series of letters with the heading, "the little moments that make up the big moments that might get forgotten." The first one, "the moment you realize you want this boy to kiss you" seems just right. She opens it and begins to read:

Dear Alice,
Okay, you're not going to need my help with this one. Lots of boys are going to want to kiss you. Trust me on this. Obviously, you'll

figure out who you want to kiss and who you don't want to kiss. But when a boy is kissing you, maybe for the first time, maybe not, other things start to happen. I don't think I have to be too graphic here.

Just remember, he can't help it.

    Love,
    Dad

Alice laughs. Her father is writing to her about kissing and also more than kissing and he's funny; she forgot how funny he is. Maybe one of these letters includes his manual on farting and all the special names he has for different kinds of farts: frips and gribbles and spilbers.

He's funny, she remembers with relief. He was funny and full of life and loved to work hard and get dirty and eat ice cream and play baseball and play with his kids. She remembers his patience those spring twilights playing catch with her and with Henry, the endless pitches to Henry for batting practice, his patience with her in the garden, in the workshop, his delight in teaching her things. Did she really like to garden or did she like to elicit that delight in her father? Does it matter? He was so easy to please. Stand up straight, tell the truth, do your best.

She sees a letter she doesn't remember noticing before: "Dad's words to live by," and opens it right up. Just exactly what she was thinking about.

Dear Alice,

Cogitate on this list when you're in the mood, but not too much and not too often. You know all of this already; these are just little reminders. These are probably the things that my father or my mother said to me; there's nothing original here. But most if not all of these ideas have stood the test of time.

In his perfect block printing, here it is, his list:

Cultivate gratitude.
Think for yourself.
Treat all people equally.
Respect your body.
Don't be afraid to ask questions.
Ask for help when you need it.
Be your own best friend.
Don't be afraid to fail.
Do one thing at a time.
Learn how to dance.
Write thank-you notes.
Good manners never go out of style.
Treat your family and your friends like gold.
Give more than you receive.
Aim high.

If she closes her eyes, she can hear him, in each of these words and phrases, she can hear him.

June 19th

School has ended. Alice kept up with classes, more or less, from home. The readings and assignments for English were no big deal, and her English teacher, Mrs. Cole, even came by the house twice to talk to her about themes and possible essay questions for the final. Henry helped with history, and her mom hired a tutor for math and science, this incredibly shy eleventh grader named Kimmie. They stretched the rules and let her log her running miles for gym credit, and chorus is just pass/fail anyway. When it came to exam time, Gram sat with her in the kitchen every afternoon for a week as she took her finals, one by one.

The day after graduation, John Kimball drove over to say good-bye. He was leaving for basic training later that day.

Angie, who had never really met John before, or couldn't remember meeting him at the funeral, fights back sudden tears when Alice introduces them. She holds on to his hand for a long moment, just looking at him.

"Be careful, okay?" she says, before releasing his hand.

"Yes, ma'am."

When Alice walks him to his car he surprises her and takes her hand, pulling her into a hug.

"I've had really bad timing with you. Maybe one day you'll give me another chance."

Alice steps away, looks at him. She knows, now, that you can't send a boy into the unknown with nothing to hold on to.

"Maybe you'll visit when you're home on leave."

"That could be a year."

"I know. I'll still be in high school, remember?"

He laughs.

"Getting less interesting to you with each passing day, probably," she laughs back at him.

"You could write to me."

"About what? Trigonometry? Homeroom? Track practice?"

"That wouldn't be so bad. Everybody says letters, real letters . . ."

"That's just like my dad: *'You can't carry an e-mail in your pocket.'*"

He hands her a piece of paper with his address.

"I'm not expecting . . . ," he says.

"I know."

He looks at his hands.

"You know I want to kiss you."

"Are you asking permission?"

"Well, after last time . . ."

"I don't . . ." She hesitates, looking at him, and realizes she's memorizing him.

"What?"

"I don't think that's such a good idea," she manages.

He reaches out and touches her face, his palm against her cheek, his thumb pressed against her lips.

"That's okay."

Knowing that her mother is watching, and Ellie, too, for that matter, and possibly Henry down the street, she stands on tiptoe to kiss him, surprising both of them. It's a quick kiss, a child's kiss thrown into the heart of this boy, not a promise, not a pledge, maybe just hope or a prayer.

"I'll write to you," he says, before he ducks into his car and drives away.

There are signs of life everywhere. The garden is thriving, the grass in the yard is growing like crazy; Alice has already had to cut it three times. They are eating peas and radishes and lettuce from the garden almost every night. Alice has planted the warm-weather crops: tomatoes and basil, and the marigolds and zinnias are already budded out. Matt would be proud.

Uncle Eddie has taught Alice how to rotate tires and inspect brakes and brake pads, and the two of them, with Henry's help, have installed the pair of horizontal windows in the west wall of the workshop. Alice can see the sunsets now, just like Matt always wanted.

During another driving lesson, which took a lot of wheedling on Alice's part after the incident with the Mercedes, Alice enlisted Uncle Eddie's help with her plan to go to Small Point. First she begged to be allowed to take the car on her own, with Henry along as a sort of safety guarantee, of course, but Uncle Eddie wouldn't buy it. He reminded her that she can't get her license until she turns sixteen in

October, and there's no way in hell he'd authorize an out-of-state trip without a license. Then he convinced her to take her family along, that she might actually need them on this trip.

In preparation, Henry and Alice and Ellie have spent hours and hours in the workshop together, making small boats out of scraps of wood. Henry and Alice had long discussions about design, arguing back and forth about flat bottoms versus keels, et cetera. They made paper, then cardboard boats, planning to implement the best designs in wood. But they ended up just winging it and making boats with the pieces of wood that they have, with glue guns and staple guns and the occasional nail. Ellie was the inspiration. She didn't need discussions or prototypes; she just picked out pieces of wood and started to put them together. Her boat is finished and painted and it even has a sail. And a name, of course: *Bibliobibuli,* one who reads too much.

Ellie has also made a mini dictionary of long words. She cut and stapled the pages and then copied out all of her favorites. She does not yet have a superlong word for every single letter of the alphabet, but almost.

"Guess what?" Ellie says one afternoon in the workshop.

"What?"

"I want to be a *neologist* when I grow up."

"What's that?" Henry asks.

"Someone who makes up new words."

"Perfect."

June 21st

They are driving to Maine: Alice, Angie, Ellie, Uncle Eddie, and Gram. The boats are packed in a box in the trunk. Alice wanted Henry to be with them, but had to concede the point of "family only," and being too squashed in the car. She asked each of them to bring a memento for Matt, something small enough to fit in the palm of their hand. She suspects that Ellie may have spilled the beans to Gram about the boats, but that's okay.

Courtesy of Uncle Eddie, they are in a 1982 pale yellow Cadillac convertible. The seats are so comfy it's hard to stay awake. Gram packed lunch and dinner in a cooler. They'll spend the night in a bed and breakfast because Mom says Gram's too old to camp.

They left at noon, stopped once in Massachusetts, and shortly after sunset they make the turn down the Phippsburg peninsula heading to Small Point. The minute they make the turn, Alice makes them roll down all the windows. She closes her eyes and breathes in the salt water, the bracken and the piney smells. She leans her forehead against the back of Uncle Eddie's seat.

And Matt is alive in front of her, he is driving and she is in the back-seat with her forehead resting against him, like this, just like this. She remembers the murmur of her parents' voices in the dark car, Ellie curled up asleep on the seat beside her, Matt with one hand on the wheel and one hand lightly twined in the hair at the nape of Angie's neck. And Alice, part of it, part of that feeling, by a thread, by her forehead just touching his shoulder.

It is twilight. It is the solstice. It is a clear, calm night.

"Can I drive?" she asks.

"What?"

"I want to drive the rest of the way."

Uncle Eddie pulls over. Alice slides into the driver's seat; Mom takes her place in the back and pulls Ellie onto her lap so Uncle Eddie can sit beside Alice.

Alice drives the curving two-lane road slowly, ticking off each land-mark as they pass: the turn-offs to the state park, to Secret Beach; Sebasco, with the snack bar that makes the best lobster rolls in Maine; the general store, the granite house, the house with two white barns.

She makes the turn onto the causeway to Hermit Island, drives past the Kelp Shed, and carefully maneuvers the sharp turn up the single-track dirt lane leading to the beaches, the Devil's Bathtub, and the campsites beyond. It's midweek; the campground is not even half full. Alice parks next to a picnic table.

They pile out of the car, pull on sweaters, and head down to the beach with the picnic basket, a ground tarp, and some blankets. Alice, Ellie, and Uncle Eddie scrounge the beach and the dunes for wood to make a fire. They roast hot dogs, eat Gram's famous potato salad and cherry pie, and wait for full dark.

Clambering up the rocks, Alice stops at the top. The sky is thick with stars, just as she imagined it would be, there is a sliver of a moon low in the sky, and the Devil's Bathtub is nearly full as the tide reaches its peak. She finds a flat rock to use as a staging area for the boats. She has brought scraps of kindling and paper and matches. Uncle Eddie has his arm around Gram and is guiding her with a flashlight. Mom and Ellie are holding hands.

Alice sets the cardboard box down on the rocks. There are six boats, one for each of them, and one for Henry.

"Okay," Alice begins, and finds she needs to stop for a moment to collect herself. "Okay, so I thought we'd each launch a boat with a wish for Dad. Wherever he is, whatever you believe. If there's something you want to put on the boat, I think it'll work. Ellie has a book that she made."

"A dictionary," Ellie pipes up.

"We tested Ellie's boat in the bathtub to make sure it won't capsize. So the boats should all be able to carry a little something. After you make your wish, we'll light each one on fire, and set it afloat in the water."

Alice opens the box and Alice and Ellie unwrap the boats and set them out on the flat rock. Ellie's *Bibliobibuli* with its pink hull and white sail almost glows in the dark. Henry's bright red tugboat

Fernticle lies alongside Alice's blue skiff, *Jillick*. Ellie hands the yellow barge named *Penny* to Gram, the orange tug named *Tupelo Honey* to Uncle Eddie, and a graceful little green skiff with a pink and yellow striped sail named *Bliss* to Angie.

"Did you make these?" Gram wants to know.

"They're beautiful," Angie says.

"What the heck does *fernticle* mean?" Uncle Eddie asks.

"Freckle!" Ellie shouts.

"*Jillick?*"

"To skip a stone across water!"

"*Bibliobibuli?*"

"One who reads too much!"

"Really beautiful," Angie says again, picking up *Bliss* and turning the boat over and over in her hands. "I had no idea."

"Do you like the names, Gram?" Ellie asks.

"I love the names, sweetheart."

Alice pulls a photograph from her pocket.

"Ellie," Alice asks, "should we launch them one by one or all together?"

"All together. We make our wishes and then light them all at once so no boat will be lonely."

"Okay. I'll start with Henry. This is a photo of Henry and Dad and me having a catch in the backyard when we're about six. Henry's wish is that there's baseball in Dad's heaven."

She puts the photo on Henry's boat.

"I made Daddy a dictionary of my favorite long words. It's illustrated. My wish . . . Do I have to say it out loud?"

"Only if you want to."

Ellie considers, then: "My wish is that Daddy will get to see me when I'm almost grown up like Alice and I'm wearing a beautiful dress and going to my first dance."

Ellie ties the dictionary to *Bibliobibuli* with a piece of twine.

Uncle Eddie pulls a feather from his shirt pocket. As he starts to speak, he finds he can't trust his voice. He coughs and clears his throat and pulls out a handkerchief. He looks at the boats and the rocks and the water and the night sky, at his mother and his sister and his nieces and he feels, as he has perhaps not allowed himself to feel before now, the enormity of Matt's absence. Finally he says:

"My wish is that if you're worried about Angie and the girls up there in your baseball playing heaven, Matt Bliss, I'm gonna do my best to be there for them right here on earth. Not like I could ever fill your shoes. But I'll do whatever I can."

He weaves the feather into the rigging of *Tupelo Honey*.

Gram has made a miniature cherry pie that she has carried carefully in its own little handmade paper box.

"I know cherry pie is your favorite, Matt. I wish you all the cherry pie you want every single day. But mostly, I wish you were right here with us. Somehow maybe you are."

The tiny pie sits like a crown in the middle of the yellow barge.

"Mom . . . ?"

Angie had no idea that this is what Alice has been up to. The request for this trip on this day was, frankly, one big headache. Alice was secretive about almost all of the details and would not compromise on one single element, except for staying in the B&B instead of camping, and even that was a fight. And the more stubborn Alice got, point by point, the more irritated Angie got. But here they are, and Angie can see the plan, she can see the care and design and love in the plan, and now that it's her turn she finds she can't even begin to speak. She looks at her daughter and she looks at the boats, the boats made, she now realizes, in Matt's workshop, on Matt's workbench, with Matt's tools. And the choice of this day, the solstice, and Alice's stubbornness about timing, because she needed to time the boats with the tide, is so exactly like Matt it could make her cry.

Angie kneels beside her little boat. She has a letter in her hands from their college days when they thought they would live forever. She found the letter in her lingerie drawer, jumbled in with the girls' letters to Santa and handmade anniversary and birthday cards. She has read it so many times in the past few days she could recite it by heart.

She thinks, I will always love you, Matt. She closes her eyes and wishes it were last summer, before any of this had happened, she wishes and wishes and wishes that she could have him back. When she opens her eyes she realizes she doesn't want to let any single bit of him go, not this letter, not this night, not this beautiful boat. She looks at Alice, who is waiting patiently. She looks at the boat again. *Bliss*. How perfect. Matt Bliss, she thinks, you should be here for this, you should see your daughter now. She folds the letter and slips it into the boat.

Alice has a small envelope in one hand and a sand dollar the size of a dime in the other.

"This is some dirt from our garden and one of the tiniest sand dollars we ever found together right here on this beach. I hope there are tomatoes in heaven, Dad. I hope you can see our boats on the water tonight. We're lighting them up just for you."

Alice pours the earth into the hull of *Jillick* and places the sand dollar on top.

Alice and Ellie carefully lay their tinder and their scraps of paper on each boat. One by one they light them on fire and launch them into the water. The boats wobble a bit when they enter the water, and Alice has a moment of panic before they steady themselves. They cluster together at first, floating like a small regatta, magically aflame.

Angie takes Ellie's hand and watches Alice, still kneeling where they launched their fleet at the narrow, closed end of the Devil's Bathtub. The tide is turning now, pulling the boats out to sea, where they begin to fan out a bit, each one responding to the current and the wind and the tide. *Bibliobibuli* and *Bliss* are in the lead, it's almost as if their sails actually work, followed by *Penny*. *Tupelo Honey* wallows along bringing up the rear. *Jillick* and *Fernticle* are in the middle, their decks burning brightest of all until the sails on *Bibliobibuli* and *Bliss* catch fire in a spectacular burst of light.

Angie wants to call them all back, or she wants them to stay just as they are. Uncle Eddie is in the unaccustomed position of having a slow-motion method of transport and finds himself wishing his boat would hurry it up. Ellie is thinking that maybe she shouldn't have burned the dictionary she worked so long to make. Alice is looking at the burning boats and wondering if it is at all possible that they will make it out to open ocean before they sink; and wondering at the same time, if it is possible that any of this, the boats, the flames bright in the darkness, could reach her father? Can anything she will do or say for the rest of her life reach her father?

She looks back over her shoulder at her mother, Ellie, Uncle Eddie, Gram, and they are all caught and held in this moment. All their hopes and their wishes launched on fragile boats, lit on fire and shining like stars in an upside-down sky. Stars floating on the water. Just for a moment, a moment longer. Here. And then gone.

ACKNOWLEDGMENTS

With thanks to:

* David and Kate, for everything, always.
* The Kleban Foundation for giving me two years to write.
* Paulette Haupt, commissioner and producer of *Alice Unwrapped*, the musical that inspired *Alice Bliss;* Jenny Giering, composer for *Alice Unwrapped* for the magic of her music and for making Alice sing.
* Rachel Kadish, Ann Ziergiebel, Angela Marvin, Jane Potter, Lillian Hsu, Kim Garcia, Liza Rutherford, and Lynn Barclay, my first readers.
* Melanie Kroupa, for seeing the potential.
* Carol Green for giving me space to write, and so much more, in Truro.
* Beth Hartley for information and insights about teens and grief.
* Molly Ziergiebel for information and insights about running.
* My agent, Stephanie Cabot, as well as Sarah Burnes and the entire staff at The Gernert Company.
* My editor, Pamela Dorman, and also her assistant editor, Julie Miesionczek.
* The team at Viking Penguin, with special thanks to Hal Fessenden.

picador.com

blog
videos
interviews
extracts